RICH BEYOND OUR DREAMS

RICH BEYOND OUR DREAMS

Carol Wensby-Scott

Macdonald

A Macdonald Book

First published in Great Britain in 1991 by
Macdonald & Co (Publishers) Ltd
London & Sydney
Reprinted 1991

Reproduced, printed and bound in Great Britain by
BPCC Hazell Books
Aylesbury, Bucks, England
Member of BPCC Ltd.

British Library Cataloguing in Publication Data
Wensby-Scott Karel
   Rich beyond our dreams.
   I. Title
   823'.914 [F]

ISBN 0-356-17655-X

Macdonald & Co (Publishers) Ltd
165 Great Dover Street
London SE1 4YA

A member of Maxwell Macmillan Pergamon Publishing Corporation

PART ONE
MAX
1926

Chapter 1

I came home on a chill wet afternoon in the late spring of 1926. It had been a long journey; two weeks overland from Mirzapur to Bombay; four weeks by steamship to Southampton. Then by train to Newcastle where I'd hired a car — a battered open tourer that had seen better days, but this last part of the journey I wanted to eke out. I had dreamed of this moment for years.

Then a few miles along the Hexham road, I realised the car had been a mistake. I had forgotten the unpredictability of the English weather; furtive sunshine and sudden squalls of rain. And the wind — my God, I had forgotten the wind — gusting down from the moors with an edge like a knife. I felt the cold intensely after the dry heat of India, and I was tired beyond belief, so that the bleak grandeur of the moorland, the distant hills, passed me by in a meaningless blur. Not much further now though. Another half a mile and I'd be able to see the house. Twenty minutes at the most and I'd be through the door.

The familiar excitement rose up inside me. It had always been special to me, the moment of coming home, the moment I came over the brow of the hill and saw the house in the valley below me. For as long as I could remember I'd been obsessed with the house. I'd never overcome my longing to possess it. It mattered to me that nine generations of Claremonts had been born there, that the Pretender had supped there on his way to Culloden, that the carving in the chapel was by Grinling Gibbons. Just the fact that it was still there meant something to me. The house was a survivor as indeed was the very name of Claremont itself. We were an old Catholic family who could boast direct descent from a henchman of the Conqueror's and even if honours and titles

3

had passed us by — as they had all Catholics that had been stubborn enough to cling to their faith — it was quite something to be able to say that there'd been a Claremont in every major battle since Hastings. We could even lay claim to a martyr or two; Pascal Claremont, a recusant, had been burnt at the stake during the Elizabethan purge; Richard Claremont had lost his heart and his head to the cause of the Scottish Queen. We'd never been really wealthy, at least not after the Reformation, not till my grandfather had thrown his stove pipe hat over a windmill and gone into partnership with the Frenchman André Deuchar and built one of the first steamships to come out of the Tyne. Our real pride was in our survival, that despite confiscation, persecution, war, death and income tax, a Claremont still lorded it over the same land that our Norman ancestor had first crushed beneath his tyrant's heel.

That this land belonged to my elder brother Hugo had only added to its allure. I coveted Blanchland as passionately and intensely as I later came to covet his wife, viewing it with a lustful lover's eye; Blanchland, naked and virginal in the depths of winter, Blanchland, lush and wanton in the summer sun. I remembered all the other homecomings stretching back over the years; from prep school, from Ampleforth, from Oxford, and even now, at twenty-four, a lieutenant in the 14th Hussars, I still approached the moment with the same feeling of eager longing. I was back, I was home. I was at Blanchland.

And suddenly there it was, the great sprawling house rising from the banks of the Derwent, an architectural nightmare welded together with ivy and dry rot, the result of every style and vogue in houses since the Conquest. From a distance it looked impressive, all towers and turrets and battlemented walls but closer inspection revealed an embarrassing incongruity of design. The main house was Elizabethan on medieval foundations, a development of the original twelfth-century hall. This had later sprouted austere and classical Georgian wings on to which had been grafted a lavish ballroom in the Renaissance style. Grim Victorian servants' quarters cowered at the rear and, to perpetuate this heterogeneity of style and taste, Hugo had added a pavilion

4

designed by Victor Horta, all *trompe-l'œil* panels, wrought iron and glass. This excrescence went by the name of Decorative Art.

But then my brother Hugo had never had any taste. He'd never had any real feeling for beauty. I remembered on my last leave how bitterly we'd quarrelled. Inspired by the pavilion, Hugo had wanted to extend Horta's designs to the interior of the house ... I couldn't help smiling. Of course, that wasn't going to happen any more. Hugo was dead. Blanchland belonged to me now.

I pulled the car on to the verge and sat, just staring out over the familiar and beloved landscape; the great sweep of Blanchland Moor bounded by lush river valleys; Devil's Water to the west; the Tyne to the north; to the south, the Derwent and Weardale beyond.

I lit a cigarette and closed my eyes. Quite calmly and without emotion I began to think about Hugo and instantly felt guilty about my complete lack of feeling. I suppose I should have felt something — my only brother dead at twenty-seven. But to be perfectly honest, Hugo and I had never got on; to say that I disliked him would have been an understatement. I suppose normal sibling rivalry had come into it somewhere but for me at least it had grown to be more than that. Perhaps because we had been so physically alike. I resented that and had made a point of demonstrating that although we looked alike that was where the resemblance ended and we were completely different in every other way. Unfortunately, being three years older than me, Hugo had first crack at the whip and had established himself as a model of filial devotion and virtue, leaving me with no choice but to be the bad hat, a part, I had to admit, I had performed with excellence so far.

Of course, it wasn't just one-sided. In fact my first memory of Hugo seemed to be of him peering down at me with hostile eyes. And our first real conversation, oh yes, I remembered that ... I had been five, Hugo eight.

'I'm older than you,' Hugo had pointed out. 'And that makes me better. I shall always be first.'

And he had been — without effort, without trying, at home, at school, even physically he'd managed to be

5

superior. I was tall, six-foot-four, but Hugo had been taller, just by an inch — and stronger, and cleverer, more amusing, more confident — or so Hugo had always managed to make it appear. Naturally, I had grown up believing myself to be a rather poor copy of Hugo, not so blond, not so tall — almost but not quite. My parents, perhaps unconsciously, seemed to confirm this belief. We had originally been a large family, my mother, true to the tenets of the Catholic faith, being pregnant every other year. Two sons were stillborn, an elder brother Basil had been carried off at fourteen; two girls, Hilary and Clarissa, died in infancy. That left Hugo and myself, Veronica in between and Helen who was the youngest. But it was Hugo and Veronica that really mattered. One got the impression that, having produced two perfect children already, by the time Helen and I were born we were somehow surplus to requirements. At least, we always felt that anyway, that we were superfluous, the reserve team, second best. Of course, as far as myself was concerned, I could quite understand their preference. I was possessed of what is described as a mercurial temperament. I suffered from fits of what my father called 'Byronic depression', climbing one moment to ecstatic heights only to plunge to the depths of abysmal gloom. I had never discovered moderation, that enviable state. It was all or nothing with me and so far it had been very much of the latter. In contrast, Hugo was wonderfully predictable, unimaginative in the extreme. Hugo was sunny, I was morose; he was as amiable as I was quarrelsome. Even at school I had always lived in his shadow. Hugo had excelled at athletics and sport. The cups and medals that cluttered his room bore witness to his coxing the Ampleforth eight three years in a row and he'd been captain of the first XI at only fifteen. The fact that I had been awarded a distinction for my translation of Homer from the original Greek seemed to have completely escaped everyone's notice. And even after we left school he continued to outshine me. I hadn't been old enough to enlist for the war but Hugo had volunteered almost immediately. Naturally, he distinguished himself, being mentioned in despatches at the battles of Verdun and the Somme. I wasn't surprised when he came home with the Military Cross. It was always like that; the perfect soldier, the perfect son, a perfect brother for Veronica, the perfect daughter. In contrast, Helen and I were both thought difficult. I was labelled sullen and quarrelsome, Helen was regarded as insular and shy. This blatant favouritism tended to draw us together though we both reacted differently to the pressure to conform. Helen retreated into a fairy-tale world of eternal childhood; I came out of my corner, fighting.

Of course, I knew I couldn't win. It wasn't just Hugo I was up against, but the Church, convention, society as a whole. By the time I was fifteen I had acquired the reputation of being something of a rebel, and then at sixteen I put myself totally beyond the pale. I dared to question the Church's morality and the dogma of Rome, and receiving no answer that satisfied me I declared for Darwin and professed myself an atheist and quite openly refuted the faith. An heretic in the family was just too much, so that when our father died in 1920 at the early age of fifty-two, I was not too surprised that, as well as inheriting Blanchland, Hugo got full control of Claremont Deuchar, the family shipbuilding business. But for Hugo to have got everything, absolutely everything. The injustice of that rankled, even today. Then and now, it hadn't been right.

I had been eighteen then, in my last year at Ampleforth, old enough to be thinking about my future. Hugo made it quite clear that I wasn't included in his. Of course, on the surface he appeared magnanimous. Blanchland would always be my home, and in the same way there'd always be a place for me in the firm. But grudgingly, dutifully, making me feel like an intruder, a hanger-on. I knew then that I had to get out, as far away from Hugo as I possibly could, before I did him any real harm. That sounds melodramatic now, but I had discovered at an early age that I was capable of violence. Both Hugo and I had a natural tendency towards it, except that Hugo's was of the verbal kind. He was a master of the sneer, the veiled insult. It was a kind of passive sadism that took pleasure in other people's humiliation. Particularly he enjoyed humiliating me, provoking me to outbursts of uncontrollable rage, for which, as a child, I was severely punished. I was thirteen before I discovered the answer, that

7

the only way to shut my brother up was to hit him. The satisfaction was enormous; the satisfaction of seeing his cut and bruised lip, and even better, of seeing the naked fear in his eyes, of knowing that he was a coward. The satisfaction had sustained me all through the inevitable retribution. That was another kind of violence, the wordless assault of my mother's cold eyes. Her voice, long afterwards, when I emerged from my room after two hungry days, explaining to me with infinite patience that what made us different, what made us gentlemen and above the common herd, was our ability to control our baser instincts. And yes, in retrospect I can understand her being appalled. My mother was a bastion of that peculiar stoicism for which the English are famed and she had raised her children in a culture which abhorred open and public display, so that beauty had to be endured in the same way as pain, silently, secretly, behind closed doors. Her only passion was religion. She was a pillar of the Church, possessed of that strange charity which poured thousands into the overflowing coffers of Rome and yet wouldn't have hesitated to double a poor tenant's rent. The centre of her universe was Rome. She saw the world from the summit of the Princian Hill. She loved to surround herself with theologians and *religieuse*; humble Jesuits, *monsignori* — occasionally the coup of a cardinal's hat, so that at times our drawing room resembled a papal conclave. It was as if, as soon as she'd realised that Father wasn't going to measure up, she'd embraced Christ as a substitute spouse — now there was a man one could look up to; a man who could raise the dead, turn water into wine, well, of course, poor Father just couldn't compete.

Father had never counted. He'd always been a shadowy figure on the periphery of our lives. Far more of an influence was Uncle Gerard, Lord Ansty, the third generation beneficiary of Lloyd George who hadn't quite got the hang of *noblesse oblige*. When he was sober, which wasn't often, he would lecture us on the merits of doing the done thing. His other weakness was cricket and he lived his life by M.C.C. rules. His conversation was always laced with cricketing jargon — keeping a straight bat; hard innings; sticky wicket and so on. He even referred to God as the Universal Umpire.

To Uncle Gerard life was as simple as that. It was just a question of keeping a straight bat, playing the game and maintaining a stiff upper lip when you were bowled out. So between Uncle Gerard and my mother, I learnt, gradually, to play the game. I learnt to control my temper, to master those sudden outbursts of killing rage. I paid lip service to the phlegmatic tradition of which they were so proud, but beneath the impeccable Anglo-Saxon façade I showed to the world, I retained all the bloodthirsty barbarism of a Celt.

In 1921 I left Ampleforth, and went up to Oxford, although the family even quarrelled about that. My repressed romanticism and flair for languages inclined me to read classics whereas Mother wanted me to take theology. Uncle Gerard favoured the law and Hugo suggested something useful like mathematics. Uncle Gerard won and resentfully I went up to Oriel to prepare for the Bar, whereupon I proceeded to drink my way through the first two years till I was ignominiously sent down after being involved in a brawl. Consequently, I returned home from Oxford at the end of 1923 with no qualifications except a knowledge of every decent vineyard north of the Loire and the ability to drink most other men under the table. On an income of less than three hundred a year, there was nothing for it but to take Hugo up on his generous offer — as he'd said, a place could always be found for me at Claremont Deuchar. And it seemed the perfect time. The shipbuilding industry was still enjoying the post-war boom. Orders were coming thick and fast. And although I had had no real experience, I felt I knew as much about it as Hugo did. Our father had always included us in his visits to the yards, explaining the process to us step by step. Hugo had been bored but I had been fascinated. It caught my imagination, the idea of a stately liner rising from a single strip of steel. But I'd forgotten about Hugo, about working under his dominance, his critical eye. Inevitably, we quarrelled over the firm as we did over Blanchland. At least we were alike in that; neither of us was prepared to share.

After six months I decided it was better to get out, to make a clean break once and for all. The army seemed the only other answer. As Hugo pointed out, the perfect answer

9

for my tendency to violence, the legitimate outlet for my need of physical release. And it was in the army that I discovered sex, that other outlet for passion and physical release. Sex made me passive, temporarily at least. I found that I enjoyed the warmth and closeness of a woman's body; to be able to touch and be touched without censure or reproof. For a long time I felt guilty, vaguely unclean. I wasn't able to escape from the strictures of my childhood when even the most natural gestures were frowned upon and physical contact beyond the commonplace was forbidden. But overall, it proved, for me, to be the perfect therapy. Briefly, in a woman's arms, I found release from the moral straitjacket of my upbringing; I found relief from the anger and passion I had been forbidden to express. I was free, without restraint, without guilt or inhibitions. And beyond the obvious satisfaction of my lust, I discovered that all women, even the plain ones, had a fascination for me. I liked them out of bed as well as in. I liked their warmth and softness, that subtle combination of fragility and strength. I liked the way they always smelt of flowers, pot-pourri and soap. I liked the sound of their voices, the way they laughed — and because I liked women so much I was sensitive to the fact that my brother Hugo didn't like them at all.

I flung away my cigarette stub and started up the car. Slowly, in low gear, I descended the hill. I was in no hurry now. I could take my time, think over my plans. I'd have to resign my commission, there was no doubt about that. Running Blanchland and Claremont Deuchar would be a full time job — I intended taking over from Hugo in every way. Then for the first time it occurred to me to speculate exactly how my brother had died. I didn't have any details. I'd been coming home on leave in any case and had been halfway across the Indian Ocean when Uncle Gerard's wire had come; 'Regret to inform you. Tragic accident. Hugo dead. Make all speed. — Gerard Ansty.' That was all I had to go on. The possibilities were numerous. Broken his neck out hunting was by far the most likely cause, or driving too fast in that flashy foreign car. It would be something like that, something sudden and violent. Hugo wouldn't have died easily.

10

And how would dear Marcia be taking it? I couldn't imagine my brother's wife in the part of a grieving widow. As a whore perhaps or a courtesan. Yes, usually when I thought about Marcia my thoughts ran along those lines. I smiled as I felt the inevitable stirring in my groin. Thinking about Marcia always had that effect. I suppose I had wanted her from the first moment I saw her even though she was already my brother's wife. She was beautiful, voluptuous, with that inborn sensuality that all French women seem to have. And twenty to my sixteen years, but that had only added to her allure. She was the sophisticated, sexually experienced woman that all young men crave; a raw virgin would have had absolutely no appeal.

Of course, at sixteen I had believed myself passionately in love, and it was only later that I realised that my infatuation was based on lust. At that age I wasn't old enough to know the difference. On the whole, though, my adolescent years had been thoroughly miserable, a constant battle against the physical manifestation of male desire. From fourteen onwards I seemed to be in a state of permanent erection that no amount of masturbation could ever dispel. This was a severe social handicap in any case, but with Marcia's arrival it swelled — forgive the pun — to mammoth proportions that no amount of cold baths and brisk walks could overcome. By seventeen my desire for my sister-in-law had become a definite fixation. Blanchland was the first grand passion of my life; the second was Marcia, my brother's wife.

Looking back, I can see that if Marcia had been a different sort of woman my adolescent passion would probably have burnt itself out. But Marcia collected admirers, both young and old. She was neither surprised nor offended that a man wished to sleep with her; the surprise would have been that they did not. But that was a part of her fascination for me. One instinctively knew that she enjoyed making love, that she was capable of enormous passion. Though to be fair she wasn't promiscuous in the usual sense. She hadn't to my knowledge ever been unfaithful to Hugo — but she gave the impression that she might like to be, that for the right man, in the right circumstances, she could be available.

Naturally, at home, her marriage to Hugo had raised a few

11

eyebrows. Hugo had been expected to marry advanta-geously, a known family, preferably out of the top drawer, so when he brought home this unknown French girl that he'd met and married in Paris at the end of the war, we were all transfixed with shock. Mother had loathed her on sight; because she was a foreigner and obviously not of our class, and later on because after several years of marriage she had failed to produce the horde of children that were every Catholic's due. By this time I didn't have any illusions about Marcia myself. She was a woman who lived entirely through her senses and for the gratification of these senses. On the whole I felt she was a calculating bitch; rather greedy like a child, and though she wasn't intelligent in the accepted sense, she was clever, quick witted, almost cunning. Strangely enough, this only increased my desire. Beside Marcia all other women seemed colourless and bland. I wanted her. I had always wanted her — because she was beautiful, because, like me, she didn't quite fit in, but mostly because she belonged to Hugo. Then as I swung through the tall gates of Blanchland, I laughed out loud. Not any more she didn't. Nothing belonged to Hugo any more.

It wasn't my usual reception, the family coming out on to the steps to greet me. Even the house didn't welcome me as it usually did. It had a sulky and secretive look, and the rooms appeared colourless and dim. And Uncle Gerard was there, my mother's brother. I could hear his voice quite clearly as I stood in the hall, high-pitched and fretful, slurred by drink.

I entered the drawing room unannounced and stood for a moment on the threshold. They were all there except Marcia; Uncle Gerard still talking, glass in hand. Father Devine, our priest, my sisters Veronica and Helen. But it was my mother that I looked at. Was it my mother? This thin, haggard woman with the frozen expression who stared at me with cold dry eyes. She stared at me for a long time as if she didn't know who I was. Then painfully she smiled. 'Maxwell, my dear. Welcome home.'

It was said warmly enough but she made no effort to take my hands, to respond to the light kiss I dropped on her cheek. For a few moments we all stood there making stiff desultory conversation. I felt like a stranger, some vague acquaintance who'd dropped in at an awkward time.

I looked at my sisters. Vee stood by the window looking restless and bored; Helen couldn't look at me at all. Suddenly I knew that something was desperately wrong, something over and above their obvious grief. And apparently it was up to Uncle Gerard to break the news. Murmuring some vague excuse, my mother and her entourage rapidly left the room. Suddenly Uncle Gerard and I were alone.

I turned to face him. 'What's wrong?' I demanded sharply.

Uncle Gerard cleared his throat. 'Have a drink, my boy. And sit down, won't you ...'

'I don't want a drink,' I said grimly. 'And I don't want to sit down. I just want to know what's going on.'

Nevertheless I sat down and allowed a glass of whisky to be put into my hand. Uncle Gerard tugged nervously at his untidy moustache. 'It's difficult to know where to start,' he began hesitantly. 'Everything's still in something of a tangle. But the long and the short of it is that Hugo ...' he hesitated again, 'Hugo's left us in a bit of a mess. No last will and testament, nothing like that — not that I suppose it would make much difference. There's not going to be much left as I see it.'

A cold sensation crept along my spine. 'I'm not sure that I follow you, Uncle Gerard,' I managed to say. 'What exactly are you getting at?'

He took a pull at his drink. 'Well, to put it bluntly, my boy — we're on a sticky wicket financially. The firm's in Queer Street. Apparently the Receiver has had to be called in'. He shook his head. 'We don't know all the details yet. Ridgeway, your legal man, has promised to look in later on. He'll be able to explain it better than I can.' He looked across at me uneasily, expecting me to speak, but my voice wouldn't function. My mind was frozen with shock.

He went on in his whisky-and-soda voice. 'I have to confess, it knocked me all of a heap. Hugo always seemed so wonderfully competent. None of us ever dreamt that he didn't have everything well in hand.' He helped himself to another large whisky. 'You know, I just can't understand why

13

Hugo didn't come to me. I could probably have advised him if nothing else. But to let things get so out of hand. And then....' His vacant blue eyes misted with tears. 'Waste of a damn fine boy, a damn fine boy. Always had a great deal of time for Hugo.' He sat down heavily, cradling his glass in his hands. 'Of course, we've covered up as best we could. The Coroner has been jolly obliging. Didn't make too much of a fuss. And Father Devine's been an absolute brick — backed us up all round. But there's talk, of course. Bound to be.'

Suddenly I felt I wasn't part of this conversation, as if I had missed some vital, all important point. I put down my glass. 'Uncle Gerard,' I said slowly. 'Exactly how did Hugo die?'

He stared at me blankly. 'My God. Don't you know? Hasn't anyone told you? Hugo shot himself. He committed suicide.'

Chapter 2

Ridgeway left just after six and three hours later I was still sitting there, at Hugo's desk, in Hugo's chair, in the very room where, in the best tradition of a failed English gentleman, he had put a bullet through his head. Well, good for you, Hugo, I thought viciously. It's the only sensible thing you've ever done.

It seemed something to celebrate so I opened yet another bottle of champagne. I should have been drunk, in fact I should have been unconscious. I had striven for oblivion but all I had managed was to make myself feel vaguely sick; the nightmare of my situation remained undiminished. Just for a moment I could understand how Hugo must have felt. I could quite imagine the sudden madness that had driven him to *felo de se*. I had mixed views upon suicide. On the one hand it seemed an act of the most appalling cowardice, and yet it must take superhuman courage to place a loaded revolver against one's head and actually pull the trigger. Perhaps the cowardice lay in leaving one's family to bear the disgrace, to survive the stigma of 'unsound mind'. It was that which had affected my mother the most, not just the fact of Hugo's death, but the manner of it, the fact he had died unshriven, outside the Church, the fact he had succumbed to the 'ultimate despair'. I could picture her now, kneeling in the chapel with Father Devine. The air would be heavy with incense, ablaze with candles lit for Hugo's soul to illumine his way through purgatory. I repressed a sneer. Nobody could say that the Claremonts didn't take their religion seriously, even to the indulgence of their very own priest. Well, I thought savagely, he could go for a start, and I could see that one of the benefits of insolvency would be to rid myself of useless dross like Father Devine whose only purpose, as far

15

as I could see, was to encourage my mother in her fanatical obsession with the Catholic faith.

I was prejudiced of course. As far as the Church was concerned I had long fallen from grace and I had never made any secret of my dislike for the priest. I disliked his fanatical Jesuit face, the hot dry smell that emanated from his armpits. I felt he was an apostle of flagellation, that he longed for the old days of religious persecution. He would have found a masochistic ecstacy in being burnt at the stake. I also suspected that he drank; masturbated; rummaged under the cassocks of innocent young choirboys; but most of all I disliked him because his fanatical teaching had destroyed any relationship I might have had with God. Yes, Father Devine could go, along with the other servants that had always been part of our life. And then what? Where in Heaven's name did we go from there. The future was an enormous void.

Despairingly I stared around the dark panelled walls, as Hugo must have done before me. This had been our father's study once; before the modern de Veschi desk and the hideous Bugatti chairs. The walls were decorated with engravings of the more important ships to come out of the Claremont yards. Our first ship, the *Aurora*, a strange hybrid of sail and steam; the *Cosmos*, the *Hercules*, the *Adelaide*, the *Siam*, clumsy-looking vessels of pre-war design with straight stems and eliptical sterns and single upright funnels. Then the engravings gave way to a series of photographs, a half dozen ships looking very much the same, the B-class steamers that Claremont had specialised in.

I thought again of my father, remembering him sitting here; serious, reticent, slowly spoken, as if it were a tremendous effort to speak at all and the words needed to be deeply considered before he uttered them. Strangely enough, I had loved my father. He had been a gentleman in the true sense of the word. He abhorred strife; he never quarrelled; I'd never even known him raise his voice. He should never have married though, or more particularly, he shouldn't have married my mother. Not that he wasn't a religious man but to my father religion was honesty, obligation, responsibility towards his fellow man and generally doing the decent thing.

16

To my mother it was schism and sin, privation and persecution. It was scourges, hair shirts, the penitential lash. To get her own way, my mother was capable of the most astonishing cruelty, her actions always justified as being 'for our own good'. So Torquemada must have justified the Inquisition but to me it was just another example of the monstrous things people did to each other, all in the name of religion and love. You see, my mother was an aristocrat in the real sense of the word. Having been the Honourable Ursula Ansty before her marriage, the daughter of a Victorian industrialist who'd made enough money out of nuts and bolts to buy a peerage from Lloyd George, she had inflated ideas of her status. Frankly, she was a snob, standing politically to the far right of Lucrezia Borgia and her single aim in life was to put as much distance between herself and the nuts and bolts as was humanly possible. Her marriage to my father was a compromise, his unsavoury association with trade offset by a blood line that practically preceded the Flood. To my mother, a gentleman's occupation was riding to hounds, shooting pheasant and grouse, with a little salmon- and trout-fishing in between. And if he really needed to do something, well, he managed his estate, chaired local committees or, as a last resort, he stood for parliament. He certainly did not, like Father, openly engage in the distasteful business of making money. And this was the creed she had passed on to Hugo who needed no encouragement at all to take his ease. Consequently, after Hugo had taken over, Claremont Deuchar had soon ceased to be a front rank yard. I suppose it had only been a matter of time before things went badly wrong.

For the hundredth time I went back over the conversation I'd had with Ridgeway, though perhaps conversation wasn't really the right word. Ridgeway had talked and I had listened as in his soft understated voice he had destroyed my world.

'Of course, one can quite understand your brother's difficulty. It's commonplace now and a good many shipbuilding firms are all in the same boat.' He had smiled feebly at the unintentional pun. 'After the war, as you know, there was something of a boom. Ships lost in action had to be replaced. Owners were fighting to get their vessels on the stocks.

17

Naturally, many firms expanded to cope with the work; new equipment, more modern up-to-date techniques. And then of course, everything dried up. The Washington treaty on disarmament put paid to the naval programme ...' He went on in this vein for some considerable time; explaining, excusing; even in death Hugo seemed to command absolute loyalty.

'Where Hugo erred was in expanding too quickly. He borrowed instead of staying within the limits of his capital. And then when things went wrong he borrowed again ... The outcome, I'm afraid, was most unfortunate.'

Now we were getting round to it, how bad the situation really was. I was prepared for disaster but not on such an enormous scale.

Ridgeway went on. 'The trading loss for 1924 was some twenty thousand pounds, plus an overall deficit since 1921 of seventy thousand. And added to that the 1st Mortgage Debenture Stock held by Rochester Mercantile, so that I'm afraid we're talking about a total liability of some hundred and fifty thousand pounds.' He paused and allowed the enormity of that to sink in. 'Now, of course, there are the firm's considerable assets to be set against that; the yards themselves, the offices in North Shields, such vessels, albeit unfinished, as we have upon the stocks ...'

I spoke for the first time, interrupting him sharply. 'Blanchland itself won't be affected though. Claremont Deuchar is a limited company. The family's personal assets can't be touched.'

'Ah yes. Well, I was coming to that. In the normal way that would be so, except that your brother took out a form of mortgage against the estate — entirely against my advice, I might add.'

'Could he do that?' I demanded. 'Legally, I mean? Surely Blanchland is entailed?'

'Well, yes, again, that is so, but the terms of the entail are rather vague, really only ensuring that the estate passes in preference to the next male heir. The incumbent always had, during his lifetime, full power to mortgage or raise money against the estate in any way he thought fit. I'm sorry, Maxwell,' he added in his stiff legal voice. 'I'm afraid there'll be no choice but to sell.'

18

So there it was; rich man to poor man in less than an hour; a tradition, a heritage, completely destroyed.

I went out walking. It didn't matter that it was dark. I knew my way around the estate blindfold.

I went down to the river and sat on the high bank room where Hugo and I had used to fish. *Hugo and I* — how ridiculous, but I was almost beginning to miss him. I'd hated him so thoroughly and for so long.

I stared down at the river; dark water lapping, seductive, inviting. I wondered why, if Hugo had had to kill himself, why he hadn't chosen to drown. So much more considerate I felt; no noise, no mess, no awkward explanations. People drowned in rivers all the time. So much more dignified too; his corpse drifting gently downstream like Arthur to Avalon — our mother watching from the window like the Lady of Shallot.

I gave a silly giggle and wished that I'd brought the champagne out. Thinking about Hugo sobered me. I couldn't believe that he was dead. I still sensed his presence. I still felt that I had to be on my guard, that he was lurking about somewhere trying to get back into my life. Perhaps if I'd actually seen his body it would have made it more real. I tried to visualise him in the act. I closed my eyes and imagined him coolly loading the revolver and placing it against his head. I saw his eyes squeeze themselves shut as he braced himself — and then suddenly they flew open. In my mind's eye I saw their expression of terror and dread and I knew then that at the very moment he'd pulled the trigger he had changed his mind. The split second before he died he had decided that he wanted to live ...

I leapt to my feet in horror. I felt he was there, behind me, embodied in the long shadow stretched behind me on the grass.

I ran; lurching, staggering, slithering over the grass — and then I stopped, ashamed of myself. I'd never run away from a fight with Hugo before. I wheeled round to face whatever was there. But of course there was nothing. Nothing to fight, nothing to fight for. Hugo, the bastard, had won after all. He'd still managed to cheat me. He'd given the lie to the old adage that you can't take it with you. Hugo had, everything

19

that I'd ever wanted — everything that is except Marcia.

I always thought afterwards that if I hadn't had so much to drink ... But people always say that about situations and events that they'd prefer to forget. 'I was drunk — I don't remember — I didn't know what I was doing.' But of course I did know; I had been vaguely planning Marcia's seduction for years although now it was more than the satisfaction of an adolescent passion. It was revenge, blood geld, the need to possess something of Hugo's.

Yet the circumstances were hardly propitious — this only occurred to me as I stood outside her door. I was drunk beyond a socially acceptable level; unshaven, and as I hadn't been able to face dinner I hadn't bothered to change and still wore my army uniform. And the object of my desire was my brother's wife, a widow of barely three weeks' standing who hadn't set eyes on me for more than a year. I felt that was a challenge in anybody's book and consequently I hesitated, seriously considering the possibility of a rebuff. But then, on the credit side, I knew that she didn't find me completely unattractive. I was too like Hugo to be physically repellant. And she would be feeling vulnerable, in need of a friend. She was bound to feel alone without Hugo's protection. And as a last resort there was always the champagne — I had great faith in the potency of that particular wine. Gin was depressing; whisky inflamed, but champagne created a mood of instant euphoria; it had a glamour that few women could resist. Besides, I wasn't going to blunder in like any over-sexed bull. I shouldn't make a move without positive encouragement. And if, after all, things did go disastrously wrong, I could always plead that I'd 'been under the influence', which of course I was.

Shifting the champagne and glasses to my other hand, I knocked discreetly on her door. There was a pause before she answered, just the one word, 'Enter'. My knees turned to water at the sound of her voice. Amazing how the French can endow the most ordinary words with an air of complete sensuality.

I opened the door and went in but didn't venture beyond the threshold. She was lying on the bed wrapped in an extravagant garment of satin and feathers. Magazines

20

surrounded her; there was a half-eaten box of chocolates by her hand. My spirits soared. No widow's weeds then or mourning black. I hadn't actually expected that there would be.

'Hello, Marcia,' I said casually. 'I hope I'm not disturbing you, only as I missed you at dinner I thought I ought to call in.'

For a few moments she just stared at me, then slowly she smiled, an amused, satisfied curve of her lips, that told me that my presence wasn't entirely unwelcome. So far, so good. I closed the door.

She slid from the bed. 'Don't tell me you have come to offer your condolences, Max.'

'No,' I said, smiling. 'In fact, quite the reverse. I thought you might like to help me finish the champagne. We might as well drink it before the bailiffs move in.'

She curled herself in the corner of a long low couch. 'Are things really so bad then, Max?'

I sat down in a chair, resisting the temptation to sit beside her. Her effect upon me was as potent as ever; all my youthful dreams came rushing back. She looked marvellous; her blonde hair short and fashionably shingled; her eyes, grey and luminous beneath finely plucked brows with their amused and knowledgeable expression. She had the body of a Gibson Girl which of course wasn't fashionable. She had breasts which weren't 'in' but they looked wonderful to me.

'Yes. I'm afraid so,' I said ruefully, and gave her a brief resumé of what Ridgeway had told me. I felt it better to get the bad news out of the way.

She looked appalled. 'So I will get nothing then? Everything will go to pay the debts?'

I had to be honest. 'Well, you'll get what's left of Hugo's personal fortune,' though I already knew from Ridgeway that this was practically nothing.

'What about the house, the furniture? That must be worth a lot?'

I frowned, my ardour fractionally cooling at being reminded so forcibly of her materialistic streak. 'Well, you wouldn't have got that in any case,' I explained. 'Blanchland and the estate are all entailed, which means that they pass

21

intact from eldest son to eldest son. If you and Hugo had had a son, Blanchland would have gone to him.'

'So who gets it now?'

'Hugo's creditors get it now,' I answered bitterly. 'He borrowed money against it, so now it will have to be sold.'

'And the contents,' she persisted with that blunt tenacity that I was one day to know so well.

'Well I suppose, technically, they belong to me. But even if there's anything left, it'll probably have to be sold. We shall need something to live on.'

She was silent for a while. I could see her mind working, assessing the situation from her point of view. In retrospect, that should have warned me.

'And where shall you live if you have to leave Blanchland?' she asked at last.

I opened the champagne and poured her a generous glass. 'That depends on how much is left. Of course, as a last resort we could go to Uncle Gerard's, but I promise you it will be a last resort,' I smiled at her reassuringly. 'Don't worry. We won't be left without a roof over our heads.'

Marcia shrugged. 'It will not matter to me,' she said coolly. 'I shall not be going with you.'

My heart plunged. I felt sick with disappointment. I hadn't realised until then quite how far I'd ventured along this particular road, how much I'd counted on stepping into Hugo's shoes in every possible way. With typical male conceit I had assumed that she would turn to me for protection. Marcia was the kind of woman who would always need a protector, whether it was father, husband, lover or son. She was incomplete without a man beside her. Naturally, I had assumed I would be that man. I had imagined inheriting Marcia in the same way as I had imagined inheriting Blanchland. Now it seemed that I wasn't to have either.

At last I managed to speak, to keep my voice steady. 'Where will you go then?' I enquired casually.

She gave a small bitter smile. 'As you say, Max, that depends on how much money is left. London perhaps — or if the worst comes to the worst I can always go back to France.'

'But how will you manage? You've no real family, no

22

friends. I just can't imagine you as the sort of person who could survive alone.'

She looked at me coldly. 'And how would you know? You don't know what sort of person I am, Max. In fact, you don't know anything about me at all.'

That was true. I didn't. None of us did. Her circumstances before she'd married Hugo were extremely vague. She said her family were all dead — *dans la guerre* — apart from a cousin who lived outside Marseilles. It was this lack of background which had formed the foundation of my mother's extreme dislike. There were other things of course. By English standards Marcia was considered completely unacceptable. Her taste in dress was vulgar, her jewellery erred on the ostentatious side, her flamboyant personality and ready laughter was considered unrefined. Of course it helped being French. The English never expected foreigners to know how to behave so any defects in social behaviour could be partially excused. But I could quite see why Hugo had married her. Her sexual charms were obvious. She made them obvious in a deliciously sluttish way. Hugo would have liked that. He'd always had rather a thing about tarts, possibly because they required less effort. It wasn't quite like that with me. To a degree sexual desire transcends all considerations of race and class. Only to sustain it did it need something more and I always felt that after one night with Marcia I would have had all that there was. But that one night I was determined to have.

'No. You're quite right,' I smiled at her ruefully. 'I don't know anything about you — except that you're beautiful and generous and that, with one thing and another, you've had a pretty rotten time. We've all treated you pretty badly, haven't we? I don't blame you in the least for wanting to get away.'

Tears misted her eyes. They looked like pools of shimmering water in which I could happily have drowned. 'You've always been kind, Max,' she said with a catch in her voice. 'It's the others who hate me — so much that in the end they made Hugo hate me too.'

I was incredibly moved. I had never seen this vulnerable side of her before and I gazed at her with tenderness and compassion. I was full of champagne and consequently full of romance and chivalry. Suddenly all my cynicism fell away. I was sixteen again; back in those days of looking and longing when a smile from her could send me shivering with excitement to my bed.

'I'm so sorry,' I said softly. 'I didn't realise you were so unhappy here.'

She smiled suddenly. 'Why should you have. Hugo was always very careful to keep up appearances. He would have hated for anyone to have known there was anything wrong. It would have looked, you see, as if he'd made a mistake.'

'I think it was you who made the mistake, marrying him at all. Hugo wasn't capable of appreciating a woman of your sensitive temperament.'

She looked amused. 'And you are?'

'Yes,' I answered softly. 'I'm quite sure I am.'

There was a pause, then she said in her sensual voice. 'But then a man does not look for the same virtues in a mistress as he does in a wife.'

So there it was; everything out in the open at last. She knew what I wanted and her open admission that she knew seemed to me to signify her willingness. From then on the situation seemed to be out of my hands. She leant towards me and I breathed the scent she always used; exotic, erotic; French, of course.

'You're very like Hugo, at least physically you are. You know, just for a moment, when you walked into the room, I thought ...'

'Do we have to talk about Hugo,' I said weakly.

'Yes. Why not? He's dead, isn't he? I can say what I like about him now.'

It was said with such vehemence that for a moment I was shocked. *De mortuis nil nisis bonum*, after all.

She laughed at my expression. 'You see, you're conventional after all — just like Hugo.' Her speculative glance flickered over my face and settled tantalisingly on my mouth. 'I had imagined that you would be more daring, that you wouldn't care anything about what people think, that when you wanted something you just reached out and took it.'

I couldn't breathe. I couldn't speak. I couldn't miss the

24

invitation in her voice and eyes. And yet for some reason, I hesitated — All those years of longing, those passionate dreams, all suddenly within my grasp. I was here, in her bedroom; beneath the thin robe I knew she was naked. And yet I hesitated, as if warned by some premonition that what I was about to do would have repercussions for the rest of my life.

Then she reached out and touched me, just the ends of her fingers carelessly brushing my sleeve. She murmured, 'I wonder if you make love like Hugo did?'

I managed to speak. 'How did he make love?'

'Oh, very rarely.' She laughed. 'And then furtively, guiltily, as if he were ashamed.'

Well, I felt I could do a bit better than that.

'It was the last thing he did, you know, before he died. He made love to me here. He hadn't done that in nearly a year. And then he went downstairs, into the study and killed himself.'

I shivered. I wasn't sure which revolted me most, the idea of him copulating with Marcia or blowing his brains out. Neither were conducive to my erotic state of mind.

'And he was a bully, you know. He liked to hurt ...'

I leant towards her, my lips brushing her cheek. 'I won't hurt you, Marcia darling.'

But of course I did. All that anger and disappointment had to come out somewhere. I needed to hurt as I felt I'd been hurt myself. And I couldn't forget Hugo, the thought of him ... furtively, guiltily ... And added to that was the terror that I might prove inadequate, that all those years of passive longing might suddenly prove too much. Normally, on these occasions, I felt that I managed to acquit myself tolerably well. I was an experienced lover in the physical sense, in perfect control of my reflexes. But with all the other women, I had acquired the habit of completely detaching my mind from my body. I laid aside conscience and inhibitions in the same way as I laid aside my clothes: intellectually and emotionally, I wasn't there. But this wasn't any other woman. This was Marcia, my brother's wife, for years the object of my secret and guilty passion. I totally lost control.

In the cold light of day the guilt was overwhelming —

25

when I woke and saw her ravished mouth, the shadow of bruising upon her breasts. She was still asleep and I did not wake her. Silently I slid from the bed and into my clothes and embarked on the long furtive journey back to my room, every step haunted by visions of Father Devine leaping from the shadows and denouncing me as fornicator and pervert, ravisher of my brother's wife.

I ran myself a tepid bath, as if by immersing myself I would be cleansed from my sin. My head throbbed with the aftermath of gin and champagne, and I couldn't stop thinking about Marcia, about what I had done. Would she expect me to marry her? I wasn't even sure that legally I could. Wasn't it some sort of incest to marry your brother's wife? And in my confused and guilty state I wasn't even sure that I wanted to now. Last night I had, but last night had been the fulfilment of a schoolboy fantasy. I wasn't a boy any more but a man of twenty-four with no money and less prospects. Marriage was the last thing on my mind.

With an effort I managed to pull myself together. I had a strenuous day ahead; meetings with Ridgeway, the Receiver and Rochester Mercantile. In the meantime there was the ordeal of breakfast to be faced — and somehow I had to tell my mother about Blanchland.

Naturally, with my inbred papist tendency towards doom and disaster, I felt they all knew about Marcia the minute I entered the room. I was immediately conscious of an air of extreme disapproval.

Marcia wasn't there although she never came down to breakfast in any case, and Uncle Gerard had gone out riding. But my mother and sisters were down, and Father Devine — he knew, of course. I was sure he knew; priests always knew everything. And so strong was the urge, the habit of confession, that for a moment I had an hysterical vision of flinging myself on my knees beside his chair. 'Father. Forgive me. I have sinned most grievously. I have fucked my brother's wife.'

Avoiding the circle of eyes I helped myself to a plateful of congealed scrambled egg which I had no intention of eating. I went through the motions though and picked up my fork. Then my mother said pointedly in her impersonal voice,

26

'And how are you feeling this morning, Maxwell?'

I understood then that the disapproval was because of my indulgence in the bottle the previous night. 'I'm very well, thank you, Mother,' I replied.

'You surprise me, Maxwell. I wouldn't have believed it possible, judging by the amount of alcohol you consumed.'

'Drowning my sorrows,' I said flippantly.

Her eyes grew cold. 'Well, that will not solve anything, getting drunk. And in case you have forgotten, it's not the way we do things here. Claremonts face up to their responsibilities.'

The hypocrisy appalled me. 'Like Hugo did?' I snapped.

She grew very pale, transparent almost. 'I consider that remark in the worst possible taste, that you should allude to your brother's tragic death at all. But if we must discuss it, then let me say that my feeling is that Hugo took what he felt to be the only honourable course.'

I saw red then. 'Honourable,' I yelled. 'What's honourable about leaving your family to face a mountain of debt? What's honourable about leaving other people to clear up the mess?'

'Oh, for God's sake, Max,' Veronica drawled. 'Must you always be so dramatic?'

I leapt to my feet. 'So you think I'm being dramatic, do you? You think I'm exaggerating? Well, let me just make a few things clear. Today I shall be forced to sit back helplessly whilst the company that our father and grandfather made a success is sold over my head at probably half of its real worth. Do you understand that? After today, Claremont Deuchar won't exist. It will have all been swallowed up by Rochester's bank.'

There was silence. I saw my mother moisten her lips, then she said in the voice that she used to children and old men. 'Yes, of course I understand, Maxwell. And I don't deny that the situation gives cause for concern — And neither do I deny that your brother may have made a few errors of judgement...'

'Errors! They weren't errors. They were blunders, disasters, colossal mistakes. The firm had been running down ever since he took over.'

'Nevertheless, I don't see that we can blame Hugo entirely.'

'Why not?' I yelled. 'Why can't we blame Hugo? He made the decisions. He was in control.'

Suddenly Veronica sprang to her feet. 'You're enjoying this, aren't you?' she hissed at me. 'You wouldn't have dared say any of this if Hugo had been alive. But just because he's not here to defend himself . . .'

'And whose fault is that,' I enquired malevolently. 'It was his choice to put a bullet through his head.'

'You beast,' Veronica screamed. 'You always hated him, didn't you? You were always jealous because he was better than you.'

I stared at her with sudden deadly calm. No one could have guessed my murderous hatred. 'Well, I know you always thought so, Vee. At least you were always telling me how wonderful he was; perfect, without a fault.' I smiled at her. 'I wonder if you'll still think so when you have to go out into the world and find yourself a job. Oh, don't look so surprised, Vee. Hasn't it occurred to you that we're all going to have to work for a living now. Once the company is sold we'll have no income.'

'Well, that won't affect me,' Veronica said like the selfish bitch she was. 'Richard and I will be married as soon as we decently can. I shall be living at Chirton.'

'And what about Mother and Helen? Am I expected to keep them out of my army pay? I can barely keep myself.'

Veronica shrugged. 'They'll still have the rents from the estate. Not as much as they're used to, I realise that . . .'

I closed my eyes. I had meant to break it gently, to choose the right time, except that there wasn't really a right time for something like that. Now was as good as any.

I said slowly and furiously — somehow it helped being angry. 'I can see that Ridgeway hasn't made the situation completely clear. The estate will have to be sold. Blanchland, the farms, the cottages as well. Everything will have to go to pay off the debts. Not my debts, I might add,' I glared at Veronica, 'but wonderful, perfect, bloody Hugo's debts.'

Her eyes dilated with shock but she kept her voice steady. 'Well, that's all right,' she said with childish bravado. 'It doesn't matter to us. Mother and Helen can come to Chirton with me.'

'I don't want to live at Chirton,' Helen whispered. 'I want to stay here, at Blanchland.'

'Well, of course, we all want that, Helen,' my mother said in such a terrible voice that for a moment I couldn't bear to look at her. She seemed to have visibly shrunk, actually diminished in size so that her clothes hung loosely about her.

She looked at me. I could see how much it hurt to ask. 'Are you sure, Max? Lawyers are such a pessimistic breed. Are you sure there is nothing to be done?'

'Yes, I'm sure,' I answered in a tight angry voice. 'Hugo mortgaged Blanchland as security for the loan. We either sell of our own accord or they'll foreclose.'

Nobody spoke. The silence seemed to stretch on and on, then Father Devine said in his soft pious voice. 'God will answer. All is in His hands ...'

'And you can keep quiet,' I turned on him viciously. 'You've been a drain on this family for long enough, so unless you can earn your keep for once and come up with one of those miracles you're always ranting about, I suggest you pack your things and find someone else to sponge off.'

I looked at my mother, sitting mute and still. 'There's only one more thing that I want to say, and that is that somehow, someday, I'm going to get us out of this mess. I'll get Blanchland back if it's the last thing I do. But, in the meantime, I'm not going to have Hugo venerated like some saint. I don't even want to hear his name mentioned.'

I stormed out into the hall and bawled at Henry, the footman, to bring my hat.

'Max, please wait.' Helen came running after me. 'Don't be too hard on them, darling. They're really very upset.'

She slipped her arm through mine. 'Come on. Let's walk. You need to cool down.'

We walked in silence, down the steps on to the terrace and into the Elizabethan box maze. I gave her hand an affectionate squeeze. If I loved anyone it was Helen. Just looking at her made me feel optimistic and relaxed. She wasn't a looker like Vee. She was slender and frail, insubstantial and childlike. All Helen's beauty came from within and to the end of my life she remained the only really good person I have ever known. Her goodness was her weakness. She saw

29

her own sweet disposition reflected in everyone else which meant the family bullied and exploited her whenever they got the chance. She was deeply religious which should have put us forever at odds. But Helen's simple faith was quite different to our mother's dogmatic and bigoted beliefs. Helen believed, as our Father had, in the inherent decency of mankind, and besides, she saw her faith as an intensely private thing, not something to be paraded and forcibly rammed down people's throats. Consequently, it was something we never dicussed.

We sat down on the rustic bench at the centre of the labyrinth on which generations of Claremont children had carved their initials. It was a tradition, proof that we'd been able to find our way through the maze alone.

I traced my own — and beside them, larger, bolder — well, they would be wouldn't they — the entwined H.E.C. of my brother, Hugo.

'Did he say anything to you?' I asked Helen quietly. 'Hugo, I mean. Before he died.'

'No. I don't think he said anything to anyone. He was with Marcia just before he died. Perhaps he spoke to her ...'

'It just doesn't seem like Hugo, does it? I mean to kill himself. I can hardly believe it. I still keep expecting him to pop up from somewhere and say it was all a huge practical joke. I mean, I've never known Hugo take anything that seriously.'

'He took failure seriously,' Helen said. 'He couldn't face us, you see. He couldn't face you. He couldn't bear the thought of being publicly humiliated ...'

'So he thought he'd let me have the privilege instead. Well, that's certainly in character, pushing his responsibilities on to someone else. I expect he knew that if he didn't kill himself I'd do the job for him. That's the worst thing, Helen. That he's gone. He's escaped. I shan't even have the satisfaction of hitting him.'

Helen looked at me with troubled eyes. 'Oh Max,' she said in a sad little voice. 'You'll have to learn to forgive him, you know, or he'll haunt you for the rest of your life.'

30

Chapter 3

I drove the leaking tourer back to Newcastle, then hired a cab to take me to North Shields. It seemed an extravagance — a tram would have more suited my present financial state — but today would be my last day of self-indulgence, and besides I didn't feel ready to advertise my penury just yet.

I sat back in the creaking leather interior and, so vividly were the memories of childhood ingrained; that it seemed like only yesterday that I had driven this way with my father and Hugo. I remembered Hugo had looked very grown up in his new Norfolk suit, a small but exact replica of our father. David and Absolom, the fair, favoured son. I had sulked in the corner like Amnon.

I stared from the window, much as I had done then. On the surface everything seemed just the same. The huge cranes still reminded me of a flock of monstrous skeletal birds. There were still acres of workshops, factories, railways converging; import jetties and coal staiths; slipways sloping down to the water's edge. But the usual clamour and bustle was strangely subdued, and I didn't remember so many men standing idle before; hundreds of them, hanging around the shipyard gates hoping to be set on for the day. I felt a stab of sympathy. I knew how they felt. Like me, they'd known better days.

The cab crawled through High Walker, past Armstrong Whitworth's naval yard, desolate since the Washington Treaty. Then into Wallsend; past Swan Hunter's from where the *Mauretania* had been launched; past the turbine works of Parsons Marine, I was surprised that I remembered everything so well, that I could so clearly anticipate the line of the river. Beyond Willington Quay it deepened and widened, enough to accommodate huge Cunarders drawing thirty-three feet. Massive gantries straddled the complex of docks; the Northumberland and Albert Edward, and across the river on the Durham side, Tyne Dock and Jarrow Slake; the grey little town of Hebburn.

I couldn't resist turning off for a last look at our yards. The gates were locked and I peered through the bars at the empty buildings; mould lofts and drawing offices, furnace and plater shops; the towering hydraulic cranes. It was the silence that was so depressing. I always remembered the yards as a place of noise and movement; air hammers rattling over white-hot rivets, thousands of men shouting above the scream of machinery. And now silence, stagnant water, the raw tinge of rust ... Suddenly I felt sick and angry. My God, if Hugo hadn't had the decency to pull the trigger himself, I'd have certainly volunteered for the job.

Ridgeway was already waiting for me in Hugo's plush office and he spent a few moments explaining the form. Apparently my presence there was a mere formality. I was to have no voice in the proceedings at all. It was then I got my first inkling of what poverty meant — not just the lack of money itself, but the lack of esteem, of dignity. People were able to treat one with contempt.

The Receiver arrived, a dour little man in an ill-fitting suit who looked as if he attended funerals as a recreation. He shook hands with Ridgeway but made no attempt to do so with me. I got the impression that social niceties were not wasted on individuals who so grossly mismanaged their financial affairs. I felt a queer mixture of anger and amusement. Poor old Hugo, I thought bitterly, to have missed all this.

Then the Rochester contingent arrived; lawyers and clerks flanking a thin young man. I felt surprised. I had expected Edward Rochester himself till I remembered that he had died two years ago. This was his son John — or Jack as Hugo had always called him. I couldn't remember whether I'd ever met him or not. I'd usually given Hugo's friends a fairly wide berth but I fancied I would have remembered that pale ascetic face with its dark intense eyes. He looked more like a fourteenth-century martyr than the chairman of a bank.

We shook hands formally. His hands were soft in an

unpleasant, feminine way. His manner was vaguely apologetic. It crossed my mind for an instant to throw myself on his mercy, to plead for just a little more time ... But time to do what? I hadn't the faintest idea how one went about raising such a vast sum of money.

The moment passed. The meeting proceeded. I thought, on the whole, I kept my temper well as everything was ruthlessly converted into pounds, shillings and pence and my entire world was suddenly reduced to a double column of figures. The only concession I gained was permission to handle the sale of Blanchland myself rather than have it put up for auction. Apart from that, it was made abundantly clear in a very subtle way that congenital poverty was one thing, but to have had money and lost it was an unforgivable sin. It seemed failure carried a worse stigma than suicide.

Then suddenly it was all over. I had turned to leave when Jack Rochester called me back.

'Claremont. I wonder if you could spare me a moment?'

I hesitated fractionally. I wasn't in the mood for sympathy and it was as I suspected. He said how sorry he was, how shocked he was and how convinced he was that Hugo's death could only have been an accident — meaning that he knew perfectly well that he'd blown his brains out. I heard him out and thanked him politely. I turned to go but once again he made an effort to detain me.

'Look here,' he said awkwardly. 'I feel thoroughly rotten about this. If there'd been any other way, if it had just been up to me ... But my board insisted ...'

'Yes, I understand,' I said shortly. 'Please don't apologise.'

'Well, Hugo and I were good pals, you know. I feel I'm partly to blame for allowing him to get so much out of his depth.' He hesitated briefly. 'Look, would you think it rude of me if I asked if you had any plans — as to what you're going to do now, I mean?'

I looked at him coldly. 'Would you think it rude of me if I asked why you wished to know?'

He flushed painfully. 'I'm not being inquisitive. I merely asked because I understand you're giving up the army and I thought, if you've nothing definite on, well, I'd like to make you a proposition.'

I waited. He went on; 'Well, I wondered if you'd consider coming to join us at Rochester's.'

'In what capacity?' I enquired drily.

'As my personal assistant, actually. I've been on the look-out for somebody ever since my father died but the right chap has never seemed to come along.'

'And what makes you think that I'm the right chap?'

'Well, you're one of us for one thing. It's always so much easier to deal with one's own sort, don't you think? And you've obviously got a good brain. You read law at Oxford, didn't you?'

'I'm afraid all I read at Oxford were the labels on bottles of Holland gin. I'm sure Hugo told you that I was sent down.'

Rochester grinned. 'Well, at least that's a qualification even I can appreciate. I'm sure we'd get on very well.'

'I don't have any experience,' I continued to object. 'I've spent most of my time in the army.'

'That doesn't matter. You'll soon get the hang of things, in fact, it might be an advantage. Having no experience means that you've no preconceived ideas to overcome. And it's really all quite straightforward once you know the ropes. As a merchant bank, we deal with companies and trusts rather than members of the public. Local rather than national; shipping and ordinance, coal and steel. We facilitate expansion schemes, arrange take-over bids. Occasionally we act as an issuing house and float new companies on a modest scale. All you'd really have to do is trail around with me and take notes, make sure I wasn't late for meetings and things like that.' He looked at me. 'Well, what do you say? A thousand a year to start. Surely, it's worth a try?'

My first instinct was to say no. This smacked of charity, the old school tie. I knew quite well that his offer was prompted by his former friendship with Hugo. And then there was my pride, already battered and smarting from my recent treatment at the Receiver's hands. To work for Rochester's, the very people that had pulled the plug ... But then on the other hand, pride was a luxury only rich men could afford. I needed a job badly and a thousand a year was a princely salary. I reminded myself that there were worse things I could do.

I said cautiously. 'I'm afraid I couldn't be of any use to you for at least a month. As you probably know, my affairs are still in some confusion.'

'That's all right,' Rochester smiled. 'Take your time. Shall we say the beginning of July?'

I shook hands with him again. 'Thank you,' I said as graciously as I could. 'I'm very much obliged.'

It was late when I got back, nearly eight o'clock, and they'd had to begin dinner without me. Everything seemed ridiculously normal; Davenport plates, Dover sole, a dry smoky Chablis. And my mother talking in her calm expressionless voice; about the weather, the garden, how she hoped to have a good crop of peaches from the hothouse this year. I felt slightly sick. It was as if the scene at the breakfast table had never occurred, as if she hadn't heard a word I'd said. Even more sickening was the way everyone humoured her, murmuring agreement whenever it seemed necessary. I looked at their faces; Helen looked distressed, Uncle Gerard bored. Veronica was pale and kept pressing her lips together as if she were trying not to cry. Eventually I looked at Marcia, having finally plucked up the courage to meet her eyes. She gave me her familiar provocative smile and I felt my body sag with relief. So that was all right then. I was still in favour. I hadn't disgraced myself absolutely.

We took our coffee in the drawing room. Uncle Gerard fiddled with the wireless and we listened to the news. It was all bad; unemployment rising; the threat of a national strike; trade figures down for the second consecutive year.

'Damn socialists,' Uncle Gerard muttered. 'No wonder the Empire's going to the dogs. There'll be trouble in India soon, you mark my words. That chap Ghandi's stirring things up.'

I wasn't really listening. With a Philistine's eye, I appraised the contents of the room, wondering how much I'd get if I had to sell. Of course, I wouldn't *have* to. Ridgeway had made it quite clear that the bank had no claim to my personal property. The bank could take the house but the contents were solely mine under the entail. But he'd expressed doubt as to whether even the sale of the yards and the estate would be sufficient to settle things up. Personally, after meeting Rochester this morning, I didn't think the bank would press their claims beyond that, but to remain in their debt, at least to me, was absolutely unthinkable. And in any case, we'd need something to live on. My salary from Rochester's, princely though it was, hardly put me in the millionaire class.

So I was going to have to grit my teeth and put a few pieces up at the rooms. I glanced around me, trying to make up my mind what things I would miss the least. It was an impossible choice. Everything meant something. Everything had a past. Like the house itself, the furnishings were a pot-pourri of several different styles; the taste and fancy of every owner over hundreds of years, a collection of oddments that, by virtue of their beauty and antiquity and their absolute right to be there, somehow blended into a pleasing whole. Of course, there were one or two really good pieces; the early French prie-dieu that was reputed to have belonged to Madame de Montespan, the Turner landscape that had been a gift from the artist. It was like that all over the house; Dutch marquetry and Louis Quinze rubbing shoulders with objects of little or no intrinsic value but things that in their own way were priceless to us. There were the family portraits, dark and gloomy — apart from the Holbein and the Millais of grandmother, I couldn't see anybody wanting those. People weren't interested in other people's ancestors, were they? And the sword that Eugene de Claremont had wielded at Crecy, my great grandfather's collection of model ships — it was unthinkable that we should ever part with these.

I felt depression creeping over me and turned my thoughts to something else. On the whole I was feeling more relaxed. Rochester's offer had been a godsend; at least now I had achieved the respectable status of being employed. And his terms had been generous, far more than I was worth. I only hoped I could live up to his expectations.

I looked at my mother. I hadn't told her yet. Perhaps it was time I broke the news.

I cleared my throat. 'By the way,' I announced casually. 'I've got a job.'

Silence. Then my mother slowly raised her eyes. 'A job!'

36

she said aghast, as if I had informed her I had got some fatal disease. 'Doing what, may I ask?'

'Working for Rochester's actually. Jack Rochester needs a personal assistant. He seems to think I can do the job.'

I thought she was going to faint. She actually put out a hand as if to steady herself. 'You can't be serious, Max? I can't believe that you have so little pride!'

'You have some other suggestion then?' I demanded coldly.

She put aside her cup. 'Yes, as a matter of fact, I do.' She glanced round at her brother. 'I was thinking, Gerard. Couldn't Max do something for you down at Ansty. You're always complaining you don't have enough help on the estate ...'

'Oh, I see,' I interrupted furiously. 'Sponging off our relatives is more socially acceptable than doing an honest job of work?'

'It's more acceptable to keep things in the family than to let the whole world know how we are placed.'

'And you think that people haven't already guessed?' I asked incredulously. 'My God, we must be the main talking point for miles.'

Suddenly Veronica jumped up and rushed blindly from the room. My mother glared at me. 'What's the matter with Vee,' I asked in surprise.

It was Marcia who answered. 'Apparently the Honourable Richard isn't so honourable after all. He broke off their engagement this morning.'

'He hasn't broken it off,' my mother insisted. 'The wedding has been — well, postponed ...'

Marcia gave a derisive laugh. 'Postponed until Richard thinks of a way out that won't reflect too badly on him.'

Well, I couldn't say I was completely surprised. The Veres were Catholics like ourselves; the elder Vere a baronet and very conscious of his dignity and Richard himself was on the threshold of a promising political career. A suicide amongst one's prospective in-laws was bad enough; insolvency as well must have been the last straw.

I bit down on my anger. I supposed we'd have to get used to this sort of thing, being treated shabbily by our former

37

friends. I felt sorry for Vee though and furious on her behalf. Whatever our differences, she was still my sister. I really didn't feel I could let it go.

'I think,' I said slowly, 'that perhaps I should have a word with Vere.'

'No, Max. Please,' my mother looked at me sternly. 'Don't interfere. It won't do any good, and perhaps if we let things settle down Richard may come round.'

I was even more enraged by this show of meekness. Keep quiet; say nothing; turn the other cheek. I saw this as part of the Church's negative philosophy, the blind total faith that left everything in God's hands and resulted in complete and utter apathy. God will answer; all was His will, and in the meantime, whilst we waited for divine guidance, Claremont Deuchar was in liquidation, Blanchland was about to go under the hammer and Veronica had been jilted by that bounder Vere.

'My God,' I said, fuming. 'You have the nerve to ask me whether I have any pride, and yet you're perfectly willing to let Richard Vere treat Veronica like dirt. I'm to keep quiet in the hope that when the scandal dies down he might have the courage to marry her?'

'It's a different thing altogether,' she answered sharply. 'Richard just needs a little time to sort himself out; he's under extreme pressure from his family. If we're patient and don't make a fuss, everything will eventually sort itself out. Whereas for you openly to associate yourself with the people that have ruined us ...'

'Rochester's didn't ruin us,' I snapped. 'Hugo did.'

She looked at me with those cold pale eyes. 'I thought you didn't want to hear your brother's name mentioned. It seems it is you who are obsessed with him, not I.'

She turned to Uncle Gerard before I could speak. 'What did you think of my suggestion then, Gerard? I'm sure it would be a help to you having Max around. in fact, I was thinking that if we have to leave Blanchland as Maxwell seems to think, we might all come to Ansty till things sort themselves out.'

Uncle Gerard actually turned pale — and I didn't blame him — at the thought of being saddled with his impecunious relatives. 'Well, naturally Ursula,' he mumbled. 'I want to do what I can. But to be perfectly honest, since the war, we haven't been that flush. The upkeep of Ansty takes a fair slice of the cake, and what with taxes and what not ... And then there's Felicity to be considered. She has her hands full with the twins ... Of course, I wouldn't see you without a roof over your heads ...'

My mother's face hardened. 'Well, that's generous of you, Gerard, but I wouldn't dream of imposing. I wouldn't want to put dear Felicity out.'

Uncle Gerard flushed. 'Well, quite frankly, Ursula, running away to Ansty wouldn't be any answer really. You're going to have to face up to things in the end.'

My mother looked at me. 'Well, Maxwell, as we appear to have been abandoned by both family and friends, have you made any plans as to where we shall live?'

'I thought we could rent somewhere,' I said. 'Just till we see how things are going to work out. It seems more sensible to rent and conserve whatever capital we might have. We'll need something to live on. My salary from Rochester's won't support five people, at least not in any sort of style.'

'Five!' Mother exclaimed. 'Surely there are just your sisters and ourselves?'

'And Marcia,' I reminded her. 'As it doesn't appear that Hugo provided for her adequately, she's our responsibility as well.'

'Marcia! Oh, I shouldn't think Marcia would wish to remain with us. She's still quite young. She'll soon find another husband. After all, there's nothing really to keep her here. It's not as if there were any children.'

She always spoke to Marcia like this, indirectly, through a third person, as if Marcia wasn't there. I glanced in her direction and saw she was amused.

'Yes, you're quite right,' she said in her languid voice. 'There is nothing to keep me here now that Hugo is gone. And besides,' she added, 'I wouldn't dream of being another burden upon Max. I, at least, am capable of earning a living.'

My mother smiled unpleasantly. 'Quite, Marcia. And I can easily imagine in what way.'

'I say,' said Uncle Gerard, 'Steady on.'

Marcia smiled. 'Oh that's all right, Gerard. I'm quite used

39

to insinuations of that kind. You see, it's her only consolation for the fact that Hugo disobeyed her, that he married me without consulting her first. It helps you see, to think he was lured away against his will by the temptations of the flesh. What she can't face up to is the fact that she drove him away with her possessiveness, her cloying affection. He would have married anyone just to escape her.' Marcia gave her quick malicious smile. 'He hated her, you see — and that's why she hates me, because I'm the only one that really knows.'

For a moment I thought my mother hadn't heard what she'd said, then she looked up and I saw the dangerous glitter of her eyes. 'Marcia, my dear,' she said in her most chilling voice, 'you were a slut when you came into this house and you'll still be a slut when you go. Frankly, I'd like that to be as soon as possible.'

She rose to her feet and called to Helen to see her up to her room. Then Uncle Gerard muttered something about turning in. Marcia and I were left alone.

'Get me a drink, will you, Max?' Marcia stood abruptly and went to stand by the hearth.

'I think there's only brandy. Will that do?'

She half smiled. 'Admirably. Please make it a large one.'

I handed her the glass and we stood for a moment side by side. 'Is it true?' I asked her. 'Did Hugo really feel like that — about Mother, I mean?'

'Yes. It's perfectly true. He was afraid of her in a strange sort of way. That's why he married me in France. He knew he would never have the courage to go through with it here.'

'How strange,' I said musingly. 'I always rather resented him for being the favourite son. It seems I might have had a lucky escape.'

She smiled. 'You won't escape from me so easily.'

'I'm not sure that I want to try.'

She turned her face up towards me. 'You look tired, Max,' she said with amusement in her voice. 'I think that what you need is a good night's sleep.'

I felt my pulse quicken, that familiar ache. 'And am I going to get one?'

Her hand reached out and caressed my cheek. 'No, I don't think so. Not for a long time yet.'

And so I embarked upon ten days during which I alternated violently between heaven and hell. Hell was seeing strangers come to look at Blanchland with covetous eyes. Heaven was Marcia; the nights, every night, that we spent together, becoming more obsessed, more involved, more enraptured with her body. Of course, it couldn't last, neither the heaven nor the hell, and strangely enough, both came to an end together. On the twelfth of June I received a letter from Ridgeway saying that a buyer had been found. The very next day Marcia left me.

I'm not sure now which affected me the most. I'd always known, of course, that I'd have to give up Blanchland. But I'd been so sure of Marcia, too sure perhaps, and recalling the last night we spent together, I could see that all the signs had been there.

She'd been on edge, openly uneasy; for the very first time since our affair had begun, she hadn't wanted to make love. I soon discovered the cause. She'd seen Ridgeway that morning about the finalisation of Hugo's personal estate, and as I'd expected it hadn't amounted to much; a few hundred pounds, the red Bugatti and his collection of silver cups.

I watched her as she walked up and down the room brandishing Ridgeway's cheque. She was talking all the time, occasionally lapsing into voluble French. One would have thought she'd been cheated out of millions.

At first I was amused. Marcia could make a drama out of anything. She enjoyed scenes almost as much as most people loathed them. One put this down to her being Continental and I was used to these mildly histrionic displays. It was rather like watching an amateur actress perform. When she paused for breath I felt that I should applaud. After a while I got bored. The part wasn't really worthy of her. The script was trite, her lines banal, and as always she was over-acting.

'Oh, for God's sake, Marcia. Stop complaining. You got more than my mother and sisters did.'

'And so I should,' she said shrewishly. 'I was his wife. It's not a great deal to show for eight years of marriage, is it?'

I didn't answer. I was beginning to dislike this conversation intensely. She made it sound as if she felt she should have been paid by the hour.

41

She read my thoughts from my expression. 'Oh, of course, I forgot,' she sneered. 'It's vulgar and cheap to talk about money. But perhaps you'll find out, now that you haven't got any, that money isn't vulgar at all. Only being without it is.

'And don't think I don't know what is irritating you,' she went on. 'You think I ought to share it, don't you? Well, I'm not going to, I shall need every penny if I'm ever to get away.'

'Get away?' I said blankly. 'From whom? From me?'

'Yes, if you like. From you, from all of you. There's no future for me here.' She looked at me scornfully. 'I thought you were a realist, Max. How long do you think we can go on before someone finds out? Don't you realise how intolerable my position here is? I had little enough status as Hugo's wife. I shall have none at all as your mistress.'

I roused myself. I hadn't been following the script. This was obviously my cue for a proposal. I'd considered it of course, several times, but on a purely practical level the idea of marrying Marcia was totally bizarre. It wasn't just the thought of family opposition that deterred me — I'd been opposing them in some way for all of my life. It was rather that I'd come to the conclusion that Marcia wasn't the sort of woman one married, not if you were as impecunious as I was. Poverty and domesticity would have completely dulled her allure. But then, on the other hand, I didn't think at this juncture that I wanted to give her up. I needed her. I had come to rely on her physically, in the way that one becomes dependent on some habit-forming drug. One resented the dependency but preferred it to the excruciating pain of withdrawal. As she'd pointed out, it would be impossible for her to continue as my mistress once we had left Blanchland. What would pass unnoticed in a thirty-room house couldn't be overlooked in a suburban villa. No, I didn't want to marry her. I was perfectly happy with the way things were. I tried a delaying tactic.

'You won't always just be a mistress,' I promised her grandly. 'I'd marry you now if I had anything to offer . . .'

'Marry!' She flung back her head and laughed out loud. 'Oh Max. You fool.'

I was stung by her scorn. This wasn't what I had expected.

'Yes. Why not?' I said coldly. 'Or don't I measure up to Hugo?'

She stared at me with an odd expression. 'Poor Max,' she said softly. 'He's still able to torment you, isn't he? He's been dead for three months but you don't seem to be able to bury him. You're still trying to compete. You're still trying to win . . .'

'I have won,' I shouted, losing my temper completely. 'I'm the one that's got you.'

'Is that how you see me then? As some sort of trophy, some sort of prize?' She rounded on me furiously. 'That's why I can't marry you — because it would be like I was still married to Hugo as well. He'd always be there between us. I want to forget Hugo. I want to start again. Can't you see that if I married you, hardly anything would have changed for me. I'd still be Mrs Claremont. I'd still be surrounded by people who despise me. I'd still be the French slut who corrupted her son — and not just one son, but both of them. Do you think she would forgive me that?'

'Marcia, please.' This was all getting completely out of hand. I could see that I'd miscalculated completely. 'Listen to me,' I said, taking her hands. 'We'll sort something out. There's obviously an answer.'

'Oh yes, Max. There's an answer. And that's for you to come away with me.' She looked up appealingly into my face. 'Come with me. We'll go to London, anywhere. We can start again. Once Blanchland is sold there is nothing to keep you here . . .'

'There's my mother . . .'

'And what do you think you owe to her? She had no time for you when Hugo was around.'

'I still can't abandon her, not the way things are. And then there's Veronica and Helen.'

'Give them half the money then. Whatever you get after everything is sold up. That's fair, isn't it? They can't expect any more than that. You'll have done the best you could.'

Just for an instant I was tempted but no longer than that. Running away wasn't an option that had ever been open to me. I was too well schooled in duty and honour for it ever to have crossed my mind. I shook my head. 'Marcia, for God's sake. You know I couldn't do that.'

She pulled her hands away. Her expression was distant. 'No, of course not. I shouldn't have asked. I can see that I shall have to manage alone.'

It was a direct appeal to my conscience, my sense of honour. 'No, you won't,' I said chivalrously. 'I'll think of something. Just give me some time. At least wait for a week or two before you make up your mind.'

But she hadn't waited. When I got home the following evening my mother was waiting with the news.

'Marcia's gone,' she announced triumphantly. 'And taken everything of value she could lay her hands on.' She went on, oblivious to the stricken expression on my face. I had never heard her talk so much for years.

'Of course, I knew she had no morals, but even I never thought she'd stoop to theft. Veronica's ruby bracelet; Helen's pearls, every ornament and scrap of silver from her room ...' She glowed with righteousness, with moral strength. This was the supreme vindication, the justification for all those years of suspicion and dislike. She had been right. After all, she had been right.

'... She must have sneaked out when the rest of us were all at morning mass. She took Hugo's car of course. It's only out of respect for Hugo's memory that I haven't informed the police. But of course, she knew that. She knew that we couldn't stand up to any more scandal. ...'

I listened, stunned by anger and disbelief. I couldn't speak, I couldn't think, I couldn't believe that she'd left me without a word. I was convinced there'd be a note for me somewhere.

There was nothing in my room, and still deluding myself, I went along to hers. Nothing, less than nothing. She had done a very thorough job. No vestige of her presence remained.

I consoled myself that at least my humiliation was entirely private. No one else knew how completely I'd been fooled. Somehow I got through dinner — of course they talked of nothing else. I said the least that could be said without betraying myself.

I went to bed early, and it only occurred to me then that this would be the first night since my homecoming that I'd slept alone. I didn't sleep though. I lay awake and formulated for myself a new set of rules. Rule One; never take anything for granted. Rule Two; never, ever, trust a woman.

At the end of June, Blanchland, like the shipyards, finally passed out of Claremont hands. We had been fortunate — as Ridgeway kept saying with irritating regularity — in that a buyer had been found quickly who was not only prepared to pay the price but to pay handsomely for a large part of the contents as well. I met them just once; a mill owner from Lancashire and his plump dowdy wife. I knew just by looking at them that they wouldn't be happy there. They looked so out of place in those coldly elegant rooms. And I didn't want them to be happy. I viewed them merely as temporary and unwelcome guests. It didn't matter whose name was on the title deeds. Blanchland would always belong to me.

And things could have been worse. All our debts were paid, there was a surplus of some two thousand pounds in cash and such furniture as we'd decided to keep but didn't have room for was sent down for storage at Ansty. We were far from destitute and I'd rented a modest house in Jesmond, a dreary edifice of yellow stucco and harsh red brick at the end of the short carriage drive girt with laurels that gave the house its name. Naturally, I hated it.

So throughout all of June and most of July, such domestic matters occupied my time and Marcia continued to occupy my thoughts. There'd still been no word from her and by now of course I'd given up hope. I hadn't given up wanting her though. I couldn't get rid of the feeling that what Marcia and I had begun was a long way from being finished. It was a weakness that was to dog me throughout my life; once I had possessed something, however briefly, I was unable to let it go.

Then at the beginning of July, two weeks before the new owners were due to move in, I went back to Blanchland for the last time.

It was raining, a fine soft drizzle that beaded the long windows of the house like tears. I quite felt like crying myself. The house had never seemed so beautiful or desirable. I had never felt so desolate in all my life.

I walked through all the uninhabited rooms except that in my imagination, they weren't empty to me. Spurred feet rang on the medieval flags of the hall, from the Jacobean panelling in the dining room emerged Claremonts clad in doublet and hose; and in the ballroom — Claremonts in crinolines, in swallow tails and white waistcoats, spinning beneath the chandeliers to the strains of a Strauss waltz.

I emerged again into the hall staring up at the ribbed and vaulted ceiling. The sun poured in through the high arched window, flooding the gallery and staircase with pale amber light. The silence was absolute, taut and strained like a pent-up breath, as if the house was waiting, listening ... Suddenly I knew what it wanted to hear me say.

'I'll be back,' I said loudly and solemnly into the silence. 'Somehow, someday, I'll be back.'

Chapter 4

I began work for Rochester's at the beginning of the month with feelings of both enthusiasm and trepidation. On the one hand a career in banking certainly appealed to me. After my recent skirmish with insolvency, it seemed only sensible to throw in one's lot with the winning side. On the other hand I wasn't completely confident that I could pull it off. I still only had a layman's idea of what banks actually did, although I consoled myself with the thought that I wasn't going in totally cold. At Rochester's invitation I had spent the odd few days at the bank, to get acquainted with the world of high finance. I had to admit myself fascinated, and on subsequent visits my fascination had increased as I began to understand the real power of money. It was the investment side of things that really appealed to me, the danger and excitement of playing the market. It was like playing roulette for fantastically high stakes. It was keeping a cool head when the index plunged, knowing that before you'd even got back behind your desk, millions of pounds could have changed hands. In theory, at least, I felt all this with a little practice to be quite within my grasp, and thus it was with reasonable confidence, attired in morning coat and silk top hat, that I presented myself at the bank's Pilgrim Street offices.

It was an impressive building; all Doric columns and wonderfully etched glass; a discreet brass plate proclaimed their business. The banking hall was even more impressive; a sea of tesselated marble divided by tall fluted pillars like the nave of a church — a temple of Mammon as Father Devine would have said, served by pin-striped acolytes who made their devotions at polished mahogany desks. The high priests dwelt upstairs in offices hushed by deep carpets and velvet drapes. I was to share one of these inner sanctums with John

Fortesque Rochester, known to his intimates as Jack.

In the years since, I've often recalled that very first day when I walked so blithely and innocently towards disaster. It's difficult now not to colour those first impressions with hindsight, to portray Jack Rochester as the man I eventually discovered him to be. I think it's true to say though that I was wary of him from the start. Something about him disturbed me intensely, so that I was always vaguely uneasy whenever we were alone. I found myself reluctant to meet his eyes.

Within a week of working alongside him I discovered that he had no real interest in the bank. I sensed he resented the dull routine and paperwork, and, though he was capable of the odd flash of brilliance when something particularly tricky turned up, on the whole I felt he was bored. It soon became clear that he was chairman in name only. The bank was controlled by his mother, Edward Rochester's widow, who despite spending half the year in the South of France had her fingers very firmly on the pulse. Out of curiosity I looked up Hugo's file and saw that it was Lydia Rochester who had insisted that Blanchland be put up as partial security for the loan. It was her signature on the petition for bankruptcy. So here, if anyone, was the person responsible for the fall of my house. The trouble was, I couldn't feel like that. I didn't blame Rochester's — I blamed Hugo. Besides, I couldn't help feeling a grudging admiration for a woman who had run rings round Hugo in the financial sense. I decided I was quite looking forward to meeting this shrewd martinet. At least I knew now who I was working for.

But to be fair to Rochester he treated me well, as a friend and an equal, and my duties to begin with were far from onerous. Financially things were quiet. None of the banks were lending except to established clients and predictions were for the slump in industry to continue. It was part of my job to keep Rochester informed on the state of the market and the price movements of the major shares. I set to with fervour, eager to learn as I planned to supplement my income with a little judicious speculation. I rather regretted now letting Ridgeway persuade me to the safe option of buying annuities with the two thousand pounds. It was capital I needed now, not income.

The bank's own investment policy was equally tame; government stocks, long gilts, Four per cent War loan; fixed interest stocks with a guaranteed yield. My own interest was in equities, ordinary shares which carried a certain element of risk; the greater the risk, the greater the profit. Given large enough financial resources, the market could be manipulated to a certain degree. Wholesale dumping of stock could push prices down. Conversely, heavy buying could send them up. And all manner of outside influences had to be taken into account; a stringent budget, a run on the pound, a change of government, all could take the edge off the most promising share. And it was still what the pundits termed a bear market. Prices were still falling, especially in heavy industrial stocks; Armstrong–Whitworth down to three shillings as against three pounds just after the war. In theory at least it was the time to buy. Ideally, one bought at the bottom and sold at the top, though this rarely worked out in practice. Not that I had the wherewithal to do anything just yet. I still had to accumulate sufficient capital. But as soon as I had and the market picked up, I intended to try my hand at a little 'stagging', buying and selling new issues within a few days for a small but instant profit. In the meantime, I contented myself with imaginary speculation, picking a dozen companies at random and attempting to predict the price movements of their shares.

At the end of the month I reviewed my progress which was summed up in the single word 'nil'. My predictions had fallen disastrously flat. If I had been dealing in actual money I would have lost thousands.

I went home depressed, walking up Grey Street to catch the seven o'clock tram. I paused outside the Eldon Grill; the smell of good food, good wine, a woman's laughter . . .

On impulse I went in and extravagantly ordered chops and a bottle of Bordeaux which I consumed with hedonistic relish. I had forgotten the taste of a really good wine, the way it ran like fire through my blood. I smiled at the waitress who blushed and giggled. I noticed she was pretty with remarkably good legs.

I'd forgotten about that too. Since Marcia I'd led a monastic existence. Father Devine would have been proud of my total abstinence. It was still there, though, smothered, suppressed, like my appetite for good food and vintage wine. I thought of Marcia, something I normally tried not to do — of Hugo and Blanchland and that ugly red-brick villa I now called home.

Abruptly, I finished the wine and called for the bill, tipping the waitress the best part of a shilling. Then to compound my extravagance I called for a taxi. The fact I would need to walk to work for the rest of the month was suddenly quite immaterial.

Only Veronica was still up, curled in her dressing gown by a spluttering gas fire. 'You'll be for it in the morning,' she said waspishly. 'We held dinner up for an entire half hour. Yours is congealing in the pantry if you still want it.'

'I've already eaten,' I said grandly, still buoyed up with Laffite '85. 'And drunk quite a bit too — and even better, I spent my last one and six on a taxi.'

Veronica glared. 'Don't you think that's a little inconsiderate, seeing that the rest of us have to live within our means?'

'Don't you mean live within my means,' I snapped back and regretted it instantly. 'Sorry,' I added ruefully. 'I didn't mean to say that.'

'Yes, you did,' Veronica cried. 'I suppose it makes you feel good, the fact that we're all dependent on you. I suppose you think we should all be grateful. Well, I'm not grateful. I really couldn't care less what happens to me.'

I bit back the sarcastic retort that rose to my lips. I had always found it particularly easy to quarrel with Veronica. As Helen brought out the best in me, so Veronica inspired the worst. Vee had everything except brains, but I supposed when you looked like that intellect was superfluous. Personally, I found Veronica's kind of beauty a little chilling. It was a purely physical thing, a perfection of feature, eyes and skin masking a completely ruthless personality. She had no mind of her own, no real principles or standards and her ideas and opinions were always second hand, gleaned from the trashy romantic novels in which she immersed herself. She was a virgin I was certain, but only because she saw her purity as a powerful bargaining counter in her relationships with men.

50

Otherwise, I felt she would have been completely immoral. But perhaps that was unfair. I reminded myself, that she'd had a pretty rough time. We never mentioned Richard Vere or the shabby way he had treated her. It must have been the final humiliation, coming as it did on top of everything else. Since coming to Jesmond, she'd hardly been out of the house.

'You ought to get out more, Vee,' I suggested casually. 'Do you know, you're becoming a virtual recluse. What good does it do, cutting yourself off like this?'

She gave a bitter little smile. 'Really, Max. Sometimes you are incredibly naive. You don't think it's me who's doing the cutting, do you? Don't you know that being jilted carries a similar social stigma to being divorced. One has become something of a social embarrassment, you see.'

'Oh rot!' I exclaimed. 'It's hardly your fault.'

'That doesn't matter. People are terrified of saying the wrong thing, of mentioning Hugo or Richard or Blanchland. It's so much easier not to have to say anything at all. Of course, nobody is actually rude. There's just that slight hesitation before they acknowledge me, then a few moment's trite conversation before they politely excuse themselves and drift off elsewhere. I wouldn't care if we weren't so infernally hard up. In normal circumstances I'd have ordered myself a half-dozen new frocks and thrown a lavish party to celebrate my new freedom.' She gave her brittle unhappy smile. 'That's the worst thing, you know. Not being able to brazen it out, not to be able to pretend that I don't care. I never realised that money was so desperately important.'

'I'm sorry, Vee,' I said and meant it. 'I hadn't realised that things were so difficult.'

'Well, they're not for you, are they? You've got your job. Mother has the Church and Helen's perfectly happy playing at keeping house. But what have I got, Max? No real friends, no real prospects. I'm twenty-six years old; unmarried — worse than that, I've been jilted ...' She got up and began pacing, wrapping her arms around herself as if she were cold. 'My God, Max. Sometimes I don't think I'll be able to stand it much longer. This house, this place; Mother always complaining and Helen so bloody cheerful I could scream.

51

I'd get a job if there was anything I was qualified to do. I feel so useless, Max. So utterly helpless.'

I was genuinely moved. I'd never seen her so depressed and vulnerable before. In fact, I'd always been rather irritated by her self-sufficiency.

'Oh Vee,' I said sympathetically. 'I wish there was something I could do.'

She swung round to face me. 'Well, perhaps there is, Max. You must meet lots of rich men at a place like Rochester's. Couldn't you introduce me to a few of your wealthy clients.'

I laughed. 'You're not serious?'

'Perfectly,' she said, resuming her seat. 'I've thought about it a very great deal and the only solution as far as I can see is to find myself a rich husband. You see, I've got to have money, Max, and if I can't earn it then I'll have to marry it. It's as simple as that.'

She reached for my cigarette case and helped herself. 'And don't look at me like that,' she added, exhaling smoke.

'Like what?'

'Down your nose — as if I'd just suggested selling myself on the nearest street corner.'

I shook my head. 'I wasn't thinking anything like that. In fact, I was thinking how handicapped people like us are when it comes to making our own way. We were always taught to despise money rather, weren't we? It was all right to be socially ambitious but it wasn't the done thing to pursue money in the same way. Up till now I'd never thought much about it except as a means of maintaining a way of life. I've never wanted a lot, just enough, you know — and yet really, underneath, it's all that matters. It rather saps one's confidence to discover that, after all this time, we've got it wrong.'

Veronica looked at me with her hard pale eyes. 'Yes,' she said. 'Money is all that matters. It's all I really care about now.'

I gave a grim smile. 'Well, that's one thing we agree on anyway, Vee. Money is all that counts.'

The next day I walked the two miles from Jesmond Dene to the bank in Grey Street, my penance for the previous night's rash indulgence.

52

The morning passed agreeably, spent out of the office which I always preferred. I was making enquiries on behalf of the bank regarding one Sydney Elsworth, a prospective client that Rochester was due to see later that afternoon. I already knew something about him. Information, I was sure, was the key to financial success, and to this end I had compiled dossiers of all the major financiers, their companies and boards. Sydney Elsworth featured largely.

I ended the morning at the Stock Exchange in Pilgrim Street, a provincial outpost of its London counterpart. Apart from size and volume of business, in all other aspects it was virtually the same. Jobbers stood on their pitches all talking at once, brokers rushed between them buying and selling. What really intrigued me was that no money changed hands unless the order was in government stock. All bargains on the floor were done 'for the account', which meant a buyer had credit for ten days before he needed to settle. I felt, probably like millions before me, that I should be able to exploit this to my advantage. Theoretically, I could buy any amount of shares without parting with a penny, sell them on before settlement day, and the broker would send me a cheque for the difference. Of course, this only worked if the shares went up. If they remained static then one was liable for the broker's fee. But if they had fallen, the losses could be enormous.

I returned to the bank, disconsolate, having seen the Australian Railway Stock I had been convinced would recover fall another two points. I worked through lunch, collating the material I had gathered. At two o'clock Rochester called me into his office.

'So tell me what you've found out about Mr Elsworth, Max.' Jack Rochester crossed his elegant pin-striped legs. 'I've heard that he's something of a sharp customer.'

I opened my file and began to read aloud: 'Sydney John Elsworth, aged forty-one, unmarried, no family that I can trace. President of Boston Marine, Hudson River Trading, Excelsior Line' — I reeled off a list of a dozen American corporations — 'But he's not American as we thought. Apparently he was born here in the north-east, though I've drawn a complete blank on his early life except for a rumour

53

that he once worked as a welder in the Sunderland yards. Emigrated to America in 1904. Nothing known till he surfaced in 1906 as a partner in Boston Marine and two years later he had a controlling interest. Between 1910 and 1918 he bought out a half-dozen small shipping firms and welded them into the Excelsior Line. He obviously made a packet out of the war and afterwards switched to property and land speculation. He was made a director of the Styvesant Property Development Corporation in 1920 and headed a group of New York financiers in a bid to gain control of a number of real-estate companies which were formed into the Manhattan Land and Investment Trust. He seems to specialise in a form of asset stripping; taking over small companies, usually by means of share exchange, obtaining advances from subsidiaries, then pledging their assets and using the funds to speculate again. Since returning to England a year ago he has acquired the entire share capital of Tyne and Wear Steam Navigation, seventy five per cent of the Pegasus Line and sixty per cent of North Securities and Land Investment Trust.'

'Mmm,' said Rochester thoughtfully. 'A big fish to surface in our small pond. Obviously he's not here to touch us for a loan ...' He broke off abruptly as our visitor was announced and Sydney Elsworth walked into my life.

He was exactly what I had expected; tall, broad-shouldered, more American than the Americans, reeking of prosperity and newly acquired wealth. Nevertheless, I was impressed.

Introductions were made — he spoke with the classless American drawl. Whisky and cigars were handed round. Remarks were passed as to the weather and so on.

'Now then, Mr Elsworth,' Rochester began smoothly. 'How may we help you?'

'I don't know yet that you can,' Elsworth said, smiling. 'That's what I'm here to find out.'

Rochester's expression grew strained. 'Well, how do you think we can help you then?' he said with a faint edge to his voice. 'Perhaps you could begin by letting me have a few essential details.'

Elsworth looked amused. 'May I suggest that we pass over

the usual preliminaries, Mr Rochester. I'm sure that we've both done our homework. If you're any sort of businessman you'll be as well informed about me as I am about you.'

Rochester stared at him. I could see he was ruffled. It was the first time I had ever seen him out of countenance. 'Go on, Mr Elsworth,' he said at last. 'You have my full attention.'

'I'll come straight to the point, Rochester,' said Elsworth bluntly. 'I want to make a deal — although I dare say by British standards my method of approach will seem completely unorthodox. To put it briefly, I'm interested in acquiring the stock of a company which are clients of your bank. I also understand you are a director.'

'Mr Elsworth,' said Rochester stiffly, 'as you say, your approach is entirely unorthodox. I'm afraid I couldn't possibly divulge information regarding a client.'

'It isn't information I need, Mr Rochester,' Elsworth drawled. 'Frankly, I know all there is to know about the Kellerman Line: share capital of just under a million sterling, fixed and current assets of a million and a half of which four hundred thousand is current liabilities, plus, say, three hundred thousand for tax and repayment of holders of Preference shares. Ordinary shares are standing at five per cent over par and yielding seven per cent on a seven per cent dividend. Trading figures for the last year were only two hundred thousand which means that Kellerman's are under-capitalised, under-valued and under-managed.'

Rochester's eyes grew chilly. 'Seeing as you are so well informed, Mr Elsworth, I do not see of what other assistance I could be.'

'You can bring me the board,' Elsworth said. 'Yourself and the other four directors hold forty per cent of the common stock. I hold five per cent, so between us it wouldn't be hard to build up a controlling interest. Of course, I could make my bid in the normal way, but from my point of view I'd prefer not to alert the market and see the shares go wild and perhaps risk another bidder stepping in. Naturally,' he added, 'you and your fellow directors would be compensated for any inconvenience.'

Rochester cleared his throat. 'Well naturally, I'm prepared

to put your proposition before my fellow directors, but really, I can't promise any more than that. I can only say again that my first loyalty must be to the clients of my bank.'

'I understand,' said Elsworth. 'Perhaps I forgot to mention that I was thinking of making a substantial deposit myself.' He opened his pocket book and slid a cheque across the desk.

Rochester stared down at the cheque but he didn't pick it up. I could see by the slight lift of his brows it was for an impressive amount. 'Well, of course,' he said after a moment's pause, 'the bank is always happy to welcome new business. If you are certain, I'll have a clerk attend to it at once.'

Silence. Then Elsworth said in a quietly menacing voice, 'I'm not used to being dealt with by clerks, Mr Rochester.'

'Well, I'm sorry, Mr Elsworth, but you see, that's the way we do things here. No preference is given. The bank does not judge a client's merit on the size of his account.'

'I see.' Elsworth leant forward slowly and retrieved his cheque.'

'Now, if there's nothing else ...' Rochester rose to his feet in a clear gesture of dismissal. 'Max, would you be so good as to show Mr Elsworth out.'

I rushed to open the door, tactfully averting my eyes from Elsworth's grim face. Strangely, I felt vaguely embarrassed by Rochester's condescending treatment of him. Of course, Jack was quite right. Respectable institutions like banks couldn't countenance bribes but I felt he could have handled it in a different way.

Outside the door Elsworth paused, staring down into the great whispering vault of the banking hall. Then, as he reached the head of the staircase, he started to whistle. The shrill strains of 'Yankee Doodle Dandy' echoed and reverberated around the marble hall. He couldn't have caused more of a sensation if he'd removed his clothes. All conversation ceased, every eye looked up. Amidst shocked and outraged silence we descended the stairs and crossed the hall. Elsworth continued to whistle softly through his teeth whilst I suppressed an hysterical desire to laugh.

We reached the tall double-doors of stained and etched

glass. Usually this was as far as I went. Another minion took over on the other side and ushered the client through the foyer and out into the street. It was purely impulse that made me follow Elsworth through.

'Can I get you a taxi, Mr Elsworth?'

'Thank you, but I think I'd prefer to walk.'

I must have looked apologetic because he said with a rueful smile. 'It's all right. I've been thrown out of far better places than this and by far better men than Rochester, you know.' He took a cigar from his inside pocket, bit off the end and spat it out. 'I suppose he was exercising the Englishman's prerogative of telling a damn Yankee to go to Hell. But I'm not a damn Yankee, I'm a hard headed stubborn Northerner, Sunderland bred, and I've been running up against supercilious bastards like Rochester all my life.' He looked at me and grinned. 'If you're a betting man, don't put your money on your boss. I'll get Kellerman's and he knows I will. He's just giving himself breathing space in case he can think up a better deal. I guarantee he's up there now buying every Kellerman share he can get his hands on. Well, tell him not to be too greedy, otherwise I might change my mind and pull out of the bid, and then he'd be left with thousands of shares that nobody wants.'

He turned and looked at me. 'Anyway, what's your name — apart from Max?'

'Claremont,' I replied. 'Max Claremont.'

He continued to stare at me with that hard appraising glance. I felt suddenly that he knew all about me down to the small change in my pocket and the holes in my shoes.

'Well, Max Claremont, if you want to do yourself a bit of good, buy yourself a few Kellerman shares on the account and sell them as soon as they reach twenty-eight. Twenty-eight, mind — that's my top end.' He smiled. 'That's the secret, Max, not just knowing when to buy but when to sell.'

'Thank you, sir,' I said. 'I'll remember that.'

He nodded. 'See that you do.' Then he held out his hand. 'Well, goodbye, Max Claremont. I'll see you again.'

I returned to my office. Rochester was speaking urgently into the 'phone. 'Yes, but use out-of-town brokers if you possibly can. And small blocks, just a hundred shares at a

57

time. Usual drill; fictitious names; spread things as thinly as you can. And you might contact the other members of the Kellerman board. Arrange for a meeting a.s.a.p. In fact, suggest that they join me for dinner at my club tonight.'

He looked up as I slid into position behind my desk. 'Well, Max,' he said happily, replacing the telephone on its hook, 'what did you think of Mr Elsworth then? Ghastly, wasn't he? But then that type usually are. I fancy Mr Elsworth comes from the school of self-made men who attempt to cling to both their money and their humble roots and preface every sentence with banal phrases like "I'm working class and proud of it", and then proceed to behave in a most unworking-class fashion, buying houses in the country; marrying Society girls and putting their sons' names down for Eton.' He gave his soft sneering laugh. 'That's their real problem, not knowing what side of the fence they're on. On the one hand they're terrified of being thought upstarts and of having people snigger behind their backs, but on the other, what's the good of having money if you can't spend it on the really good things in life. What lets them down is their need to keep proving that they're as good as the next man and that their money isn't unacceptable just because they've earned it.'

I said, as I found myself rather taken with Elsworth; 'Well, in a way one can rather admire that.'

'Oh, one does,' said Rochester. 'It would be all right if they were just content to be filthy rich but they all want to be acknowledged as gentlemen as well. They don't understand that it isn't quite as easy as that.'

I bent my head over my work and applied myself to four per cent War Loan until five o'clock. Then I walked round to the Exchange in time for call-over. Kellerman's still stood at twenty-one and a half, twenty-one and three-quarters, depending on whether one wanted to buy or sell. For a few minutes I still hesitated, wandering apparently aimlessly from pitch to pitch. Then I squared my shoulders, and casually, as if it were something I did every day, I bought a thousand Kellerman shares on account.

Chapter 5

The Claremonts had been invited out — albeit only for cocktails at the Rochesters', to mark Mrs Rochester's return from the South of France, but I felt we had emerged from the social vacuum to which the scandal of Hugo's death and bankruptcy had consigned us.

As I dressed in my room it was almost like old times, except that my evening clothes reeked unpleasantly of camphor and I had to struggle alone with the tedious business of collar and studs. I glanced at my reflection, adjusting my tie which seemed to have a persistent tendency to list to port. I looked exactly as I felt; optimistic, confident, a man of means. The fact that the 'means' only amounted to a few hundred pounds didn't dampen my good humour in the least. Compared to my previous financial state, I was fabulously wealthy. And it had all been so easy. Just a few fraught days spent constantly consulting the office tape, seeing the price rise, fall back, creep up again, then leap to twenty-eight shillings as Elsworth publicly announced his bid. I sold immediately, though it was tempting to hang on till the shares finally peaked as they did two days later at thirty-two shillings. Amazingly, Rochester and the Kellerman board still hung out, though Elsworth had received thirty per cent acceptances from the other shareholders. From listening at doors I knew that Rochester hoped to force Elsworth up to thirty-five, and for a few days longer the shares continued to rise, struggling up to thirty-two, only to fall back almost immediately to thirty, then plummet disastrously, as Elsworth quietly withdrew his bid, to settle below their original level at nineteen. Kellerman's panicked. The bank panicked. An extraordinary shareholders' meeting was called, and after a rowdy exchange the board were under orders to get Elsworth back round the table, where, after three days' wrangling they finally, to Rochester's chagrin and my delight, accepted his original offer of twenty-eight.

Of course, it's always tempting in these situations to carry on speculating how much one might have made if one had done this or hadn't done that. I persuaded myself that I was perfectly content with my modest profit of three hundred pounds, less duty and commission, which I immediately re-invested in five hundred of Elsworth's Excelsior Line Shares, knowing the price would move up when the successful outcome of the Kellerman bid was announced. The shares performed even better than I had hoped, rising three and sixpence in a single day. There was more to come I suspected but I bought and sold again within twenty-four hours, feeling it more prudent to cut and run than hang out for the ultimate profit. As it was I was richer by nearly four hundred pounds. I felt sure Elsworth would have advised me to quit whilst I was ahead.

I went downstairs. The girls were waiting and I surveyed them with fraternal pride; Helen, slim and boyish with her cropped shining hair; Veronica looking stunning in a beaded Worth dress, a relic of better days. The only sour note was our mother's disapproval as she watched us from the sitting-room door. She wasn't coming, of course, reminding us that officially we were still in mourning, though I felt this was a moot point of etiquette. Did one accord the same respect to a suicide as one did to someone who'd died a natural death? Seeing Hugo had precipitated the event by a good fifty years, I felt the family had more than done their bit.

We travelled by taxi to Eldon Square where the Rochesters had their town house.

Rochester met us at the door for which I was grateful. For Veronica's sake especially, I had rather dreaded making an entrance; the turning heads, the whispered asides — 'Of course, the brother committed suicide, you know ... Richard Vere dropped her like a hot brick ...'

'Max. Glad to see you.' Rochester shook my hand. 'Veronica, my dear. You're looking marvellous.' He paused and his soulful eyes swept over Helen. 'Helen? It can't be. The last time I saw you, you wore pigtails.'

I laughed, Helen blushed, Veronica gave her languid cock-tail-party smile; pink champagne was brought to us on a silver tray. Then Rochester whisked Helen away to dance. Veronica and I turned to face the scrutiny of the other guests. There seemed to be few people that I knew, yet everyone seemed to know us. Our presence was acknowl-edged by curious stares, cautious nods and the occasional wary smile.

'Well, that wasn't too bad, was it?' I murmured to Veronica as we moved through the throng. 'At least they're not turning their backs.'

Veronica shrugged. 'I wouldn't have cared if they had. There's nobody here I particularly want to talk to.'

We sipped our cocktails. I lit a cigarette. Everyone seemed to be talking and laughing at once. A band played loudly in another room. Then Veronica nudged me gently in the ribs. 'Who's our fellow outcast?' she enquired.

I followed her glance and saw Elsworth standing alone. Like us, though for different reasons, he was being given the cold shoulder. I was surprised to see him. I couldn't imagine why Rochester had even asked him here ... And then, of course, I understood. This was Rochester's subtle way of putting Elsworth in his place, of reminding him that within the confines of the bank he and his money might be king, but here neither were of any account.

I felt a flicker of compassion. The English class system, rigorously maintained by those at the very top to the disad-vantage of those at the very bottom, was a strict social hier-archy which people like Elsworth had yet to fathom. The pecking order was thus; lower classes equalled the dregs; working class lower middle class — poor but respectable; middle class — trade; upper middle class — still trade but trade with a great deal of money, and so on, until one reached the dizzy heights of peerage and monarchy. These were the stations into which people were born, and though a certain amount of movement was possible between the lower ranks — people who didn't count in any case — on the whole, you remained where an accident of birth had placed you. There were exceptions, people who attempted to crash

their way in, people like Elsworth who felt that their money
entitled them to take a step up. It never worked, of course.
There were so many pitfalls; accent for one thing, those
upper-class English vowel sounds to which one had to be
bred. Dress too, not so much what one wore but the way one
wore it — casually, comfortably, when things had been
properly broken in. My father had never worn a garment
publicly till it was at least three months old. And here was
Elsworth, stiff and self conscious in his over-cut American
suit, with his lapels a fraction too wide, his hair a shade too
long and exposing far too much of his shirt below his sleeves.
Naturally, he'd been spotted at once.

I went over to him immediately and held out my hand. 'Mr
Elsworth. How are you? May I introduce you to my sister,
Veronica? Veronica — may I present Mr Sydney Elsworth of
Sunderland and New York.'

Elsworth smiled and visibly relaxed as I had intended him
to. Then he turned to Veronica and bowed over her hand.
'I'm deeply honoured to make your acquaintance, Miss
Claremont.'

Veronica, scenting money, lit up as if she'd been plugged
into the mains. 'How do you do, Mr Elsworth. Max has told
me so much about you.'

Elsworth smiled. 'Nothing too much to my detriment, I
hope?'

Veronica gave him a cool vampish glance. 'Well that
would depend on what one regarded as detrimental, Mr
Elsworth. Personally, I think a little vice in a man is exciting.'

Elsworth looked amused. 'Well, I must try to live up to
your expectations, Miss Claremont.'

'Oh please call me Veronica, everybody does. It seems so
stuffy to bother about formality these days.'

It soon became evident that I was superfluous and I drifted
off. I was quite glad to be alone and, helping myself to
another glass of champagne, I surveyed my surroundings
with approval; chandeliers dripping with crystal, Aubusson
rugs, a collection of paintings quite worthy of the Tate —
extravagant, extrovert, yet still remaining within the bounds
of good taste. I thought grimly of Blanchland, in my imagination desecrated by the mill-owner's appalling taste;

department-store furniture, books by the yard, everything excruciatingly modern. No doubt they were already regretting exchanging the comfort of their Yorkshire farm-house for Blanchland's cold austerity. Another classic example of the middle classes trying to ape the gentry and making themselves thoroughly miserable in the process. It was love of heritage that made one endure cold draughty rooms and inadequate plumbing. One had to be bred to the discomfort of somewhere like Blanchland.

Another glass of champagne. My feeling of physical well-being substantially increased. I looked at the women in their expensive skimpy frocks. One or two of them looked back at me. Inevitably, thoughts of Marcia crept into my mind. Whatever else she hadn't been, she'd certainly been a consummate lover. Occasionally, once in a lifetime, a man meets a woman like that; love turns to hate, respect to contempt, but the desire never diminishes. I felt like that about Marcia; liar, cheat, thief that she was, I wouldn't have hesitated again to share her bed.

Suddenly, without warning, I felt acutely depressed as I always did when I thought too long and too hard about Marcia. My temperament wasn't suited to long periods of celibacy. It was essential to my health to have a mistress of some sort, and in the past, as a reasonably personable young gentleman of reasonably independent means, I had encountered no real difficulty. Of course, there were alternative ways of finding relief. One could pay for it or resort to self-gratification, though neither had ever particularly appealed to me. Prostitution was sordid and offended against my romantic ideals and masturbation was something no gentleman indulged in past the age of sixteen.

And then I saw her, an unknown face glimpsed over the shoulder of a fellow guest; dark sleek waves of hair bound by a silver fillet, a luscious smiling mouth. I shifted my position to get a better view. She wasn't young. She could have been any age between thirty and forty — at this distance it was difficult to tell.

Then as if she had become aware of my intense scrutiny, she turned her head. As soon as our eyes met I knew that we were going to be lovers. It was just a question of when and

63

where, of how long I would take to make the first move, of how long she would take keeping up a respectable pretence of resistance. No time at all it seemed, for within minutes of that first glance she was walking towards me.

A shiver of excitement ran up my spine. My eyes ravished her supple body. I had a sudden vision of her naked in my arms.

Then she was standing before me. I could smell her perfume. 'You're Max Claremont, aren't you?' She held out her hand. 'I'm Jack's mother, Lydia Rochester.'

I was speechless with shock. I couldn't believe my ears, Jack's mother. Oh my God! What a blunder.

'Mrs Rochester. You must forgive me,' I said in an effort to redeem myself. 'You took me by surprise. I rather expect everybody's mother to look like my own.'

She looked at me, smiling, and now of course I could see the resemblance; those dark unfathomable eyes, the pale ivory skin that looked so incongruous upon her son.

She ignored my rather clumsy compliment. We resorted to respectable cocktail-party conversation. 'Jack tells me that you were in the army before you joined him at the bank, Mr Claremont.'

'Yes, I was. The 14th Hussars. Mostly we were based in India.'

She nodded. 'That accounts for the fact that we've never met before. I knew your brother Hugo, of course ...' She paused. 'I was sorry to hear about his death.'

'I wasn't.' I said, aggressive as always at the mention of his name. 'In fact, it was the best piece of news I've ever had.'

Her eyes grew chilly at this breach of good taste. 'You're very blunt, Mr Claremont,' she remarked coolly.

'I'm a realist, Mrs Rochester,' I replied, remaining equally cool. 'Invariably the two go together.'

There was a pause whilst she looked at me as if I were a schoolboy she'd caught being sick on the floor. 'Well, you must excuse me, Mr Claremont,' she said with a polite but frigid smile. 'I must attend to my other guests.'

She walked away. Suddenly I was alone with an empty glass in my hand and a sick feeling in the pit of my stomach.

The evening dragged on. I drank more champagne. I talked to people and couldn't remember anything they said.

And all the time, on the periphery of my vision, Lydia Rochester was moving confidently among her guests; laughing, smiling, exhaling blue smoke from a Black Russian cigarette. I felt the stirrings of obsessive desire.

I encountered her once more, as I was on the point of leaving. 'Goodnight, Mr Claremont. I hope you've had an enjoyable evening.' Then her hand, briefly, coolly, clasping mine. Her eyes, amused and mocking.

I was ready for her this time. The well-rehearsed line flowed easily off my tongue. 'Indeed yes, Mrs Rochester ...' I paused. 'Though not as enjoyable as it might have been. I'm afraid that was entirely my fault.'

It worked. She smiled. There came into her eyes a speculative look. 'Well, we must see if we can't do better next time.'

I bowed. 'I shall look forward to that,' I murmured.

In the car going home I was silent and withdrawn, preoccupied with emotional and erotic thoughts. I listened, half listened, without much interest as Veronica, who had drunk far too much, recounted at great length her conquest of Elsworth.

'Really!' I exclaimed suddenly, jarred by her voice. 'So when is the wedding? Should I have my morning suit sponged and pressed?'

Veronica smiled archly. 'My dear, if I marry Sydney Elsworth, you'll be able to afford a new one.'

'You're seeing him again then? He's asked you to lunch?'

'Dinner actually,' she said with that smug little smile that reminded me so vividly of Hugo.

'My word!' I sneered. 'You're not wasting any time, are you, Vee?' Then I added maliciously, knowing it was the one way to wipe the satisfaction from her face. 'Obviously you're not going to let Elsworth get away as easily as you did Vere.'

Her face flamed at this reference to her broken engagement. 'Well, someone has to attempt to restore the family fortunes,' she snapped. 'It's obviously something we can't leave to you.'

'Unfortunately, I don't have the advantages of your sex, my dear, of being able to sell myself off to the highest bidder. As a man, I have to work for it.'

'And you don't think I'm having to work for it?' she

65

snapped. 'Do you think I enjoy having to be pleasant to someone like Sydney Elsworth? My God, if I wasn't so desperate, I wouldn't look at him.'

'Oh stop it, you two,' Helen said suddenly. 'Please don't quarrel, Max. Don't spoil everything now.'

I looked at her. 'I'm sorry,' I said and patted her hand. 'You had a good time then, did you?'

Helen blushed and her eyes sparkled. 'Yes, I did. Everyone was such tremendous fun.'

'Especially Jack Rochester,' Veronica smirked. 'I noticed that he was paying you a great deal of attention.'

Helen blushed. 'Don't be silly, Vee. He was just being kind. He knew that I didn't know anyone very much.'

Veronica gave a derisive smile. 'Don't be so naive, Helen. No man is kind. By nature they are selfish, egotistical, vain and weak and totally committed to proving their superiority. And as there is only one place a man feels truly superior to a woman, his whole life is spent in devising various ploys for getting her there ...'

'Well, I can imagine that has been your own personal experience, Veronica. You don't exactly appeal to a man's finer feelings. It's different with Helen ...'

'Is it?' Veronica gave her sister a pitying look. 'You'll learn, Helen. You'll learn.'

By the time I reached the bank the next morning I had managed to pull myself together. Lydia Rochester was taboo, off limits, out of bounds. To pursue her in any way would not only jeopardise my future at the bank but would give rise to an almighty scandal. A liaison with one's employer's wife, conducted with tact and discretion, was socially, if not approved of, at least permissible. But an affair with one's employer's mother, in theory, quite old enough to be my own, would have been regarded as the most enormous breach of taste. I would be socially ostracised forever.

Thinking about it — I had done nothing else — I had come to the conclusion that there must be some grievous flaw in my personality to be sexually obsessed with women so much older than myself. It had started early, as soon as I had become 'carnally aware'. At prep school it had been the

66

assistant matron who had been the object of my fantasies; at Ampleforth, the head gardener's wife. Freud would have made much of it. A mother-fixation was the obvious prognosis. No doubt Oedipus would have been dragged in. And from an intellectual viewpoint, I could see that there might be some truth in this. I had always fiercely resented my mother's obsession with Hugo; my bouts of infantile rage and difficult behaviour had perhaps merely been efforts to gain her attention, and this in turn had manifest itself as a sexual preference for mature, experienced women. It was an interesting thought but it did nothing to ease my present dilemma, that I desperately wanted to seduce my employer's mother.

I resorted to the tried and tested methods of my youth; cold baths, long walks, slavish attention to my work. Then, just as I was beginning to feel the benefit of this stringent regime, Mrs Rochester walked into my office.

'Oh, Mr Claremont. Forgive me for interrupting you. Actually, I was looking for Jack.'

I rose courteously. 'I'm afraid he isn't here, Mrs Rochester,' I said in a matter-of-fact voice. 'He's with a client over at North Shields.'

'What a pity.' She smiled. 'I had hoped to persuade him to take me to lunch.' Still smiling, she added in her wonderfully provocative voice. 'I don't suppose you would care to deputise?'

My heart leapt. My resolution dissolved. 'I should be delighted, Mrs Rochester,' I said.

She suggested le Bon Mot, exclusive and fashionable. I inwardly cringed at the thought of the bill.

'Jack tells me you were up at Oxford, Mr Claremont,' she said after we had been shown to a discreet corner table. 'Which college were you at?'

'Balliol,' I answered, wondering whether Jack had also mentioned the fact I'd been sent down.

'Really,' she smiled. 'My father was a Balliol man. In fact, he was Master of Balliol until he died. Before your time, of course, Richard Soames would have been Master when you were up.'

'You know Oxford well then, Mrs Rochester?' I asked, trying to ignore the way her mouth closed deliciously over the prongs of her fork.

67

'Yes. Very well. I was born there, you see' — a pause while the waiter removed our plates. 'We lived there until my father died and then my mother and I came north. My mother's people were from Newcastle.'

Another pause. I refilled our glasses. The waiter brought dessert.

'Your sister is very charming — your younger sister, Helen, I mean.'

'Yes, she is,' I smiled. 'I'm very fond of Helen.'

'Yes. Jack seems fond of her too. I notice how much he seems to enjoy her company.'

I looked up. There was something in her voice, a note almost of anxiety. 'You object to that, Mrs Rochester?'

'Oh no. Far from it. I'm pleased to see Jack taking an interest in someone. He's never really done so before.'

I digested this remark, together with a mouthful of lemon water-ice — both set my teeth on edge. Helen and Jack Rochester! I couldn't say that I cared for that, but then I didn't really care for the idea of Helen loving anyone but me. I'd always been over-protective and possessive. Of course, I hoped she'd marry one day, a decent chap, not exactly someone of my choice but at least someone I thoroughly approved of. I didn't approve of Rochester although he was eligible in every way. But there was something about him, an air of degeneracy, a hint of vice ...

'Well, it's kind of Jack to take an interest in Helen,' I said at last. 'She's always found it difficult to make friends, and of course, now, with things the way they are with us ...'

'Yes,' she cut in, 'I was going to speak to you about that. I —' she paused and gave me a regretful smile, 'well, I just wanted to say how sorry I am about Blanchland. I really wish there had been some other way. From a personal point of view one can't help feeling a little responsible — but of course, in a bank one has one's shareholders to consider. It was really too large an amount for us to think of writing off.'

Her sympathy enfolded me like a warm soft cloud. 'Please don't apologise,' I said. 'I understand perfectly. I've never held the bank responsible. If anyone was to blame, it was my brother Hugo.'

'That's generous of you, Mr Claremont, but really the

68

debts should never have been allowed to reach such an amount. That's what I meant when I said I felt responsible. I'm afraid Jack was something of a fool as far as your brother was concerned.'

'Yes,' I remarked drily. 'Most people were.'

'Well, please let me know if there's anything I can do. I really feel I should do something to make amends.'

'No, please' — by now her sympathy was becoming tiresome. It wasn't the emotion I had intended to arouse. I changed the subject and we talked for a while about the current vogue for pre-Raphaelite art. My infatuation increased. Even discounting my feelings of lust, she was the sort of woman I admired enormously. She was intelligent, educated, a woman of intellect and greater inner strength. Suddenly I didn't care whose damn mother she was. I couldn't wait to get her into bed.

But as luncheon progressed I could see it was going to be hard work. So far there was nothing between us but the width of the table and every time I came anywhere near approaching an intimate note the waiter intervened. This time it was to ask whether we would take our coffee at the table or in the salon.

She glanced at her watch. 'Actually, I don't think I shall have time for coffee. I have an appointment at two o'clock. Do you mind?'

'Not at all,' I said with as much grace as I could — Of course I bloody well minded. But I was acutely aware that I had to let her make all the running. All the moves would have to come from her.

'No, please stay and have your coffee,' she protested as I rose to my feet. 'You mustn't let me spoil your lunch.'

'But you must let me escort you to your car,' I protested.

'No, please don't bother. The car's just outside. Really, Mr Claremont, I insist.'

I subsided meekly, aware of the faint but definite edge to her voice. 'Well, goodbye Mrs Rochester,' I said lamely.

Disconsolately I drank my coffee, smoked a cigarette, and then discovered on leaving and to my utter chagrin that she'd already paid the bill. I went back to the bank feeling like a dance-hall gigolo.

69

Chapter 6

I went back to Blanchland at the end of October, though I had made up my mind even before I left, that it was going to be for the last time. I was beginning to find these secretive visits depressing. All this furtive lurking was both undignified and demoralising, and what had begun as a purely romantic notion — this monthly pilgrimage to the house to renew my vow — had somehow acquired an air of the faintly ridiculous. I had made another vow. The only way I would return to Blanchland again was with the keys of the door in my hand.

Still, I couldn't resist one last look. It was Sunday and I had nothing better to do except accompany my mother to Matins and Vespers. That in itself was incentive enough.

I had hardly set out when the weather closed in; the sun abruptly obscured by a leaden grey pall. I had intended to leave the car at Riding Mill and walk to Blanchland across the moors. However, I abandoned that idea as soon as the weather changed, driving down into Blanchland village itself, something I had not previously done.

I had forgotten the charm of the mellow stone houses that had sprung up over six centuries on the old monastic site. I knew the history well of course. Once a Premonstratensian abbey had flourished here, founded by the White Canons that had given the area its name. The abbey had long disappeared except for the gate but the neat houses retained something of a cloistered look. There was a peaceful ordered feeling to the narrow streets.

I went down to the river and looked across at the house. I couldn't see much; lawns mottled with dead leaves; the glitter of windows through the thinning trees, plumes of smoke from the banks of chimneys. It was enough. Memory supplied all the details and in my imagination I could still

70

walk between the high beech hedges, I could still lie in the orchard eating sour green apples, I could breathe the heavy scent of my mother's rose garden. The roses would be finished though. It would be chrysanthemums now, great mop-headed blooms of bronze and yellow . . .

Suddenly I was overcome by a sickening feeling of nostalgia, a longing for the safe and secure days of my childhood: Sunday tea on the lawns; my mother in a bustled dress and a Gainsborough hat, my father in blazer and flannels. Memories flooded over me; Hugo and I smart as paint in our Sunday suits, Veronica preening, Helen laughing with chocolate around her mouth. It was then I realised that the Blanchland I had known was lost to me forever. What I longed for was just a dream. Strangers were there now, for the first time in over five hundred years. Even if, by some miracle, I regained possession of the house, nothing would ever be the same.

I walked back to the car, a second-hand two-seater Singer I had bought with my ill-gotten gains from the Kellerman deal. A rash and unnecessary purchase — my mother's words. — but I had seen it in the nature of an investment though not necessarily one of a financial kind. The car served a dual purpose. Apart from giving me the freedom to come and go as I pleased, it also allowed me greater access to Lydia Rochester.

Up until then I had rather frowned upon Helen's friendship with Jack Rochester until I realised it was purely of the platonic kind. Helen was just one of a crowd invited to the race meetings, weekend tennis parties and riverside picnics with which Rochester amused himself when his presence was not necessary at the bank. His attitude towards Helen reassured me even more, Rochester referring to her as a 'brick' and a 'good sport', sentiments, I felt, so lacking in carnal interest as instantly to put my mind at rest.

Thus satisfied that Rochester's intentions towards my sister were strictly honourable, I had set about the serious business of seducing his mother. To this end, I took full advantage of his generous hospitality and every other weekend motored out to Farnfield, the Rochester's country place, purely in the hope of seeing her.

71

My imagination had run riot, visualising the two of us walking quietly together in the sunlit grounds or drinking champagne on the terrace, discoursing intimately and erotically on the merits of Wagner, whilst the 'children' exhausted themselves playing tennis.

The reality, of course, was quite different and after two weekends of knocking balls about, drinking pink gin, making trite conversation with giggling girls, without even so much as a glimpse of her, I was beginning to give up hope.

It only occurred to me then that she was deliberately avoiding me, that what I had taken to be the start of a grand passion was nothing more than a mild flirtation to her. I knew there were women like that, who led you on with smiles and glances, who made promises with their eyes they never intended to keep. Probably it was fashionable for women like her to have a tame young man in tow, only I hadn't been as tame as she'd expected.

Then suddenly, quite without warning, everything changed. I was working late at the bank one evening on some papers that were needed for an early meeting at Lloyds, and was on the point of leaving when Rochester telephoned to say he'd been held up.

'Be a good chap, Max, and drop the papers off at Eldon Square. With luck, I'll have time to go through them before tomorrow morning. I'll telephone the Mater to say you'll be round ...'

'Yes, of course. It's no trouble.' I was practically fainting with delight.

'See you at Lloyds then. Nine o'clock sharp.'

'Yes. Nine o'clock. I'll be there.'

I replaced the telephone, smoothed my hair, and within fifteen minutes I was being shown into the Rochester's drawing room.

'Mr Claremont. How nice!' Her voice was pleasant, assured, indifferent.

'Jack asked me to drop some papers round,' I said, establishing my credentials immediately.

'Yes, I know. He telephoned.' She looked at me with that amused worldly stare. 'Can I offer you a cocktail?'

'Thank you. That would be nice,' I answered casually.

She mixed the drinks herself rather than calling a servant. I took this as an encouraging sign. We were actually alone, though this affected me so overwhelmingly that I had difficulty in looking at her without betraying a disgustingly ravenous expression. I turned my attention to the paintings on the walls, pausing before an exquisite Russian icon.

'It's rather fine, isn't it?' she said, coming towards me with two White Ladies in her hands. 'Fifteenth century, or so I'm told. Do you care for that sort of thing, Mr Claremont?'

'No, not really,' I answered, desperately wishing she would stop calling me Mr Claremont. 'My mother would though. She's very fond of religious art.'

'Oh yes, of course. I forgot. Your people are Catholic, aren't they?'

I raised my eyebrows. 'You make it sound like some sort of disease.'

'Do I? I'm sorry, I didn't mean to offend you.'

'I'm not offended. I gave up religion of any kind some years ago.'

'Nevertheless, it was rude of me to mention the subject in the first place.' She seated herself and crossed her long elegant legs. 'I only did so because, in a way, I have Catholic connections myself. Edward, my late husband, was a Catholic, you know — and naturally, Jack took his father's faith . . .'

'But you didn't?' I took the chair opposite her. 'That's unusual, isn't it? Most women who marry Catholics convert.'

She gave a cynical little smile. 'I'm afraid I don't convert very easily, Mr Claremont. Besides I don't feel Catholicism has a great deal to offer women. There seems to be only two states of grace for women as far as the Church is concerned; virginity and maternity, although how one gets from one to the other without committing mortal sin I have never yet been able to fathom.'

I laughed and my longing to possess her substantially increased. Not only was she the most desirable woman I had ever met but she was amusing, cultured, sophisticated and literate. I could see that I was going to have to exert myself.

'You've read Darwin, I suppose?' I enquired with a knowledgeable smile.

'Yes, of course. Remember that I was brought up in Oxford. He's almost compulsory reading there.'

'And your conclusions?'

'Well, technically one can't dispute his theory, although I must admit my vanity is pained at the thought of descent from an anonymous globule of mucous. And of course, it's much easier to embrace atheism when one is very young ...'

She held out her empty glass. 'Would you mind, Mr Claremont?'

'No. Of course not.' I moved across the room in such a state of anticipation and excitement that my hand could barely grasp the shaker — My God! This was exceeding my wildest dreams. I was aware of her watching me, wondering perhaps if I was worth the risk. I made mine a small one. I was going to make damn sure that I was.

'Thank you.' She took the glass and raised it slowly to her lips. Her eyes surveyed me thoughtfully across the rim. Then suddenly she said, 'How old are you, Mr Claremont?'

'Twenty-four,' I said, 'And please call me Max.'

'That's indecently young,' she said wryly. 'You're only a year older than Jack.'

I could see this was going to be a problem. Obviously it disturbed her, the difference in our age. I said in my smoothest manner, 'Don't they say there's no such thing as age, only experience.'

'And you think you are experienced?'

'In some things,' I countered. 'Perhaps mature would be a better word. At least I don't believe in the concept that there is beauty only in youth.'

'But it's true, I'm afraid, at least as far as women are concerned.'

'Every woman is beautiful at sixteen, Mrs Rochester. It's being beautiful at forty that counts.'

She smiled. 'Is that a compliment?'

'Yes, it is.'

'Thank you,' she said softly and sipped her drink.

We were silent for a long time, too long in fact; a note of awkwardness had now crept between us. I saw her glance at her watch. 'Really, I ought to be getting changed. I'm dining out this evening.'

74

I took a deep breath. It was now or never.

'Actually,' I heard myself say in an off-hand voice. 'I had hoped I could persuade you to dine with me one evening.'

I knew immediately I had overstepped the mark. She looked at me. 'Dine with you!' I thought she was going to laugh.

'Yes,' I said belligerently. 'Why not?'

She gave me a scathing look. 'If you are as mature as you say you are, you wouldn't need to ask that.'

I was beginning to lose my temper. 'Please don't treat me like a schoolboy,' I said quietly.

'Well, don't you think you're behaving like one?'

'Is that what you think? That my feelings for you are the result of some juvenile crush?'

'It's what I would prefer to think,' she answered coldly.

I'd gone too far to think of backing down now. 'What is it you're afraid of?' I challenged her outright, believing attack to be the best method of defence.

'At the moment, Mr Claremont' — her voice was like a lash of a whip — 'of saying something that I might later regret.'

'I see,' I said coldly. 'Obviously I have made a mistake in thinking you enjoyed my company as much as I do yours.'

'I do enjoy your company — but not to the extent of dining out with you alone. I'm sorry if I gave you any other impression. I should have made it quite clear from the start that I do not form intimate relationships with my son's friends, especially when they also happen to be employees of the bank.'

I felt myself flushing. She couldn't have said anything more guaranteed to crush my ego. But I couldn't give up. With typical male conceit I felt I couldn't be mistaken about the look in her eyes. Then I proceeded to make the biggest mistake of my entire life. I grabbed her and pulled her into my arms, intending to smother her protests with a passionate kiss. Passion subsided swiftly as the palm of her hand cracked against my cheek.

'How dare you,' she breathed. 'How dare you treat me like some cheap little tart.'

I thought for a moment I was going to burst into tears or at least be sick on the floor. I have never felt so foolish, so immature and childish.

'I'm sorry,' I said stiffly, trying to salvage something of my battered dignity. 'Please forgive me. I shall understand perfectly if you'd prefer that I no longer called.'

She smiled. 'Don't be silly,' she said, making me feel about sixteen. 'I shan't give it another thought and neither must you. And you must call whenever you please, otherwise Jack will be curious. Now,' she rose briskly and held out her hand. 'Let's forget all about it, shall we, Mr Claremont. I'd like us still to be friends.'

And so we were friends and in consequence I avoided her as if we were mortal enemies. On the rare occasions that we met, she was always civil and charming; I was always courteous and polite. By now of course, I knew the worst. I was in love with Lydia Rochester.

I drove home disconsolately, putting the Singer through its paces along the Military Road, pushing her to a top speed of forty. Not that I was in any hurry to get back. Mother would be at Mass, Helen was over at Farnfield, and Veronica was out with Elsworth. I had to hand it to Vee though. If I was lagging in the romantic stakes, Veronica was practically breasting the tape. Of course, the advantages of a rich brother-in-law were not lost on me. No doubt he could be persuaded to come across with a fat loan, except that I inwardly cringed at the thought of being beholden to Veronica. No. I had thought about this. The only benefit to me, if Elsworth married her, was that he would take her off my hands.

I entered the house reluctantly, my depression increasing as the walls of the narrow hallway closed around me.

'Maxwell!' My mother appeared at the top of the stairs. 'Maxwell, I need to speak to you. Will you please come up.'

My heart sank at this peremptory 'summons to the presence'. I knew from experience that it meant a lecture, a monthly accounting of my misdeeds which had something of the rite of the confessional about them. I admitted my faults, was admonished and absolved, and suffered a lengthy sermon as a penance.

Meek as a schoolboy about to submit to the cane, I slowly ascended the stairs.

'Please come in, Maxwell. Sit down, won't you?'

I did so with difficulty, manoeuvring my way around the Elizabethan four-poster bed that took up nearly half the room. And there were tables and chairs, a massive oak armoire, lurid paintings of religious scenes adorning the walls.

I sat down facing Holman Hunt's 'Massacre of the Innocents'. My mother was already seated at Madame de Montespan's *prie-dieu*, totally incongruous in the suburban bay window. She picked up a rosary and the ebony beads slid smoothly through her fingers. She looked at me but did not speak. Mother had always used silence to great effect, and as a child this subtle technique had struck terror into my soul. Now it merely made me slightly uncomfortable. Still, it was unthinkable that I should speak first. So I waited and the rosary continued to rattle through her fingers. Then after a pause the length of a Pater Noster, she spoke.

'It is your sisters that I wish to speak to you about, Maxwell, as it seems to me that you are signally failing in your duty towards them. Naturally, I appreciate that our circumstances are not what they were but that is absolutely no reason to lower our standards. Therefore, I am surprised that you should allow, I might even say condone, your sister Veronica's association with this Elsworth person.' (I might mention that only a favoured few whom my mother acknowledged were referred to as people. The rest of the world were merely persons.)

'What's the matter with Elsworth?' I demanded, knowing perfectly well. 'He seems to be a decent enough chap.'

'He's a Protestant, for one thing,' she answered acidly.

'That's an assumption on your part. Frankly, I don't think Elsworth has any particular religion at all.'

'That's even worse — to have absolutely no faith at all. And, in any case, there are other differences besides religion. Surely I don't have to spell it out. It must be perfectly obvious that he isn't our sort. He could hardly be described as a gentleman.'

I gave an exclamation of disgust. 'What is more important

77

to you, Mother — Veronica's happiness or a son-in-law with an entry in Debrett.'

'The two are synonymous, Maxwell. There is nothing so likely as to cause unhappiness than marrying out of one's class.'

I looked at her with distaste; at her icy well-bred features with their haughty expression. 'I really don't think it's my place to interfere, Mother. Veronica is nearly twenty-seven years old, quite old enough, I would have thought, to make her own decisions.'

She regarded me coldly, even with contempt. 'I thought that might be your attitude, Maxwell. You've always had an aptitude for shrugging off your responsibilities, and you've never really cared for Veronica in any case. But I thought you might have been more particular about your younger sister. You've always seemed especially fond of Helen, and yet you can countenance her gadding about unchaperoned, coming and going at all hours of the day and night ...'

'Mother,' I said wearily. 'Nobody has bothered with chaperones since the end of the war. This is 1926. Girls come and go as they like these days.'

'Girls of good breeding and decent family do not.'

'You're living in the past. How else is Helen going to meet people of her own age? It's no life for her being cooped up here all day. Quite frankly, I think she's entitled to a little fun.'

'Fun! Oh I see. So that is the sole criterion these days, is it? Nothing of duty or conscience or obligation.'

'For goodness sake, Mother! She's only seventeen.'

'Exactly my point. Far too young to be mixing with the Rochesters and their rackety crowd. She's at an impressionable age, an age when her head can be easily turned. You know perfectly well that I had planned for Helen to enter a religious order as soon as she was eighteen. In fact, I have already spoken to the order about the possibility of Helen taking her vows.'

'Have you spoken to Helen though? That would seem far more to the point.'

'It isn't necessary to speak to Helen. I know what she wants. Her path is with God. She's wanted to enter the reli-

78

gious life since she was a child.'

'Only because you bullied her into it. Only because you made it perfectly clear that, short of openly defying you, she didn't have any choice.'

'Well, is there a choice? Helen isn't strong enough, either physically or mentally, to survive the wickedness of the outside world. The religious life would protect her. She'd be safe with God ...'

'She'd be a prisoner,' I shouted. 'Cooped up with a lot of religious cranks. Can't you see that Helen needs normality. She needs to be loved, to be married ...'

'She will be married. She'll be married to the Church, a bride of Christ.'

I groaned. I felt sick. 'I won't let you do it. I won't let you shut Helen away just to gratify your obsession with a God that doesn't exist.'

She gave me her pained martyr's smile. 'I shall ignore that blasphemy. I should have known better than to attempt to discuss Helen's future with you. You've always refused to recognise and accept the fact that Helen is not exactly of this world.'

'There's nothing wrong with Helen that a normal happy life wouldn't put right. It's you who haven't allowed her to develop. It's you who has kept her a dependent child, filling her mind with religious clap-trap, convincing her that there's no other life outside the Church.'

'For Helen there isn't. You can protest all you like but you know that Helen wouldn't be capable of standing up to the rigours of a normal life. She could never cope with marriage and childbirth.' Her pale eyes strayed to the silver-mounted photograph of Hugo. 'Far better that she leads a useful life of prayer.'

I understood immediately. 'Oh I see,' I said bitterly. 'Helen is to be sacrificed to save Hugo from purgatory. When you say a life of prayer you mean prayers to rescue Hugo from the fires of Hell.'

'And why not? Hugo sacrificed himself for us.'

'Sacrificed himself!'

'Yes.' She turned her cold pale eyes full upon me. 'You still don't understand, do you, Maxwell? It was for our sake that Hugo took his own life, that he damned his soul. He thought, you see, that if he was out of the way, people would leave us alone. He thought that the debts and everything would die with him ...'

I maintained a cynical silence as she transformed Hugo's sordid little exit into a virtuous and noble act. And I was beginning to see that Hugo dead was going to be just as much a nuisance as Hugo alive. Already he seemed to be a candidate for martyrdom.

I interrupted her eventually, irritated beyond belief. 'Mother,' I said with heavy patience. 'Hugo killed himself because he was too much of a coward to go on living. He couldn't face up to being a failure and that's exactly what he was — as a businessman, a husband and, worst of all, as a Claremont. Things would be a great deal easier if you could admit that.'

Chapter 7

It is always tempting, looking back on an event after so many years, to endow the moments leading up to it with a mystic significance. In spite of all that has happened I am still something of a romantic, and even in the face of my professed atheism I have a secret need to believe that my life, if not actually ordered by some deity, has at least some preordained purpose and pattern. The alternative is to think of myself as a helpless amoeba being swept relentlessly along on the tide of life, and that idea definitely does not appeal.

But despite a relentless search for omens and portents which could perhaps have warned me of my fate, October the fourteenth began like any other day, remarkable only for the fact that it was the eight hundred and fifty-ninth anniversary of the Battle of Hastings and my sister Veronica's twenty-seventh birthday.

I had ringed the date on my desk calendar to remind me to take some offering home. Flowers were usual, though I doubted that my modest affordable posy would be noticed among the hot-house flowers that Elsworth sent by the score. The engagement had been announced and Vee was sporting a four-carat diamond that wouldn't have looked out of place in the Imperial State Crown. And not just Vee; I had been the recipient of a gold cigarette case; Helen had had a triple row of pearls. Mother's gift still awaited her, unknown and unwrapped, as she had taken herself off to Ansty at the news of the engagement, refusing to receive 'that man'. The wedding, promising to be a disgustingly lavish affair, was set for the following spring. All in all, it looked as if the Claremont fortunes were looking up.

I left the bank early that day. I was virtually my own master now, Rochester turning up just one day a week unless

81

anything urgent cropped up. Things were quiet all round. The bank rate up, investment down. Nobody wanted to borrow except those in real need which meant of course that nobody wanted to lend. It was the first rule of high finance. A rich man could raise ten million overnight but a poor man had difficulty borrowing a pound.

Since buying the car I had felt myself to be very much in the latter category — a balance of three hundred and four pounds in my account at the bank; a thousand virtually worthless Armstrong shares, purchased at what I was convinced was the bottom price, only to see them sink a further six points within the week. It was just a temporary set-back, of course; everyone said so. In the long term Armstrong's was basically sound. The government wouldn't allow their number one armaments manufacturer to go to the wall and predictions were for a merger, probably with Vickers who were also suffering from the cult of pacifist thinking. It was just a question of hanging on and hoping for another war.

Still, on the credit side, I was acquiring a rich and influential brother-in-law who had dropped hints about 'letting me in' on his next deal. Emotionally too, I felt on a steadier keel. I hadn't seen Lydia Rochester for nearly three weeks as she was staying with friends in London prior to going abroad. And in her absence I had managed to convince myself of the folly of yearning after a woman nearly twenty years my senior. I had convinced myself that this nagging ache at the thought of her would eventually pass. Oh yes, I was quite over all that. I prided myself on my strength of will which was variously interpreted as obstinacy, stubbornness, sheer pig-headedness. It all meant the same thing. When I made myself a promise, I kept it.

So all in all, as I drove home on that fateful day, I was in reasonably high spirits, completely unaware that after today all the decency and kindness in me would have died. After today I would never be the same person again.

I was met at the door by an ashen-faced Veronica. 'Thank God you're back! I've been at my wits' end.'

I followed her into the small sitting room. 'What's the

matter? What's up? It's not Mother?'

'No. It's not Mother.' She lit a cigarette and I saw that her hand was shaking. 'It's Helen. The silly little fool's got herself pregnant.'

The room tilted. A vile bitter fluid rose up in my throat. 'Pregnant!' I said stupidly. 'What the hell do you mean?'

'Surely I don't have to explain the facts of life to you. She's pregnant. Expecting a child, Jack Rochester's child. Is that clear enough for you, Max?'

She flung her cigarette away and went on talking — naturally, about herself. 'My God! This is all I need. I don't think this family could survive another scandal. This will just about finish Mother off. And Heaven knows what I'm going to tell Sydney ...'

I found my voice. 'Is she quite sure? I mean ...'

'Well, Helen's never quite sure about anything, is she? But I'm sure. I wouldn't have sent her to see Rochester if I'd had any doubts.'

'Rochester knows then?'

'Oh yes, he knows. Helen saw him this morning, naturally expecting him to do the decent thing and propose. Well, he made a proposal all right. He gave her the name and address of a doctor who could "fix things".

Abortion! I was still enough of a Catholic to feel revulsion and outrage. 'Where's Helen?' I demanded. 'I want to see her.'

Veronica grabbed my arm. 'She's upstairs, asleep, and I want her to stay that way. I had to give her a sleeping pill to get her off as it was.' She looked at me with her hard pale eyes. 'Your job is to go and see Rochester and get him to toe the line. You must insist that he marries her. Helen's not some cheap floosie he can just ignore.'

'Yes. All right,' I agreed numbly, still trying to reconcile myself to this ghastly revelation. Helen, that innocent child ...

'And keep your head, Max. Don't lose your temper like you usually do. Remember, he must agree to marry her. It's the only solution.'

'Yes. All right,' I said again. 'I understand.'

I drove very slowly, with careful co-ordination, against the chaotic turmoil of my emotions. Bastard, I thought: filthy, lecherous, underhand bastard — all that jolly good pals stuff, when all the time he'd been ...

With an effort I controlled the sudden upsurge of rage. For Helen's sake I needed to keep calm, to keep my head. As Veronica had said, nothing would be gained by losing my temper. These things happened, I told myself, and I couldn't completely exonerate myself from blame. I had allowed it to happen, perhaps even encouraged it to happen in my mad passion for Lydia Rochester. And besides, I wasn't such a hypocrite as to browbeat a fellow for seducing my sister when I had entertained similar ideas towards his mother. But there was a great deal of difference between a seventeen-year-old virgin and an experienced married woman. And Lydia Rochester wasn't pregnant — and if she had been, I'd have done the decent thing. I wouldn't have suggested a bloody abortion ...

I stopped the car. My hands were shaking. I wound the window down to let in some air. I had a sudden urge to turn the car round and drive back to Jesmond. That would have been the sensible thing to do: leave things till the morning, till I'd had a chance to cool off. Except that it would have seemed cowardly to turn tail, as if I didn't have the nerve. Not to be in control of one's actions was the ultimate weakness.

Uncle Gerard was always saying 'If you cannot control yourself, Maxwell, how can you ever hope to control others.' Self control was the answer to every crisis. Stiff upper lips, *esprit de corps*, smile while the bastards were hammering the nails in. And no doubt, he would also have reminded me that as a gentleman I had a certain code to uphold. There were certain ways of doing things, of tackling delicate situations like these, and barging in and accusing Rochester of rape would certainly not have been on his list.

After all, he would have reasoned, we were both gentlemen, we both knew the form, and if the matter was approached in a civilised and gentlemanly fashion Rochester would have no choice but to do the decent thing.

So inspired by this philosophy, I started up the engine and moved away, one perfectly controlled machine in perfect

84

control of another. By the time I reached Eldon Square, my manner was so calm as to be almost comatose. Uncle Gerard would have been proud of me.

'Is Mr Rochester at home, Mellon?' I enquired casually of the butler who answered the door.

Mellon looked doubtful. 'Well, he did say he didn't wish to be disturbed, Mr Claremont.'

'Oh, he'll see me, I think, Mellon.' Skilfully I intruded my foot in the door. 'It's urgent business, you know. I'm afraid it really can't wait till the morning.'

He stood back. 'Of course, Mr Claremont. I'll tell him you're here.'

'That's all right, Mellon,' I was already halfway across the hall. 'I'll find my own way. I shan't be keeping him more than a few minutes.'

He was in the library, curled like a cat in a deep leather chair. It was obvious that he'd been drinking heavily.

He smiled when he saw me. 'Ah Max! I've been expecting you. Did you leave the shotgun with Mellon or is it to be pistols at dawn?'

'I'm sorry,' he added quickly as he saw my expression. 'I don't suppose you're in the mood for clever remarks.' He waved his hand towards an array of bottles and glasses. 'Have a drink, won't you?' He smiled weakly. 'I'm afraid I've finished the whisky but I think there's some brandy left.'

Somewhat soothed by his apologetic and contrite manner, I accepted a chair and a glass of brandy. 'Obviously,' I said when he had resumed his seat, 'you're aware of why I'm here?'

'Well, it's rather apparent, isn't it? Outrage in your every gesture and glance.' He slopped a quantity of brandy into his glass. 'And if you've come to give me the thrashing I deserve — feel free, my dear chap. I shan't put up a fight. In fact, fifty lashes might come as something of a relief.'

I frowned. I was beginning to be irritated by his flippant manner. I couldn't see any grounds whatever for humour. But remembering that I was a gentleman I refused to be provoked and, adopting my mother's tactic of a demoralising silence, I waited for him to speak.

He got to his feet eventually. 'Look, Max — I can't tell you

85

how sorry I am. It's the last thing in the world that I wanted to happen.'

'Well, it has happened,' I said in a crisp and businesslike fashion. 'The question now is what are you going to do about it?'

He was silent. I glared at him. 'Now look here, Rochester. I'm not going to take a moral stance over this. We're both men of the world in that respect. But Helen isn't some dreary housemaid you've got into trouble. You can't pay her off as if she were some cheap tart.'

'I know that,' he said quietly. 'And please don't misunderstand me. I'm very fond of Helen. She's a dear, sweet girl' — he paused — 'but I can't marry her. I can't marry anyone.'

My mind leapt ahead, drawing ghastly conclusions from this cryptic remark. He had syphilis! He had some dreadful incurable hereditary disease! There was insanity in the family!

'Don't you think,' I said slowly,' that you owe it to me to explain that remark?'

He made no answer except a distressed movement of his head.

'You must tell me,' I persisted. 'In the circumstances I have an absolute right to know.'

'You wouldn't understand. Nobody ever does. Can't you just accept that if I married Helen I'd be doing her more harm than I've done already. I should make her life thoroughly miserable.' He looked at me. 'I couldn't ever be a husband to her in the real sense of the word.'

'In what way?' I enquired drily. 'You seem to have fulfilled all the requirements so far.'

He actually had the nerve to laugh, a silly suppressed giggle that made me want to knock him off his feet. I took a good look at him then. His appearance was ghastly; his face flushed and feverish, his voice pitched high, and to my horror, there were tears in his eyes.

Rigid with embarrassment, I averted my eyes. 'For God's sake!' I muttered. 'Pull yourself together.'

He swung round to face me. 'All right. You want to know ...' His eyes were dark and large in his pale intense face. 'Don't you know already? Can't you guess? For Christ's sake — Hugo was your brother!'

86

Comprehension dawned slowly. At first I had no idea what he was talking about. Then suddenly I became aware of his passive and feminine glance, of his moist full lips ...

'Yes. That's right.' Rochester said in his soft drunkard's voice. 'Hugo and I were lovers. We had been for several years.'

I stared at him, rigid with shock. Hugo! Big, blond, heroic Hugo! A queer! A nancy! Oh my God ...

He made a movement towards me and instinctively I recoiled. A hot tide of revulsion rose up in my throat.

Rochester smiled painfully. 'Well, yes, that's the stock reaction. I suppose I shouldn't be too surprised.' He gave a queer hiccuping laugh. 'It's all right. It isn't contagious. I haven't got leprosy, you know.'

I would have gone then except that I couldn't seem to co-ordinate my limbs very well. I should have gone then. Rochester seemed to take my continued presence as a licence to further unburden his soul. With mounting horror I saw that I was to be the recipient of confidences of the most unwelcome kind.

'It isn't easy, you know,' he said in a weary voice. 'It isn't something that one chooses to be. It isn't like a physical deformity that one is aware of from birth. It seems to creep up on you gradually. One moment you're just like everyone else — and then, well, you know that something isn't quite right but you've no idea of what it is. I was seventeen before I really understood. You know how it is. Everyone plays around at school a bit. It's like tossing yourself off, almost mandatory. But everyone grows out of it as soon as a willing female comes into view. Except that somehow I never grew out of it, the desire to touch myself, to touch other boys. That's the worst moment, when you know for certain that you're not completely normal. Then after that comes the loneliness, the sense of isolation, the constant fear of discovery. You have to be so careful, constantly on your guard in case a word or a look gives you away. It alters one's whole personality. Life becomes a complete pretence ...'

He went on talking. I tried not to listen. I wasn't even sure if he was talking to me or just to himself. I felt like a priest in the confessional, duty-bound to let him get the thing off his

87

chest, after which I would absolve him and administer penance.

'... And then suddenly there was Hugo — and oh the joy of knowing that I wasn't alone. Better than any sexual pleasure was the knowledge that there was someone who knew and understood. Of course, we fought it. We both made efforts at normality. Hugo married Marcia and I knocked around with various girls. They didn't interest me though, not in that way. I could never think of them as more than good pals. I tried prostitutes of course, but that didn't work either. You see, when it came to it — I — well, I just couldn't manage it. But Helen was different, so slim and boyish, so innocent and virginal. I realised then, of course. It had to be a virgin, at least the first time. It horrified me to think of a woman making a comparison, knowing by experience that I was no good ...'

'And so,' I yelled suddenly in a choked angry voice: 'You thought you'd experiment on my sister just to see if you could raise it ...'

I hit him then and once I'd heard his shrill yelp of pain I couldn't stop hitting him. I lost control, I forgot I was a gentleman, I forgot about the rules and playing the game. I wanted to kill him and I probably would have succeeded if Mellon and the servants hadn't intervened.

The parlourmaid was screaming. Mellon and the footman pinioned my arms. I would have fought them too if I hadn't caught sight of Rochester's smashed and bloody face. A measure of sanity returned. I felt Uncle Gerard's restraining hand ...

Slowly I got to my feet. Mellon and the footman stood back cautiously as fastidiously, with a handkerchief, I cleaned Rochester's blood from my hands.

Then I heard myself saying in a perfectly normal voice: 'I think you had better call a doctor, Mellon. Mr Rochester seems unwell.'

I walked home. I didn't dare trust myself behind the wheel of a car. I felt slightly drunk; euphoric with righteousness; ecstatic with virtue. My God, I'd taught him a lesson, hadn't I? I'd given the little pervert the whipping he deserved. He'd think

88

twice now before he indulged his depraved taste for virgins.

I was still congratulating myself when I turned into the Avenue. It was only then that the possible consequences actually occurred to me. I could see this was going to be something of a Pyrrhic victory. I was finished at the bank of course, that went without saying. In fact, I'd be lucky when Rochester had finished with me to find any employment at all. I knew the way Rochester settled his scores; a quiet word here, an insinuation there and the respectable business world would close its doors.

Of course, I held a few cards myself in that respect. If just a whisper leaked out of Rochester's homosexual tendencies, he would become a social outcast overnight. Unfortunately, I couldn't see how I could slander Rochester without dragging my brother in ...

I bit hard on my lip. Just the thought of Hugo inflamed me and filled me with moral righteousness and disgust. Eventually though, I knew I was going to have to think about him and try to come to terms with what he had been. I could see how it might have happened. I had experienced myself, at school, the sadistic suppression of what in reality was only healthy adolescent lust: cold baths, bromide and beatings, mortification of the flesh, the infliction of pain to quell the longing for pleasure so that to some people they became as one. And for others, the fear of women as a source of corruption was so deeply instilled, that they became incapable of the sexual act altogether. A few turned in desperation to their own sex and I supposed it could have been like that with Hugo. And of course, thinking about it, it seemed obvious now; all that swagger and bluster, that overt virility, that fanatical pursuit of physical excellence. It had all been a sham, a colossal pretence, a cover for his unspeakable weakness. I felt it was fortunate that our mother still remained at Ansty. In my present mood I couldn't have resisted informing her that her beloved idol had feet of clay, that after all, she'd picked the wrong son. I felt a sudden lifting of my spirits, an overwhelming sensation of relief. This was the vindication I'd been seeking all my life. Hugo hadn't been perfect, a hero, a god — he'd just been a pathetic disgusting little queer.

89

I arrived home with my mind still churning with these pleasurably vindictive thoughts and it wasn't till I actually reached 'The Laurels' that my agreeable mood fell away. I had almost forgotten about Helen, about the purpose of my visit to Eldon Square. And Veronica, waiting like Salome for Rochester's head on a plate ... I squared my shoulders and went in.

'Where the devil have you been?' Veronica flew into the hall at the sound of my key. 'Do you realise how long you've been gone ...'

She broke off at the sight of me. I hadn't realised there was blood on my clothes. 'Oh my God!' she whispered. 'What have you done?'

I pushed past her into the sitting room. 'I've given Rochester what he deserved — a damned good hiding.'

'You fool! You bloody fool. I should have known better than to let you tackle him. You've never been able to keep your temper...'

'Yes, well, remember that before you say anything else, Veronica.'

I slopped gin into a glass. 'Anyway, my thrashing Rochester was purely a last resort. He wasn't going to marry Helen in any case, and even if he had been I wouldn't have allowed it.'

'What do you mean — wouldn't allow it? Why on earth not?'

I shook my head. 'Not now, Vee. I couldn't go into it all again. We'll just have to think of something else, that's all. Rochester is definitely out of it.'

She sank down in a chair. 'Oh God! What in Heaven's name am I going to tell Sydney ...'

'To hell with Sydney,' I yelled. 'Don't you ever think of anyone except yourself?'

She leapt to her feet. 'Myself!' she cried indignantly. 'Is that what you think? Well, correct me if I'm wrong, Max, but as I see it we're all in one hell of a mess. We've no money to speak of. You've got no job. Helen is pregnant and without a husband. Don't you see? We need Sydney. At least we need his money. He's our lifeline at the moment.'

I was silent, digesting this unpalatable fact.

'All right then,' said Veronica, taking my silence as capitulation to her point of view. 'Now, as you say, we'll have to think of something else, and to be perfectly honest, Max, there's only one other sensible solution' — she hesitated, just for an instant — 'Helen will have to get rid of it.'

I regarded her stonily, making no effort to hide my hostility and distaste. My God, I thought, you're a callous bitch. We were at a major crisis in our lives, and here was Veronica, looking as cool as if she had just suggested afternoon tea instead of what, to the Catholic mentality, virtually amounted to infanticide.

'It's no good looking at me like that, Max, as if I've just crawled out from under a stone. I'm only trying to do what's best.'

'Best for whom, Veronica?' I enquired dryly. 'For you and Sydney perhaps?'

'Best for Helen,' she answered sharply. 'The alternative is having the child and then being forced to give it up or being branded an unmarried mother for the rest of her life. And best for the child as well. It isn't easy facing up to the stigma of bastardy.'

I shook my head. 'No,' I said decisively. 'It's out of the question. Helen would never agree, and besides I wouldn't allow it. She's too young to be faced with a decision like that.'

'I see,' said Veronica with a steely note in her voice. 'Well, seeing as you won't *allow* her to marry Rochester or *allow* her to get rid of the child — you'd better come up with something else, because she can't stay here. *I'm* not going to allow that.'

'I'll take her down to Ansty then,' I snapped. 'She can stay there till the child is born.'

'Oh wonderful!' Veronica sneered. 'That's a really marvellous idea. I can just see Uncle Gerard and Aunt Felicity jumping at the chance to show off their pregnant unmarried niece. And what are you going to tell Mother?'

'I don't know,' I answered wearily. 'I can't think any more.' I finished the gin and repressed the urge to pour another one. 'Let's leave it for now, Vee. We'll talk again in the morning. I'm going up to see Helen.'

'Helen!' I called to her from the doorway of the darkened room. 'Helen. Are you awake?'

She didn't answer me but I saw her put out a hand to turn on the light.

'Are you all right?' I looked at her searchingly. Somehow I expected the signs of her ravishment to show on her face. I half expected her to look knowing, worldly, old. Instead she seemed bewildered and a little frightened.

'Yes, I'm fine,' she answered and attempted a smile but I was sickened to see how she avoided my eyes. For the first time in our lives, my presence embarrassed her.

I didn't know what to say. I was at a loss as to how to bring the subject up. The easy unconstrained familiarity we had always shared had gone. Before I had just been her brother, her confidant, her friend. I was still all these things but now I was also a man, the opposite sex. Somehow it raised a barrier between us.

'Vee's told me,' I began awkwardly.

She nodded and I saw her eyes fill with tears.

I swallowed hard. I wanted to take her in my arms and weep with her. I wanted to comfort her physically as I had always done but I knew instinctively that such gestures between us were things of the past. Rochester had deprived her of more than her virginity. He'd taken away her confidence and trust in men.

I cleared my throat. There were so many questions I wanted to ask but I didn't think I could bear to hear the answers. I thought the best approach was to be brisk and businesslike, to minimise the entire affair. 'I thought we might go down to Ansty tomorrow,' I suggested brightly. 'It'll do you good to get away.'

She bit her lip anxiously. 'What about Mother. What are you going to tell her?'

'The truth of course. It's not something we're going to be able to conceal.'

'No. No, of course not.' She turned her face away. I saw her shoulders quiver in an effort at self-control.

'Come on, old girl,' I said, trying to strike a balance

92

between maudlin sentimentality and being completely off-hand. 'It's going to be all right. I'll be with you. You won't have to face up to everything alone.'

She smiled weakly and we talked for a while longer. We didn't mention Rochester — in fact we didn't actually refer to the fact that she was pregnant at all. It was as if we were children again, retreating from unpleasant reality into our own private world. I used phrases like 'when you are better', 'when you're feeling more like yourself again', as if she were the consumptive heroine in a penny-dreadful romance and needed to go to Ansty purely for the sake of her health. I found it easier like that, to put off the reality for as long as I could.

I left her sleeping and went along to my own room; buff-coloured walls, the smell of damp, hideous lace curtains masking the glare from the street lamp outside.

I lay down on the bed, physically and mentally exhausted but with sleep still a million miles away. Where did I go from here? Ansty — and the promise of my mother's accusing face. She wouldn't blame Helen of course. I would be the villian and I resigned myself to the prospect of endless recriminations; 'Well I expected something like this ... If only you had listened to me ... This would never have happened if Hugo had been alive ...' And she would be right. If Hugo had been alive, I wouldn't even be here. I'd still be in the army thousands of miles away ... I turned my face into the pillow. Hugo! Bloody Hugo! Dead or alive, wherever I turned, Hugo was always there.

Then I stiffened as I heard a car pull up outside; doors slamming, footsteps — I sat up. I looked at my watch. Eleven o'clock. Not Sydney surely at this late hour? No, not Sydney, Sydney wouldn't have hammered the door in that aggressive way.

My mouth was suddenly dry. For a moment I was overcome by sheer blind panic. Surely Rochester hadn't been such a fool ...

Then a tap at my door; Veronica's stricken voice.

'Max will you come? It's the police.'

Silence whilst I gathered my wits together, while I forced my trembling hands to be still.

93

'Max!'

'Yes. All right. I'm coming.'

I opened the door and saw Veronica's face and its sickly pallor. 'It's the police, Max,' she whispered. 'They're downstairs.'

'Yes, I know. I heard you.' I straightened my tie. 'Go and sit with Helen. Under no circumstances allow her to come downstairs. I'll handle everything. You understand?'

She nodded. 'All right — but what do they want? You didn't kill him, did you?'

I smiled painfully. I wished that I had now. It had never occurred to me that he would involve the police. Obviously revenge had been more important than avoiding a scandal and I winced inwardly at the thought of the resultant publicity; banner headlines in the Sunday tabloids; my name, Helen's name, sniggered and leered over ... I felt my temper rising, the familiar pressure building up in my head. Yes, I wished that I had finished him off now. He'd have kept his damned mouth shut then.

And then, just as I began my descent of the stairs, I realised the significance of Veronica's question. Had I killed him? Unknowingly, accidentally ... Was that why the police were here?

It was an unfortunate moment for the thought to come into my mind, just as I came into view of the two constables waiting in the hall. I must have looked guilty. I felt the hot colour suffusing my face.

'Mr Claremont? Mr Maxwell Claremont?' One of the officers stepped forward to the foot of the stairs.

I paused. It gave me a moment to recover myself. Then I said in my smoothest Oxford voice. 'Good evening, officer. How may I help you?'

He looked mildly disconcerted as if I wasn't what he had been expecting at all. He cleared his throat. 'Perhaps we could go somewhere private, sir?'

'Certainly.' I led the way into the sitting room and took up a proprietory stance by the hearth whilst I mentally rehearsed my defence against manslaughter. 'Now, what seems to be the trouble, Constable?'

He pulled out the statutory notebook and again cleared his

94

throat. 'A complaint has been laid by a Mr John Fortesque Rochester' — I almost fainted with relief. Not dead then. Corpses didn't make complaints — 'that at approximately six-thirty this evening you called at his residence in Eldon Square and assaulted him, causing his nose to be broken and two fractured ribs.'

He looked at me, expecting me to speak, and when I remained silent he enquired respectfully. 'Do you admit the offence, sir?'

There was no point in denying it. 'Well, I hit him, Constable. I'll admit to that.' I hesitated. 'Did Mr Rochester tell you why?'

He consulted his notebook. 'Yes, sir. He did. He said that he had asked you to call regarding some discrepancy in the bank's accounts, and that when you were unable to explain the matter to his satisfaction, he dismissed you, at which point you became violent and assaulted him.'

I couldn't help smiling. I couldn't have put the thing together better myself. Especially, I liked the bit about the discrepancy in the accounts, the subtle mixture of fraud and violent assault was quite damning. Of course, he'd gambled on the fact that as an officer and a gentleman I'd be reluctant to completely refute the charge. The alternative was dragging my already much-pilloried family in, publicly branding my sister as a fallen woman and my late-lamented brother as a queer. As an officer and a gentleman the choice was quite clear. I had none. I did the decent and honourable thing.

'Yes, that's quite right. Constable,' I said crisply. 'So where do we go from here?'

He put away his notebook, stuck out his chest and said in what I assumed was his official voice; 'I'm afraid I shall have to ask you to accompany me to the police station, sir — and I have to caution you....'

I accompanied him to the police station, leaving Veronica white-lipped and almost in tears with instructions to telephone Ridgeway.

Within an hour I had been formally charged and was only mildly put out at having to suffer the indignity of a night in a cell until some reputable person of standing could be found

95

to stand bail. But on the whole I thought I stood up to it all very well. Uncle Gerard would have been proud of me. My upper lip was so stiff that I suspected rigor mortis, and even when the door slammed and I was left alone in the fetid dingy cell, I continued to play the game. Scorning sleep, I sat bolt upright on the hard, unyielding bed and quietly and methodically plotted my revenge.

Chapter 8

Ridgeway turned up the next morning at eight o'clock and I was released on a surety of five hundred pounds. By nine o'clock I was sitting beside him in the back of his ancient sedan, my skin crawling with imaginary vermin, my lungs full of the sickening smell of urine and carbolic. I was obsessed with changing my clothes and having a bath.

'It'll mean a court appearance, I'm afraid. There's no way round that. We'll try and keep it within the magistrates' jurisdiction, unless of course you'd prefer to go for trial?'

'No,' I said sharply. 'I just want to get it over with as quickly as possible.'

'We're going to offer a plea of guilty then?'

'Yes, of course,' I said. 'I am.'

Ridgeway pursed his lips. 'It's a pity we can't plead undue provocation.' He hesitated and I knew instinctively that Veronica had told him about Helen. 'I suppose we can't?' he added hopefully.

I answered him shortly. 'No, we can't.'

We drove in silence for a while, one of mild disapproval on Ridgeway's part. At least he said: 'Maxwell, my boy, much as I applaud your motives in taking this line, I'm not sure that it's entirely wise.' He turned and looked at me. 'I like to think of myself as a little more than your family's legal advisor. Your father and I were friends for many years. We were at school together, in fact.' He paused. 'I remind you of this purely to assure you that I have nothing but your best interests at heart. You see, I find myself somewhat on the horns of a dilemma. As your legal advisor, I should make every endeavour to have you acquitted of this charge or at least use every means to minimise the penalty. But then, on the other hand, as a family friend and Helen's godfather ...'

He broke off, looking distressed.

'I understand,' I said, 'It's difficult, I know. But I'm not rushing into this in a mood of blind chivalry. Whatever happens, whatever punishment I receive, it'll be over with fairly quickly. If I drag Helen into this, she'll be punished for the rest of her life. A man can stand a certain amount of disgrace but a woman can't, especially of the moral kind. Technically I'm guilty, anyway. Even if Rochester had lied about my motives, I did assault him. In the end it comes down to the same thing.'

'Well, that's not strictly true,' Ridgeway observed. 'The court would take a very different view of a man who loses his temper in defence of his young sister's honour as opposed to one who lashes out because he's been caught in an act of petty pilfering — and that's how things stand at the moment.'

'I can't help that,' I persisted stubbornly. 'Helen is my responsibility till she comes of age. I've got to do what's best for her.'

Silence again, but after a while I couldn't resist asking: 'What will happen, do you think? What sort of punishment will I get?'

'Oh nothing too drastic. They won't ship you to the colonies, if that's what you mean.' Ridgeway smiled his thin legal smile. 'Looking on the bright side; it's a first offence; you're of previous good character, an Oxford man with an unblemished army record. Probably you'll get a good stiff wigging and bound over to keep the peace. It rather depends on who we get. If old Cummings is on the bench then we're home and dry. Cummings is an Ampleforth man ...'

'So is Rochester,' I reminded him.

'Well, that wouldn't matter too much if it wasn't for the complication of this suggestion of dishonesty. We keep coming back to that you see. I know Reggie Cummings and normally he'd take a dim view of an Ampleforth man not being able to settle a personal difference without resorting to the rigor of the law.' He glanced at me. 'Of course, there's no foundation ...'

'None whatsoever,' I said firmly. 'The allegation is absurd. It wouldn't stand up to even the barest scrutiny.'

'Well, that's interesting,' Ridegway mused. 'I shall have to work on that. It isn't a formal charge as yet, so possibly I could get it removed from the deposition. If I can, then it'll virtually be plain sailing, my boy, because if we don't get Cummings it'll probably be Grey or Sinclair and they were both at Oxford, Balliol men too. Sinclair's ex-army, not your regiment unfortunately but a cavalry man nevertheless.' He smiled confidently. 'Yes, I think I might be able to do something, you know. It's all a matter of *esprit de corps* in the end.'

I wanted to laugh. It seemed absurd. Apparently all I had to worry about was which tie I should wear for the trial.

I wore the old school tie, though as it turned out the choice was purely academic. I didn't get Cummings, the Ampleforth old boy, nor the Balliol men, Grey and Sinclair. The prosecution, I suspected at Rochester's instigation, had anticipated the bias of local men and had shipped in a hard-headed industrialist who looked as if he would have as much respect for an Ampleforth tie as he would for the Panamanian flag.

Nevertheless, I was reasonably confident as I stood in the dock ten days later. Ridgeway had done his stuff and the fraud charge had been dropped for lack of evidence and Actual Bodily Harm had been whittled down to Common Assault. In fact, I was congratulating myself that I had handled everything remarkably well. Mother still remained in blissful ignorance at Ansty, although eventually of course she would have to be faced. I'd have preferred to have had Helen out of the way too, but she'd refused point blank to go to Ansty without me and had driven myself and Veronica almost insane arguing bitterly against my refusal to involve her. I was quite convinced in my own mind, though, that I'd made the right decision. The reaction in our own social circle had been particularly gratifying. Opinion had come down very much on my side and the general feeling was that Rochester had got beaten fair and square in a scrap; and, well, if a chap couldn't take a beating without whining to the police ... Elsworth particularly had been delighted. 'Good for you, Claremont.' He'd slapped me on the back. 'You should have hit him harder.'

So all in all, I wasn't feeling too bad. I'd had a few

moments of panic in the cell downstairs, but then confined spaces had always had that effect on me. I recovered my optimism the minute I stepped in the dock. After all, I wasn't really a criminal, was I?

I glanced quickly round the courtroom. Apart from Ridgeway there didn't seem to be a single face that I knew. That was how I wanted it. This wasn't an occasion when I felt I needed an audience, and for that reason Veronica and Helen had remained at home. I was vaguely surprised not to see Rochester. As the instigator of the charge against me, I would have thought his presence almost mandatory — and besides, I wouldn't have thought he could have resisted the opportunity to gloat. To believe that he was too ashamed to face me was to credit him with feelings of decency I knew he didn't possess.

And then I saw her; half hidden by a pillar, her face shadowed by the wide brim of her hat, but unmistakably Lydia Rochester.

My composure deserted me. I felt the humiliation of her presence was too much to bear. It was obvious why she'd come — to revel in my discomfiture, to crow over the shame. I could imagine her smiling, that dry mocking smile I knew so well ... And then she looked at me and I saw that she wasn't smiling, that her expression was one of compassion and distress. I looked away. I didn't know which was harder to bear, her anger or her pity.

'Maxwell Francis Vivien Claremont ...'

I attempted to pull myself together. The charge was being read and in my confusion I said 'Guilty' before he'd finished.

I looked around for something solid to fix my eyes upon. There was a clock on the wall; a white stark face with roman numerals. It had a loud and distinctive tick.

The prosecuting counsel rose. I kept my eyes fixed on the clock. It took him exactly four and a half minutes to turn me into a violent, uncontrollable, remorseless thug who had battered his employer almost to the point of death merely because I had been dismissed from my post.

Then it was Ridgeway's turn, and he made much of my background, my army career, the unfortunate circumstances of my brother's death. I glanced at the magistrate as

100

Ridgeway sat down. He seemed unimpressed. He didn't even seem to be paying attention.

Then at last he spoke, without lifting his head or even looking at me. 'Young man, you are here today accused of what seems to me to be an unprovoked assault of the most savage kind. Much has been made of your unfortunate circumstances in that as sole provider for your mother and two sisters, to be suddenly dismissed from your employment constitutes a reasonable excuse for your behaviour. But I'm afraid if we conceded the right of every employee who received the sack to launch a vicious attack on his employer, then commerce and industry would grind to a halt.

'I have also been asked to take your previous good character and conduct into account. This I am not inclined to do, as to me it seems even more reprehensible that a young man of your privileged background and education should have fallen foul of the law.'

He looked at me then. 'Young man, I think you need to be taught a lesson — therefore I sentence you to six months' imprisonment ...'

I said nothing. My expression remained fixed and aloof. I was aware of nothing except the slow ticking of the clock and the tears on Lydia Rochester's face.

PART TWO
VERONICA
1926–1927

Chapter 1

I remember staring out of the window at the houses across the street. They were exact replicas of the one in which I stood; the same bay windows filmed with lace, the same high hedges of laurel and privet ... Ordinary little houses full of ordinary little people except that we weren't ordinary any more.

I sat down unsteadily. Ridgeway had just left. In my hand I held Max's scribbled note bequeathing me the two-seater and the three hundred pounds hidden in his dressing chest upstairs. It read like a testament, as if he were dead. There was a small parcel too; his signet ring and his pocket watch, a handful of loose change. I quite expected to find it labelled 'Deceased's Effects' with instructions about the funeral.

I read the note again: instructions to take Helen down to Ansty straight away. Something about Durham — that was where they were taking him — and he would really prefer it if we didn't come down ...

Oh my God. Prison! I couldn't believe it. People like the Claremonts didn't get sent to prison. I only had the vaguest idea of what the word actually meant. Visions of men shackled with chains rose up before me; men with cropped hair sewing mailbags with arrows on their suits; rough men, common men, thieves and murderers — but not men like my brother Max.

Tears of self-pity and frustration filled my eyes. I didn't know what to do. There was no one to turn to. I'd never had to face anything like this on my own. My normal strategy when faced with unpleasantness was just not to think about it. I had survived the trauma of Hugo's suicide and my broken engagement by the simple expedient of just putting it out of my mind and letting everyone else do the thinking.

But there wasn't anyone else now. I had to face the ghastly fact that I was alone ... I glanced venomously at Helen. This was all her fault. It was her stupidity that had driven Max to this mad and chivalrous gesture and I wondered with a certain amount of bitterness if he would have sacrificed his freedom so readily for me. Helen had always been special, particularly to Max. She'd always been indulged and protected.

And there was no doubt of course that Helen was different. It would be too unkind of me to say that she was simple-minded. More charitable to describe her as an eternal child. The fact of the matter was that my sister Helen had never really grown up; emotionally and intellectually she was a girl of twelve. Of course, as far as the family were concerned, this slight defect in her personality was cancelled out by her artlessness, her good nature and her piety. They all treated her like a small playful kitten whose charm and appeal was so overwhelming that one overlooked the occasional puddle on the floor. Personally, I had never felt like that. I had never been taken in by that Alice-in-Wonderland pose. I viewed her flawless disposition with suspicion; her saintliness got on my nerves, and such appalling naivety, such childlike innocence, were to my mind quite abnormal in a girl of seventeen.

Not that I blamed her for being sexually naive. None of us were ever told anything except to abjure lust and beware carnality and put aside the temptations of the flesh. What these temptations actually were one had to glean from medical text books and the grubby well-thumbed novels that went the rounds at school. But even allowing for ignorance, one was always vaguely aware from puberty onwards that every man, excepting one's immediate family, was a potential seducer and hell and damnation lurked in every admiring smile. Helen's problem was that she had never acquired this awareness. She had absolutely no conception of how beastly and deceitful men could be.

I gritted my teeth against the sound of her weeping. In the past I had always rather envied Helen's ability for instant and copious tears. It was so easy, wasn't it? To give up, to break down. And of course Helen wept so beautifully. No red-

106

rimmed eyes or stuffed-up nose, just tears spilling out from those limpid pools and coursing effortlessly down her cheeks. . .

'For goodness' sake, Helen! Stop that appalling row. Snivelling isn't going to get us anywhere, is it?'

She sat up, flushing. 'I'm sorry,' she murmured. 'You're right, Vee, I must try and pull myself together. It's just that I feel so dreadfully guilty. We shouldn't have let him do it, Vee. We should have insisted that he tell the truth.'

'It's no good thinking about what we should have done,' I snapped. 'We've got to think of what we're going to do now.'

'What can we do?' Helen whispered.

'I don't know yet. I'm thinking. Oh my God, what a mess.'

Helen's head drooped. 'I'm sorry, Vee. It's all my fault, isn't it?'

'Well, I have to agree with you there, Helen,' I retorted acidly. 'For goodness' sake, how could you have been such a gullible fool?'

'I don't know,' she said with that quiet simple dignity that so enraged me. 'He said he loved me. He said it was what people did when they loved one another.'

'So they do — but they usually wait until they're married first.'

'I felt he needed me. He needed me to belong to him. It was important to him and it wasn't important to me so I didn't see why not.'

I groaned inwardly. How typically naive. She had surrendered her virtue as easily and as casually as if she were giving a warm coat to a beggar standing at the door.

I sighed with exasperation. 'But surely you must have realised. We've had fornication rammed down our throats often enough.'

'I didn't know it was the same thing. I didn't understand . . .'

Well of course, there we had it. Helen didn't understand anything very much. In fact her ignorance of her own body verged on the pitiful. She'd never even have realised that she was pregnant at all if I hadn't spotted her being sick in the mornings and, after careful enquiry, discovered that what should be happening regularly every month suddenly wasn't happening at all.

107

I opened my mouth to speak. Harsh words of recrimination burned my tongue. I didn't say them. I knew that I couldn't bear to hear her say 'sorry' again — in fact, her very presence irritated me beyond endurance; that look of mute suffering, that quiet despair...

'Helen,' I said with forced concern. 'Why don't you go and lie down for a bit? You'll feel better when you've had some sleep.'

She smiled her meek and angelic smile. 'Yes, I will if you don't mind, Vee,' She paused at the door. 'You'll be all right?'

'Yes. Yes, I'll be fine'. At least I was as soon as I'd poured myself a large sherry. Then after another cigarette I was able to think, to make some plans for minimising the disaster. Mother first. How, what and when was I going to tell her? As Ansty had no telephone that would mean a wire, although I imagined the wording might prove a little tricky: '*Come at once. Helen pregnant. Max in prison. Veronica out of her mind.*'

I smiled grimly. No that wouldn't do; Mother would have a coronary on the spot. A letter then, or alternatively I could go down to Ansty and tell her myself. I didn't relish the task. There'd be an almighty fuss, recriminations all round. Naturally, I'd come in for a good bit of the flak. On the one hand I felt I should get Helen down to Ansty as soon as possible so that she could fade into the obscurity of the Yorkshire Dales. But on the other I didn't actually want to come clean yet and I could hardly deposit her there like an unwanted parcel. There would need to be explanations, excuses, which at the moment I didn't feel I wanted to give. After all, I had to think of myself.

I poured myself another sherry. I really wasn't any good at this sort of thing. I didn't have the brains for successful intrigue or forward planning. I wasn't a purist like Max who found beauty in truth, however ghastly — frankly, I preferred a lie every time. To this end I read avidly, immersing myself in romantic novels where I was guaranteed a happy ending. And when I was really depressed, I would sneak off to the Stoll Picture Theatre in Westgate Road and sit in the anonymous darkness to live out the fantasy of a glamorous and exciting life. I was Pola Negri resisting the advances of Ramon Navarre. I was Clara Bow swooning in the arms of Valentino. Of course, I knew I couldn't escape the truth, but as the truth was usually unpleasant, inconvenient and depressing I felt quite justified in postponing facing up to it for as long as I could. But instinctively I knew this truth wasn't going to go away. I was actually going to have to do something.

I lit yet another cigarette. Personally, I felt Rochester's suggestion was the only sensible one but I had to admit that there were drawbacks. Apart from the difficulty of persuading Helen to compound her sin with one more grievous still, I hadn't the faintest idea how to set about it. What else then? What did people of our sort usually do? Pack the offending party off to an anonymous south-coast resort and mutter about sanitoriums and tuberculosis? But that would need money which was something, at the moment, we didn't have. Of course, when Sydney and I were married — I paused in my machinations — always supposing that he still wanted a wife with a convict in the family.

I felt a moment of complete panic. One could perhaps survive being jilted once but twice was out of the question. It would be the end for me socially. I would be a complete laughing stock. And I could quite see it happening! Sydney backing off as Richard had done when he realised his fiancée was becoming a social liability rather than the asset he had imagined.

Then the telephone rang. I leapt up to answer it.

'Veronica?'

'Sydney!' I was amazed how relieved I felt at the sound of his voice.

'I'm so sorry, Veronica. I've just heard about Max. Is there anything I can do?'

'Yes. There is.' I laughed shakily. 'You can take me out to dinner tonight. I can't stand being in this ghastly house a moment longer.'

There was the faintest pause, just a fraction of a second's hesitation. I thought: My God, he doesn't want to. He doesn't want to be seen in public with me...

Then he said; 'Of course, Veronica. If that's what you

109

want. I'll pick you up about seven, shall I?'

'Yes. That will be wonderful ...' the conversation ended lamely. I hung up the receiver feeling faintly sick. I felt that all my worst fears had been confirmed.

You see, even then I had no illusions about Sydney, any more than he had about me. From the very first our relationship had been a practical one. I was marrying Sydney for his money; Sydney was marrying me for social prestige. In short, I got a charge account at Asprey's and he got invited into the Royal Enclosure at Ascot. Of course, I despised him for his aspirations but I didn't resent them. I didn't care about him enough to feel used.

In fact I didn't care about any man very much. I had only ever really loved two men in my life; my brother Hugo and Richard Vere and both of them had abandoned me. I now felt terribly insecure, conscious that in some way I had completely failed and even more conscious that to my mother, failure was the eighth deadly sin. You see, Mother demanded perfection, second best just wouldn't do. There were no prizes in life for runners-up. Hugo and I had been especially singled out to aspire to these dizzy heights and we grew up believing that we were better than everyone else. We knew we had to be better because we'd been taught to believe that there were no degrees of success. One made it to the top or one didn't make it at all. Being anywhere else on the ladder just didn't count. Consequently, I had never attempted anything at which I'd only be moderately good so that in the end I attempted nothing at all. And Hugo, poor darling Hugo, making himself thoroughly miserable in the pursuit of excellence, driven by the need to shine in Mother's eyes. I understood perfectly well why my brother had killed himself. The fear of failure and our mother was too deeply ingrained. Failure was something that couldn't possibly be faced.

I also quite understood why Richard had let me down too. Richard had his standards and those standards had demanded a virtuous, well-bred, intensely respectable wife, untarnished by even a breath of scandal. Well, it went without saying that after Hugo's suicide and the family being dragged through the bankruptcy courts I no longer fitted the bill. Sydney, on the other hand, was a businessman; he knew a bargain when he saw one and was prepared to accept slightly damaged goods knowing that the perfect article would have been out of his reach. But even Sydney had his standards and like all the *nouveaux riches* he was fanatically keen on doing the done thing. To have one's prospective wife so continually the subject of gossip and scandal was not the done thing at all.

With a sinking heart I saw all my negotiable assets fast falling away, my stock dropping with every fresh disaster. Suicide, bankruptcy, a convicted felon for a brother — and Helen would round it all off nicely by giving birth to Jack Rochester's bastard.

Reaction set in. I was suddenly angry, quivering with rage at the injustice of it all. I was sick of everyone indulging themselves at my expense, of continually being the victim of other people's thoughtless actions. I'd always lived decently. I conformed slavishly. I was conventional to the point of utter tedium. If I had any faults they were pride and vanity but these were hardly mortal sins. I wasn't like Max, an out-and-out heretic. And I wasn't like Helen — my God, I certainly wasn't like Helen! I was still *virgo intacta* at twenty-seven and likely to be so at thirty-seven the way things were going ...

I lit another cigarette. I could see that I was on the verge of becoming obsessive about Helen. Whenever I thought about her I felt slightly sick. As far as holding our heads up in decent society was concerned it would be the last straw. When people found out — and they would find out because, whatever elaborate measures one took to cover these things up, the truth always came out in the end.

I stubbed out the cigarette with savage finality. Well, as long as it didn't come out before I'd got Sydney safely up the aisle. It was Helen's bad luck after that.

I dressed for dinner carefully. Sydney liked women to look chic and expensive, something that was beginning to prove extremely difficult in view of my rapidly diminishing wardrobe. Of course, this need not have been a problem. Sydney could be generous to a fault and I need only have dropped the tiniest hint to have been inundated with Schiaparelli gowns. But I still had my standards and to have allowed him to buy me anything more intimate than scarves and gloves would have permitted a familiarity that could have been misconstrued. So having selected a couple of evening frocks that weren't too obviously last year's, I dithered for ten minutes between a Worth green georgette and a Molyneux cream silk before I finally sat down in front of the mirror.

There was no doubt about it, I looked a wreck; in fact, I looked positively ghastly. My hair needed shingling; there was a growth of hair down the back of my neck, dark shadows beneath my eyes and, to cap it all, I detected the beginnings of a spot on my chin.

I stared at the ugly blemish and tears filled my eyes. For some reason the spot utterly demoralised me. The more I looked at it, the more it seemed to assume the proportions of a cancerous growth. Of course I was being quite ridiculous. I realised that, but I so hated physical imperfection, particularly in myself. I never felt totally confident unless I was perfectly turned out.

This obsession with my looks went back a long way. I had been a beautiful infant, an even more beautiful child and the description had followed me throughout my life. People remarked on it; how beautiful I was. They never said that I was intelligent or witty or even that I possessed an engaging personality. It seemed I had nothing to commend me but my dazzling good looks and to be possessed of just this single, tenuous, ever diminishing asset had always made me feel vaguely insecure. I felt that when I was old, when I was no longer beautiful, I would no longer be of any account. But growing old and ugly was the smallest of my fears. I was afraid of being poor, of being alone; unmarried and childless. I was afraid of being ill, of dying a painful and sordid death — and most of all I was afraid that when a combination of these things had made life completely unbearable, I should follow Hugo's example and kill myself.

Of course, I realised that all these phobias and fears were the result of shock, that my loss of self-esteem was purely temporary and had a perfectly rational explanation. The first

112

blow to my confidence had obviously been my brother's death; the second, that not only had he committed suicide in the physical sense but also financially, morally and socially as well. It had left me reeling; the loss of Blanchland, the farms, the family business — and even worse, the realisation that without all these things I was simply nobody. For the first time in my life I felt vulnerable and exposed whereas before I had always felt so safe.

I hadn't worried though. After all, I was soon to be the Honourable Mrs Vere. At least that part of my life was going according to plan. Like Hugo, I had been expected to make a brilliant match. Mother had some rather feudal ideas on the subject of marriage. One was expected to marry for social advantage as well as for love, and after Hugo had blotted his copy book by marrying Marcia, the full onus of making this perfect alliance had rather devolved upon me.

Richard Vere had been perfect; well-bred, well-connected, of the one true faith. He was also wealthy, heir to a title and incredibly handsome in a pale understated, thoroughly English way. Of course I had loved him. We had everything in common and I had looked forward complacently to being eventually Lady Vere, mistress of Chirton, and probably the wife of a future prime minister as well. The discovery that Richard didn't love me — at least not enough to share my family's shame and disgrace, had been the final and totally devastating blow to a confidence that at best, I realised now, was only superficial.

Consequently, I now thought of myself as being unlucky with men. There was Richard of course, and before Richard I had been practically engaged to Philip Ainsworth till he'd broken his neck at Hexham point-to-point. And before Philip there'd been Charles who'd got himself killed in the last year of the war; a succession of men who'd either died or walked out on me resulted in my still being single at twenty-six. Of course, that was no age I kept telling myself, except that all my contemporaries were married and had children by now. It was an example of how low I had fallen in my own estimation that I regarded Sydney as my final hope.

I set to work feverishly on the spot. I particularly wanted to look ravishing tonight as insurance against the possibility of Sydney cooling off at the prospect of a convict in the family. Not that I cared a damn personally whether he found me attractive or not except in so far as it contributed to his desire to marry me. I hadn't thought too deeply about that side of things, although I was by no means naive. I had read Marie Stopes' *Married Love* from cover to cover, and although I had just a few reservations about Mrs Stopes' ideas of conjugal bliss I felt I certainly knew what I was letting myself in for.

And Sydney wasn't totally unattractive. In fact, I suppose by Hollywood standards he would have been considered handsome in a Douglas Fairbanks sort of way. He wasn't my type though. For one thing he was fifteen years older than me and for another I'd never cared for men with what I called 'Irish' good looks. If I felt any attraction at all it was for that definite aura of power. One instinctively knew that there wasn't much he would stop at to get his own way. For some reason that made me feel safe and I desperately wanted to feel safe again. That meant having all the things I'd been used to all my life. It meant living somewhere like Blanchland or Ansty, having a house in town. It mean horses and cars and furs and jewels.

And in exchange for all that, I was prepared to overlook the fact that Sydney was brash, flamboyant, uncultured and vulgar, that he talked with a spurious New York accent and wore suits that made him look like a Chicago racketeer. He was also something of a paradox. On the one hand he appeared open handed and unpretentious, on the other he could be secretive and mean. He never spoke about his past, his family, his friends and met all my tentative questions with an evasive smile. I knew he had a large estate near Sunderland though he'd never offered to take me there. I found this strange as I assumed that when we were married this would be our home. So I was left to draw my own conclusions, that his past embarrassed him, that if he had any family they embarrassed him too, and any friends he might have had had been left behind in New York. I told myself it didn't matter. All I needed to know was that Sydney was seriously rich and could keep me in the manner to which I was accustomed.

I returned pensively to the contemplation of my reflection

114

again. An improvement — but despite the discreet camouflage of powder and rouge, I felt I still looked tense and washed out.

I finished dressing, wishing now that I'd chosen the green georgette; cream silk seemed to emphasise the sallowness of my complexion. Then the final touch. I slipped on Sydney's flamboyant rose-cut diamond.

I stared at it thoughtfully. It was incredibly vulgar of course, just that little bit too showy to be considered good taste. I felt that when we were married I wouldn't wear it so much ... When we were married. When I was the respectable Mrs Sydney Elsworth instead of Veronica Claremont, the gossip's delight. I closed my eyes and suddenly, inexplicably, I began to cry.

I had managed to pull myself together by the time Sydney arrived and make the necessary repairs to my ravaged complexion. I felt ghastly though, unattractive and shabby, and to make matters worse at the very last minute I'd discovered a grease stain on my shoe. I'd quarrelled with Helen too. There'd been another tearful scene. She hadn't approved of me going out in public whilst my only brother languished in a cell in Durham gaol. Of course, she was right. I was asking for trouble in that respect; to thrust myself on Society without allowing a decent interval for the initial sensation to die down would be considered a breach of taste. But I felt I had no choice except to brazen it out. I didn't dare give in. I didn't dare allow people to see that I was vulnerable.

I certainly didn't dare let Sydney see that I was vulnerable and I was my usual smiling and confident self as I sank back into the Bentley's sumptuous interior. It seemed that Sydney intended to brazen it out too. He informed me casually that we were to dine at Maxways, fashionable and expensive. All our friends were bound to be there.

For a moment though, standing in the crowded foyer waiting to be shown to our table, I almost lost my nerve. I was quite sure that everyone was staring at me, whispering about me behind their hands. And of course they were. As we threaded our way through the maze of tables, I was aware

115

of small silences falling at my approach, of furtive outbreaks of comment in my wake. I behaved beautifully though, moving through them with my head held high, an amused smile on my lips as if I enjoyed being the focus of attention, the object of all their eyes. I almost thought I'd pulled it off when I saw Sylvia Townsend coming towards me. My heart sank, Sylvia was a bitch of the very first water besides being one of Jack Rochester's crowd.

'Vee darling!' Her clarion voice turned every head. 'I see the Claremonts have made the headlines again.'

Her eyes swept over me from my lacklustre hair to the stained satin shoes. 'I was just saying to Ronnie that it's a pity you're not in the theatre where you could put all this free publicity to some good use. Still, if it's any consolation, you're keeping everyone vastly amused. We're all agog to see what delicious new scandal you're going to entertain us with next.'

She swept on amid subdued laughter and left me still formulating my cutting reply. Everyone was smiling and despite my rage and chagrin I smiled too. The alternative was to make an even greater spectacle of myself than Sylvia already had. It was a sure sign of my diminishing prestige that she had dared to attack me publicly.

We reached our table. Sydney ordered champagne, vintage of course. I stared at the menu whilst I composed myself. Then when the waiter had gone, I looked up, smiling.

'I'm sorry about that, Sydney,' I said airily. 'I'm afraid it's something you're going to have to get used to.'

He raised an eyebrow. 'I thought the Townsends were friends of yours?'

I smiled bitterly. 'They're also friends of the Rochesters. It seems that people are taking sides.'

'I see.'

I glanced at him sharply, unnerved by his tone and his grim expression. Of course, he wouldn't like that, and I could see him speculating on what effect an open rift with Rochester would have on his business. For some reason this angered me far more than the demoralising scene with Sylvia, and although I told myself it was unwise to antagonise him when my prestige was at such a low ebb, I couldn't resist

116

reminding him of where his loyalty should lie.

'By the way,' I enquired in an off-hand voice. 'Do you still bank with Rochesters?'

'Yes,' he answered evenly. 'Among others.'

'You don't think that's perhaps a trifle disloyal?'

He frowned. 'To whom?'

'To me. To Max. After all, it's due to Rochester that my brother has been sent to prison.'

Sydney smiled. 'I'm afraid that where money is concerned, Veronica, I only have one loyalty and that's to myself. Besides, before I committed myself I should want to know the truth about what really happened between Max and Jack Rochester.'

He had slipped it into the conversation so adroitly that I was taken completely by surprise, and my voice betrayed my consternation. 'The truth! What do you mean?' I blustered.

He gave me a long hard look. 'I'm not a complete fool, Veronica. I know Rochester well enough to know that if he was going to sack Max he wouldn't have asked him round to Eldon Square to break the news over a cosy gin and tonic. And even if he had, Max wouldn't have cared a damn — he certainly wouldn't have cared enough to beat his brains out.'

I was saved from commenting on this by the advent of the waiter. I ordered the first thing that came into my head. It was only a brief respite. As soon as we were alone again, Sydney continued.

'It's quite obvious that something far more serious was involved. Naturally, I'm curious to know what it is.'

Another pause whilst bowls of clear consommé were set before us.

'Come on, Veronica. Surely you can trust me?' He smiled disarmingly. 'Not more skeletons in the family cupboard, surely? I'm beginning to wonder what I've let myself in for.'

I stared into my soup. If he hadn't said that I might actually have told him — if we hadn't been in that ghastly restaurant; if Sylvia's sneering voice hadn't been ringing in my ears ...

I looked him straight in the eye. 'I haven't the faintest idea what you're talking about.' I lied coolly. 'If Max had some other motive for what he did then he certainly didn't confide in me.'

117

'I see,' he said slowly and I saw from his expression that he probably did.

Like all inexperienced liars I couldn't leave it at that. I had to attempt to justify myself. 'I don't think you do, Sydney,' I went on glibly. 'You're judging Max's reaction from your own point of view. You don't know Max. He's always had the most devilish temper ...'

'So have I,' Sydney said mildly. 'And I've been known to lose it when confronted with a bare-faced lie. I don't like lies, Veronica. It might be as well to remember that.'

I set down my spoon with a clatter. 'Now, look here, Sydney ...' I broke off as I realised we were on the verge of a serious quarrel and I was so demoralised by the entire evening's events that it occurred to me to wonder whether he'd engineered it deliberately. It was so much easier to tell someone to go to Hell than to say that you no longer wanted to marry them.

'Sydney,' I said wearily. 'I'm not going to argue. I'm really not up to it tonight.'

We finished the soup in silence and I began half-heartedly to pick at salmon en croute whilst Sydney savagely filleted his trout. I could see that he was furious and the knowledge unnerved me and filled me with uncertainty as to what he might do. Sydney wasn't a gentleman, born and bred to the rigid etiquette that precluded quarrelling in public and raising one's voice above a certain pitch. I felt he was perfectly capable of making a scene and I visualised him walking out on me; leaving me sitting here whilst I summoned up the courage to run the gauntlet of the inevitable, amused and sneering glances...

I gulped down a complete half glass of champagne and in an effort to distract him said the first stupid thing that came into my head: 'Actually Sydney, I was thinking I shall have to go down to Ansty to break the news to Mother. If you have the time, I thought perhaps you might take me down in the car?'

I could see he was soothed by the mention of the ancestral pile. 'Yes, of course,' he said stiffly but I saw his mouth relax. 'When did you want to go?'

'Well, I thought it you're free we could motor down

118

tomorrow, stay overnight and come back the following day.'

'What about your uncle, Lord Ansty — won't he mind us descending on him unannounced?'

'Heavens no. We've been descending unannounced for as long as I can remember. Ansty is my second home.'

'Really!' Sydney said with distinct sarcasm in his voice. 'You're very fortunate to have had a choice.'

My spirits plunged. Obviously my attempt to divert him by dangling the prospect of Ansty hadn't worked. He was still sulking over this business about Max. The thought made me nervous. This was a side of Sydney I'd never seen before; this stubborn determination to have his own way. I wasn't quite sure how to deal with it.

Of course, in normal circumstances I'd have told him to go to Hell, but in normal circumstances I wouldn't have been engaged to marry him and I certainly wouldn't have stood for being patronised. It came home to me then, exactly how tenuous my position was. This wasn't a love match; I wasn't even sure that he liked me sometimes; he was marrying me purely to enhance his own social prestige. And it had to be faced, as mine diminished I became less and less of a catch and I wished now I hadn't insisted on such a long engagement. Once we were married it wouldn't matter what people said, it wouldn't matter if they found out about Helen...

Helen! The very name seemed to me to be synonymous with disaster. I thought about her sitting at home like a time bomb getting ready to go off. My God, the gossips would have a field day. We'd be the talking point of every cocktail and dinner party; every conversation would begin with; 'Have you heard about Helen Claremont?' and finish with smug pronouncements about 'instability' and 'bad blood'.

I said suddenly on impulse, primed by nerves and a further glass of champagne: 'Sydney, I don't think I want to wait until April. Couldn't we be married now? Just a quiet affair ...'

I felt his shrewd and amused glance upon my face. 'Well of course I'm flattered by your impatience — but what's the rush?'

I felt my cheeks burn. How dare he speak to me in that condescending fashion! How dare he be so crude!

119

He lit one of his disgustingly ostentatious cigars. 'What's the matter, Veronica? Do you think I'm going to get cold feet like the Honourable Richard?'

I could have died. So he knew about Richard? Well of course he knew — everyone knew.

I found my voice. 'It's possible, isn't it?' I tried to sound casual. 'You saw what happened with Sylvia just now. I can't imagine that a wife who's fast becoming a social leper would be of any use to you.'

He didn't say, 'I don't give a damn what people say,' or any of the things that I wanted him to. He just shrugged. 'That'll pass. They'll soon forget. In a few weeks' time they'll have found some other poor devil to tear to bits.'

Foolishly I persisted. 'I just don't think an elaborate wedding would be appropriate in the circumstances. Max isn't here . . .'

'He will be in April. And that's another reason for sticking to the original date. Max is to be the best man.'

'Oh for God's sake!' I snapped. 'Can't you find yourself another best man? Don't you have any friends of your own?'

His eyes hardened. 'No, I haven't — at least none that you would find acceptable, my dear.'

I bit my lip. I was making the most appalling hash of this. 'I'm sorry,' I said meekly. 'I didn't mean to be rude. It's just that with things the way they are, I think I would prefer to be married quietly, just an ordinary civil ceremony if necessary . . .'

'I thought you were anxious not to provoke comment! Surely to rush of to a registry office would do just that, and of the worst possible kind. Besides, I was rather looking forward to a Society wedding.' He fixed me with that cold uncompromising stare. 'I only intend to get married once, Veronica, and therefore I intend to do it properly.'

Looking into his eyes, I realised my mistake. I had allowed him to see how desperate I was, how terrified I was of losing him. And he was having second thoughts, that was obvious. A month ago he would have jumped at the chance of getting married at once. Now he was grateful for a breathing space. You see, I knew all the signs. I'd been through it all with Richard; the sudden coolness in his manner, the tendency to

120

quarrel over the most trivial things whilst he looked for an excuse to renege that wouldn't make him seem too much of a cad. I could have supplied him with that instantly. I could have told him that there was yet another delicious scandal on the way, that my sister who had the morals of a bitch on heat was already three months pregnant ... You see, it all came back to Helen in the end. I made up my mind there and then that somehow she had to be persuaded to do the sensible thing.

Chapter 2

'But why can't I come with you? Max said that I should go to Ansty. He was going to take me today.'

Helen sat tearfully on the end of my bed whilst I packed a small overnight bag and considered how I was going to answer her. I played for time by checking over the contents of my case; the beaded Worth gown, tweeds, cashmere twinset and sensible shoes — if I needed riding clothes I could borrow them from Aunt Felicity.

Then I turned to look at Helen. She was now sprawled on the bed in an abandoned pose, her arms flung up above her head. She looked such a child. It was hard to believe that she was actually pregnant, but if one looked hard enough one could already detect a slight thickening of her figure, an almost imperceptible enlargement of her immature breasts.

I pursed my lips, imagining how she might look in six months' time, that slight body bloated with Rochester's bastard. But that wasn't going to happen now, I'd made my mind up about that. Of course, I realised I couldn't force Helen to get rid of the child but I could make the prospect of continuing with the pregnancy so thoroughly unpleasant that she'd be thankful for any way out. The plan was to make her feel cheap, guilty, frightened and alone at which point I would come to the rescue and suggest the only sensible thing to do.

My thoughts were pure heresy, I realised that, but for years, intellectually at least, I hadn't believed in God, or at least I hadn't believed in the fiction served up by Father Devine. Emotionally, of course, it was quite a different thing. One never lost that deep-seated sense of fear and guilt, the belief that one's actions were being observed and judged and that punishment and retribution were the inevitable wages of

122

sin. It seemed to me that I had to choose between the possibility of Hell and Damnation in a life to come or the absolute
certainty of experiencing it here.

I sat down on the bed. 'Listen Helen,' I began: 'About
going to Ansty. I think, you know, it might be best if we put
that off for a while.' I rearranged some china ornaments that
stood on the table by the bed. 'Just for a week or two, just till
I've worked out the best way to tackle things.'

I paused whilst I convinced myself that this was as much
for Helen's good as it was for mine, then I went on in a
mildly accusing voice; 'Mother's not getting any younger,
you know, and she's had so many dreadful shocks already.
It'll be bad enough having to tell her about Max, I'm not sure
she'll be able to cope with the news about you as well.'

Helen looked uncomfortable but she didn't speak. I could
see this was something she hadn't cared to think about.

'You see, Helen,' I went on, determined to labour the
point, 'that's something one has to take into consideration
whenever we feel like indulging ourselves. We have to
consider the effect of our actions upon other people's lives. I
hate to keep harping on the fact that you were foolish and
naive enough to get yourself pregnant — but really, you
know, it was you who had all the pleasure and yet it's your
family who has to bear the shame and disgrace.

'You didn't think of that, did you? Any more than you've
thought about what it'll be like for you once your condition
becomes common knowledge as it surely will be within the
next few weeks. You'll be finished socially — I suppose you
realise that? You'll be completely ostracised even by people
you've thought of as friends. People have their own reput-
ations to consider, and to be seen to consort openly with
someone who's had — well, shall we say, a severe moral lapse
— it might look as if they condoned that sort of thing, as if
they were equally shameless in their behaviour . . .'

From the corner of my eye I saw a shudder pass through
her body. 'I'm telling you all this for your own good, Helen.
It's so much easier to face up to things when one is
completely prepared.'

Helen shook her head miserably. 'I didn't know, Vee.
Really I didn't. I didn't realise I was being so terribly wicked.'

123

Feeling like Judas I kissed her. 'No, of course you didn't. We all understand that. But you do understand why it might be better to postpone going down to Ansty? All the worry might make Mother ill — and there's no point in upsetting her before we need to, is there? You do see that, Helen, don't you?'

I gritted my teeth as she raised her eyes to my face. She looked so helpless, so defenceless, so trusting. 'Yes, of course, Vee,' she whispered. 'I do understand. I'll do whatever you say. I don't want to be any more trouble.'

I patted her hand. 'I think you'll find that's best in the long run.'

'Now, I've arranged for Kitty to sleep in for the night and I've got you some new books from the library.' I rose to my feet. 'So you'll be all right, won't you?'

She nodded bleakly and I went quickly from the room, refusing to be moved by that white tragic face. I wasn't going to be sentimental. I wasn't going to let emotion or affection or family feeling stand in my way. It was survival of the fittest as far as I could see — and I was going to survive, I promised myself that, even at the peril of my immortal soul.

Half an hour later I was speeding down the Great North Road heading for Yorkshire with a smile on my face and a fur rug over my knees, determined that for the next few hours at least I wasn't going to think about Helen or Max or any of the other tiresome problems that beset me. And yet as the familiar landmarks sped by, I couldn't help remembering that the last time I had motored down to Ansty I had been with Richard. I remembered his hands on the wheel, the small frown of concentration as he took a bend; I remembered being blissfully and deliriously happy...

I stared fixedly ahead. I wasn't going to think about Richard either.

'Veronica. There's a crossroads coming up.'

'Oh yes, of course.' I was supposed to be navigator, an unfortunate decision which had resulted in us taking the wrong turning twice. 'It's left here, I think, the Shipley Road ...'

'Well, is it or isn't it?' Sydney said irritably. 'I should have

124

thought you would have known the road like the back of your hand.'

'Well, I do — but Simmons, our chauffeur, usually drove us down and Richard ...' My voice tailed off. I really had to stop thinking about Richard. It would be disastrous to start making comparisons now. And yet it was impossible not to and I found myself giving Sydney a sly appraising glance. Dressed in a long motoring coat and Oxford cap he looked almost dashing, and he might easily have passed for a gentleman except for his hands. I studied them with interest as they lay on the wheel; strong, square and slightly brutal, I tried to imagine them touching me and felt a mixture of fear, delight, excitement and panic, and I was just thinking that things might not be so bad when he said in the tetchy voice he'd used all day:

'You're quite sure your people aren't going to mind us dropping in out of the blue. I think we should have tele-graphed them that we were coming ...'

'Oh Sydney, don't fuss'. I sensed he was faintly nervous about meeting Uncle Gerard and Aunt Felicity and suddenly that made me nervous too. It occurred to me that perhaps it wasn't exactly an auspicious moment to introduce him to the family at the same time as breaking the news about Max. Everyone was bound to be gloomy and down in the dumps. Perhaps I wouldn't mention it until it was time to leave...

'Veronica! Right or left? Don't they have signposts in this part of the world.'

'Left,' I said decisively. I had my bearings now. 'Then you'll come to another crossroads where we turn right. Ansty is about another five miles beyond that.'

My nervousness increased as we drew nearer to the house, and as usual I began to chatter inanely. 'Actually the house isn't strictly Georgian at all. Great-grandfather Ansty didn't start building it till 1824 but it's a very good copy; elegance without the inconvenience. Apparently the plumbing is par-ticularly good — turn right here, Sydney, then follow the road for about two miles.

'Of course, everything's incredibly shabby now but that's only due to lack of cash. In great-grandfather's day it was quite palatial. He built it just after he married Elizabeth

125

Reckington-Cairns, apparently for the brood of sons he expected her to give him. Unfortunately there was only one, my grandfather, Gerard the first. He married Violet Estolan but she died shortly after my mother was born. He then devoted himself to politics and spending what was left of his father's money. He was created a baron in 1906 and died three years later, leaving poor Uncle Gerard with Ansty and a mountain of debt. In fact, there was a time when everyone thought Ansty might have to be sold, but Uncle Gerard rescued the situation by marring Aunt Felicity who had money of her own. Of course, that's all gone now. They're still frightfully hard up. The upkeep of Ansty is enormous.'

Sydney began to look interested. 'How do they manage then?'

'Not terribly well, I'm afraid. Uncle Gerard plays at farming but he's not very good. They have the rents from the estate but probably that doesn't go very far with a place the size of Ansty. When things were all right with us, Mother used to help them out quite a bit. Mother adores Ansty. She'd do anything to keep it in the family.'

'And yet you didn't all go and live there when your brother died? That would have seemed the natural thing.'

'Well, Mother would have liked to but Aunt Felicity put her foot down about that. You see, Mother and Felicity have never got on, basically because both of them wanted to be mistress of Ansty and Mother always was until Felicity came along. When we were children we spent as much time at Ansty as we did at Blanchland, because for a long time my brother Hugo was the obvious heir. Uncle Gerard married late and for years after that the marriage was childless so it seemed a foregone conclusion that Hugo would inherit Ansty and the title as well. So when Aunt Felicity suddenly produced the twins, Russell and Philippa, Mother was absolutely livid. Consequently, she was beastly to Aunt Felicity for years, so that as soon as Felicity got the chance to be beastly to Mother, she grabbed at it with both hands. Not that it's ever stopped Mother inviting herself down whenever she feels like it and she feels like it quite a lot of the time.'

I paused. I felt he was no longer listening. As we turned in through the lodge gates I saw his eyes roaming acquisitively over the green sweep of the park. I saw him mentally evaluating and appraising, so that by the time we'd travelled the mile-long drive, I felt he knew Ansty down to the last hectare.

Then we emerged from the trees and saw the house: the long elegant facade moated by terraces, flights of steps like stone waterfalls spilling down to the lawns.

'Well,' I said, smiling at him. 'What do you think?'

He didn't speak at once but an extraordinary expression crossed his face, a look of blind admiration mingled with envy and resentment.

I could see why he was impressed. Ansty was built on a lavish scale. Even with its peeling paint it shrieked wealth and ostentation. My father had always said it was the typical overstatement of a man who had been born in a back-to-back along the Shields road, which was probably why it appealed so vastly to Sydney.

'It's perfect,' he said at last. 'Quite, quite perfect.' Then he added casually; 'I don't suppose your people could be persuaded to sell?'

I laughed. 'Heavens, no. Uncle Gerard would never sell. That's why he's so poverty stricken, because he feels it's so important to keep the estate in the family.'

'I am family,' Sydney said. 'Or at least I will be as soon as we're married.'

I suddenly felt uneasy. There was something in his voice, a look in his eyes . . . 'He won't sell, Sydney,' I said sharply. 'To you or anyone else, so there's no point in even bringing the subject up.'

Sydney smiled. 'We'll see,' he murmured. 'We'll see.'

We were greeted by the five-year-old twins, Russell and Philippa, who although they were my cousins always called me Aunt Vee.

'Hello, you two! Where's everybody got to?'

Russell, who was always spokesman, stepped forward. 'Mummy's out with the dogs, Daddy's in the library. Nanny is in the kitchen having tea with Blake and cook and we're supposed to be in the nursery.'

'Well, can you go and see if Blake has finished his tea as

127

there are some bags that need to be brought in?'

'Yes, all right.' Russell looked at Sydney. 'Are you Aunt Vee's new boyfriend?'

'Yes, I am,' answered Sydney solemnly.

'What happened to the other one?'

'Russell, please!' I protested but Sydney just laughed.

'Aunt Veronica sent him away. She thought I was nicer.'

'Well, I don't think you're nicer. Uncle Richard always gave us a coin when he came.'

'Russell, you little beast,' I cried.

Sydney, quite seriously, said; 'How much?'

'A shilling.'

'Each?'

'Yes, of course.'

Sydney slipped his hand into his pocket. 'A florin is nicer than a shilling, don't you think?'

Russell considered. 'Half a crown would be nicer still.'

Sydney grinned and paid up and Russell retired triumphant from the negotiations to summon Blake to fetch our bags.

I sighed ruefully. 'I'm sorry. I forgot to warn you that Russell was such a mercenary little beast.'

Sydney smiled. 'Oh, there's no need to apologise. He's made me feel almost at home.'

'Veronica, my dear!' Uncle Gerard emerged from the library looking everyone's idea of a peer of the realm in threadbare flannels and a moth-eaten Guernsey.

'Hello, you old fraud,' I kissed him affectionately and then introduced Sydney.

They shook hands gravely. Uncle Gerard with obvious relief as if he had expected a cigar-smoking cowboy in a ten-gallon hat.

We were invited into the library. 'There's a fire in here and I dare say you could do with a spot of something to warm you up.'

I made my excuses. 'I really ought to go up and let Mother know that I'm here.' I knew if I put it off for a moment I'd lose my nerve.

Outside Mother's door I paused, a little breathless. To be perfectly honest, I was rather dreading this. Mother was intimidating at the best of times and she'd obviously still be sulking over my engagement to Sydney. She'd be furious about me asking him here although, on the plus side, the news about Max was bound to take the wind out of her sails. Still, I had to be careful and play things down all round. I had to tell her about Max without involving Helen; I had to make Sydney look like Sir Galahad instead of Bugsy Malone; I had to convince her that this marriage was essential to our survival ... I sighed, squared my shoulders and went in.

'Veronica!' She looked surprised. 'What on earth are you doing here?'

She was sitting by the fire, a teacup in her hand, a book on her knees; Kip the ancient spaniel dozed at her feet. She looked as if she were posed for a portrait entitled 'English-woman Taking Tea'. It occurred to me then that I had never seen my mother looking anything else than elegant. I had never seen her with her hair even mildly disordered or her face without its discreet veil of powder and rouge. Even her expression was always controlled and neat.

I closed the door and her smile became tinged with alarm. 'What's wrong? There's something wrong, isn't there?'

'Yes, I'm afraid so. Something rather unfortunate has happened. It's Max ...' I hesitated and promptly forgot my lines. It all came out in a muddled rush. 'Rochester sacked him and Max lost his temper. There was a fight and well — Max gave him a thrashing ...' I paused for breath. 'Rochester had him arrested and — and well, yesterday, Max was sentenced to six months in prison ...'

I waited for a reaction and briefly her eyes widened and her mouth grew thin — then suddenly she reached down and stroked the sleeping dog. 'I see,' she said calmly. 'Well, I can't say I'm surprised. Something like this was bound to happen.'

I stared at her in disbelief. 'Is that all you've got to say?'

'What can I say?'

'Well, that you were sorry or something.'

'I'm not sorry for Maxwell. Why should I be? From what you say everything has been of his own doing.' She picked up the teapot and continued in exactly the same tone of voice. 'Would you like some tea? Shall I ring for another cup?'

'No,' I said faintly. 'I don't want any tea, thank you.'

She refilled her own cup and added a thin slice of lemon. 'Where is he now?' The chilly interrogation continued.

'Durham, I think. Yes of course, Durham. He said he didn't want any of us going down.'

'Well, I should think that goes without saying,' Mother said coolly. 'I have no intention of allowing either you or Helen to rub shoulders with criminal riff-raff.' She sipped at her tea. 'Is Helen with you?'

'No,' I mumbled. 'She was upset about Max. She didn't want to come. I got the maid to stay overnight.'

Mother pursed her lips. 'Yes, I see. Well, of course Helen was always inclined to make a hero of Max. I hope this will have changed her mind.'

Oh God, I thought. If you only knew what a hero he was.

'You came on the train then?'

'Actually, no' — I hesitated — 'Sydney brought me down in the car.'

She paused with the teacup halfway to her lips. 'Sydney! Sydney Elsworth! That man is here?'

'Yes,' I replied defiantly. 'Sydney's here — and I wish you'd stop referring to him as "that man".'

Her eyes grew chilly. 'You still intend going through with this marriage then?'

'Yes, of course. I've never been more intent on anything in my life. I only hope that Sydney intends on going through with it too.'

'You're making a mistake, Veronica, rushing into marriage with someone you hardly know, someone who a year ago you wouldn't have even wanted to know. Why can't you just wait decently for someone of our own sort to come along?'

That did it. My nerve broke. Angrily I jumped to my feet. 'Richard was our own sort and he couldn't get out quickly enough. That's the trouble with our "own sort", Mother, they want to marry their own sort too and when you're part of a family that is broke, prone to suicide and beating their employers up, that makes me the other sort. Think about that before you start looking down your nose at Sydney.'

She looked at me with cold disdain. 'Well, of course, if

that's how you're going to think of yourself that's how people will see you.'

'It's how I feel,' I cried. 'It's how everyone makes me feel.' I shook my head as she began to speak. 'It's no good keeping on about it. I've made up my mind to marry Sydney...

'Look, Mother,' I added in a conciliatory voice. 'I'm not asking you to be nice to him. Just be civil, that's all.'

'I am always civil, Veronica. Even to the boot boy I am civil. But if you're asking me to conceal my distaste for the idea of Mr Elsworth as a son-in-law, well I'm afraid it just can't be done.'

We stared at each other in silence and then I gave up. 'Well, you must please yourself, Mother,' I said grimly and headed for the door. '*I* certainly intend to do so from now on.'

Dinner was over, an indifferently cooked saddle of mutton followed by cabinet pudding and a vintage Meursault Charmes that had been kept a year too long. Conversation had been desultory. Mother hadn't come down which had been both an irritation and a relief. Uncle Gerard had talked about sheep and pigs and how he was seriously thinking of going over to arable. Aunt Felicity talked about horses and dogs whilst Sydney and I made polite noises.

We retired to the drawing room and I held my breath. I knew that at some point in the evening, Aunt Felicity would submit Sydney to the third degree: Did he ride? Did he hunt? Did he play canasta or bridge? Where *exactly* were his people from?

We settled down with our coffee. Blake came round with brandy and liqueurs, then Aunt Felicity fixed Sydney with an inquisitional eye. 'I understand that you are an American, Mr Elsworth?'

'No, I've lived in America for the last twenty years but originally I hail from Sunderland.'

'Really,' Aunt Felicity said in a voice that equated Sunderland with the Bombay slums. 'You still have family there, perhaps?'

'I have no family,' Sydney answered shortly. 'My parents died when I was fifteen.'

131

'Oh, I'm so sorry,' murmured Aunt Felicity but I could see she was relieved. At least she was to be spared the cloth-capped proletariat trampling all over her Turkestan rugs.

'Veronica tells me you're a financier, Mr Elsworth,' she gave her fluttering and girlish laugh, 'although I'm never actually sure what that means.'

'It means he uses money to make more money,' Uncle Gerard said, making it sound only one step removed from usury.

'Really. How fascinating,' Aunt Felicity murmured vaguely.

We lapsed into silence, then Uncle Gerard asked Sydney what he'd done in the war. I could see the evening heading towards a disastrous conclusion.

Then Sydney smiled at Aunt Felicity. 'This is a very fine house, if I may say so, Lady Ansty.'

'Well, of course it used to be,' she answered wistfully. 'But I'm afraid one can't get the servants any more. All the girls seem to want to work in factories or shops. And the upkeep is enormous. You've no idea. We have to keep half the rooms shut up as it is.'

'And how many rooms are there, ma'am?' Sydney had suddenly become terribly colonial, exhibiting that ingenuous curiosity at which the Americans excel. I felt any minute he was going to say something like 'cute' or 'swell'.

'About forty principal rooms — but then there are all the servants' quarters, kitchens, pantries and so on.' Aunt Felicity sighed. 'Sometimes one wonders whether one wouldn't be happier in a little bungalow by the sea.'

'You've never thought of selling?' Sydney enquired.

'My dear, I think about it all the time but of course Gerard won't even consider it.'

'It's a question of heritage,' Uncle Gerard said thickly. 'Of keeping things together for the next generation. I see it as a sort of sacred trust.'

'I entirely agree, sir. These old mansions should be kept going as long as they can. Being in real estate myself, I've seen what can happen when they have to be sold off. The houses are turned into schools and institutions, the estates

132

broken up; land sold off for housing and factory development, woodland cleared for timber.'

'How appalling,' breathed Aunt Felicity. 'It sounds almost like rape.'

'Yes, it's a great pity,' said Sydney gravely. 'But unfortunately that's what's happening these days. It would be a tragedy if it ever happened to Ansty.'

'Oh it won't happen here, I can promise you that. I'd rather let the place fall down than have some beastly developer carve it up.' Uncle Gerard looked depressed. 'That's probably what will happen,' he pronounced gloomily. 'The roof in the east wing isn't going to hold out much longer, though where we're going to get the money, I just don't know. The trouble is, money's not been really worth anything since the end of the war. What used to be considered a tidy income just doesn't go anywhere these days.'

Sydney nodded and looked concerned. 'Look sir ...' he hesitated. 'I hope you don't think I'm presuming on so short an acquaintance, but as Veronica and I are to be married soon ...' he smiled diffidently, 'if there's anything I can do — if I could help in any way — I mean, if you should need a temporary loan ...'

Uncle Gerard frowned. 'Well, that's generous of you, Mr Elsworth, but I really don't think ...'

'Oh, for Heaven's sake, Gerard. We can't afford to be proud.' Aunt Felicity beamed at Sydney. 'I think it's very kind of Mr Elsworth to be concerned.'

'Well, I'd like to help,' Sydney gave his frank ingenuous smile. 'And naturally, any loan would be virtually interest free.'

Well of course he had them eating out of his hand after that. I was speechless with admiration, irritated too, that Uncle Gerard and Aunt Felicity should fall for, what seemed to me, such a transparent ploy. It was perfectly obvious what he was up to. The loan was the first step, his foot in the door, and it struck me as vaguely sinister, how easily Sydney was able to manipulate situations, how completely people succumbed to his spurious charm. It was frightening too, the ruthlessness and decisiveness with which he pursued his aims. After just one look he had set his heart on Ansty. The fact that it appeared unattainable just spurred him on. He had us all summed up and had settled on Aunt Felicity as the weak link in the chain. Throughout the rest of the evening I watched, enthralled, as the barriers of class and prejudice fell. Aunt Felicity invited him to join the Hunt, Uncle Gerard broached the port normally reserved for cabinet ministers and dukes. I felt I ought to say something. I felt at least I should try and put them on their guard but I found that I didn't have the courage.

I went to bed in a mood of both irritation and elation. Of course Sydney was wasting his time with regard to Ansty. I knew that Uncle Gerard would never sell. But I couldn't help admiring the masterful way he went about things and I could see how incredibly safe I would feel once we were married. I'd be able to forget about Hugo and I'd be so secure and happy that the thought of Richard Vere would never cross my mind. I snuggled down in the four-poster and allowed myself to relax — and then of course I remembered Helen.

Chapter 3

I renewed my attack upon Helen within hours of returning home, undeterred by her wan and fragile appearance. Appearances were deceptive, though, for she seemed in a placid and disgustingly tranquil frame of mind — clearly I was going to have to be savage.

Consequently, I maintained a grim and brooding silence until at last she was forced to ask; 'How was Mother then, Vee?'

I sighed and allowed a tragic look to cross my face. 'As well as can be expected under the circumstances, I suppose. Naturally, she was awfully cut up over this business with Max.' I was amazed at how easy I found it to lie.

'When is she coming home?'

'She didn't actually say. I suppose she needs some time to pull herself together. Certainly not before the end of the month.'

Helen bit her lip. 'You didn't tell her about me, then?'

'No, I didn't,' I said flatly. 'Frankly, I don't think she could have stood another shock.' I paused and allowed the significance of that to sink in. 'And to be perfectly honest,' I continued, 'I think it's a responsibility you should bear yourself. You can't expect other people to do your dirty work.'

Her eyes filled with tears. 'Oh Vee, don't be beastly.'

'I'm not being beastly. It's time you grew up and faced a few unpleasant facts. After all, you managed to get yourself into this mess without any help from me so you can jolly well get out of it in the same way.' Brutally I added; 'And I really don't see why I should take the responsibility for making Mother ill. After all, she's had the most frightful time these past six months. Finding out about you might possibly be the last straw.'

135

She grew pale and I saw her shoulders slump. Tears seeped slowly from the corners of her eyes. 'So what I suggest you do,' I went on in a matter-of-fact voice, 'if you haven't the courage to tell her face to face, is write to Mother and break the news as gently as you can — and as soon as you can. Obviously, there are certain arrangements that will have to be made.'

'Arrangements?' she whispered. 'What sort of arrangements?'

'Well, you can't stay here, can you?' I pointed out cruelly. 'And Uncle Gerard and Aunt Felicity won't want you at Ansty. After all, they've got the twins to think of. They're of an age now where they might ask awkward questions.'

'Where will I go then?'

'Well, they have special places for girls in your predicament, I believe. Like nursing homes, you know, except they are run by the Church. You'll just have to go to one of those until the baby is born and arrangements can be made for its adoption.'

'Adoption!' I knew from the distress in her voice that it had never occurred to her that she might have to give the child up.

'Well, you don't think you'll be able to keep it do you?' I flung her a pitying look. 'Can you imagine Mother agreeing for Rochester's bastard to be brought up in our house?'

'Of course,' I added quietly as I saw the mutinous look cross her face. 'No one could actually force you to give the child up. I mean, that would have to be your decision. But if you did decide to keep it against the family's advice — well, you couldn't expect any support from us, could you? You'd have to make a new life, somewhere else, on your own. You'd have to pretend you were widowed or something like that, because, you see, Society, at all levels reserves a particularly unpleasant retribution for unmarried mothers. You'd be a complete outcast, if anyone found out — and of course, they would, eventually ...'

Her defensive position collapsed. She dropped her head in her hands. 'Oh Vee. You've got to help me. What on earth am I going to do?'

I smiled. I had thought for a moment she was never going

136

to ask. 'Helen,' I took her hands. 'Listen, my dear, I don't know if you'll understand what I'm going to say, but you don't actually have to go through with any of this. There is an alternative, you know.'

She looked at me with wide innocent eyes. 'What sort of alternative?'

'It's just a small operation. Nothing too dreadful. They just take the baby away, you see.'

'What happens to it then?'

'Well, it goes to Heaven, to be with God.'

'You mean it's dead,' she said quietly. 'To take the baby away they have to kill it first.' She shook her head. 'I couldn't do that, Vee. That would be the most terrible sin.'

'So is fornication,' I remarked acidly, 'but that didn't seem to put you off.'

Helen flushed. 'It's not the same thing. It's not half so bad.'

'Well, that depends how you look at it, Helen. When you sinned with Jack Rochester you did so for pleasure alone, purely for the gratification of self. Now that seems to me far worse than sinning to save other people from worry and pain. If you did this thing, you wouldn't be doing it just for yourself, would you? You'd be making a sacrifice in order to protect your family.

'You see, Helen,' I continued when I felt she'd taken that in, 'You've been wicked and so you must be punished, for without penance we can never be truly absolved. You remember Father Devine telling us that, don't you? That only through punishment and sacrifice can we hope for real absolution?' I went on to point out that the alternative was a lifetime tortured by remorse and guilt. 'I mean, just think how you'd feel if the shame and disgrace made Mother ill. What if she actually died? You'd never forgive yourself, would you?'

She shook her head numbly. I could see she was weakening. I paused for a few seconds and then played my ace card. 'And what about Max?' I demanded. 'I thought you cared about him.'

'I do,' Helen cried. 'Of course I do.'

'But not enough to make this sacrifice for him? My God,

137

Helen, he made a big enough one for you.'

'Max wouldn't want me to do it. He wouldn't allow me to do it.'

'Well, that's just where you're wrong, Helen,' I lied glibly. 'Max and I discussed it when we knew that Rochester wouldn't marry you. He agreed with me that it was the most sensible thing to do. He didn't mention it because he felt that you didn't have the strength to make a decision like that.' I knelt down beside her. 'But you have got the strength, haven't you? You could do it for Max. And it's all so quick and easy these days. Just a simple operation. No worse than having a tooth out really.'

I was pushing too hard. I saw her physically recoil.

'At least let me make some enquiries.' I added casually. 'Have you still got the card Rochester gave you? The name of the doctor he thought could help?'

'I — yes. Somewhere ...'

'Well, let's go and dig it out, shall we? And then I'll go and see him myself and find out what's involved. You see, you needn't be bothered with anything at all. I'll make all the arrangements myself.' I gave her my most brilliant and reassuring smile. 'You can leave absolutely everything to me.'

I didn't waste any time. The next morning I set off immediately after breakfast and by ten o'clock I was staring thoughtfully at a highly polished brass plate: Dr Marcus Goldman, 15, The Leazes. Well, that was reassuring, a decent address. I had feared some ghastly backstreet off the Scotswood Road.

I was even more reassured on entering his consulting rooms; a well-furnished waiting room, all the right smells, an efficient-looking nurse in starched linen. And Dr Goldman himself, plump and bespectacled, exuding an air of quiet paternal benevolence. I was immensely relieved. When one thinks of abortionists one thinks of awful squalid drunkards who've been struck off. This obviously wasn't the case.

He extended a firm, well scrubbed hand. 'Miss Claremont? How may I help you?'

I cleared my throat, uncertain how to begin. 'It's — well, it's rather a delicate matter, you see?'

'Yes.' He smiled encouragingly.

138

'It's my sister, my younger sister.' I gave him a direct look. 'She finds herself in a rather unfortunate predicament.'

'I see.'

'I was told that you might be able to help.'

He still smiled but his eyes took on a cautious look. 'And may I ask who told you, Miss Claremont?'

'The — er — gentleman in question. Mr Rochester. Mr Jack Rochester.

'Ah yes.' He looked relieved. 'I know Mr Rochester.' He unscrewed the cap of his fountain pen. 'And how long has your sister suffered from her complaint?'

'Oh, just under three months I would think.'

He nodded. 'Well, yes, in those circumstances I believe I can assist you. Perhaps you could make an appointment for your sister to see me.'

I hesitated. 'Well, actually I'd rather not. I'd rather hoped we could fix everything up here and now? Helen is terribly highly strung, you see. She's inclined to get herself worked up quite unnecessarily. It really would be better if she only had to come here just once.'

'I see. Well, of course, if you think so. I presume she is perfectly healthy in all other respects?'

'Oh yes. Absolutely. She's only seventeen.'

He made some notes. I sat looking at his square capable hands. Then he murmured without looking at me; 'There will, of course, be a fee.'

'Yes,' I swallowed. 'If you'll just let me know how much.'

His eyes flickered over my expensive cashmere suit.

'Two hundred and fifty guineas — in cash, in advance.' He smiled. 'I'm sure you appreciate that for this kind of treatment we are unable to take cheques.'

I concealed my dismay. *Two hundred and fifty guineas!* Nearly all the money I had. 'I'll bring it with me,' I said airily. 'When?'

He consulted a diary. 'Shall we say in three days time; Thursday, the 2nd of November at 12 o'clock?' He rose, smiling blandly, 'My nurse will inform you of the necessary preparations.'

So there it was, all settled in such a calm and clinical way that I hadn't the slightest qualm. All that was necessary now

139

was to keep Helen diverted for the next three days; it was imperative that she didn't have time to think. I didn't want to think either, for despite my deep conviction that I was doing the right thing, I was aware of a mounting disquiet reminding me that what I was doing was criminal; sacrilegious; murder.

Thursday came, the 2nd of November. I woke with an abominable headache and my nerves on edge. This was it then! In a few hours' time the whole wretched business would be over. Everything would be back to normal. It was then that I had my first real attack of conscience. Up until that point I had regarded the issue of bringing Helen around to my way of thinking merely as an intellectual trial of strength. I had convinced myself that practically and logically it was absolutely the right and proper thing to do. Helen was just not mature enough to suffer the fearful trauma of bearing an illegitimate child. Emotionally, she was little more than a child herself, so from that point of view I had never had any doubts. And yet here I was at the eleventh hour, no longer able to suppress the fact that I had badgered and bullied an innocent young girl and exploited her simple childish faith so that she believed in some strange and inexplicable way that it was God's will she kill her own child.

I leapt from the bed. Nerves, just nerves. Perfectly natural in the circumstances. I should have been prepared for an attack of cold feet. Telling myself sternly that I wasn't going to give way now. I dressed and went quickly along to Helen's room.

She was kneeling by the bed, her lips moving in silent prayer. I could see she'd been crying. She lifted her head and gave me a watery smile. That did it. I felt a monster. The brisk cheerful words died on my lips.

'Oh Helen,' I went and sat on the bed and took her hands. 'You don't have to go through with it if you don't want to. Really, I shan't be cross.'

Looking like Joan of Arc about to be tied to the stake, she gave me a brave and tearful smile. 'I'm all right, Vee. Honestly I am. I promise I won't let you down.'

I winced. My God, I'd done a magnificent job. She was so completely under my domination, so pathetically eager to please. I bit my lip. All I had to say was that I'd changed my

140

mind, that somehow, we'd find another solution. But I said nothing. I did nothing and an hour later I drove her in guilty silence to Dr Goldman's consulting rooms.

'You're sure, Helen?' I said as I helped her out of the car. 'You're absolutely sure this is what you want?'

'Yes, I'm sure, Vee.' She smiled beautifully. 'Don't worry. I'm not afraid. I feel, you know, that God is with me.'

And so in a virtual state of grace she ascended the steps. I knocked at the door and delivered Helen and her child into the hands of the executioner.

I had two hours to kill. Originally I had intended to do some shopping at Fenwicks, but now such a frivolous exercise seemed positively obscene. Instead I drove to the Town Moor and sat in the car, smoking cigarette after cigarette and justifying my course of action. It really was all for the best. I had done absolutely the right thing. In six months' time Helen would thank me. After all, everybody benefited, not just me. Helen could go back to being Alice in Wonderland, Mother would remain in blissful ignorance and Max's noble sacrifice wouldn't have been in vain; a monumental scandal would have been averted all round. Of course, I'd have some explaining to do when Max came home. I'd have to say that Helen had had a fall, just simply say that she'd miscarried. It was perfectly feasible; these things happened all the time, and probably he'd be so relieved that he wouldn't bother to pursue it. I smiled, feeling happier. Max would never know. Nobody would ever know ... I paused in the act of raising a cigarette to my lips. Nobody would ever know — unless Helen told them, and immediately I saw the flaw in my perfect plan. Helen would never be able to keep her mouth shut. She'd be dying to unburden herself, burning to confess. She'd tell Max, of course, and Max would tell Sydney ... Suddenly I realised that it wasn't over at all. I had merely exchanged one nightmare situation for another. Instead of being terrified that people would find out that Helen was pregnant, I would now be terrified that they'd find out that she'd been aborted and that I was the one who had procured it.

I took a deep breath. Relax. Calm down. I was getting

141

things out of proportion again. Even if Max did find out he was unlikely to tell Sydney — unless he saw it as a subtle way of punishing me. I juggled frantically with dates. Max was due for release on April the 24th, Sydney and I were to be married on the 30th. That meant nearly a week of wondering and worrying that Helen would spill the beans. I envisaged being jilted again, left standing at the altar. I imagined the laughter, the humiliation...

I started the car. I was being completely ridiculous, letting a fevered imagination get entirely out of hand. After all, if I had been able to badger Helen into imperilling her soul, surely I could bully her into keeping quiet.

So feeling calmer, that I had the situation perfectly in hand, I drove slowly back to Leazes Avenue.

My tentative knock was answered almost immediately and I was startled to find Helen practically thrust into my arms.

'She's a little groggy from the anaesthetic,' Starched Uniform said. 'But she'll be as right as rain in a couple of days.'

I looked at her in astonishment. Obviously I wasn't going to be asked in. Then of course I realised, Helen was now incriminating evidence and needed to be got off the premises with all speed.

I began to protest and found myself addressing an abruptly closed door. Helen sagged against me; 'Oh Vee,' she whispered. 'Please take me home.'

I looked at her then. She looked absolutely ghastly. Her face was white and sweating. 'Yes, of course,' I muttered and put my arm around her. Hurriedly I got her down the steps and into the car.

'Are you all right?'

She nodded and closed her eyes.

'Was it awful?'

'Yes. Yes, it was.'

'Well, it's all over now,' I said briskly. 'You'll soon forget.'

She turned and looked at me then and as our eyes met I knew what a terrible thing I'd done. Her expression was awful. She looked cowed and violated, as if she were the victim of some unspeakable rape. She wouldn't forget. I wouldn't forget. It would be between us for the rest of our lives.

142

The drive home seemed to take hours, though in reality it was no more than fifteen minutes before the door of the Laurels closed behind us.

'Now up to bed with you.' I spoke as if she were a child with the mumps. 'What you need is a good long rest.'

She didn't speak. She didn't even move until I took her arm and guided her towards the stairs. I wished suddenly that she would cry. I could have coped with tears, hysterics even, but this stricken inanimate silence unnerved me.

I began to help her undress when suddenly she stopped me. 'It's all right, Vee. I can manage. I'd rather, you know.'

'Yes, of course,' I murmured, feeling awkward and insensitive. I hovered uncertainly. 'Would you like some tea?'

'No, thank you.' She gave me that faint brave shaming smile. 'Later, perhaps. I really just want to sleep.'

I went downstairs into the sitting room. It was bitterly cold. Of course, having given the maid the day off, none of the fires was laid so that I had to grovel for half an hour with paper and sticks. At the third attempt I achieved a grudging blaze. Then I looked in the cupboard to see if there was anything to drink. I poured a large gin and added bitters until it was the right shade of pink. The gin bucked me up. I felt instantly more cheerful. Of course Helen would get over it, given enough time. She was young, resilient. Of course she'd forget. She'd be herself again in no time.

I picked up the book that I had begun the previous night and read until gin, exhaustion and the coy doings of Ethel M Dell's imbecilic heroine combined finally to put me to sleep.

It was dark when I awoke. I peered at the clock and saw it was nearly nine — I'd been asleep for over five hours. I stretched cramped and frozen limbs. The fire was out and my teeth were chattering with the cold. I remember vaguely noticing as I drew the curtains that it had begun to snow.

I put on the kettle to make tea and then went upstairs to see Helen. 'Rise and shine,' I said brightly as I went towards the bed. 'I expect you're ready for a cup of tea now, aren't you?'

I touched her shoulder lightly. She was as cold as ice. 'Come on, Helen, wake up. It's nine o'clock.'

I was suddenly aware of her utter stillness, the frightening rapidity with which she breathed. I shook her more roughly. 'Helen! Helen! Wake up!' Then I switched on the light and saw her face, grey and ghastly, beaded with sweat. She wasn't asleep. She was unconscious.

Oh my God! I wanted to scream, just to open my mouth and let all the fear and panic out. I gritted my teeth. I must keep calm. I mustn't panic. I must think things through in my usual rational way. Now obviously I needed help. I wasn't going to be able to cope with this all on my own. I would have to telephone Dr Goldman, ask him to call. And then it occurred to me that he probably wouldn't want to do that. He wouldn't want to admit that Helen had been his patient at all. I'd have to insist, that was all. We were in this together. I certainly wasn't going to take all the responsibility myself.

I ran downstairs to the telephone and rummaged for his card in my bag before I realised that he wouldn't be in his consulting rooms at this time of night and I hadn't the faintest idea where he lived.

I tried the exchange; 'Yes, Dr Marcus Goldman. No, I don't have an address but there can't be too many Dr Goldmans surely?'

I groped for a cigarette. Really, my nerves were quite gone. What on earth would I do if I was unable to contact him?

'Trying to connect you?' I almost swooned with joy as I heard the ringing tone but my relief was short-lived as the telephone was answered and his housekeeper's voice informed me that Dr Goldman was not at home.

'When will he be back?' It was hard to keep the hysteria from my voice.

'I really couldn't say.'

'Do you know where he is? Would it be possible for me to telephone him there?'

'I'm afraid not. He's dining out with friends and they don't have a telephone, but if it's an urgent medical matter, I can put you in touch with another physician.'

'No, it's all right,' I said quickly. Obviously I couldn't risk that. 'I must speak to Dr Goldman personally. Perhaps you could ask him to telephone me the minute he gets in. It's very important that I speak to him. I'll be waiting for his call.'

144

I waited, smoking my last cigarette, then ransacking Max's room to see if he'd left any there. I finished the last of the gin too, drinking it neat out of the bottle, and in between I drifted fretfully between Helen's room and the telephone in the hall. At eleven o'clock I knew I couldn't wait any longer. I needed medical help urgently. There was nothing for it but to, call Peter Gilly, our family doctor. And tell him what? That Helen had had an illegal abortion which had somehow gone wrong? I wouldn't need to tell him — he'd know, he'd guess, the minute he made his examination. Or would he? There was no real reason why he should immediately jump to the conclusion that Helen was the victim of a bungled abortion. Of course, he might guess that she'd been pregnant, it didn't matter about that. It was how the pregnancy had ended I had to conceal.

I went to telephone. I knew I had to think very carefully about what I was going to say. How far could I trust Dr Gilly? If the worst came to the worst, could be be persauded, for old times' sake, to be discreet? On the plus side was the fact that he was a friend of the family and he'd known all of us for years. On the minus side was the possibility that though he might be prepared to protect Helen and myself, he would draw the line at protecting Dr Goldman. Therefore, I decided I couldn't risk confiding in him yet. I'd have to continue to bluff the thing out.

'Dr Gilly? It's Veronica Claremont. I'm so sorry to disturb you at this time of night, but I'm rather worried about Helen. You see, I'd been out shopping all afternoon and when I came home she complained of feeling unwell. She said something about having a fall but as there seemed to be no bones broken I sent her straight to bed. Well, I've just been up to her to take her some tea and I can't seem to waken her ...'

He arrived within twenty minutes and I waited downstairs, sick with apprehension and fear, rehearsing lines which seemed feebler and more unbelievable by the minute. I felt I knew exactly what he'd say. He wouldn't come straight out with it. It was a delicate subject, to be approached in a subtle, roundabout way; 'Veronica, my dear, I don't quite know how to put this but ...'

He didn't say anything like that. He came crashing into the

room, his face grim and angry. 'You should have called me hours ago. The child's practically at death's door. Didn't you at least have the sense to keep the room warm? Surely you're capable of lighting a fire?'

'I'm sorry,' I began. 'I didn't realise ...'

He cut off my excuses with an impatient movement of his hand. 'Where's the telephone,' he demanded. 'You're going to need a good nurse. I'd prefer to get her into a hospital immediately but I daren't risk moving her. She's in very deep shock. She must have been haemorrhaging for hours judging by the amount of blood she's lost. She needs a transfusion badly, though to introduce large quantities of blood when she's in such a weak state might put too much strain on her heart. I've given her an injection of adrenaline. That'll help to bring her round ...'

I stared at him blankly. He's trying to frighten me, I thought. Obviously he knows and he's making it seem worse, so that when he pounced with his question I'd break down and confess. He pounced; 'Veronica. Are you aware that Helen has recently had a pregnancy terminated?'

At least he said something like that. I couldn't hear him very well. There was this awful roaring noise in my ears. But I heard myself, lying superbly in a shocked and indignant voice. And I continued to lie superbly, especially to myself. Helen was going to be all right. She was young. She was strong. Of course she'd pull through. You see, I had to believe that. I had to continue to pretend that nothing was really wrong. I had to shut everything else out and concentrate all my thoughts on the belief that Helen would survive, because I knew that if she didn't then neither would I. So I refused to acknowledge what I saw in Peter Gilly's eyes. I refused to admit that whilst I'd slept, guzzled gin and dithered for hours about whether to get help or not, Helen had been slowly bleeding to death. And so I clung to my pathetic belief right until the end. Even when Father Clement, the parish priest, arrived, I couldn't let go of that slender thread of hope. I prayed of course, desperately, hypocritically, invoking the Holy Mother and all the Saints, promising to live like a saint myself, if only Helen could be saved. And it seemed for a moment that my prayers had been answered when Dr Gilly came to tell me that Helen had regained consciousness and was asking for me.

Of course, I was overjoyed. I almost wept with relief and then suddenly, terrifyingly, the fear of discovery was back and I found myself thinking that I had to get to Helen before she said anything incriminating. I went quickly upstairs. Father Clement was still with her and I waited impatiently for him to open the door.

Then suddenly the door opened and the priest was there, smelling of stale incense and candle wax with retribution in his eyes. 'I'm afraid she's gone,' he said in a soft and sorrowful voice. 'Thankfully she was able to make her peace with God ...' His gaze fastened accusingly upon my face. 'I only hope that you can do the same.'

Chapter 4

Helen was buried quietly at Ansty on November the 7th and ten days later, equally quietly, I married Sydney. It caused comment of course, a wedding so hard on the heels of Helen's tragic death was considered an appalling breach of taste. I was past caring by then. The strain of the last few weeks was beginning to tell. I had given Sydney an ultimatum; either he married me immediately or the whole thing was off. It was a desperate gamble but I was desperate, enough to risk Sydney calling my bluff. I just couldn't face up to more weeks of uncertainty, constantly wondering if Sydney would find out about Helen or not. I argued that this wasn't likely. Peter Gilly knew, or at least he knew that Helen had been pregnant and subsequently aborted, but I had pleaded my ignorance so convincingly that he had agreed, for Mother's sake, to hush the whole thing up and issue a death certificate accordingly. Only the priest knew of my involvement but I wasn't too concerned about that. Priests were bound by the seal of the confessional and anything Helen had said in *articulo mortis* could never be divulged. That just left Max, and stoically I volunteered to go down to Durham to break the news. You see, it was imperative that Max should be convinced along with everyone else that Helen's death had been no more than a tragic accident. I anticipated difficulties. Max wouldn't be fobbed off with glib explanations and I couldn't play the complete innocent as I had with Dr Gilly. I had to hope that Max would be so completely devastated with grief and shock that explanations would be the last thing on his mind.

Nevertheless, it was in a nervous and uneasy frame of mind that I drove down to Durham the day after Helen's funeral. Fortunately, I was to be spared the usual grim formalities. Uncle Gerard had telephoned the Governor who was a member of his club and I had been granted the privilege of seeing Max alone. Even so, I found it a ghastly experience; the terrible feeling of claustrophobia, the lack of air, struggling not to breathe the unspeakably fetid prison smell. And I couldn't help thinking that if Peter Gilly hadn't been so decent and I had been less accomplished as a liar, I might have found myself in a similar establishment. Gritting my teeth, I trailed after the warder down endless dingy corridors, our progress constantly impeded by the unlocking and relocking of doors until I was eventually shown into a small windowless room.

'Hello Max,' I said. Was it Max? This tall thin spectre with the dead expressionless eyes? It was like looking at a photographic negative, everything was reversed. His fair hair had darkened to a nondescript brown, his tanned healthy skin had faded to a sickly yellow. And his clothes! Sack-like garments stamped with broad black arrows, and ridiculously I thought of St Sebastian. Here was a martyr indeed.

Then our eyes met and I suddenly realised why he had been so insistent that none of the family should come. I would always see him like this now. This one shocking image would superimpose itself over the familiar figure that I'd known for years. And from now on, every time our eyes met he would remember and resent that I had seen him like this. It was as if I had caught him naked, engaged in some unspeakable and despicable sexual act. The memory would always be a source of shame and embarrassment, a grisly, ghastly secret between us.

'I'm so sorry, Max,' I whispered. 'But I had to come.'

'You needn't have bothered,' he said abruptly. 'If you've come to tell me about Helen, I already know.'

That took the wind right out of my sails. How did he know? How much did he know? I blurted out the obvious question.

'Lydia Rochester told me.' He gave an ironical smile. 'She wrote me a letter of condolence.'

I couldn't conceal my chagrin or my utter surprise. 'Lydia Rochester! My God, she has a nerve.'

'Yes, I suppose one could look at it like that. Actually, I

149

thought it was rather decent of her in the circumstances.'

I licked my lips nervously. I didn't like this. Things weren't going the way I'd planned at all. 'I'm sorry,' I said again. 'I should have come straight away — but there was so much to do. We were all so shocked.'

He nodded and then said disconcertingly. 'I don't suppose you've got a cigarette, have you?'

'Yes, of course.' I handed him my case and he helped himself. Then he sat back and regarded me through a haze of blue smoke. 'All right, Vee,' he said harshly. 'What happened?'

I took my time before answering, knowing that he was listening acutely to every word I said. I needed a few moments to retrench, to replan my strategy. Lydia Rochester's letter had robbed me of the element of surprise. He'd had time to think, to formulate questions. I had to be absolutely sure of my answers.

'Well, to be perfectly frank,' I admitted, 'I'm not really sure what happened. I just came home and found Helen in bed. She said she didn't feel well, but considering her condition, I didn't think too much about that; she quite often went to bed during the day. It wasn't till I went to wake her, at about nine o'clock, that I realised anything was wrong.' That monumental lie over with, I proceeded with a sequence of events which was very near to the truth, omitting my telephone call to Dr Goldman and the fact that I'd dithered for two hours before calling Peter Gilly out.

Then I paused dramatically. I thought a show of emotion was called for here. 'Oh Max, it was dreadful, I just didn't know. It never occurred to me that she was actually ...'

He cut off my performance with a sharp movement of his hand. 'So what you're saying is that Helen died of shock and loss of blood following a miscarriage.'

I nodded mutely and pulled a handkerchief from my bag.

'And Peter Gilly was quite satisfied with that?'

'Yes. Why shouldn't he be?'

'Well, it all seems rather odd, don't you think? Strong healthy girls like Helen don't miscarry for no apparent reason. And even allowing that she did, I can't believe that it's an absolutely painless experience. She would have called

150

out, surely. She'd have called to you for help.'

'I don't know,' I stammered. 'Perhaps she did and I didn't hear her. You see, I dozed off myself ...' I plunged on with my fantasy, getting more and more out of my depth. Max kept interrupting me. Why had Helen been in the house alone? Where was Kitty? Where was I? Why hadn't I taken her down to Ansty as we'd originally planned? And he was obsessed with Peter Gilly, what he'd thought and said. I could see he wasn't satisfied. I could see that he wasn't going to be able to leave things alone. He'd brood on it, turn everything I'd said over and over in his mind and then, as soon as he was released, he'd go and see Peter Gilly and I would be caught out in a deliberate lie. Gilly knew that Helen hadn't just merely miscarried and, although I trusted him not to reveal the truth to the world at large, I knew he wouldn't hesitate to be frank with Max. And then Max would wonder why I had lied. Why would I conceal the fact that Helen had had an abortion if I wasn't personally involved ... It was this muddled and panic-stricken thinking that led me to make my first real mistake. I needed a scapegoat. I needed someone on to whom I could divert the blame — and I suddenly thought of Jack Rochester.

I stopped talking at once and stared down at my hands. 'Max,' I began again in a small fearful voice. 'I don't know how to tell you this. I didn't want to tell you, at least not while you were in here.' I drew a deep breath. 'But you're going to have to know — you see, Peter Gilly thinks Helen might have had an abortion. Of course, I blame myself. Obviously Rochester managed to get to Helen behind my back ...'

Max suddenly twisted sideways in the chair. 'Oh my God!' He dropped his head in his hands. 'I should have killed him. I should have killed him while I had the chance.'

'Please Max,' I laid a restraining hand on his arm. 'For Goodness' sake, don't think of doing anything foolish. After all, we've absolutely no proof and he'd obviously deny it. And I really think, for Helen's sake, that it would be better to let sleeping dogs lie. Nothing will bring her back, will it?'

He lifted his head and looked at me with frightening calm. 'Don't worry, Vee. I shan't take the chance of ending up in

151

here again. It'll have to be something far more subtle next time.'

I took the 'next time' philosophically. Making a threat was one thing, carrying it out quite another, and I was convinced that by the time Max was released, when he'd had time to calm down, he'd realise the only sensible course was to put the whole frightful business behind him.

I allowed a few moments to elapse before I ventured to change the subject. 'Actually there's something else I have to tell you that you probably won't like either. Sydney and I are to be married next week.'

He didn't say anything. I wasn't even sure that he'd heard me. 'Of course, everyone thinks it's positively indecent. Mother has said she'll never speak to me again.' I smiled wanly. 'I'm not sure whether that's a bonus or not.'

I lit cigarettes for both of us. 'It seems the only practical thing to do. Obviously, I can't stay on at the Laurels on my own and Mother refuses to budge from Ansty. Actually, Sydney wondered if it wouldn't be better if we gave up the lease. I can't imagine you'd want to go back there. Naturally, you'll make your home with us when you're released, so there doesn't really seem any point in keeping it on.'

'What? Oh yes.' He spoke in a disinterested voice. 'Whatever you think is best.'

The meeting ended on this almost commonplace note and I left in a mood of light-hearted relief, quite unaware that for the second time in my life, my actions would result in disaster.

'I, Veronica Theresa, take thee, Sydney John ...'

We were married quietly at Ansty in the family chapel, flying full in the face of Mother's furious opposition — I gained a husband and lost a parent simultaneously. It was a ghastly wedding all round, just the bare essentials. I wore a severe and sober Paquin suit and Sydney wore a grim expression. But I couldn't have cared less. I was triumphant. I had done it. I was home and dry, past the post — all sorts of ridiculous clichés went through my mind. What mattered was that I was safe. I was Mrs Sydney Elsworth, protected by his money, sheltered by his name. I would never feel insecure or frightened again.

152

We left almost immediately for the Continent, not intending to return till the first week of the new year. I was so relieved to get away that I practically floated across the Channel on a tide of rapture and champagne, travelling overnight to Paris where I raided the couture salons on the Rue de la Paix. Then Nice, Cannes, a week in Toulon, then Christmas in Biarritz.

Sydney proved to be an ardent lover. His ideas on conjugal rights were somewhat theatrical, i.e. performances twice nightly and matinées. I seemed to spend the days in a haze of Veuve Cliquot and the nights in a stupor of physical exhaustion.

Eventually, I had to come down to earth. We returned to England the first week of the new year and I began in earnest the life for which I had sacrificed my pride, my principles and the life of my seventeen-year-old sister and her unborn child. Not an auspicious beginning but my vanity at that time had assumed megalomaniac proportions. I felt that everything would be all right if I spent enough money, drank enough champagne and never, ever thought about Helen.

I was happy. Of course I was happy — except for a vague nagging unease, an occasional pang of guilt. Up until then fear and anxiety had suppressed any real feeling of guilt. I had been too busy looking back over my shoulder to give a thought to the nightmare that might lie ahead. And it would be too ironic, that just as I was feeling safe, just as I felt I was no longer threatened, I should be stricken with pangs of conscience. I couldn't accept that. It was just reaction, I thought. All those weeks of worry and panic and then suddenly not having to worry and panic at all. And then, added to that, the realisation that, after just nearly three months of marriage, being Mrs Sydney Elsworth wasn't coming up to my expectations at all.

I blamed Sydney at first. The very first day we arrived home he provoked a quarrel. I had been vaguely depressed ever since I glimpsed the English coastline and as we travelled north I went into a positive decline. Harden Hall was the last straw, Sydney's idea of a pleasant surprise. I loathed it on sight; grotesque and Gothic, it squatted like a huge carbuncle on the banks of the Wear. It was the shock, I suppose, that made me over-react. One moment I had been sunning myself on the French Riviera and the next I was standing shivering in a vast ugly Victorian drawing room cluttered with the vast, ugly Victorian furniture that Sydney had bought lock, stock and barrel from the previous owners.

'But Sydney!' I exclaimed. 'It's positively ghastly. What on earth possessed you to buy such a mausoleum.'

Sydney paused in the act of pouring out sherry. 'What's wrong with it?' he demanded in an aggressive voice.

'Well, everything,' I said. 'Absolutely everything. It's the most vulgar house I've ever seen.' I went to stand by the window. 'What a hideous view. I can actually see the docks.' I fitted a cigarette into a holder and waited for Sydney to supply a match. 'Really, you know, darling, we'll have to do better than this. Nobody of any consequence lives in Sunderland and there's nothing more socially damning than having a squalid address. I'll start looking for somewhere else straight away.'

'Well, I'm sorry you don't like it, Veronica,' Sydney said in a quiet and level voice. 'But I do. So this is where we are going to live.'

I turned to face him. 'You can't be serious, Sydney? What's so special about this place? It's only a house. You can't possibly be attached to it in any way.'

'As a matter of fact I am.' He gave a self-conscious smile. 'It was Roger Cookson's place. I used to work for Cookson you know — in those shipyards that are part of the "hideous view".' He smiled, half to himself. 'I used to pass this house on my way to the yards and every day I would look up and think ...'

'Yes, I understand all that, Sydney,' I said impatiently. 'But surely now that you've made the point that you've come up in the world, we can move on to something a bit more civilised.'

'No, we can't,' he snapped. 'This is where I want to live.'

'I see,' I said in a cold little voice. 'Obviously, my wishes don't count.'

'Of course they count. But not to the exclusion of everything and everybody else.' He broke off and I could see that

154

he was struggling not to lose his temper. 'Look, Veronica. I know that at the moment this doesn't suit you ...'

'Doesn't suit me!' I shrilled. 'My God, that's an understatement. I think it's the most hideous house I've ever seen.'

'That's a rather sweeping statement considering you've only seen two rooms.'

'That's more than enough.' I shook my head. 'No. It's no good, Sydney. I can't possibly live here. I absolutely refuse ...'

'Refuse!' Sydney exploded. 'You've got a bloody short memory, haven't you? Don't I seem to remember something about your promising to love, honour and obey. Well, I'll not hold you to the first two, but on the last I'm going to damn well insist.'

I stared at him coldly, appalled at his language and loss of self-control. 'Really, Sydney,' I said with a contemptuous curl of my lip. 'It's bad enough being able to see the docks through the window without having their foul language brought into the house,'

He took a menacing step towards me. 'You haven't heard anything yet. I'll say what I damn well like in my own damn house. I'll not have you giving the orders.'

I stared at his white and furious face. Instinctively I knew this was one of those moments of choice, that what I said and did now would affect my whole future. Sydney was making a stand, asserting his masculine authority. I knew I should back down. I should burst into tears or employ some other utterly feminine device. But he'd chosen a very bad moment to play the heavy-handed husband. I was cold, exhausted, nervy and depressed and absolutely fed up with always having to compromise. I decided that I was going to make a stand too. We were married now. I was in a position to assert myself. I was going to start as I meant to go on.

'Sydney,' I said coolly. 'I hope you don't think I'm going to be one of those meek submissive wives without any mind of their own.'

It was his turn to look surprised. He had been waiting for me to make my usual apologetic retreat. 'No, I don't expect that,' he said, retreating a little himself. 'I expect you to be reasonable and just for once to consider a point of view other

155

than your own. This house means something to me, Veronica. I've wanted to own it since I was fifteen years old.'

'Oh, I understand perfectly why you want to live here, Sydney. You want to strut through the rooms and remember your threadbare and impecunious youth. Well, personally, darling, it's something I'd rather forget.'

I saw his face whiten and his big hands clench themselves down by his sides. He took a step towards me and for one wild, incredulous moment I thought he was going to hit me. Then slowly he relaxed and said in a chilling voice, 'I'm not going to argue with you, Veronica. The subject is closed.' He glared at me. 'We're going to live at the Hall whether you like it or not, so I suggest you start getting used to it, unless of course you'd prefer to make alternative arrangements.'

So there it was. The honeymoon was barely over and I was on course for divorce. This fed my growing neurosis, my terror of failure. I was overwhelmed with self-pity. Not only had I married a selfish inconsiderate beast, I was to be walled up in this ghastly mausoleum. I decided I was going to be unwell and retired fainting to my room. A doctor was called — not Peter Gilly, I couldn't have faced that — who immediately diagnosed mental and physical exhaustion and prescribed a week's absolute rest. So I lay back on my pillows and played at being the 'delicate wife'. It was the first time I had ever used this useful feminine device and I could quite see why so many women became 'invalids' after they'd married. Illness was a refuge from bullying husbands, sexual harrassment, an escape from the pressures of an unhappy life. Then after two days I decided that such an obvious ruse was unworthy of my intelligence. It was the sort of ploy used by women when sympathy was the only emotion they could arouse and who could get attention in no other way. Besides, I was bored, and as a means of bringing Sydney to heel it had proved quite useless. His brief, dutiful visits to my bedside had made it quite clear that he wasn't going to be swayed by a languishing neurotic wife who constantly took to her bed. Sydney's interest in bed was purely physical and I could see that sex was going to be a far more powerful means of barter. Sydney was the kind of man who was always in the mood. I would have to get the point over that what put me in the mood was spending vast quantities of money, drinking vast quantities of champagne and generally getting my own way about everything. I reconsidered my position. Quite clearly I wasn't going to get my own way about the house. If it was to be Harden Hall or nothing, then obviously it had to be Harden Hall. And once having accepted that, things really didn't seem too bad. I could even begin to view the Hall as a challenge. I brightened considerably, envisaging the vast amount of money I would need to spend to bring the place up to scratch. And we'd need more servants; a butler, naturally, and I'd have to replace the cook. Then two footmen at least, a chauffeur, gardeners and odd job men; a personal maid for me and a valet for Sydney. I felt quite excited as I made my extravagant plans.

I leapt from the bed and immersed myself reluctantly in a tepid bath, making a mental note about the inadequate plumbing. Then I descended on the servants' hall and gave the cook a week's notice, informing the remainder that the armistice was over and the reign of terror about to begin. I then telephoned a domestic agency and announced my requirements. I had the two footmen within the hour, a chauffeur and a cook-housekeeper were to arrive the following day and a butler was to present himself at the end of the week.

When Sydney arrived home, I was waiting for him in my new Edward Molyneux gown, a cocktail in my hand and a come-hither look in my eye.

'Veronica!' He looked amused. 'What a miraculous recovery. I hadn't expected to see you up for days.'

'Darling,' I smiled my most seductive smile. 'Forgive me for being so incredibly childish.' I offered my mouth for his kiss. 'All right, I give in. You're the boss,' I added coquettishly. 'Tell me that I'm forgiven.'

He raised his eyebrows. 'Well, of course you are, my dear.'

I poured him a White Lady I'd mixed myself. 'Of course, you were quite right on insisting that we live at the Hall. It'll be a perfectly good house once it's had a bit of a face-lift. In fact, I'm quite looking forward to taking it on.'

'I thought you said it was squalid,' Sydney remarked dryly.

'I said it was a squalid address. But then, come to that, so

157

are Bayswater and Chelsea, but they're incredibly fashionable just now.' I gave him my most brilliant and alluring
smile. 'I intend to set a trend. Soon everyone will be clam-
ouring to live in Sunderland.'

His laughter was a good sign. He rarely did so. I was
discovering how difficult he found it to relax. 'Besides, you
won't even recognise it in a few months' time ...' I chattered
on, outlining my elaborate plans, spending thousands by the
minute...

'Veronica!' He stopped me suddenly. 'How much is this
going to cost?'

I stared at him. 'Goodness knows. I hadn't thought. Does
it matter?'

'Well, it might be an idea to stick to some sort of budget.'

'Budget!' I stared at him aghast as if he'd uttered some
awful profanity. 'But you more or less said I was to have
carte blanche.'

He looked irritated. 'I meant that you could have a free
hand with the decor. Naturally I expect you to keep things
within certain limits.'

Well, that immediately put the damper on things. I had
ghastly visions of having to rummage in bargain basements
for remnants, of eternally having to do tiresome sums. 'Oh
well,' I said peevishly, 'If I'm going to have to stint ...'

'Well, let's discuss it, shall we?'

'What's there to discuss. You said the other night ...'

'Well, we both said things then that we didn't mean.' He
took some time lighting a cigar. 'To be perfectly honest, I
bought this house on a whim; it appealed to my mood at the
time. And you're quite right, it's not suitable but it'll do for
now. That's why I don't want to commit too much time and
money on doing it up. It seems pointless if we're going to
move on elsewhere.'

'Well, why didn't you say so?' I screeched in rage. 'I said
I'd start looking for somewhere else.'

'You don't need to look. I've found what I want.'

I stared at him intently. There was something in his voice,
a curious inflexion ... 'Sydney,' I said sharply, 'I hope you're
not getting any silly ideas about Ansty.'

He looked at me innocently. 'Such as?'

158

'Such as thinking you can badger Uncle Gerard into selling up.'

'I'm not going to badger anyone, as you put it, into doing anything. But if you want to know what I think, I don't think your people are going to be able to keep things up. I just want first refusal, that's all, seeing as it's my money that's paying for the restoration of the East Wing. As for the Hall, as I said, within reason you can please yourself what you do. Just don't get too enthusiastic, that's all. One way or another, we're bound to be moving on.'

'Oh, I see,' I said witheringly. 'I'm supposed to be thrilled at the prospect of being trailed around like a gypsy. Well, I'm sorry Sydney, but it won't do ...'

'Veronica!' I knew by the heavy, laborious way he pronounced my name that I was in for a dreary lecture. 'Perhaps we ought to get a few things straight between us. We ought to have it quite clear in our minds what we expect of one another so as to prevent any more unpleasant scenes. Now, I fully understand that you've been used to money and being generally indulged and in that respect I don't expect you to change. But naturally, I expect certain things in return. Firstly, a wife who doesn't question every decision I make; secondly, a wife who takes a certain amount of interest in how I make the money she's so ready to spend, in the way of making yourself agreeable to such business associates as I may occasionally bring home. I also expect you to provide me with children and a stable home ...' He fixed me with his cold stare. 'Are there any of these terms with which you feel you cannot comply?'

'No,' I answered icily, hating him more and more. 'You've made everything perfectly clear.' I added bitterly; 'Where do I sign?'

Then we went into dinner and struggled in near silence through an excrutiatingly bad meal. At nine o'clock, Sydney excused himself and went into his study to await a long-distance call from New York. I poured myself a large brandy and went up to bed and cried myself to sleep.

So the battle lines were drawn and we began our silent war of attrition. On the surface we were entirely pleasant and polite but we looked for small subtle means of causing pain.

159

It soon became clear that Sydney wasn't going to allow marriage to alter his routine. It was business as usual; days spent between his offices and the docks, evenings glued to the TransLux which he'd had installed at enormous expense. I was often alone, frequently bored and consequently I had far too much time to think. I thought about Helen, going over and over that last day in my mind; if only I'd done this, if I hadn't done that — and the last straw was reading the announcement in *The Times* of the engagement of my former fiancé to the Honourable Janet Secombe. I shut myself in my room, consumed an entire bottle of sherry. My unhappiness was now complete.

In desperation I decided to distract myself by taking an interest in the house. After all, it seemed I was to be stuck there until Sydney made up his mind where our future was to be and good furniture was good furniture wherever you were. So out went all the hideous Victorian junk. In came painters and decorators to wash the dingy walls with delicate pastels and strong greens and blues. It was a dark house, built in the typical Victorian manner so as to admit the very minimum of light. There were four principal rooms on the ground floor; a morning room, a drawing room with French doors leading out on to the lawns, a dining room panelled in gloomy oak and a library whose walls were lined with neat rows of books which had obviously never been read. I couldn't help thinking of the glorious Vanburgh library at Blanchland; of Hugo and I sprawled by the fire sharing our tea with the dogs, of Max reading aloud in his clear beautiful voice, and Helen — but I wasn't going to think about Helen, was I? Helen, like Hugo and the Vanburgh library, belonged to the past. It was the future that mattered now.

And at first the days passed quite easily. I was absorbed with my task and found that I had quite a flair for design. Sydney was easily pleased. Providing it was old and looked expensive he was inclined to leave everything to me. He took a vague interest in art in a Philistine way. As in all things he expected value for money and bought paintings by the square inch as he bought books by the yard, so that frequently I had to alter my plans to incorporate a gargantuan portrait or a vast biblical scene.

160

Then at the end of February, when the army of workmen made habitation of the Hall impossible, we moved temporarily into the Clarendon Mansions flat. This made it more difficult to ignore each other in such a comparatively small space. The intervals between our bouts of mild sparring grew shorter. Consequently, I was relieved when Sydney announced he was going over to Belfast to see about the commissioning of a new ship. I decided to take advantage of my freedom and spend a week in Town. The following Monday saw me comfortably esconced at the Ritz from where I sallied forth every morning to Sotherby's rooms. After lunch I tackled Harrods and the Bond Street galleries and by Thursday I had acquired vast quantities of china, linen and glass, a pair of exquisite Chinese lacquer cabinets, a French Empire couch, two drawings by Augustus John and a rather superlative Burne Jones. Then on Friday I met Richard Vere.

'Veronica!' I turned instantly, immediately recognising his voice. I was on the first floor at Harrods, in the perfumery department and suddenly there he was, Richard Sebastian Bourbon Vere, Member of Parliament for Hexham, bounder and cad.

'Veronica,' he said again with his warm possessive smile. 'It's been ages, hasn't it? I can't remember the last time.'

I could though, the day he had hedged and prevaricated until pride had demanded that I set him free, 'Richard,' I forced a smile. 'How lovely to see you.'

We stood awkwardly for a moment. 'You're looking very well,' he observed quietly. 'You're married now, I understand.'

'Yes,' I gave what I hoped was an ecstatic smile.

'Happily?'

'Yes. Yes, of course.'

Another pause. I tried not to look at him. I had forgotten how incredibly handsome he was.

'Look,' he said awkwardly. 'Could we have some tea or something? I'd like to talk. There's a restaurant downstairs, isn't there?'

We went downstairs and sat in embarrassed silence over a pot of Earl Grey and a plate of cream cakes.

Richard smiled sheepishly. 'This is awful, isn't it? Now that we're here, I really don't know what I wanted to say.'

'Perhaps,' I blurted out suddenly, 'you were going to apologise for the despicable way you treated me.'

He flushed. 'I'm sure I deserve that. I can't blame you for feeling bitter.'

Bitter! I didn't like that. The word conjured up visions of a sour, disappointed, sexually frustrated old maid. I remembered that I was supposed to be a happily married woman. I wasn't supposed to care. I gave a bright, carefree laugh. 'Oh, Richard, I'm only teasing you. It really doesn't matter any more. Quite frankly, I think we both had a lucky escape.'

'You think so?' Richard said, his wonderful blue eyes intent on my face.

'Of course.' I speared a chocolate eclair on to my plate. 'Janet Secombe will make you a far more suitable wife. She's quiet' — I meant dull — 'conventional' — I meant boring — 'and I'm sure she'll never embarrass you by having opinions of her own.' I meant she was a stupid, mindless cretin.

'And as for me, well I couldn't be happier. Sydney's an absolute darling. He spoils me frightfully which is probably the wrong thing to do, but it's so much easier, isn't it, Richard,' I added pointedly, 'being married to someone incredibly rich?'

He missed the point and said pompously; 'Well of course, if that's the sort of thing that's important to you.'

'It was important to you,' I snapped. 'You weren't so keen to marry when you discovered I would be penniless.'

'That's not true,' he protested. 'It wasn't because of that.' He was silent for a moment, then he looked up at me with that diffident, boyish smile. 'If it's any consolation, Vee, I've missed you terribly. I had hoped that we could at least be friends.'

Friends! I could have slapped him. How dare he suggest something so dreary and tame. Then I saw the way he was looking at me and the acid rejoinder died on my lips. At least he still desired me. My vanity was soothed.

Silence again but this time it was of an entirely different kind. Silence because what we wanted to say could never be said and saying nothing was better than small talk.

162

Then the inevitable question. 'When are you returning north again?'

'Tomorrow. Tomorrow afternoon. I'm catching the one o'clock train.'

'That's a pity.' He lowered his eyes. 'I had hoped you might be staying till the end of the week. I shall be going back myself then. You see, I try to divide my time equally between the House and my constituency. Two weeks in town, two weeks on the home front.' His eyes focused on my mouth. 'It would have been nice to have travelled together.'

So potent was his effect on me that for one brief moment I actually toyed with the idea of delaying my departure for a week. It was, of course, only a momentary lapse. Richard Vere, like all unpleasant memories, belonged firmly in the past and the past was something I never thought about. I knew the sensible thing to do, the only thing to do, was to pick up my bag, thank him politely for tea and then walk out of his life just as calmly as he had once walked out of mine.

I got as far as rising to my feet. 'Yes, that would have been lovely but I really must get back.'

'What about lunch tomorrow?' he persisted gently. 'Surely you could catch a later train?'

'No, really I can't ...' fatally I hesitated which allowed Richard to slip his card into my hand.

'Well, think about it,' he said with his wonderfully sensual smile. 'Give me a ring if you find yourself free.'

I went back to the hotel, ordered dinner and a bottle of Dom Perignon to be sent up to my suite and spent the evening mulling over the unforgivable way Richard had treated me. I re-lived all the humiliation, I wallowed in the shame, I listed every slight and embarrassment I'd suffered because of him. Then the next morning I telephoned Richard's Belgravia flat.

'Richard? It's Veronica. I find that I'm free for lunch after all.'

Chapter 5

And that's how it all began — lunch at a discreet little Soho restaurant that Richard knew. It was all very respectable; incredibly tame. We were just two old friends meeting casually for lunch but underneath, of course, we knew.

I returned home that same evening in an excitable frame of mind. I had half resolved not to see Richard again. After all, we would both be taking the most tremendous risk. I had my marriage to think of and Richard had Janet and his political career. But that's what made it so irresistible, the danger, the excitement, so that when he telephoned the following Thursday and suggested that I meet him for tea at the Bodega Rooms, well naturally I didn't hesitate.

An intimate little dinner was obviously the next step, far more difficult to arrange and impossible to explain, but as Sydney was still in Belfast there didn't seem too much danger. The following evening I was sitting beside him as we drove along tortuous and interminable country lanes until we found a quiet little inn where we were unknown.

It was an awful meal, the food cold and the wine warm, but there was a glorious fire and soft rosy lights. And I was in love — with Richard, with myself, with the whole idea of having an affair. It was really terribly romantic.

Then Richard said as we were sipping coffee and crème de menthe: 'It's ridiculous, isn't it? I gave you up purely to avoid being involved in a scandal and yet here I am, quite calmly risking everything just for a few hours alone.' He took my hand. 'It's worth it, though, isn't it, Vee? The way I feel at the moment I'd give everything up just to have you back again.'

I smiled ecstatically. This was music to my ears, even though I didn't take a word of it seriously. I knew Richard

164

too well to believe that he meant to give anything important up. He wanted me simply because I belonged to someone else and this passionate declaration was merely a prelude to getting me into bed. But I didn't intend to give in quite as easily as that. The thought excited me, I admit, but mingled with my desire for Richard was an equally passionate lust for revenge. I wanted to make him suffer, to treat him as badly as he'd treated me. And I was confident that I had my own feelings well under control. I wasn't frigid by any means but my enjoyment of sex came principally from the feeling of power it gave me. More important than any personal gratification was the idea of enslaving Richard and making him beg.

I turned and gave him a long smouldering look. 'Richard,' I breathed. 'Please don't say things like that.' I stared down at my hands and Sydney's gargantuan diamond gave me a conspiratorial wink. 'In fact, I've been thinking, I'm not sure that we should see each other any more. It really doesn't do any good, does it?'

'Oh God, Vee,' Richard groaned. 'Please don't say that. I couldn't bear to lose you again.'

'But we have to be practical, Richard,' I said with a catch in my throat. 'We had our chance and we threw it away. Now we've just got to get on with our lives as best we can.'

'And what sort of life is that going to be? Both of us saddled with people we don't love?'

'But it's better than torturing ourselves over a life we can never have.'

'All right.' A note of desperation crept into his voice. 'I agree that we can never be man and wife but that doesn't mean we can't have any happiness at all. We could have the next best thing.'

I looked at him coldly. 'You mean you want me to be your mistress, I suppose.'

He flushed. 'Well, I wouldn't have put it quite as crudely as that. You make it sound so sordid.'

'That's because it is sordid. In fact it's more than sordid, it's downright insulting. You renege on our engagement and then offer me some hole-in-the-corner clandestine affair ...' I stood up. 'Please take me home, Richard. I really think that this has gone far enough.'

165

Oh the joy of seeing that pleading look on his face. 'Veronica. Please. Sit down. Just listen.'

I resumed my seat. He took both my hands. 'Veronica darling, I'm not asking for anything that you don't want to give. I love you. I know that now and I can't tell you the agony of thinking of you married to someone else. That's my own fault, I know. By my own stupidity I've ruined both our lives. But perhaps we can salvage something. For me at least it would be more bearable if we could just see each other now and again. That's all I ask, that we can be together sometimes, that occasionally, when it suits you, we can have an evening like this.'

For an undemonstrative and usually uncommunicative Englishman, this was really quite a speech and I couldn't help but be moved by such a passionate appeal. Besides, I felt I had made my point and that, having dictated the terms of our relationship, I could afford to be fairly generous. I spent the rest of the evening being generally alluring, reminding him that, apart from being vastly decorative, I was also sophisticated, charming and amusing in comparison with the worthy Janet.

We drove home like lovers, my head pillowed on his shoulder as he manoeuvred the huge Lagonda round hairpin bends. We said a lingering goodnight in the darkness and privacy of the car and, although he'd kissed me a hundred times before, this time it was different, his tongue shockingly and intimately exploring my mouth.

'Richard,' I disentangled myself before the situation got out of hand. 'Richard, I hope you know what you're doing. If ever we were found out you'd be quite ruined, you know.'

He gazed at me fatuously. 'I don't honestly think I care.'

I smiled. Really! Men were such fools.

Richard returned to London at the end of the week and we agreed that we shouldn't communicate for the fortnight he was in town but arranged to meet for lunch the day following his return. I was quite glad of the respite. For one thing Sydney was home again, and besides, I needed time to think. I knew that sooner or later I was going to have to decide whether to sleep with Richard or not. I couldn't decide which would be the more devastating, to spurn him whilst his nose was still pressed longingly against the shop window or to do so after he'd sampled the excellence of the goods. I decided that the latter would be more wounding to the male ego, apart from relishing the role of a *femme fatale.* And why not? I thought. It didn't seem to me a moral issue. What seemed more immoral was, having strenuously preserved my virginity for twenty-six years, I had yielded it up in a matter of moments to a man I didn't love. I felt that having, so to speak, unlocked the door, did it matter who I allowed over the threshold? But then, on the other hand, I didn't want to fall victim to that dubious male morality that allowed men to be promiscuous but labelled women as tarts. And leaving passion aside, I could see that, on a practical level, it wasn't going to be as easy as that. There was the all important question of 'where'? If I was going to commit adultery I intended to do it in style. Consequently, I had already discounted sordid little clinches in the back of a car. Hotels were out too, being only marginally less squalid, conjuring up visions of leering desk clerks and stained crumpled sheets. Of course there was the Clarendon Mansions flat, risky because the porter would see everyone that came and went and it was rather too close to home to be comfortable. And even more important than 'where' was 'when' and 'how'? There were only so many excuses a married woman could make for wanting to go out at night without her husband. The only alternative was waiting for business to take Sydney a safe distance out of town. Really, it was all too complicated, and I was just beginning to wonder if it was all worthwhile when fate, in the unlikely guise of Aunt Felicity, stepped in and the issue seemed decided for me.

We had removed back to the Hall and I was supervising the hanging of the drawing room curtains when suddenly Lady Ansty was announced.

'Veronica, my dear!' Aunt Felicity strode across my new carpet as if it were a tract of the Yorkshire moors and despite the chic town hat and business-like suit she still looked determinedly rustic.

'Forgive me for just dropping in on you like this but I really only came up on the spur of the moment. I always think snap decisions are best, don't you? I find that if I start thinking about tiresome things like times of arrival and frequency of trains, it all seems too much of a bother.'

She flung herself down in the most substantial chair. 'I don't suppose you could rustle up a morsel to eat, could you, my dear? I always seem to descend upon people at entirely the wrong time — too late for lunch and too early for tea. I had meant to lunch on the train coming up but I refuse to pay five shillings for lamb cutlets and Bakewell tart. Really, it's quite extortionate.'

She paused for breath and in the interim I ordered coffee and sandwiches. I was rather unnerved by her inclination to chatter so much. She only did so when she was nervous.

'There's nothing wrong is there, Aunt Felicity?' I enquired.

'Oh no. Well, only the usual trials and tribulations of family life. Gerard's rather liverish at the moment but then he always is at this time of the year. He finds February so interminably dreary in the country. The shooting's over and he doesn't care to hunt. And of course we're still frightfully hard up despite Sydney's generosity in lending us the money to re-roof the East Wing. It's just a drop in the ocean when one considers the work that needs to be done. And then Russell's due to start at prep school at the beginning of next year, though Heaven knows where we're going to find the fees.' She wolfed another sandwich, then said with the ease born of long practice, 'Actually, I know this will seem a frightful cheek as Sydney's already been so kind but we were rather wondering if he'd be able to help.'

'In what way?' I enquired guardedly, knowing perfectly well that I was being primed for a touch.

'Well — er — by way of another loan really.'

I pursed my lips. This was getting embarrassing, this queue of impecunious relatives with their hands held out. 'What's happened to the five thousand pounds that you've already had?' I demanded coldly.

Aunt Felicity looked vague. 'Well, there have been things to settle up — outstanding bills, you see. And of course, the workmen have started on the East Wing roof — but really, you know, Vee, money just doesn't go anywhere. When one

168

thinks of the work needed to put Ansty right, five thousand pounds isn't going to be nearly enough. So I've talked it over with Gerard and it seems so much more sensible to have everything done at once as Sydney suggested instead of attacking each job piecemeal. Of course, we'd want it to be a proper business arrangement. We certainly wouldn't expect to borrow that amount of money completely interest free.'

'How much were you thinking about?'

'We thought about twenty thousand actually. Yes, I know it seems a lot,' she added quickly as she saw my surprise. 'But when you parcel it all out, it only just goes round. And we felt we ought to do the thing properly or not do it at all. I mean, as Sydney quite rightly said, it's no good tackling a job like Ansty by halves.'

I poured more coffee. 'How do you intend paying it back?'

'Well, that's our plan, you see, to use the money to completely modernise the estate and then we can put all the rents up and with the increased revenue from the farms, pay back the loan out of that.'

I looked dubious, having heard some of Aunt Felicity's money-making schemes before. 'Well, of course I'll put it to Sydney.'

'Would you, dear? That's awfully good of you. I thought you could put the proposition to him and gauge his reaction. If it's favourable then perhaps he could come down next weekend and thrash out the details with Gerard.'

Of course. I saw the possibilities instantly. If only I could persuade Sydney to go down to Ansty alone — wonderful, remote, inaccessible Ansty. Without a telephone Sydney would never be able to check up on where I was.

I gave Aunt Felicity a radiant smile. 'Yes, I'll ask him,' I said happily. 'I'm sure it'll be all right.'

I tackled him straightaway, before we sat down to dinner that night. 'By the way,' I said casually, 'Aunt Felicity called.'

'Oh!' He looked up. 'Nothing wrong, I hope?'

'Only the usual,' I answered dryly. 'Apparently Uncle Gerard wants to arrange another loan.'

'Does he now,' he said thoughtfully. 'Did he say how much?'

'Well, Aunt Felicity said something about twenty

169

thousand pounds.' Briefly I outlined Aunt Felicity's plans. 'So she wondered if you'd be able to get down next weekend to talk things over with Uncle Gerard.'

'Yes, why not. You haven't got anything planned have you?'

'Actually,' I said carefully, 'would you mind if I didn't come? Apart from the fact that Mother and I are bound to row, I'm not sure that I care to look on whilst you take advantage of my family.'

He raised his eyebrows. 'In what way?'

'By charging them extortionate rates of interest or something beastly like that.'

'I haven't even decided to lend them the money yet, but if I do I shall charge them exactly the same rate of interest that they'd get from a bank.' He paused. 'And like a bank, I should want some sort of security.'

'Security?' I echoed.

'Yes. Security. I should have to insist on a mortgage on Ansty as security for the loan. It's perfectly normal banking practice.'

'But you're not a bank,' I protested. 'You're supposed to be family.'

'I'm a businessman, Veronica, and I think it's reasonable to want to protect myself. It's a perfectly legitimate piece of business. A ten year mortgage at two per cent and I can promise you that they won't get a better deal anywhere else. It's up to them after that. If they keep the repayments up, then everything's fine — if they don't ...'

'If they don't, you'll foreclose and put them out on the street.'

'Don't be ridiculous, Veronica. I should do nothing of the sort. Naturally, I should allow Gerard and Felicity to live there for as long as they wished.'

'But eventually, when they died, Ansty would belong to you?'

He lit one of his foul cigars. 'Frankly, I hadn't anticipated waiting that long. If, as I think likely, they do default, then I don't see any reason why we shouldn't make Ansty our home. There's room enough for us all to live there quite comfortably, and besides I should want to keep an eye on

170

things. I can't see old Gerard bothering himself too much about keeping the place up once he knows that I'm next in the queue.'

'Well, exactly,' I said. 'What about Russell and Philippa? It seems rather hard on them.'

'They're kids. They'll survive. And let's face it, Veronica, if I don't step in, all they'll inherit is a pile of death-watch beetle and dry rot. It'll still be their home if they want it to be. It'll still be in the family, which is better than having it fall down around their ears or sold off to repay creditors like your place was. Doing it my way, at least everyone gets a little piece of what they want. If you think about it, it might turn out to be a suitable arrangement all round.'

Well, I could quite see how it would suit Sydney; master of Ansty with titled relatives on tap. I wasn't so sure that it would suit me, buried in deepest Yorkshire, miles from town, miles from my friends — from Richard. The thought recalled me to the real point of this conversation.

'I don't want anything to do with it,' I said in a self-righteous voice. 'If you are going to Ansty then you'll have to go alone. I'm afraid I can't approve of you exploiting my family in such a cold-blooded way.'

'Now, wait a minute, Veronica, I'm not exploiting anyone here. I'm not forcing anyone to do anything they don't want to. But if they want the money, well, those are my terms. They don't have to agree to them, do they?'

I stared at him stonily. If only he wouldn't stand with his hand stuffed in his pockets like that; if only he wouldn't speak with his cigar clenched between his teeth. And that smug expression, as if the whole thing were cut and dried...

'You're very sure of yourself, aren't you?' I said in an irritable voice. 'You're so sure that they're going to mess things up ... They might surprise you, you know, and pull things off.'

'They might,' he said, flinging his cigar stub into the hearth. 'But I don't think somehow that they will.'

The next few days were a nightmare; moments of glorious heart-thumping excitement as I visualised myself in Richard's arms, then hours of nerve-wracking anxiety as I anticipated

171

the consequences of getting caught. Several times I was tempted to call the whole thing off.

Friday came. I was a mass of nerves and quite unable to look Sydney straight in the eye. Not that I felt any real guilt about deceiving him, but I lived in terror that at the last moment he'd change his mind and insist on my going with him to Ansty. But everything went amazingly according to plan. At ten o'clock I waved him off like a dutiful wife and spent the next two hours torturing myself with visions of the various calamities which might bring him back. After lunch I relaxed. He was obviously well on his way. So far, so good, but it didn't do to be complacent, and carefully I revised my plans. I had told Sydney that I intended to spend the afternoon shopping in town; then possibly a cinema, perhaps I'd dine at my club ... I'd been deliberately vague so as to keep my options open in the event of anything going disastrously wrong. Not that I anticipated discovery. I felt I'd been far too cautious for that, but in the unlikely event of Sydney finding out that I'd spent the night at Clarendon Mansions I had an entirely plausible explanation ready. I hadn't felt well; a sudden headache; I hadn't felt up to driving back so I had decided, quite naturally, to stay overnight at the flat. Of course, Richard might be seen too, and his presence at the flat wasn't so easily explained. The porter was the stumbling block here. It was his business to enquire of callers which resident they wished to see and, although I felt I had minimised the risk by arranging to meet Richard around the time the porters changed shifts, I was still taking a fairly big chance. But then no plan of this kind could be absolutely foolproof. And really, if I was honest, it was the element of risk that made the venture worthwhile. It wasn't so much the idea of sleeping with Richard that I found so thrilling, but the thought that I was breaking all the rules. Probably I would have derived the same feeling of excitement from stealing a car or robbing a bank. It was as potent as alcohol, as stimulating as drugs and far more erotic than sexual intercourse. It was strange, thinking about it, that after twenty-six years of dull conformity I should have developed this craving for sensation.

So at three o'clock I got out my smart, red, two-seater car

and drove confidently into the town. I had my hair done and a manicure and on impulse bought one of the new backless gowns. Then, trembling with excitement and last-minute nerves, I went to the flat to keep my assignation with Richard.

As soon as the flat door closed behind me I began to get cold feet. Really, was it worth it? I was bound to get found out and then Sydney would divorce me, the ultimate scandal, or even worse, I might get pregnant and be in the ghastly position of not knowing who the father was ... I analysed my motives. I loved Richard — or at least I loved the man who had once asked me to marry him. I didn't love the man who had publicly humiliated me by calling it off but how was I to distinguish between the two. But I still wanted to possess him; I wanted to force him into the commitment that he had previously refused to make; I wanted to bind him to me morally if not legally. Then I would reject him, as coolly and callously as he had rejected me. I would be happy then. My honour would be satisfied. I could forget all about Richard and get on with my life.

I mixed myself a cocktail. It had its usual magical effect. I was calm. I was in control. The world took on a rosier hue. Destinies were mine to dispose of.

I had another just in case the euphoria should fade. Then I bathed and changed into the satin sheath dress, dabbed Worth's *Je Reviens* liberally behind my ears. Then at eight o'clock the doorbell rang. I poured another cocktail and put on the gramophone. Well, this was it, I thought as I went to open the door. It was too late to turn back now.

It was a complete disaster. We were both so strung up, it couldn't have been anything else. Richard was obviously terrified that he'd fail and I was equally terrified that any moment Sydney might walk in — and what terrified me more than the thought of discovery was the thought of discovery in such a humiliating state. One feels so totally vulnerable when one is naked.

I was glad when it was over and I could put on my clothes. I had exchanged my vampish attire for a Schiaparelli sweater and a simple Chanel skirt and tried to assume an equally

173

elegant and casual demeanour. After a drink and a cigarette I felt able to look Richard in the face and we exchanged a glance of mutual embarrassment.

'I've disappointed you, haven't I?' Richard said in a sulky voice. 'You're regretting it already, I can see that.'

Obviously his ego was seeking reassurance. He wanted me to say that the earth had moved, that he was much better in bed than Sydney. But I wasn't going to say that. For one thing it wasn't true and for another I felt a little coolness on my part would guarantee him coming back for more; every man wants to make a triumphant exit. I felt that here I had the complete upper hand. It was his performance that had been lacking, not mine. But then I reasoned it wouldn't do to demolish his pride utterly, so I said lightly; 'No, of course I don't regret it. But let's face it, darling,' I drawled, 'this wasn't the most inspiring of venues, was it? Frankly, I'm surprised you managed it at all.'

'Don't talk like that,' he snapped. 'It makes you sound cheap and promiscuous.'

I raised my eyebrows. 'Well, considering I have just surrendered my virtue in my husband's bed, I don't see how I can possibly refute that.'

He suddenly looked very English and upper class. 'I must say you've changed, Veronica,' he said in a stuffy voice. 'You used to be so ...'

'Trusting? Gullible? Is that what you were going to say? Well, that was before I'd been jilted,' I reminded him waspishly.

He sat down suddenly and ran a hand distractedly through his tousled blond hair. 'My God, I've made a mess of things, haven't I, Vee? I feel so guilty — subjecting you to all this. And then there's Janet. She deserves better than this — and your husband. I've never met him but from what you say he sounds a decent enough chap.'

I felt a definite flicker of unease. I didn't care for the way this conversation was going. All this guilt and recrimination ... I'd been through all this before. The next thing would be some deliberately provocative remark. Then we'd quarrel. Then he'd leave...

I said with icy composure, determined that I wasn't going to be provoked. 'Well, there's a perfectly simple answer if

174

you feel as badly as that. We just won't see each other again. If that's what you want ...'

He leapt to his feet. 'I want *you*. Surely you know that? But I don't know how I'm ever going to have you without ruining the lives of two perfectly innocent people.'

I was provoked. 'My God! I wish you'd felt so guilty about ruining mine.'

'I did feel guilty. I've never stopped feeling guilty. I've never stopped thinking about you, wondering how you were. Do you know, when Max got sent to prison I actually came round to see you? I sat for hours in the car, trying to pluck up the nerve to knock at the door.'

I stared at him bleakly. Oh Richard, I thought, if only you had. Then I wouldn't have married Sydney.

'You see, I feel I've done you enough harm already. And now I'm asking you to take these terrific risks. I'm asking you to do things that go against your conscience and religious beliefs.'

'Oh for heaven's sake, Richard.' I lost patience entirely. 'Don't you think it a bit late in the day to adopt this high moral tone, seeing as you've just turned me into an adulteress. If you want to finish the affair then all you need to do is say so. Really, it isn't that important, you know.'

He grabbed me suddenly. 'Well, it's important to me. You still don't understand what I'm getting at, do you? I love you, Vee. I've always loved you. I always will love you and I'll always want to make love to you now. That's the problem, you see. Now that I have made love to you I'm not going to be able to stop thinking about your husband doing it too. I'm going to resent you being with him instead of me, and then I'll make you miserable by making impossible demands. Where's it all going to end?'

'Right here and now if you're going to take that ridiculous attitude.' I pulled my arm free and walked away from him. 'We've got to be realistic, Richard. If we're going to continue to see each other, then there have got to be rules. I'm married to Sydney and that gives him certain rights which I have absolutely no intention of withholding. You had your chance, Richard, but you decided that your religion and your career were more important.'

175

'They were then,' he muttered. 'I feel differently now.'

'So what is it you're suggesting? What are these impossible demands you feel you're likely to make? That I leave my husband perhaps?'

'Yes. Why not? You don't love him. You said so yourself.'

'And what then? Allow him to divorce me, so that I can marry you?'

I smiled as I saw him blanch. 'No. I thought you'd draw the line at that. What else then? Hide myself away in a discreet little flat somewhere, so that you can visit me when the demands of your wife and your constituents allow you to?' I gave a scornful laugh. 'No, I'm afraid that wouldn't suit me at all, Richard. And just think of the scandal if you were found out, but then I suppose, being a man, it wouldn't affect you too much. Men are allowed to do that sort of thing, aren't they? Keep mistresses and visit whores. It's only the women who are considered immoral.

'So you see, Richard,' I went on coolly, 'this is all there is. We either continue to see each other when opportunity permits or we don't see each other at all.'

He was silent for a long time and I thought for one moment he was going to walk out. Then grudgingly, he said; 'All right, Vee. We'll do things your way. I don't really have any choice, do I?'

'Oh but you do, darling,' I gave him a teasing smile. 'That's what's so exciting about having an affair. There's not that dreary feeling of total commitment.' I stubbed out my cigarette. 'And now that we've got all that out of the way, I really think we should leave. This place makes me nervous. I certainly shan't want to come here again.'

'Where then?'

I shrugged my shoulders as if I couldn't care less. 'You'll have to think of somewhere, won't you, darling.'

'When?' he demanded. 'When will I see you again? I'm due back in London at the end of the week.'

'Oh, I'll manage something before then,' I promised airily. 'But naturally I have to fit in with Sydney's plans. It's just a question of how soon I can get away.'

He nodded. 'All right. You'll telephone me then?'

'Yes, of course. As soon as I can.'

176

Oh, the feeling of power. It was better than sex. I'd never felt so completely elated. Nevertheless, I didn't telephone him till the following Thursday, arranging to meet him for lunch the next day. Our rendezvous was to be a small isolated cottage on the outskirts of Richard's estate where he sometimes went when he needed peace and quiet to work on a speech. Well, this was more like it, an idyllic little love-nest with roses round the door, in which we sat before a blazing fire and feasted on oysters and champagne. We made love, of course, and it would be tempting to say I enjoyed the oysters more but it wouldn't have been strictly true. It would be fairer to say that my enjoyment was inhibited by an awareness of self. Even with Sydney, it was always vanity versus passion and always vanity won.

Richard returned to town the next Monday and I tried not to feel bored, although it was a definite anticlimax returning to dull domesticity and the pretence of married bliss. Sydney had come back from Ansty as pleased as punch with the mortgage deed all nicely signed up. It hadn't been all plain sailing though. Mother had made a fuss. There'd been a bit of a row. Mother had called Sydney avaricious and vulgar; Aunt Felicity had called Mother an interfering bitch. It had all worked out in the end though. Uncle Gerard had signed. It was obviously a choice between Sydney and the bailiffs, and naturally Sydney won. I should have been appalled that the family fortunes had descended to this but secretly I was rather sorry to have missed all the fun. I was getting to like the feeling of power. I definitely enjoyed feeling wicked, the idea that I had a secret life of my own. I enjoyed imagining people's reactions if they knew. Of course, I meant to be discreet. One half of me lived in terror of Sydney finding out whilst the other half wanted to shout it from the rooftops. Quite often I found myself wishing that my triumph could be public or at least wishing that there was someone I trusted enough to tell. After all, what was the point of having a secret if nobody knew.

It was unfortunate that whilst I was in one of these impulsive and wildly indiscreet moods I should have run into Sylvia Townsend.

'Vee darling. How are you? What a lovely surprise. Where

have you been hiding yourself these days?'

I bristled instantly. Hiding? She made it sound as if I was ashamed to show my face.

'Oh, I've been busy,' I said airily. 'Spending money mostly.'

Sylvia's eyes flickered over my Paquin coat with the deep sable collar and registered my tiny cloche as a Carnegie original. 'So I see,' she murmured. 'Well, you always had a flair for that.'

We exchanged a smile of pure feline malice, then she slipped her arm through mine. 'Tea,' she said, steering me determinedly across the street. 'I'll tell you all the gossip, darling, and you can tell me where you got that divine little hat.'

'And how is Sydney?' Sylvia enquired when we were settled at a table. 'I must say you're keeping him very much to yourself. We haven't seen you out together for ages.'

'Sydney prefers to live quietly,' I replied, tongue in cheek. 'His business takes up a great deal of his time.'

'Well, I must admit, Vee, that you've had us all wondering. Speculation has been rife. In fact, to be perfectly honest, considering the speed with which you rushed Sydney up the aisle — hard on the heels of Helen's funeral cortège, so to speak — we were all totally convinced you were pregnant.'

I resisted the urge to plunge the butter knife into her heart. 'How disappointing for you, Sylvia, but I'm afraid I'm not.'

'Well, absolutely, darling. I can see that now.' She took out her cigarette case. 'They're Turkish, I'm afraid. Filthy things actually, but they've got such a divinely decadent aroma.'

We lit cigarettes and Sylvia regarded me thoughtfully through the divinely decadent haze. 'Well, you're looking very well, I must say. Marriage obviously suits you — or at least, I assume it's your husband who's putting the stars in your eyes!'

I stiffened. 'That's rather a cryptic remark!'

She leaned forward and fixed me with her avid little eyes. 'Rumours, darling — divinely scandalous rumours about you and a certain gentleman you were once engaged to.' She gave a twitch of excitement. 'You've been *seen*, angel — lunching at Pattersons, swanning about in his car.'

'Well, why not?' I said coolly. 'Richard and I are old friends.'

Sylvia smiled knowingly. 'Of course, Vee. We all understand that.' Then she gave me a look of grudging admiration. 'Honestly, Vee, I don't know how you do it. I wish I had the same devastating effect on men. Of course, I always said that if you waited long enough you'd get Richard back. It was his mother who bullied him into getting engaged to Janet Secombe just the same as she bullied him into breaking it off with you. It's typical of men, isn't it? Now that you're married and out of his reach ...' She leant forward and gave me a knowing wink. 'Well, I hope you're leading him one hell of a dance, Vee ...'

I couldn't resist it. 'Well, as a matter of fact, Sylvia,' I began with a triumphant smile — and with a few careless words I sealed my fate.

Chapter 6

I was pregnant. After hysterically poring over the calendar for the umpteenth time there was absolutely no doubt — I was ten days late.

Don't panic, I told myself. It could be anything; worry, over-excitement, even guilt. But no! There's no point in pretending the earth isn't round. I knew with awful, instinctive, doom-laden certainty that I was going to have a child. But whose? The delicate question of paternity loomed. What a ghastly situation to be in.

Sydney must be the father, I told myself firmly. Looked at logically, as my brother Max would say, surely there can't be any doubt? After all, I'd only slept with Richard half a dozen times ... but it doesn't work like that, does it? It's not frequency but potency. After all Helen — oh my God, I didn't dare think about Helen ...

Frantically, I ransacked the small bureau in my bedroom where I kept an emergency bottle of gin. Panic recedes instantly. Everything falls quite magically into place. Of course! It all depends on how long I've been pregnant. If I conceived more than a month ago, then quite clearly Sydney is responsible and everything's all right. If I didn't, then a horrible question mark hangs over the whole thing. On the other hand — another tiny splash before I put the bottle away — does it really matter who the father is? There's one thing that is absolutely and incontrovertibly certain — I am the mother. The child is mine.

I found myself smiling fatuously, already envisaging the fine strong son that I was bound to produce. I decided to call him Hugo, after my brother, and it was amazing how quickly the child became a reality in my mind. And after Hugo there would be a Giles and a Gerard as well ... I quite saw myself as the powerful matriarch, wielding influence through my army of sons.

But first things first. Of course, I would have to end my affair with Richard. He was completely redundant, now there was this new excitement in my life. In fact, I'd been thinking about ending it for a while now. For one thing, I'd been vaguely worried by Sydney's behaviour lately. He'd been unusually quiet, positively withdrawn and, more important, we had only slept together once in the last two weeks which amounted practically to celibacy for someone like Sydney. I wondered if he was ill or if things were going badly on the business side but he answered my enquiries with a thoughtful look and said that everything was absolutely fine.

Of course, I've considered the obvious — does he suspect? On balance, I don't think so. Sydney isn't the type to suffer being cuckolded in silence. If there'd been anything like that on his mind, he would have been bound to have said so. Even so, I felt there was absolutely no point in pushing my luck. Besides, the novelty of being a *femme fatale* was beginning to wear off and what promised to be a grand passion had turned after all into a dreary little affair. We met twice a week for the fortnight when Richard was not in town. We made love, although that doesn't really describe what Richard and I did. We copulated — eventually — after I had indulged Richard in his rather ludicrous vice. It was quite amusing to begin with, a novelty to distract me from the boredom of real life, but like everything else it eventually palled. And after all, I'd succeeded in what I originally set out to do. I'd brought Richard to the point where he was virtually prepared to risk everything to keep me. I was tempted to give him the final push, but as I couldn't think of any way of ruining his life without ruining my own as well I had to be content with a private rather than a public revenge.

So, having made up my mind to pull the rug from under the Honourable Richard's feet, I couldn't wait to put my plan into action. Fortunately, Sydney was going to be in Leeds till Wednesday evening at least, so I arranged to meet Richard the following night. All that remained then was to decide what I should wear, and having exchanged, so to speak, sensuality for maternity, I chose a simple dress of black crêpe

181

de Chine with a white piqué collar; seductive but not obvious, alluring yet chaste. Pregnant or not, I still intended to look *ravissement.*

I caught the five o'clock train to Hexham but alighted, as always, a few stops before. This was a necessary subterfuge, to meet at a prearranged destination which we varied each time. Apart from adding to the glamour and intrigue of the occasion, I felt we were less likely to be noticed at a smaller station.

Richard was waiting for me in the car and he came to met me with the ravenous eagerness of a drug addict expecting a fix. I felt a tiny pang of regret. In a way I was rather reluctant to relinquish the delicious sensation of power. I had rather enjoyed being an object of craving and desire. But now my thoughts were turning to quite another kind of male domination, and I was remembering the influence that my own mother had exerted over my brothers' lives. I meant to be just such an influence except that instead of bullying I would coerce. I would charm and encourage, I would be just and fair ... In the meantime though, there was Richard saying that he might have to return to London early this week as he was needed to vote on an emergency bill in the House. I listened, half listened, whilst I considered at what point in the evening I would break the news.

We reached the cottage and as soon as we were inside he took me in his arms. I felt his trembling, his rapid pulse. He could hardly wait.

Then he poured the usual aphrodisiacal champagne and told me how wonderful I looked. This was routine now; the champagne, the compliments, and when we'd finished the bottle we'd go to bed and I'd give him the benefit of my limited sexual experience — I use the word limited in the strictly normal sense but Richard's sexual needs seemed far from normal to me. You see, Richard had a secret, a little peccadillo we'd discovered accidentally in a moment of play. He liked to be punished. He liked to be spanked. It had got to the point where he was virtually impotent unless I treated him like a naughty little boy. I took part in this ghastly charade purely because it increased my influence. I imagined

182

a time when the knowledge might prove useful, some point in the future when we were no longer lovers, when I could embarrass him by reminding him that I knew. It was the first rule of politics, that if one was unfortunate enough to have an unnatural vice, one indulged it with strangers and not people you might have to sit next to at dinner. But that would never have occurred to Richard. He was so sure of himself, so sure of me.

We finished the bottle. He bent to kiss me. 'Richard' — a dramatic pause — 'I don't know how I'm going to tell you this' — coldly, cruelly, with a great deal of relish — 'but I'm not going to be able to see you again.'

He gave me a quizzical look. I could see he wasn't sure whether I was serious or not and I returned his look steadily to let him see that I was. His expression darkened. 'Why not? What's wrong?'

'Everything,' I said simply. 'And if we're honest, it always has been from the very beginning. I just feel that we ought to call things off.'

'Oh, I see. Just like that, as if you were cancelling your order for *The Times*! Our relationship means as little to you as that.'

I looked bored. 'Please don't be emotional, Richard. I really couldn't bear a scene.'

'If by emotional, you mean angry, then yes I'm afraid I am. I want an explanation, Vee. Something must have happened. I want to know.'

'What's happened, Richard, is that I've come to my senses at last. I'm no longer prepared to risk losing my security for a grubby little affair that can lead nowhere.' I gave him a pitying look. 'Didn't it ever occur to you that I might get bored with these furtive hole-in-the-corner meetings? Bored with always having to sneak about?'

'And bored with me?'

'Yes, Richard, bored with you. Bored with your smugness, your insensitivity, your conceit in thinking I'm always available.'

He stared at me in silence and then quite amazingly, he smiled. 'All right, Vee,' he said with condescension in his voice. 'What is it you want?'

183

'Want?' I raised my eyebrows. 'What on earth could you offer me that I could possibly want?'

'Well, I presume all this is leading up to some kind of ultimatum. Either I give up Janet and my career ...'

'Richard,' I said, my voice cold and hard, 'the only thing I want you to give up is me.'

I had made contact at last. His eyes clouded. He looked bewildered. 'Vee, I don't understand. We were so happy.'

'You were happy, Richard, and why shouldn't you be? You've got money, a title, your career prospects are brilliant. In August you're going to marry the Foreign Secretary's daughter, so I imagine a cabinet post is just a matter of time. And then, when you were bored with your meek, submissive, sexually repressed wife, you'd have me, ready to rush round and give you six of the best so you could keep your nasty little perversion from your high-minded wife.' I smiled with pure pleasure into his stricken face. 'Quite frankly, you disgust me. Sydney might not be a gentleman, Richard, but at least he's absolutely normal in bed.'

Then I saw his expression and realised I'd gone a bit too far. He lashed out at me and I retreated. He grabbed at me and I screamed ... Then suddenly, on cue, the cavalry arrived. The door opened and in walked Sydney.

Richard released me so abruptly that I nearly fell. We both stared at Sydney in stupefied horror.

'Get into the car, Veronica,' my husband said in a terrifyingly calm voice. I couldn't move. I couldn't speak. I was totally paralysed with fright.

'Go and wait for me in the car,' Sydney said again. 'I want a few words with Mr Vere.'

I fled, blundering past both of them, not even bothering to gather up my things. I stood shivering in the darkness. I couldn't see the car — then I realised Sydney had parked it out of sight so that we wouldn't hear his approach.

Oh my God! I fumbled along the dashboard for cigarettes and matches, inhaling deeply to steady my nerves. All right! Calm down. Just sit quietly and think this one out. Fact: I'd been caught in a compromising situation but not so compromising as if I'd been caught in bed. Therein I felt lay my salvation. Sydney could think what he liked but he could

184

never prove conclusively that we'd been lovers. If I held on to that, denied it consistently ... Of course, I'd have to admit that I'd been meeting Richard now and then; for lunch, cocktails, innocent occasions like that. And yes, I'd have to own up to being foolish and gullible, letting Richard persuade me to go back to the cottage like that, but there was a world of difference between indiscretion and immorality. He couldn't divorce me for just being a fool. And on the plus side, his entrance couldn't have been more timely from my point of view. He must have seen me struggling. He must have heard me scream — well, what women wouldn't when a man she had known for years and trusted as a friend suddenly made improper and unwelcome advances!

I lit another cigarette. I was beginning to feel better until it occurred to me to wonder what Sydney and Richard were talking about. Panic rose in my throat as I envisaged Richard confessing all the sordid details — surely he wouldn't be such a fool? No, he wouldn't be, I was sure of that, but neither would he be so obliging as to admit to being the villain of the piece. I began to feel nervous again, a feeling which accelerated to pure terror as Sydney emerged from the cottage and got into the car.

'Sydney,' I began in a piteous tone of voice ...

'Shut up,' he said. 'If you've any sense left in that vain trivial mind of yours, you won't say another word.'

I didn't, and the complete silence enabled me to further embellish my defence, and so convincing did I feel my case to be that by the time we arrived at Harden Hall, I had persuaded myself that Sydney was being entirely unreasonable in his behaviour and I stormed up to my bedroom and slammed the door.

It opened a few moments later.

'Sydney,' I said with an aggrieved persecuted air, 'I know what you must be thinking ...'

'Do you, Veronica? I doubt that very much.'

I swallowed; the soft controlled voice, the soft controlled smile, both inspired terror rather than reassurance.

'Now Veronica,' he advanced towards me, smiling and calm. 'I want to hear your explanation — and before you're tempted to lie, I should tell you that I've had you followed. I

185

know everything — except why?'

Everything! My heart contracted but I clung to my resolve to admit nothing. And he could be bluffing. I had nothing to lose by trying a little bluff of my own.

I regarded him steadily. 'Well, if you know everything Sydney, then you'll know that I haven't done anything wrong. I don't deny that I've met Richard several times for lunch but it was perfectly innocent, quite casual, you know. There wasn't anything more than that in it.' I gave a scornful laugh. 'Surely you don't think I'm still in love with him, do you?'

He regarded me gravely. 'No. I don't think that. Quite honestly, I don't think you're capable of loving anyone except yourself. But you don't have to be in love with someone to sleep with them, do you? After all,' his mouth turned in an expression of amusement and regret, 'however repugnant, you've always managed to do your duty by me.'

I sensed a thaw, a crack in the ice. 'Sydney, that's not true. It isn't a bit like that.'

'Please don't add hypocrisy to your crimes, Veronica. I'd rather you just said that you were bored with being saddled with a middle-aged husband and that an affair with Vere appealed to you as a bit of fun.'

Well, I wasn't going to fall for that, was I? 'Sydney, I have never thought of myself as being *saddled* with a husband, middle-aged or otherwise. And frankly, if it ever came to the point where I was going to have an affair, it certainly wouldn't be with Richard. All right, I don't deny that it might have been at the back of my mind to lead him on a bit. I must admit I took a great deal of pleasure in rebuffing his advances. And quite obviously I was naive in thinking I could cope with a situation like that. I couldn't, as you must have seen when you walked in.' I shrugged. 'I admit to being foolish ...'

'The point is, Veronica,' Sydney interrupted this fairy tale in a chilly voice, 'the point is that you have made me look foolish too. Everybody's talking about it. That's how I found out.'

Sylvia! The bitch. Well, of course, I should have guessed.

'Sydney,' I said indignantly, 'I'm just going to say this and

186

then I'm going to bed. Yes, I have been wildly indiscreet by allowing myself to be seen out with Richard Vere. Yes I deserve a good telling off, perhaps a thrashing as well, but I don't deserve to be treated like a faithless and immoral wife. In fact, Sydney, the way I see it, if that's what you believe then that gives me licence from now on to sleep with who I like. If I've been judged and condemned, I might as well go out and commit the crime.'

'Very good, my dear.' He gave a sneering laugh. 'A wonderful performance. You're quite an actress — except that I don't believe a single word.'

I lost my temper then. It was all too much. My nerves completely went. 'Believe what you like,' I screamed hysterically, 'I couldn't care less. If that's what you want to think, I can't stop you. In fact, it probably excites you, doesn't it? The thought of someone else making love to your wife.'

'What an extremely unladylike thing to say, Veronica. In fact, I think that's where I've made my mistake.' He advanced towards me with a menacing smile. 'I've treated you too much like a lady, with too much respect — instead of the cheap little whore that you are.'

He pushed me down on the bed and his big calloused hand fastened in the neck of my dress. I knew then that he intended to degrade me and humiliate me. I didn't resist. I wasn't going to give him the satisfaction of putting up a fight. The humiliation would be his when for all his rage and cruel passion he could evoke no response.

I was wrong. The humiliation was all mine in that I loved every minute of it and that whilst he thrust and tore at me and whispered obscenities in my ear, I writhed and sobbed and begged openly for more.

Then I remembered the child, the delicate, defenceless embryo being subjected to this murderous attack. 'Sydney,' I gasped when I could free my mouth. 'Sydney. The baby. Be careful.'

He froze. 'What! What did you say?'

Instantly I realised my mistake. What a stupid time to tell him when the thought of Richard was so fresh in his mind. 'I'm pregnant,' I whispered miserably.

For a moment he remained motionless, then slowly he

187

climbed from the bed and began to put on his clothes. 'Sydney,' I said, terrified. 'Did you hear what I said?'

'Yes, I heard you. You're pregnant.' He stood up and looked down at me. 'Would it be indelicate of me to enquire who the father is?'

'Well, I expected you to say that,' I said with an attempt at dignity. 'I'm not even going to bother answering you. The question is beneath contempt.'

To my surprise he just turned his back and walked from the room. 'Sydney!' I called out in desperation as he opened the door. 'I swear to you, Sydney, the child is yours.'

He gave me a look of utter contempt. 'Yes, I suppose it might be. But don't you understand, you stupid bitch, I'll never be sure.'

Chapter 7

Max came home at the end of April. Naturally, I was glad to see him. For one thing, his presence in the house lessened the tension between Sydney and myself, but then Max brought new tensions of his own. I could never think of Max without thinking about Helen and we all knew where thinking about Helen led.

I was now two months pregnant. The date of conception had been officially confirmed — not long enough ago to be absolutely certain that Sydney was the father, but on the other hand I couldn't be certain that he was not. It was an appalling situation, not to know whether I was carrying Richard Vere's bastard or my husband's legitimate heir. Sydney obviously entertained similar thoughts although it was difficult to know what his attitude towards me really was. As a husband, I felt his natural inclination was to throw me out on to the street, but as a businessman — well, I represented a considerable investment, and men like Sydney didn't sell out just because the first dividend was poor. And of course he could never be sure that I'd slept with Richard. Logically, on a practical level, the odds were that I had, but there was still that element of doubt that he couldn't overlook. I might be telling the truth, the child might be his and quite often when he looked at me I saw the question in his eyes: was I a scheming and unprincipled bitch or was I just a vain and stupid woman? He seemed to be adopting a policy of wait and see. If I produced a black-haired, blue-eyed infant with a small pencil moustache, then everything would be all right. If, on the other hand, it was fair, with a haughty expression and wearing an Eton tie ... Oh God! I mustn't be flippant. It was far too serious for that; so serious that we hadn't made love since that wonderfully degenerate and

189

orgasmic night. I wasn't sure why; whether his indifference was meant to be a punishment or that he found his last performance an impossible act to follow or perhaps he just didn't find pregnant women desirable. Whatever the reason, there was a definite barrier between us and I wasn't sure how I was going to break it down.

Of course, Max didn't know anything about this. We'd never been close enough for me to think of confiding in him, and in any case, being a man, he'd probably side with Sydney. Anyway, Max obviously had problems of his own. It couldn't have been the simplest thing in the world, to emerge from prison and simply carry on with your life. He looked dreadful too, far more of a criminal than when he went in. The cropped hair gave him a faintly Prussian look and there was a definite air of menace about him, which if I hadn't been his sister I might have found quite thrilling. As it was I found him rather intimidating; his brooding silences had the effect of getting on my nerves. When he was in the house I wore myself out wondering what he was thinking and when he was out I worried myself sick wondering who he was with. I felt I had to keep an eye on him. I needed to know what he was up to because I knew that sooner or later Max would start thinking about Helen. It was only a matter of time before something or someone triggered him off and I was certain that Jack Rochester would be the catalyst. When Max had been safe in prison it had seemed a masterstroke to blame Rochester for Helen's fate. I had been in a tight corner and it hadn't occurred to me to ponder the consequences. Now, I was anxious about what might happen when Max and Rochester eventually came face to face. Happily, on a social level, there wasn't much chance of that. As an ex-convict, it would be some time before Max was admitted to polite society, at least until people were sure that he wasn't going to batter his host senseless because he didn't like the soup. And as for earning a living — well, it was anybody's guess what Max's reception in business circles would be. On Tyneside at least, the financial world was dominated by the Rochesters. Everyone seemed to be a friend of the Rochesters or a client or an employee. I couldn't see Max making much headway against such odds. In fact, I really felt it would be better for

190

everyone, especially me, if he made a fresh start elsewhere.

I mentioned it to Sydney, casually suggesting that, as he had business interests all over the world, couldn't he find Max something to do in Boston or New York?

He looked up from his newspaper, his eyes narrowing with that suspicious look I was beginning to hate. 'What's worrying you now, Veronica?' he said irritably. 'I thought it was all settled that Max would work here with me.'

'Well, yes, I know it was. But I've been thinking. It's going to be awkward for Max, isn't it? I mean people are bound to give him the cold shoulder for a bit and it'll be even more unpleasant for him if he comes up, as he must, against Jack Rochester.'

Sydney returned to his newspaper. 'Oh, I think Max can take care of himself. He knows what he's doing.'

'But I don't think he does,' I persisted. 'He's really not quite sane where Rochester is concerned. I'm terrified he'll do something rash. And besides,' I added when I saw this strategy was having little effect, 'some of the unpleasantness is bound to rub off on you. It might have awkward consequences from a business point of view if you're seen to be openly championing Max.'

He looked up at me then. 'My, my, Veronica. Your sense of family loyalty certainly does you credit.'

'It's not a question of loyalty,' I argued. 'It's just common sense.'

'Both of which you know absolutely nothing about.' Sydney folded his newspaper. 'Might I suggest, Veronica, that you attempt to run your own life on more conventional lines before you start interfering in other people's.'

Well, there wasn't much I could say to that. I retired, suitably chastened, defeated by the knowledge that somehow I had only managed to make things worse. And as the weeks passed, I could see that Sydney intended to be madly perverse, that he meant to isolate me and exclude me by closing ranks with Max. So I languished on my *chaise-longue*, looking at magazine photographs of gowns I couldn't wear and dying from boredom as they talked incessantly about margins and dollar parity. Sometimes these discussions lasted all evening; throughout dinner, after dinner, long after

191

I had yawned my excuses and gone off to bed where I lay sleepless and anxious, wondering how long it would be before Max ran into Jack Rochester and began raking up the whole ghastly business of Helen again.

Not that I really felt I had anything to worry about. I had anticipated all the questions and had the answers prepared. It was just a matter of being consistent, of resisting the temptation to enlarge or embellish my original story.

I waited. Nothing happened. I began to relax. Obviously Max was going to be sensible and forget about the whole thing ... And then it occurred to me how entirely out of character that was. Max had never been sensible and he certainly wasn't the forgiving type. Max was hot tempered, impetuous, outspoken and vengeful. Even prison wouldn't have changed him as completely as that. I could only come to the conclusion that he was biding his time, planning some subtle and heinous revenge. It also struck me as strange that he hadn't discussed it with me. Surely I was the one person he could confide in? But when I thought about it, I realised we hadn't had a single private conversation since he'd been home, almost as if he were avoiding me, keeping out of my way ... Reason deserted me then. I was suddenly convinced that he knew, that I was the object of his revenge rather than Rochester. Perhaps Dr Gilly had said something? Perhaps Max had talked to the priest? Perhaps, perhaps, perhaps ...

Of course, I had to know. I had to say something ...

'Max?' I cornered him in the library before dinner one night. 'I'm not disturbing you, am I?'

'No, of course not.' He smiled quite naturally — there was nothing accusing in his look. 'Will you join me in a sherry?' he asked courteously.

'Yes. Why not?' I curled myself in a deep leather chair, with a glass of Amontillado in my hand and a Sullivan and Powell smoking between my lips, and proceeded with my interrogation.

'So!' I began briskly. 'How are you settling in?'

'Oh, all right,' he answered lightly. 'It's very decent of you and Sydney to offer to put me up.'

I waved my hand airily. 'Think nothing of it. After all, we've got to stick together, haven't we Max?'

He turned and smiled at me, and for the first time in my life I felt an affection for him. It was the strangest feeling. Just for an instant I felt quite strongly the tie of blood. There was a sudden unspoken intimacy between us, a tacit acknowledgement that we both had secrets, scars to hide...

I looked away, reminding myself that my secret at least couldn't possibly be shared. 'Were you thinking of going down to Ansty, at all?' I said in a careful and casual voice.

'No, I don't think so — at least not yet.'

'Have you made any plans at all?' I persisted. 'Obviously you intend sticking things out here.'

'For the moment anyway,' he answered shortly, then he gave me a shrewd look. 'Why? Am I going to be a social embarrassment to you, Vee? Would you rather I did the decent thing and took myself off to the colonies?'

'Don't be silly,' I said. 'I didn't mean anything like that. I just thought' — I hesitated — 'Well, I just thought things might be rather difficult for you here. I mean you're not going to be able to avoid Rochester, are you?'

'I haven't got any intention of avoiding him. In fact, quite the reverse.'

'That's what I meant,' I said quickly. 'That's what I was trying to say. We don't want any more trouble, do we, Max? Really, you know, I think we've been through enough.'

He looked at me with his torpid eyes. 'There won't be any trouble, Vee. I can promise you that.'

I got up. My God, this was hard work and I needed another drink. I slopped sherry into a glass. If only he'd say something. If only he'd just mention Helen's name. I found his silence more unnerving than any amount of threats. I could see I would have to force the issue.

'Well, I'm glad to see you're being sensible, Max. I suppose it's the only thing to do in the circumstances really. Forgive and forget, if you know what I mean.'

He looked at me then. 'Forgive and forget!' He gave a harsh bark of laughter. 'What on earth made you think I felt like that?'

Careful now. Just the right amount of interest. 'Oh, I don't know,' I said casually. 'Probably the fact that you haven't seemed to want to talk about it. I thought perhaps you were

193

trying to put it out of your mind.'

He smiled thinly. 'I haven't talked about it, Vee, because I didn't feel it was something that you would want to discuss — in the circumstances, if you see what I mean.'

I didn't. What circumstances? I was just trying to work out if there was anything sinister in this remark when he said;

'For God's sake, Vee, you're pregnant yourself. I didn't feel miscarriage and abortion were really suitable subjects to raise.'

'Oh I see.' I almost fainted with relief. 'Well, thank you for being so considerate, Max, but I'm really not that sensitive, you know. And anyway, I didn't mean that you'd forgotten about Helen in the obvious sense. None of us will ever do that, but then on the other hand I can't see any point in pursuing Rochester. I mean there's nothing we can do, is there? It's not as if we can haul him up before the courts on a charge. We haven't got a shred of real proof and can't ever hope to have really.'

'At the moment, we haven't. But that doesn't mean to say that we can't ever find out the truth. Obviously there must have been other people involved besides Rochester and Helen. Helen couldn't have arranged the abortion herself and I can't see Rochester actually getting personally involved, so probably there was a third person, a woman I would think, who acted as a go-between. And then there's the doctor, if he was one, who actually performed the operation. I've talked with Peter Gilly and he seems to think that, despite the end result, it had been a reasonably professional job. I remember you saying that Rochester had given Helen somebody's name. I don't suppose you can remember who it was?'

'No,' I said quickly. 'Helen never mentioned it. But then obviously she wouldn't have confided in me.'

Max frowned. 'Well, there can't be too many doctors in Newcastle who are prepared to do that sort of thing. It's possible that a few discreet enquiries might turn him up ...'

'Max!' With an effort I kept my voice from rising. 'Look, I'm not trying to defend Rochester or anything like that — but is it worth it? Is it worth raking it all up and involving us all in a scandal again? I mean it can't help Helen, can it?

194

Nothing you could do will bring her back.'

'I know that,' he said quietly. 'I've thought of all that but it doesn't make any difference, Vee. I've got to know. For my own peace of mind I've got to know exactly what happened and how Helen died.'

I suppose I should have felt relieved that he had confided in me. Obviously, Max didn't suspect that I'd been involved — but when I thought of him poking and prying, stirring things up ... well, I'd have to cross that bridge when I came to it, I thought. After all, there was no point in meeting disaster halfway.

In the event, disaster didn't come from that quarter at all. I'd been so preoccupied with Max that I hadn't noticed Sydney growing more distant as my pregnancy progressed. Then one night before dinner as I was refreshing my glass with another champagne cocktail to quell my unease about Max dining out, Sydney suddenly said in a mildly critical voice:

'Veronica, do you think you could try not to drink quite so much.'

Stunned, I turned to face him, the empty glass still in my hand. 'For goodness' sake, Sydney! I've only had two.'

'I was referring to — how shall I put it — your extra-curricular drinking, the amount of alcohol you consume during the day. Apart from the fact that it's extremely unpleasant to have one's wife smelling so constantly of gin, I shouldn't have thought it was good for the child.'

That was the last straw. I slammed down the glass. 'Oh, so you've decided at last to acknowledge the fact that I'm pregnant and, even more amazing, to show concern for a child that you're not even sure is yours.'

'Veronica, please. Keep your voice down, the servants will hear.'

'Damn the servants,' I cried. 'I couldn't care less. Anyway, I don't expect they'd blame me if I did take a drink during the day now and then. It helps to relax me. It helps me to forget that I'm married to the sort of man that accuses his wife of infidelity just because he's caught her talking to a strange man in the lift.'

He looked at me coldly. 'Richard Vere wasn't a stranger,

and I didn't catch you in a lift, I caught you in a cosy remote cottage and, what's more, I caught you actually in his arms.'

'You caught me fighting him off. You must have heard me scream. Surely that speaks for itself.'

'Quite honestly, Veronica, what spoke for itself was the look on your face — not fear or outrage but just plain guilt.'

'Well of course I felt guilty. I wasn't so naive as not to realise that I shouldn't have been there.'

'Let's not go over it all again,' Sydney said wearily. 'I find your denials even more disturbing than your infidelity. At least Vere had the guts to tell the truth.'

I blanched. I actually felt the blood draining out of my face. 'I don't believe you,' I said faintly. 'Richard wouldn't do such a despicable thing.'

Fool! Sydney pounced instantly on this ambiguous remark. 'You mean Vere's too much of a gentleman to admit to sleeping with my wife.'

'Yes. No. I mean he wouldn't tell such a dreadful lie.'

Sydney looked at me thoughtfully. 'No, I don't believe he would. That's why, when I accused him of having an affair with you, he didn't deny it.'

'Well, he probably thought there wasn't much point. You wouldn't have believed him any more than you've believed me. Naturally, he felt guilty. He'd behaved like a cad, persuading me to go back to that cottage and then ...'

'Was it the first time he'd asked you?' Sydney demanded.

Then I made my first real blunder. The champagne must have fuddled me. I had forgotten that Sydney had said that he'd had me followed. Without even thinking, I said. 'No. It wasn't the first time he'd asked me but it was the first time I'd gone.'

'Well, that's lie number one,' Sydney said coolly. 'I happen to know that you'd been to the cottage twice before.'

I recovered amazingly quickly. 'Well, yes. That's true I suppose. But the circumstances were quite different. Once, after we'd had supper somewhere, Richard stopped off to collect some papers. And another time, during the day, but I don't think I went in ...' I blundered on. It was a marvellous effort but I was rattled and it showed.

'Poor Veronica.' Sydney said, and his voice was kind.

196

Then suddenly he stood up and came and took my hands. 'Veronica. If you told me the truth I could forgive you, you know. It's the deception that matters, not whether you did or didn't sleep with another man. That's what I can't forgive, the lies, the deceit, knowing that I can't ever trust you to tell me the truth, knowing that you don't trust me enough to be honest.'

I tried not to look at him. I was always tempted by these offers of amnesty and for one weak moment I was on the verge of owning up. Then sanity returned. I snatched my hands away and stared him straight in the eye.

'I have told you the truth. And it's cruel of you to continually persecute me like this. I really can't bear it, Sydney, and it's hardly the action of a gentleman to bully the woman who is carrying his child.' I glared at him. 'Because you see, Sydney, whatever your own private opinion, I *know* the child is yours and that's an end to the matter as far as I'm concerned. I don't ever want to discuss the matter again.'

He regarded me in thoughtful silence. 'All right, Veronica,' he said at last. 'I suppose I don't have any choice but to give you the benefit of the doubt.' His voice hardened. 'But if I ever find out that you've lied to me, not just about this, but about anything at all, however trivial, I warn you it'll be the end. You'll be out on the street, I promise you.'

He walked out and slammed the door, leaving me alone in my beautiful and fashionable drawing room with the Burne Jones gouache and the oyster-coloured sofas draped with fringed silk shawls. I shivered and reached for the gin.

I have discovered vodka; colourless, tasteless and more importantly odourless, so that I can indulge my little weakness to my heart's content and Sydney doesn't suspect a thing. In fact, it's quite amusing, the poor darling, he's convinced I've reformed. I'm most abstemious in his presence, just a small sherry before lunch, a single cocktail at six o'clock and two glasses of wine during the meal. And he can check the level of the decanters to his heart's content. I have arranged for my own secret supply. Naturally, I find all this subterfuge rather stimulating. It was really a mistake on Sydney's part to mention my drinking at all as he has now

197

transformed a perfectly innocent habit into a forbidden act, and as always I find the illicit irresistible. Once again I am breaking the rules. And really, he was making a fuss about nothing at all. It's not as if I were in danger of becoming an alcoholic or anything ridiculous like that. I enjoyed having a drink but I didn't need to. Alcohol both stimulated and relaxed and I'd come to regard drinking alone as spending time with an old and valued friend from whom I had no secrets and in whose company I could relax. Of course, later on, after Hugo was born, I intended to make an effort and give it up. But just whilst things were so awful, just whilst I felt so physically and mentally done up ... I would just think of it as medicinal; one very large vodka to be taken three times a day. After all, where was the harm in that?

You see, I knew it was all a question of waiting, of getting myself through the next few months. I was quite certain that when the child was born everything would be all right. For one thing I was positive that it would bring Sydney round. He might be able to ignore his heir whilst it was safe and anonymous in my womb but once it was a living, breathing thing ... Oh yes, I was quite sure that Sydney would come round. So I awaited the birth as if it were the advent of Christ. I saw the child as my redeemer and the answer to all my problems. Already he was having a conciliatory effect. I'd actually had a letter from Mother saying how thrilled she was at the prospect of becoming a grandmother and insisting that I come down to Ansty to discuss preparations for the christening. I could see she intended it to be a lavish affair.

So at the end of July we all trooped down to Ansty and endured the most ghastly family reunion with Mother practically ignoring poor Max whilst to Sydney she talked earnestly about the importance of his child being baptised into the Catholic faith. It seemed she was prepared to bury the hatchet at the prospect of a new recruit. Of course, it was absolute hell for me. Everyone pouring Uncle Gerard's best claret down their throats as if it were Vichy whilst I had to make two small glasses last all night. Of course I had a half bottle hidden away among my smalls but it was difficult with Sydney watching me. I felt that he was still suspicious and that the only reason he kissed me was for an opportunity to smell my breath. I had overdone things as usual. Sydney, being an atheist, didn't believe in miracles and obviously my sudden temperance had been a bit too much. Three days after we got back from Ansty there was the most frightful scene. Sydney actually accused me of being drunk just because I lost my balance coming down the stairs. It was absolute nonsense of course, but Sydney insisted on making the most tremendous fuss, shouting so loudly that all the servants could hear. Then to humiliate me further he searched my room, ransacking every cupboard and drawer. He found the vodka, a half-empty bottle which he proceeded with great ceremony to pour down the sink. It was all too tedious, quite Vaudeville really. As if I was going to be deterred by a little setback like that.

After he'd gone I locked the door and went into my dressing room for the emergency bottle I kept in a hat box on top of the wardrobe. Solemnly, I poured a large one and drank it down neat, then another and another until I realised with horror that half the bottle was gone. Even more horrifying was the fact that I still felt perfectly sober. It didn't seem to be having an effect at all. I replaced the bottle in its hiding place, then lay down on the bed. Within minutes I was sound asleep.

When I awoke it was dark and I was shivering with cold. My head ached. I felt sick, very small, very vulnerable. The room seemed to have taken on gigantic proportions and I was sure there were eyes watching me from the shadowy corners of the room. I was frightened, trembling, overcome by a feeling of utter panic. I wanted a drink. I needed a drink. Just a small one, I said to myself, just to settle my nerves.

I crawled from the bed. The floor was like a marshmallow beneath my feet. I staggered blindly through into the dressing room. Mirrored doors rose to the ceiling and suddenly the room was crowded with people all looking like me. I opened one of the doors. Sequins glittered like menacing eyes, my furs seemed like crouched animals waiting to spring. I swallowed down my mounting hysteria and dragged forward the set of mahogany steps. They were on castors and moved easily enough and carefully I mounted till I reached the little

199

platform at the top and the hat boxes were on a level with my eyes. I stared at them; striped, beribboned, flowered, gay. Oh God, I couldn't remember in which one I had hidden the bottle. I was sweating now, I felt dizzy and sick and I plunged my hand into one hat box after another until my fingers encountered the delicious coolness of glass. I couldn't even wait to get back down again. With trembling hands I raised the bottle to my lips — but before I could even take a sip, the steps slid quietly from beneath me. I heard myself screaming as I fell.

Chapter 8

Strangely enough, my first reaction when they told me I had lost the child was one of overwhelming relief. It was over, I had been punished. An eye for an eye, my child for Helen's — I needn't ever feel guilty again. Of course, that was too simple. A Catholic doesn't relinquish guilt as easily as that, and as the shock wore off I had time to think, I realised that not only had I murdered Helen's child but indirectly I had murdered my own as well. It was a terrifying moment. I could no longer deny my dependence on drink. I couldn't deny that my craving for alcohol had caused me to miscarry. And the worst thing was, despite everything, I still wanted a drink. There was still a part of my mind that kept saying if only I could have a drink then everything would be all right. Just one drink and I'd feel better. I'd be able to cope ... Without a drink there was nowhere for me to hide. So alone in my room, for the first time in my life, I faced the brutal truth. I was not only a liar, a murderer, an adulteress and a cheat, I was a disgusting alcoholic as well.

For a split second madness stared me in the face. Suddenly I knew how my brother Hugo had felt. How tempting it would be to end it now. How simple, how sensible, just to pick up a revolver and place it gently against one's head ... But I didn't have a revolver; for the moment, at least, I would have to go on living and the future stretched before me, terrifying and bleak. Of course, Sydney would divorce me, I had already accepted that. He hadn't been to see me. He hadn't even bothered to find out how I was. Losing the child must have been the last straw.

I closed my eyes, visualising myself as a drunken down-and-out, selling my body for the price of a gin ... Then the door opened and when I looked up Sydney was there, standing awkwardly at the end of the bed.

'How are you feeling, Veronica?' he said.

I smiled bravely. 'Oh, as well as can be expected.' I could feel the hysteria rising up in my throat. 'Dr Vine says I'll be quite well in a few weeks' time.'

He didn't speak but stood staring at his hands, those embarrassingly large and brutal hands. I was suddenly mesmerised by his hands; the most fantastic idea suddenly entered my head. I didn't have a revolver but I had Sydney's hands. I could imagine them fastening around my neck and squeezing hard ... Then, as if he had suddenly become aware of their size and ugliness, he thrust them behind his back. 'I'm sorry about the child,' he said in a polite, distant voice.

'Are you?' I shrilled. 'I would have thought everything had worked out quite well for you. After all, you won't have to worry now whether it was yours or not. Just tell yourself that it was Richard Vere's bastard I miscarried and things won't seem half so bad.'

He looked at me. 'Was it?'

'I wish I could put your mind at rest, Sydney, but I'm afraid it isn't as simple as that.' I giggled hysterically. 'It might have been but then on the other hand it might not. You see, the truth of it is, I don't really know.'

I thought; he'll kill me now. He'll place those big ugly hands around my throat ... But he didn't move from his place at the end of the bed. At last he said, and his voice was so quiet I could barely hear, 'Well, thank you for telling me, Veronica. I appreciate that.'

It was such an anti-climax that for a moment I couldn't speak. I thought; obviously he didn't care enough to be angry with me. Then he looked up and I saw the pain in his eyes. 'Why, Veronica? I must know why. What else could I have done to make you happy.'

It was all too much. I began to cry. I felt so ashamed. 'Oh Sydney,' I whispered, 'it wasn't your fault. I don't know why, except that Richard, like the gin, made me forget. They stopped me thinking about Helen and what I had done ...'

It all came out then, about Helen, about the child, the whole sordid story, and for once I made no attempt to spare myself. Of course, I knew it was the end. Sydney would leave

202

me. He'd insist on the divorce for which I'd just obligingly given him overwhelming grounds. And he'd tell Max about Helen and Max would tell Mother and Uncle Gerard and Aunt Felicity. I'd be utterly despised, a total outcast...

And then suddenly, to my amazement, I felt Sydney's arms around me. 'It's all right, Veronica,' he murmured into my hair. 'Everything's going to be fine now. You needn't worry any more. You're safe now, my darling. You're safe.'

And so, although I didn't deserve it, I was given another chance. Sydney loved me, really loved me, and in my relief and gratitude I found that, temporarily at least, I loved him too. I made a promise to reform. I was determined to turn over a completely new leaf. From now on I was going to make Sydney the perfect wife. I'd stop drinking for one thing and as soon as possible I would have another child. I intended to make it up to Sydney in every way. And of course, it was so wonderful to have an ally at last in this ghastly business about Max. Sydney had decided that there was nothing to be gained by confessing my part in Helen's death. As he very sensibly pointed out, Max would still feel he had a score to settle with Rochester. He wasn't going to call a truce just because he hadn't been the actual perpetrator of the final deed. Sydney told me to forget all about it, to put it completely out of my mind and Sydney made forgetting so easy. As soon as I was recovered we were to take a three-month vacation in New York. Of course, I couldn't wait, and within three weeks I was out of bed and making plans. And then, just when I thought that everything was going to be all right, just when I felt I could let go and relax, Max announced that he was going to marry Lydia Rochester.

PART THREE
LYDIA
1927–1930

August 12th, 1927, Eldon Square, Newcastle
I begin this journal with the very strong feeling that one day I shall regret having set down so clearly and uninhibitedly my most intimate thoughts. Already I feel vulnerable, the object of prying eyes, as if I were taking my clothes off before a leering voyeur. Neither am I really clear as to my reasons for wanting to do so, except that as a scholar's daughter I have perhaps inherited something of my father's belief that an answer can be found to practically everything once it has been set down clearly in black and white. Of course, I have always kept a diary of sorts; schoolgirl scribblings, the random jottings of an uninformed and undisciplined mind. Browsing through them now, I see that occasionally, a single line entry in capitals marks some momentous or important event. For example, under September 17th, 1901, one finds the brief unemotional statement that at three o'clock that afternoon my beloved father died, and similarly six days later, on the 23rd, after the simple funeral service he had stipulated in his will, my mother and I discovered that he had left us penniless, and we were forced to return to the north of England to live as pensioners in my Grandfather Fortesque's house in Eldon Square. Three months later, on the 3rd January, 1902, equally briefly and unemotionally, I made a similar note of my mother's death. 'Louisa Ann Bennet, 1849–1901. Rest in Peace, Mama.' It was a poor epitaph. A casual observer, glancing through these brief notes, might have supposed that the death of my parents hadn't affected me at all. There was a great deal more I could have said. I could have added, had I been of a more melodramatic turn of mind, that Mama had died of a broken heart, that she'd been bullied to death by her own father. Grandfather made it

207

plain from the outset, that having married 'that schoolmaster fellow' against his wishes, she couldn't come home after eighteen years and expect to be kept for nothing. He'd do his duty. He'd see we didn't starve, but beyond that we'd need to fend for ourselves. And the unforgiving, vengeful, old man was as good as his word. We were treated like servants; in fact, we weren't treated so well. After three months Mama just gave up and succumbed to a chill. I was seventeen, afraid and alone, a stranger living with another stranger in a city I neither knew nor liked. My grief and misery were beyond something so trivial as words.

I made no other entries for a time. The blank pages recall my unhappiness far more than anything I could have said. Then in the spring, about April, the name Edward Rochester begins to make its appearance. 'Mr Rochester, Grandfather's banker, came to lunch' — 'to tea' — 'to supper' — and then so frequently that his presence in the house was hardly worth noting. On June the 17th I wrote with all the brutality of youth; '*Old* Mr Rochester (ironically, he was forty-four) asked Grandfather if he could take me to the theatre on Wednesday night.' This was followed by three blank pages, and then inscribed in large capitals decorated with exclamation marks; 'Mr Rochester has asked me to marry him and I have said yes.'

One might think that a young girl who had just received her first proposal, might have been tempted to romantically embellish this brief remark. But even then I was a realist. Grandfather had made it quite plain that he didn't care for me much. Like Mama, I was a disappointment. Having been cheated of a son and heir, he had expected at the very least a grandson in lieu. I was there on sufferance, till a husband could be found who met Grandfather's rigorous standards as to birth, breeding, bank account and so on. I was left in no doubt that the choice was between marriage to Edward Rochester or continuing financial dependence upon him. As a feeble woman and heiress to his not inconsiderable fortune, I had to be protected from charlatans and rogues. I was intelligent enough to realise that it was Grandfather's money that needed to be protected rather than myself. Who better than Edward Rochester, already at the helm of the fiscal ship. It

208

seemed the lesser of two evils, and at least I would escape from Grandfather and the Victorian gloom of Eldon Square. Edward might not have been the answer to a maiden's prayer but he was kind, intelligent; he reminded me of the father I had so dearly loved, so that it seemed a suitable arrangement all round.

After my marriage the diaries took on a more important note, a daily record of the trivia of a busy and ordered life. Lunch appointments and dinner parties featured large; visits to hairdressers, dressmakers, milliners and furriers, everything necessary to the creation and continuing comfort of a wealthy banker's wife. And after Jack was born, careful notes of school holidays and sports days so that they didn't interfere with our frequent holidays abroad. The crowded impersonal pages gave nothing away, there was no hint of my boredom, no inkling that for the last twelve years of our marriage Edward's failing health had made it impossible for him to share my bed. He grew worse, a complete invalid. My social life diminished; cocktail and dinner parties were replaced by appointments to see specialists, visits to expensive clinics in London and spas abroad. In between, I stood as Edward's proxy in the day-to-day running of the bank. Then, in February 1923, Edward died and I knew real freedom for the first time in my life.

Strangely enough, my grief for Edward was quite sincere but it was for the loss of an old friend rather than a husband. I had nothing to reproach myself with. I had been a dutiful wife and mother, an excellent hostess, a first-class nurse and companion. My devotion was well rewarded. Edward left me his entire personal fortune of nearly three quarters of a million pounds and thirty-five per cent of his stock in the bank. I was suddenly rich, independent and free.

I considered my options and realised they were infinite. Within reason I could do exactly as I pleased. I reviewed my assets; apart from an income of ten thousand a year, I was still reasonably attractive to men and, after twelve years of repressing a passionate and emotional temperament, I discovered that men were very attractive to me. It occurred to me that I'd never experienced physical passion or overwhelming desire. My sexual experience had been limited to a few brief, apologetic fumblings in the dark. I couldn't help feeling cheated, that life — excitement — had passed me by. I was seized with a wild recklessness, a sudden longing to capture the wild impetuousness of youth. I made up my mind that from that moment on I was going to live every moment as if it were my last.

I took a six-month cruise on the Mediterranean. The *Mauretania* sailed from Southampton on the 12th July, by the 14th I had almost mastered my urge to sleep with half of the crew. It was inevitable, though, that I should have an affair. To use banking terminology, I had twelve years of celibacy standing to my credit. I was determined to go into the red.

I took my first lover in Florence, a young penniless artist called Mario who painted rather bad impressionist pictures but turned out to be something of a Modigliani in bed. He was the first of a succession of handsome young men with whom I amused myself over the next few months. That they were always young, at least in the beginning, was purely coincidental. I had no particular passion for youth but attractive, unmarried men over thirty were rare. Later on I came to prefer the uncomplicated, uninhibited attitude of the younger man to say nothing of his unquenchable and inexhaustible virility.

I came home a new woman, ready to take up my responsibilities again. Until Jack reached his majority, as the largest shareholder in Rochester Mercantile, I was nominally chairman of the board, and the discovery that I enjoyed power almost as much as I enjoyed sex added yet another exciting dimension to my life.

I returned to the Continent every year. It became an accepted thing that I would winter abroad. Usually it was Cannes or Biarritz. The French had perfected the art of the casual affair and I could take a lover as easily as I took a swim; impetuously, impulsively, knowing that I was unlikely to get out of my depth. I would return to England in April. May and June were spent in town, travelling north after Ascot week, usually stopping off to see friends in Oxford *en route*. Outwardly, I resumed the role of the respectable and morally irreproachable Mrs Rochester, and though my private life was as complicated as a system of double-entry book-keeping not even my closest friends were able to tell. Not that I actually cared about their opinion, but they would have cared, and out of courtesy, to spare their blushes, I kept my affairs very much to myself.

And then I met Max Claremont and everything changed. It was lust at first sight, and in any other circumstances he would have found his way speedily into my bed. He had all the qualifications; tall, blond, good-looking and young — too young, I felt. Extreme youth coupled with an outspoken temperament usually results in a tendency to be wildly indiscreet. Furthermore, he was my son's friend and an employee of the bank. One had to draw the line somewhere.

So I contented myself with a mild and harmless flirtation. It's always flattering to be the object of a young man's desire, and at first I found it amusing, the rather obvious way he pursued me. Alternatively I encouraged and rebuffed. It was a game that women of my age often played, but as with all games there were rules. It was tacitly understood that the young man in question never embarrassed the lady of his choice, that he never overstepped the bounds of propriety, and that, on the whole, he had to be content to worship from afar. The discovery that Max Claremont had no respect for rules of any kind alerted me to the danger of my position. I did the sensible thing and slapped him down before things went too far.

I was inclined to avoid him after that, partly because whenever I was in his company I was seized with a temptation to break the rules myself. As it was only weeks till my annual migration to the South of France, I decided to spend the time with friends in London and embark for the Continent from there. Out of sight didn't prove to be out of mind, though. I found myself constantly thinking about him, constantly trying not to think about him. Even when I arrived in Cannes with all its usual delicious distractions, I found I was unable to get Max completely out of my mind. I moved on to Nice long before my usual time. I had the strangest feeling that I was running away. Then in Monte Carlo, before I'd even had time to unpack my trunks, I received a wire from Jack saying that Max Claremont had tried to kill

211

him and had been arrested by the police.

It took me three days to get home and a fortune in bribes to get passage on a ship. I arrived at Eldon Square too late to do anything but minimise the disaster as best I could. Max had already been charged.

I was furious with Jack. His hysterical action in calling the police had only resulted in an unsavoury notoriety for both his family and the bank. Besides, I didn't believe a word of his fantastic story. As his mother I had a natural duty to back him up but I was well aware, that for his own protection, he was quite capable of manufacturing the most bizarre of plots. Unfortunately, I have none of the usual maternal blind spots as far as Jack is concerned. My feelings for him are a mixture of love and loathing, compassion and disgust. He is my son and I love him but strictly in the maternal sense. I have always been aware of the unpleasant side of his personality and of course I have known for years about his preference for members of his own sex. You see, my involvement with the Claremont family didn't just begin with Max. I had known his brother Hugo extremely well. I had been attracted to Hugo for exactly the same reason that I was attracted to Max. He was my type; Nietzsche's blond beast, the stereotyped hero of a Viking epic; Galahad stepping from the pages of *Morte d'Arthur* — replace the shining armour with faultlessly cut English tweeds, the white charger with a red Bugatti — and you had Hugo Claremont.

Edward was still alive then and it was hard not to contrast an ageing invalid with this paragon of physical beauty and youth. I had always been beguiled by physical beauty and Hugo was beautiful in an entirely masculine way. I knew that nothing would ever come of it, though. The thought of being unfaithful to Edward had never crossed my mind, but in the privacy of my chaste bed I had the occasional adulterous thought. I dreamt of what it must be like to lie in the arms of a man like Hugo. And it might have gone on like that if one night Edward hadn't had a bad attack and been rushed to the Royal Victoria Infirmary. I sat by his bedside till two o'clock, until I was certain he was out of danger. I went home exhausted, so tired I could hardly stand. The servants were all asleep. I had to use my key. I dragged myself upstairs, pausing as I heard familiar male laughter then Hugo's voice, breathless and passionate, coming of all places from my son Jack's room. I stood outside the door listening to those unmistakable carnal sounds, listening as Hugo Claremont made love to my son ...

I never told Jack that I knew. In fact, I made every effort to conceal my knowledge and the inevitable change in my feelings towards him that the discovery had brought. I tried to think like my father. I tried not to make judgements and take the liberal, philosophical view. After all, homosexuality hadn't been regarded as a vice by the Ancient Greeks! But that was a romantic and idealistic point of view. I was a realist and this wasn't Ancient Greece but twentieth-century England where sodomy was regarded as a criminal offence, punishable by a long and rigorous term of imprisonment. As a result my dislike of Jack's personality, my distaste for his morals, couldn't ever override my instinct to protect him. I live in constant fear that some day he'll give himself away, that he'll reveal himself to the wrong person as I'm sure he did with Max. I am still convinced that the real reason for their quarrel was based on something to do with that. Jack admits that he'd been drinking and he's inclined to be indiscreet when he's in a mood like that. I can quite imagine him blurting out his secret in the frankest way. And if he'd mentioned Hugo, or, God forbid, if he'd been insane enough to think that Max might be similarly inclined ... I could quite see Max reacting in a violent way faced with what to most normal red-blooded Englishmen was a disgusting vice.

Yes, I'm quite sure that something of that kind happened, and, if it did, then Jack behaved quite stupidly in calling the police. He would have done so in a blind panic, out of fear that Max would reveal his secret vice. By accusing Max first, by inventing the story that Max had attacked him because he had been sacked, he would cast doubt on any accusations Max might make in return. They would be dismissed merely as vengeful slander. But Max said nothing and I was so grateful for his discretion that I felt the least I could do was to attend his trial. Thank God that by this time sanity had prevailed and Jack's hysterical charge of attempted murder had been judiciously pared down to one of common assault. I

213

fully intended to speak to Max afterwards, to offer my apologies, to try in some way to make amends — at least to offer to pay his costs and any fine that the court might seek to impose. It never occurred to me that he would incur any more rigorous punishment and his imprisonment came as a horrible shock. Naturally I was devastated. I was overwhelmed by guilt, by the knowledge that I, or at least Jack, had been partially to blame. I wanted to write, to say I was sorry, to let him know at least that I understood. Several times I got as far as 'Dear Max' — or was that too familiar? 'Dear Mr Claremont' — or was that too impersonal and cold? In the end I gave up. It seemed too difficult. What on earth could I say that wouldn't seem patronising or smug? How could I be sympathetic without seeming to rub salt in the wound? He was bound to take offence. I quailed at the thought of an overtly hostile reply, or even worse, he might not reply at all.

Then an opportunity came to contact him without fear of rebuff. I wrote a formal letter of condolence when his sister Helen died, and Max replied, equally formally, but I read an invitation between those few stilted lines and was encouraged to write again. And so began an epic correspondence, or as epic as the meagre weekly ration of prison notepaper would allow. At first the letters were tentative and wary, an exchange of polite sentiments rather than points of view. Then gradually we started throwing the odd intellectual challenge down, making statements with which we knew the other would disagree. Soon we were fiercely debating music and literature, religion and politics, coming to verbal blows over philosophy and art. The brilliance of his mind impressed me. I was astounded by the soundness and maturity of his views. I could have been taking issue with my father instead of a man in his twenties. Our friendship blossomed — at the time I didn't care to think of it as anything more — so it seemed only natural that on his release from prison we should arrange to meet. Our rendezvous was in the ruins of Tynemouth Castle.

He was already there, sitting hunched in the shadow of the crumbling walls as if he had grown so used to walls that open spaces made him nervous.

214

'Hallo Max.' I had approached him silently over the soft springing turf.

'Hallo Lydia.' He rose to his feet but made no other movement towards me.

The moment fell flat. I had expected a far more intimate greeting. I had imagined he would drop a light kiss on my cheek or at the very least reach out for my hands.

Then he came out of the shadows and I saw his face. I was shocked to see how much he had aged. He could have been thirty-five rather than the twenty-five he now was. His eyes had a real hardness; his mouth seemed set in an habitually angry line. And there was an air of suppressed violence about him, like a powerful machine held permanently in low gear. Just for an instant I felt intimidated and threatened.

'Have you been waiting long?' I said awkwardly. 'I'm afraid I'm a little late.'

'It doesn't matter,' he answered, looking away. 'It's been very pleasant, sitting here in the sun.'

We fell silent and I thought: How ridiculous this is! All the countless words that had passed between us on paper and now he was here I couldn't think of anything to say. I said the first thing that came into my head. 'Well, how does it feel to be a free man?'

He smiled thinly. 'I'm not sure. I haven't really got used to it yet.'

'Well, obviously it's going to take some time to adjust.'

This dreadful conversation ground to a halt. We began to walk. Silences are always worse when you're standing still.

'Have you made any plans yet?' I asked after a while.

'No. At least, nothing definite. I have a job if I want it with my brother-in-law's firm. I'll probably take it. I don't expect to be inundated with offers.'

I winced inwardly. 'Well, if there's anything I can do, anything at all ...'

'Thank you.' He smiled at me, 'But you've been so kind already, I hardly like to impose on your friendship again.'

'Oh, please. That's what friends are for,' I volunteered quickly.

He frowned. 'Well, actually there is something. It occurs to me that if Rochester — Jack — if he still harbours a grudge

215

— well, he could make things very awkward for me. As managing director of a large commercial bank he obviously wields a great deal of influence, and if he should use that influence against me ...'

'You needn't worry about that.' I laid my hand on his arm. 'I certainly shouldn't allow Jack to harm you again. And besides, he doesn't have as much influence as he would like to think. As the major shareholder, I have a great deal more, and if Jack should ever try to use the bank to pursue a vendetta against you, he'd soon find himself up before the board.'

'I see,' Max murmured. 'That's very reassuring.'

'And to be perfectly frank, I don't think the situation will ever arise. My impression is that he'd be happy to put the entire, unfortunate episode out of his mind rather than pursue any grudge against you.'

'Well, I'm glad,' Max said. 'I certainly feel like that.' He hesitated for a moment. 'Has he ever discussed what happened between us that night?'

'No.' I waited for him to elaborate, to give his own version of events — but he said nothing which only served to confirm my theory that morally Jack had overstepped the mark. Naturally, Max would hesitate to mention the unmentionable — homosexuality wasn't a subject that a gentleman could freely discuss, but he could have taken the opportunity to score a point. It made Jack's treatment of him all the shabbier and myself all the more ashamed.

Then he was holding out his hand. We were saying goodbye. 'Thank you again, Lydia, for all you've done. I can't tell you how much your letters meant. Sometimes they were all that kept me sane.'

I stared at him blankly. This all seemed so final, as if we were never to meet again. I was shocked at how much the thought depressed me. Up until that point I had been able to delude myself that my actions had only been those of an interested friend, a necessary discharge of conscience and duty. Now I knew that I couldn't bear it if I was never to see him again. I felt in some special way that he belonged to me.

I found myself saying — how obvious in retrospect — 'Max. Do you remember that you asked me to have dinner with you once?'

216

'Yes, I remember.' He smiled ruefully. 'And you said that as a friend of your son's and an employee of the bank, it was entirely out of the question.'

'Well, you're no longer my son's friend or an employee of the bank.' I smiled faintly. 'Is it too late to change my mind?'

In the same obvious way I engineered my own seduction — if seduction is the right word, implying as it does a loss of honour and virtue, handicaps that I had abandoned long ago. Certainly it wasn't the act of a virtuous woman to invite an attractive young man to an intimate dinner *à deux* the moment her son was out of town. From the moment that Max arrived at Eldon Square, it must have been apparent that the invitation was for far more than the hospitality of my table.

I didn't intend to rush things though. There was a certain added excitement in spinning things out, in observing the proprieties until the very last moment. Throughout the meal we maintained polite and civilised conversation. Then with that formality over and Mellon and the other servants safely tucked up in bed, I led the way into the drawing room and poured brandy for us both.

'Don't you think Mellon was wonderful?' I remarked. 'He really didn't seem to turn a hair.'

Max smiled. 'You must have great faith in your servants' discretion.'

'I have great faith in their desire not to be dismissed from a well-paid job,' I answered cynically. 'Of course, servants talk, but only amongst themselves. That's the wonderful thing about the class barriers being so rigid. The gossip of the servants' hall never reaches the drawing rooms of one's friends.'

'Are you always so inconsistent?'

'Inconsistent? In what way?'

'Well, I can't help remembering the last time the two of us were alone together in this room.'

'The circumstances were a little different,' I pointed out. 'You weren't here at my invitation then.'

'Does it make so much difference?'

'Yes. To me it does. I like to make my own choices rather

217

than have them thrust upon me. I have never subscribed to the Victorian ethic that allows men to do exactly as they please and women only to do as they're told.'

'Oh, come on,' he scoffed. 'Surely those sort of attitudes went out with the war.'

'Attitudes certainly changed with the war but only the attitudes of the women themselves. They were no longer content to be chattels, the property of men.'

'That's an emotional argument rather than a factual one. The last fifty years have seen an enormous amount of legislation in favour of women.'

'You can't legislate against attitudes. It's still an unwritten law that any woman who sleeps with a man who isn't her husband is regarded by Society as some kind of whore.'

'So what you're advocating is a charter for promiscuity?'

'I don't like the word promiscuity. It implies an uncontrollable compulsion and a complete lack of taste.'

'All right. Immorality then.'

'I don't like that word either. Equality is the word I would have chosen myself; the right for women to behave in exactly the same way as man.'

'Yes. Immorally.'

I shrugged. 'What is immoral? What is thought of as immoral today will be thought of as fashionable tomorrow. Thirty years ago it was considered immoral for a woman to show her ankles and yet today we are treated to vast exhibitions of knee and thigh. How galling to spend one's youth repressing one's natural inclinations and then to have to endure an old age where the expression of those same inclinations is considered *passé.*'

'Is that a purely theoretical view or something you have put into practice?'

I hesitated. I wanted to be totally honest with Max and I suppose I also saw it as a test of his maturity. I said carefully: 'If you're asking me whether I've ever taken a lover then the answer is yes — frequently.'

'I see,' he said and his voice was cold. 'May I enquire what the terms of entry are to this exclusive club — or perhaps it isn't so exclusive after all?'

I flushed. 'You see! That's a typically masculine and

hypocritical remark. How many lovers have you had?'

'Probably not quite so many. I haven't been around for quite so long.'

I should have been angry. I should have been trembling with rage. I felt faintly surprised that when I eventually spoke my voice was so remarkably steady. 'How entirely ungallant,' I reproved him lightly. 'And besides, you have an entirely wrong impression, I was completely faithful to Edward as long as he was alive.'

'Really!' he sneered. 'You make it sound like a concession.'

I smiled faintly, remembering the twelve years I had spent in an empty bed. 'As a matter of fact, it was.'

We were silent. I took a cigarette from the box and lit it myself.

'I'd better go,' Max said, and rose to his feet.

'Yes,' I said crisply. 'I suppose you had. I'm sorry that you should find my morals so offensive. I had thought you were more intelligent than that.'

'It's not your morals I find offensive. It's the fact that you pretended to be something you were not.'

'Pretended!' I laughed. 'My God! I've been more honest with you than I've been with anybody in my life.'

'Oh yes, *now* you have, after you've deliberately humiliated me and made me feel a complete fool.'

I stared at him. 'I really don't know what you're talking about.'

'Don't you? Well, let me remind you of the occasion a year ago when you stood in this very room and lectured me about morality, when you accused me of treating you like some cheap tart. My God! I left here feeling as if I'd attempted to rape the Virgin Queen. Obviously it wasn't so much that I'd made an improper advance but that I'd failed to make the grade.'

'Oh, I see,' I snapped. 'It's your vanity that's at stake. You thought to relieve me of the burden of my chaste and widowed state only to find that somebody else has beaten you to it.' I sprang to my feet. 'Well, I'm sorry I've destroyed your illusions. But if you need so desperately to score a first then I suggest you confine your attentions to virginal school-girls and maiden aunts.'

219

I made to walk past him but he grabbed my arm. 'Don't walk out on me,' he yelled.

'Would you rather I slapped your face again?'

Then suddenly we were both silent. We both stood very still — we had made the mistake of physical contact and it was as if we were both paralysed by a numbing electrical charge.

'Lydia,' Max said faintly but I didn't reply. I looked at him, and saw the pain and longing in his eyes. Then he bent to kiss me, slowly, tentatively, as if he thought that at the last moment I might still resist. I didn't resist, and when he released me I took his hand and in silence we went upstairs.

One is naturally reticent to set down in black and white the details of intimacy, but sex plays such an important part in the decisions I have to make, that I feel I need to state clearly just how very special that side of our relationship is.

I had always felt that my crash course in copulation enabled me to make a reasonable *critique*. I'd had encounters of all kinds: some that could only be described as an exercise in technique; others, in which lack of expertise was countered by a robust enthusiasm so that one awoke the next morning feeling that one had sustained a full fifteen rounds with an amateur wrestler.

Max was different, so different that I realised all my so called experience was worth nothing at all. I realised that passion was more than two bodies writhing and gasping in the dark. It was an intensity of emotion, a depth of feeling, a madness of the senses, a wildness of the heart. Max was the ultimate experience; pure passion, perfect pleasure, the complete abandonment of self. It was the fusion of two bodies, the interlocking of two minds. For a brief instant we were so completely one that we felt each other's pleasure and pain. We made love everywhere; in hotels, in cars, in fields, on the beach. Sometimes it was almost bestial; heat and sweat, odour and pain; animals mating, dog and bitch. Sometimes it was tender, reverent and pure, as if we were innocent virgins coming together for the very first time, clumsy, unrehearsed, unsure. It wasn't love though, I told myself. It was lust, infatuation, pure sexual need. It was a last grasping at

220

the passions and desires of my unfulfilled youth. In a year's time it would be all over and I'd look back on the entire episode with a wry amused smile. You see, from the very beginning I'd acted with thoroughly good sense. I'd never deceived myself that it could ever be anything more than a passing affair, that in the long term we could be anything else but good friends. It was just a pleasurable interlude in both our lives; so that last night when Max asked me to marry him, I didn't take him seriously at all.

We had been making love and were sitting up in bed sharing our usual post-coital cigarette. As always, I was a little on edge. I have never been totally comfortable in the aftermath of illicit sex when, all passion spent, the inevitable note of embarrassment creeps in. Copulation viewed in retrospect always has an air of the faintly ridiculous — was it de Maupassant who complained of the perversity of God in making the act of human reproduction possible only by adopting the most preposterous of attitudes? Anyway, I have always felt a bit like that. Denied the oblivion of sleep, memories of one's recent abandonment are uncomfortably vivid and on a practical level one starts worrying about the servants, whether anyone will see your lover slipping out of the house. I know that Max hated it, sneaking up to my room after the servants were asleep, sneaking out again before they should wake.

'You'll have to leave soon, darling,' I reminded him gently. 'It's almost three o'clock.'

Without a word he slipped from the bed and with a connoisseur's eye I watched him dress. Physically he was quite magnificent, the perfect specimen of a young male homo sapiens at his sexual peak. I often thought of him like that, in a detached and completely clinical way. It made it easier to pour scorn on the foolish suspicion that was forming in my mind, that at the age of forty-four, when I was old enough to know better, I was falling in love with a man young enough to be my son.

I watched him slip on his shirt and grope irritably for his tie. Suddenly he said in an exasperated voice; 'Lydia. Don't you ever get tired of all this? I mean all this furtive sneaking about?'

221

'Well, of course it's a bore, darling,' I reached for the ashtray. 'But I don't see what else we can do.'

'You could marry me,' he said lightly. 'After all, why not?'

'Marry you?' I laughed. 'Darling, you're drunk.'

It was the wrong thing to say. I saw the anger suffusing his face. 'I'm perfectly sober, thank you,' he snapped.

I could see that he was. His face had that grim stubborn look which meant that we'd quarrel. 'But why, Max?' I asked, suddenly very sober myself. 'Surely we're quite happy as we are.'

He sat down on the edge of the bed to fasten his shoes. 'Well, you might be,' he said, 'but I'm certainly not. In fact, I'm fed up to the teeth with all this sneaking about.' He turned to face me. 'I resent my private life being governed by whether or not Jack is away. I resent having to fit in with your other social commitments ...'

'Darling,' I soothed, 'of course, I understand — but don't you think marriage is a rather drastic solution.' I still couldn't believe that he was serious.

'It's the only solution,' he argued stubbornly.

'Oh for God's sake, Max.' I was beginning to feel irritable and a little nervous as well. This wasn't a situation I'd ever foreseen.

He stood up to put his jacket on, then resumed his seat on the edge of the bed. 'Don't you want to marry me, Lydia? Don't you want us to be together all of the time instead of just the few hours that we can snatch?'

'Well, yes, of course I do, darling,' I murmured. 'But ...'

'Marry me then.' He leant towards me and fixed me with those hypnotic blue eyes. 'Either marry me or find someone else who's prepared to fit in with your busy schedule, some other obliging young man who doesn't mind being squeezed in between a visit to the hairdresser's and a board meeting at the bank.'

'Don't give me ultimatums, Max,' I advised him coldly. 'I should probably react in a typically perverse and feminine way and tell you to go to Hell.'

'I'm not giving you an ultimatum, I'm giving you a choice.'

'Look, darling,' I stalled. 'Let me think about it, won't you? I'm going down to Oxford for a few days at the end of the week. Can't we talk about it when I come back?'

'No, we can't,' he said stubbornly. 'I want an answer now. Things won't look any different when you come back from Oxford. You either want to marry me or you don't. It's as simple as that.'

To him, of course, it was. He was the romantic. I was the realist. I was Guinevere to his Lancelot, Helen to his Paris with Arthur and Agamemnon vicariously represented by Jack. Like all romantics he believed that the impossible was possible, that to get what you wanted you only had to reach out a hand.

'Well?' he demanded. 'Yes or no?'

I suddenly realised that he meant it and I stared at him helplessly, thinking the unthinkable, that if I said 'no' I might never see him again. He was perverse enough to throw away the half he had because he could not have the whole.

Just for a moment I allowed myself to be swept away by the romantic dream. Just for an instant I believed it was possible. We would be married, we would be together, through him I would recapture the lost world of my youth ... I found myself smiling and pulling him down towards the bed and in the split second before his mouth closed on mine, I heard myself saying, 'Yes'.

Of course, in the cold light of day I had to face up to how impossible it all was ... For one thing how on earth would I break the news to Jack? I have spent the entire morning rehearsing what I might possibly say.

'Jack darling, Max Claremont has asked me to marry him and I've decided to say yes.'

That's all I have to say, just the brief statement that as a mature intelligent woman I have taken the decision to marry again, and naturally I expect my only son to wish me every happiness. Except that as a mature intelligent woman I realise it isn't going to be as easy as that. Jack isn't going to be wildly enthusiastic about my marrying again in any case. He'll resent another man in my life on principle, especially a man who is virtually his own age and for whom, to say the least, his feelings are cool. And if that isn't reason enough to call the whole thing off, there is also the unpalatable fact that

223

a woman who marries a man young enough to be her own son runs the very real risk of becoming a laughing stock and exposing herself to the scorn and ridicule of all her friends. Whilst it would be considered scandalous for a woman of my age to indulge in a light-hearted affair with a younger man, any attempt to regularise such an irregular position would be considered more scandalous still. Marriage is seen as a moral and intensely respectable institution only to be indulged in by people of a like age, colour, religion and background. We were back to the Victorian hypocrisy that permitted a gentleman to keep a chorus girl as his mistress but didn't allow him to marry her and inflict his questionable taste on his friends.

So, to sum it all up, I am faced with the prospect of alienating my son, shocking my friends, possibly making myself a complete laughing stock. Obviously, I need to think things out carefully.

August 20th, 1927, Balliol College, Oxford

Oxford was home, the 'sweet city of dreaming spires' where, as the indulged only child of middle-aged parents, I had spent seventeen blissful and contented years. The moment I emerged from the station I felt happy and relaxed. The ancient buildings enfolded me; Magdalen, Merton, Corpus Christi and Queens; Wren's tower over Wolsey's gate, the Ashmolean, the Bodleian, Trinity. The years slid away and I was sixteen again, strolling with Mama past the shops in the High, walking with Papa in Christ Church meadow. As if it were only yesterday I remembered warm summer evenings punting on the Cherwell. I remembered the clamour of term time, the excitement of Eights Week, the endless quiet of the long vacation. Most of all I remembered the naive happy thoughts of a young girl whose future, like her past, would be comfortable and assured. It had been practically certain that I'd be offered a place at Lady Margaret Hall. I'd had a privileged education, a first-class day school supplemented with private tuition by my father at night. I was determined to follow in his footsteps and read for a history or a classics degree. I wasn't even deterred by the fact that in those days

224

women couldn't obtain an actual degree. That was just another challenge. Times were changing and I dreamed of being the first woman to be awarded a double first in Greats. And then, when I'd proved myself, I'd eventually marry, a younger version of my father, a college Fellow who would appreciate a learned and educated wife ... but then Papa died and the dream died with him. I left Oxford and wasn't able to return for another six years. I came every year now, between the end of Hilary and the start of the Michaelmas term. For a few days I would wander happily through the familiar college buildings. I could walk again with my father across the Garden Quad. I could listen to his quiet authoritative voice discoursing on the origins of the Punic Wars. I could relive the dream again and fantasise how my life might have been if he hadn't died so suddenly. Except that this time it wasn't my father who occupied my thoughts. It was Max I was thinking of as I strolled leisurely through the Oxford streets. Max had been here. He'd been an Oriel man. I kept seeing him in my mind, striding in subfuse across Front Quad, sprawled on the river bank immersed in a book ...

I held imaginary conversations with my father. 'Daddy, I've met the most wonderful man ...' I could see him nodding gravely as I explained my dilemma. He wouldn't be shocked. Nothing shocked my father except bad grammar. As he filled his pipe he would be turning it over in his mind. Eventually he'd speak, nothing profound, just the simple observation that I was at a dangerous age to fall in love. And I'd agree that at my time of life one didn't have the same resilience if things went wrong, but I'd argue that this was probably my last chance of personal happiness. After forty the opportunities dwindled.

We'd be silent for a while and then he'd smile. He'd say in his gentle and caring voice that if I loved Max and he made me happy in turn, then that was reason enough to take the chance. He'd say that happiness came so rarely that we must take it while we can.

Of course, he was right. It was as simple as that. I felt wonderfully elated and suddenly the idea of marrying Max didn't seem so completely scandalous here. Of course, scandal is scandal wherever you go, but the morals of Oxford weren't as narrow as those of a northern industrial town. The nearer one got to London the more licence one had, and perhaps the answer would be to move farther south and to live among people to whom morality was simply a word rather than a rigid code to be adhered to at all costs. It seemed the perfect answer; a fresh beginning, an escape from the inevitable censorship of close family and friends. After all, there was nothing really to keep us in the north ... And then I remembered Jack.

Of course I'm a fool about Jack, as to some degree all mothers are fools about their sons. But at least I know I'm a fool. My indulgence and tolerance aren't the result of blind devotion but more the outcome of a continual struggle to reconcile my love for the child I have borne with my antipathy to the man he has become. I feel vaguely guilty, that in some way it's my fault he hasn't come up to expectations. He seems a misfit in every way and I've always blamed myself for not being firmer with Edward about Jack going into the bank. You see, I knew he wasn't up to it. He's clever, intelligent, but he has no real grasp of money and finance and his position at the bank is only sustained by his reliance on me and a highly competent board. His real talent is for music. He's a brilliant pianist, and with the right training he would have been certain to reach the concert halls. I've always wondered — if his father hadn't forced him into a profession he disliked, if his ambition hadn't been thwarted and his talent suppressed — well, things might have turned out quite differently.

That's the first obstacle then, that morally and practically I can't abandon Jack. It's no good arguing that he's old enough now to look after himself. Jack will never be able to look after himself. He'd always be under threat from his abnormal desires, and if he was threatened then so was I. I can't turn my back on him, not even for Max.

So having made the mistake of forgetting about Jack, I then made the even bigger one of going to see Celia Richmond. Celia and I were old friends and confidantes. We'd attended the same school and were approximately the same age — although Celia insisted she was only thirty-six — and we both shared a weakness for handsome young men, except

226

that Celia's taste ran to scruffy, long-haired, artistic types. Celia herself churns out two or three ghastly daubs every year. This entitles her to call herself an artist, a vocation she adopted after a chance encounter with Wyndham Lewis at the Café Royal demonstrated that artists have a licence that ordinary mortals do not. Artists can be eccentric, permissive, undisciplined and rude. If one has talent one can get away with anything. That Celia has no talent hasn't prevented her from indulging in the fringe benefits, hence the flowing pre-Raphaelite gown and hideous Holman Hunt jewellery and the tousled male head I glimpsed through the open bedroom door.

'Darling! What a surprise. I'd quite forgotten it was your week.' Celia adroitly closed the door on her startled young man.

'I'm sorry,' I murmured. 'I should have telephoned first. I'm obviously interrupting ...'

'Well, twenty minutes ago you might have been, darling, but fortunately the critical moment has been passed. Oh don't worry about Jeremy. He'll just go back to sleep. Now, drinks, darling. Being caught *in flagrante delicto*, even by one's best friend, isn't something I can face completely sober.'

I sat down on the edge of a shell-shaped sofa submerged in an assortment of fringed and tasselled silk shawls. Celia chattered on whilst she mixed the drinks. Jeremy was the latest. He sculpted apparently in metal and bronze. Oodles of talent, quite unrecognised of course, but Celia had that well in hand. In fact, she'd practically persuaded the Regent Gallery to mount a show ...

'Now, is that all right for you, angel. Not too much gin?' Celia enthroned herself in a hideous Carlo Bugatti chair. 'Now, tell me all. Of course you're in love. I can tell by the fatuous expression on your face. Well, tell me all about him or shall I guess? Tall, blond, hard up and handsome. That's your usual type if I remember.'

'And young,' I added.

'How young?'

'Twenty-five.'

'Darling, that's not young. That's positively infantile.'

Celia screamed with laughter. 'Well, good for you, angel. He's obviously doing you the world of good, although you always do look disgustingly youthful when you're having an affair.'

I smiled nervously. 'Well, actually, it's a bit more than an affair this time, Celia. Max and I are going to be married.'

She stared at me incredulously. (I can see I'm going to have to get used to that look.) 'My dear Lydia. You're not serious. He's only a boy.'

'I'm perfectly serious,' I snapped. 'After all, why not?'

'You know perfectly well why not. Bed them but never wed them — wasn't that what we always said?'

'Celia,' I ground out my cigarette in exasperation. 'I think you've got entirely the wrong idea. Max isn't some down-at-heel gigolo I picked up in a bar. He's well bred, intelligent ...'

'And nearly twenty years younger than you. That's the point, Lydia, the point that you're obviously determined to overlook.'

'I'm not trying to overlook anything. I just thought that you would be one of the very few people to understand.'

'Oh, I do understand,' Celia drawled. 'Perhaps that's the trouble, angel, I understand too well. I've had similar offers from young men myself, you know, although usually they were far more in love with my income than with me. I didn't even mind that. What I did mind was the thought of making myself an object of derision, of living in dread that every time we went out socially some wit would ask him if his mother wanted a chair.'

'Oh for Heaven's sake, Celia ...'

'I'm perfectly serious, Lydia. I don't think you've any idea of what you're letting yourself in for. You're in your prime now, Lydia, but believe me, after this, it's all downhill. The one thing you can't do is turn back the clock. Everything's perfect between you now but you have to be practical and face the ghastly fact that when — what's his name — Max is only forty, you'll be a withered old hag of nearly sixty.'

'Don't exaggerate, Celia ...' I was getting irritable now.

'It's the truth, angel. One sees it every day. London is full of raddled old crones trying to patch themselves up to look nineteen, purely in order to keep up with a younger man.'

'I've no intention of trying to keep up ...'

'Then he'll leave you behind. Whilst you're at home tinting your hair and plastering your face with rejuvenating cream, he'll be taking the girl in the chemist shop out to lunch.

'Look, I'm sorry to be so brutal, angel, but it's far better to face the truth now, instead of later on, when you've committed yourself. Growing old is beastly and sordid in any case and usually the only consolation is that one's spouse is withering away as well. It's an unequal contest in any case. Men don't age so noticeably as us, but if you're insane enough to give him a twenty-year start ... And to be even more frank, darling, you've got to ask yourself why he's so keen to get married at all. Of course, you're a very attractive woman, Lydia, and you've never looked anything like your age, but you're also a very rich one and let's face it, darling, men of twenty-five aren't usually so eager to give up their freedom. When they do eventually decide to tie the knot it's usually to some spotless young virgin from the neighbouring estate who'll provide them with the necessary sons and heirs. I'm not saying you're past it, darling, but I wouldn't have thought pregnancy was something one wanted to contemplate at forty-four. No, I'm afraid, if it was me, I'd be looking for some ulterior motive in this rush to get you up the aisle. The obvious one, of course, is that he's after your cash, so I'd make it perfectly clear that, married or not, he won't get a sou ...'

I didn't listen. I didn't speak except to ask for another gin sling. Eventually I came away feeling old, wretched, drunk and devastated. My grand passion had been reduced to a sordid affair, Max to a grubby fortune-hunter and myself to a gullible middle-aged dupe. I couldn't face that. I might be weak on morality but I was strong on pride, so I gathered together the tattered shreds of my dignity and thought about how I would explain to Max that I couldn't marry him after all.

August 25th, 1927, Eldon Square

I left Oxford the next day and recklessly wired Max to meet my train. Fortunately, by the time I drew into Newcastle

229

Central my sense of humour had returned and I was able to look back on Celia's homily with a wry and cynical smile. I saw now that the doubts weren't mine, they were all other people's. They made gloomy predictions and offensive remarks because I was forcing them to look at something they would rather ignore. They were all so obsessed with their own ideas of respectability and doing the done thing, and what I was proposing to do wasn't the done thing at all. They were going to be looking at me with all the horror and embarrassment of guests in the Royal Enclosure at Ascot viewing a fellow guest who had suddenly decided to remove her clothes. Well, I could put up with that, in fact I rather fancied I might enjoy a little notoriety. Of course, that didn't mean I was going into this thing with my eyes completely shut. Celia had obviously given me something to think about and, although emotionally I had made my mind up, I felt I needed to go through the motions of making a rational decision. Out of habit I assessed the situation as I might have assessed an application for a loan. On the credit side was the fact that, apart from the age gap, we were eminently suited. We shared a unique physical and mental rapport. Max made me feel happy, desirable, protected and needed. What more could a woman want? On the debit side, I couldn't completely rule out the possibility that my money was an added attraction. Money was a powerful aphrodisiac. It was a complete fallacy that men were incapable of getting an erection in the absence of real desire. The Riviera teemed with dance-hall gigolos who could give the lie to that. But that was being too cynical. The kind of sex life that Max and I enjoyed couldn't possible be faked. I was fairly confident that my money was no more to Max than the icing on the cake. And even if I was wrong, when one considers the thousands that most women squander on jewellery and gowns, a handsome young husband was a much better buy. The age difference wasn't so easily dismissed. I was a confident woman, but even my confidence would be under pressure, eternally confronted with the spectre of age. It wasn't just one's looks that deteriorated; vitality waned; one's health failed — I wondered if Max had considered all this? It was obvious that we needed to talk.

I climbed into his shabby two-seater car. 'Well,' he said lightly. 'How was Oxford?'

'Oh,' I said vaguely. 'Just the same.'

I made a point of not looking at him. Once under the spell of that hypnotic blue gaze, all thoughts of a practical discussion would fade. I pretended to be looking for something in my bag, though I could feel his eyes searching my face.

He started the engine. 'Where to? Not home?'

'No. Not home, at least, not yet. I think we should talk. Perhaps we could just drive round for a bit.'

I saw him frowning. Of course he knew me too well not to know that I had something on my mind. Abruptly he turned the ignition off.

'You've changed your mind, haven't you? You're going to say that you don't want to marry me, aren't you?'

'No, I haven't changed my mind — perhaps I'm giving you a last opportunity to change yours. I want to be quite sure that you know what you're doing.' I looked at him. 'There are a great many things we haven't discussed.'

There was a moment's silence. 'Let's discuss them then,' Max said grimly. 'Money first, I suppose.'

'Well, that's one thing.' I smiled in an effort to keep things from getting too tense. 'Are you going to be able to keep me in the manner to which I am accustomed?'

He flushed. 'No. But I can keep myself, which seems to me the most important thing. I certainly shan't be sponging off you.'

I smiled at the obvious naivity of this statement, as if we were to live two separate lives. Was he to dine *table d'hôte* whilst I feasted from the *à la carte*?

'And then there's Jack,' I continued. 'You do understand that he'll still be part of my life — of our lives. I can't just walk out on him, you know.'

'I didn't ever expect you to.'

'Well, I must know how you feel about it. I don't want the two of you at daggers drawn ...'

He looked at me, his eyes clear, innocent and candid. 'Isn't that a question you should really be asking Jack. He's the one that's going to make all the fuss.'

I sighed with exasperation. I didn't seem to be getting

231

anywhere. 'Has it — has it ever occurred to you that I won't be able to give you children? Usually that's important to a man.'

'It's not important to me. In fact, I'm glad. I don't want to have to share you with anyone.'

I smiled weakly. 'Darling, you say that now ...'

'But it's only now that matters. Now is all that any of us really have. Why concern yourself with a future that might not even exist?'

'Because I'm that sort of person. I'm not used to living purely for the moment as you seem to do. I need to think about tomorrow because tomorrow always comes and I have to know that I can face it.' I paused. 'And more important, I have to know that you can face it. Do you realise that when you're only forty, I shall be sixty?'

He regarded me gravely. 'And you think that will make a difference to the way we feel about each other?'

'It'll make a difference to you. It's bound too, Max. There's nothing attractive about old age.'

'For goodness sake, Lydia, I thought what we had between us went deeper than that.' He smiled at me in the diffident way he had. 'I love you, Lydia,' he said simply. 'And I shall always love you. Can't you be content with that?'

I should have been but I wasn't. In fact, I felt more uncertain than I'd ever done before. We hadn't really discussed anything. I felt his answers had been glib, evasive even. I hadn't been able to penetrate that smooth outer façade.

'Max,' I said at last. 'Why does it have to be marriage. If loving each other is all that matters, why not stay as we are?'

'Because that's the sort of person *I* am. Because everything I've always wanted has belonged to someone else. Hugo always came first, you see. He had Blanchland, the firm, and it was only on his say-so that I was allowed to share. But I had no rights. I was always second. I always had to fit in. And unless we're married that's how it will be with us. I'll have no rights. I'll always have to fit in, take my place in the line after Jack and the bank. I can't do that. I'd rather not take part in the race at all if it means I can only ever come second or third. Just for once in my life I want to be first.'

I stared from the car window. I watched the people hurrying to and from their trains. Well-heeled businessmen in bowler hats and pin-striped suits, women in smart costumes draped with the *de rigeur* dead fox. I looked at their faces with their smug, cautious, repressed expressions. I could see these were sensible people, people who'd never known a dangerous or reckless moment in their entire lives, to whom the desire to be ordinary and respectable overcame all other desires. Faced with my choice they wouldn't have hesitated. People like that could always be depended on to do the sensible thing. And hadn't I always done the sensible thing . . .?

Then Max said softly. 'It's all right, Lydia. I understand.'

I turned to look at him. His face was pale and tense. 'I don't blame you for backing off. You're quite right, I haven't got anything at all to offer you.' He smiled painfully. 'I'm hardly what could be termed a catch, am I? I'm a social outcast with a prison record. I've no real money or prospects, and if it wasn't for Sydney I wouldn't even have a job.' He stared down at his hands. 'I had no right to ask you to share in that. It was just that I needed you so badly. I was just thinking of myself. The best thing I can do is to clear right out . . .'

'Max.' I stopped him and turned his face towards me so that I could kiss his mouth. I was more moved by the quiet humility of that small speech than by any passionate declaration of love. In fact, he couldn't have said anything more guaranteed to change my mind. He needed me. That was enough. How could I let him down?

August 28th, 1927
I had to tell Jack. I'd managed to put it off for the last two days whilst I rehearsed various little speeches designed to soften the blow. In the end, I blurted it out after dinner last night.

'Jack,' I said as we settled ourselves in the drawing room to drink our coffee. 'I've something to tell you.' I waited till I was sure I had his full attention. 'I've decided to marry again. I hope you don't mind.'

233

He froze with the brandy glass half way to his lips. 'Well, this is news. I wasn't aware that you were even engaged.' He tried to smile but I saw the displeasure clouding his eyes. 'Would it be too inquisitive of me to enquire as to the lucky man?'

I drew a deep breath. This was it, the point of no return. I was about to commit myself irrevocably, once and for all. I felt as if I were lighting the touch paper to an unexploded bomb.

'It's Max Claremont,' I said and hoped that my voice sounded casual.

'Max!'

I hadn't actually expected him to embrace me, but even so I was taken aback by the look of unutterable horror on his face.

'You're not serious?' he said in a strangled voice. 'Please tell me this is some tasteless and hideous joke.'

'I'm perfectly serious,' I replied, nettled by his attitude although I don't know what else I had expected. 'Max and I are to be married in ten days' time, just a quiet civil ceremony, and then we're to accompany his sister Veronica and her husband on their trip to New York.'

'I see!' Jack was silent for a long time, then grudgingly he smiled. 'Well, well. So that's what he's been up to. I thought he was lying rather low.' The smile developed into a bitter laugh. 'I have to hand it to him. Even I couldn't have thought up such a subtle revenge. It's quite Freudian really, when you think of it.'

He looked up at me with an unfathomable expression in his eyes. 'How long has this been going on? I must say you've kept it remarkably quiet.'

I was deceived by his tone, his apparent acquiescence. 'Oh, some time,' I admitted, quite prepared to come clean in my relief that he wasn't going to make too much of a fuss. 'I suppose it really began when I wrote to him in prison ...'

'And I presume you've slept with him?'

I flushed. 'That's not really any of your business, Jack.'

'That means that you have.' He gave me a look of bitter disgust. 'My God, he's certainly stormed the citadel in every possible way. You're not pregnant by any chance, are you?

234

That would be too much of a coincidence, I suppose.'

'Jack,' I said sharply. 'My private life is absolutely none of your concern and it's certainly not a subject I am prepared to discuss. I'm going to marry Max Claremont and that's all you need to know. I understand that you're upset because obviously there are going to be changes to both our lives. For the time being at least, Max and I intend to live here at Eldon Square ...'

'I see. And where do I fit into this cosy domestic arrangement. Shall I have to call him Papa?'

'Look darling!' I attempted a conciliatory tone, sensing the situation was likely to get out of hand. 'I realise this has all come as something of a shock, but don't you think you're over-reacting. You and Max were good friends once. Surely you could make an effort to patch things up. If you're embarrassed about what happened, then you needn't be. As far as Max is concerned it's all over and done with. He accepts that he was equally to blame and that you both behaved stupidly and both lost your heads, but that's all in the past now, don't you see?'

'And you actually believe that?' He gave me a pitying look. 'You honestly believe that you can deprive a man like Claremont of his liberty, his reputation, his name, and he'll be prepared to forgive and forget, just like that.' His voice rose to a shrill note. 'My God, I can't believe how utterly he's fooled you. Can't you see what he's doing? He's going to use you to get at me.' He sank down in a chair, hysterical laughter bubbling in his throat. 'Oh my God, what a plan, what a masterstroke. He couldn't touch me before. He had no money, no power, but the instant you marry him you'll have given him both. He'll be on the inside then. He'll be able to watch me, to listen at doors. He'll be able to threaten me without even saying a word. He'll turn you against me. He'll turn everyone against me ...'

'You're talking absolute nonsense, Jack, and as always, looking at things from entirely your own point of view, I admit it isn't an easy situation but it won't be easy for Max either, especially if you're going to behave ...'

'Oh yes, Max, bloody Max. We must think of poor old Max. Everyone always feel sorry for him. They all think I'm a complete bastard for putting him in gaol. No one ever has any sympathy for me.' He sat down heavily and dropped his head in his hands. 'You can't imagine what it's like, to have someone actually try to kill you — and he would have killed me if the servants hadn't been there. He's a killer. He's vicious and unstable. Hugo always said that he was. And you want to marry him. You expect me to be pleased. You want to put him in my father's place, in my father's bed . . . Christ! It's unnatural. It's bloody obscene.'

I lost my temper than. 'My God! You dare to use words like that to me! You dare to criticise my morals when your own wouldn't bear the slightest scrutiny! I didn't expect you to be pleased but I expected you to accept the situation as I was forced to accept the situation between you and Hugo Claremont.'

We stared at each other in shocked and painful silence, then the hot tide of humiliation flooded his face. 'I see,' he said faintly. 'I suppose I have Max to thank for telling you that?'

'Max didn't tell me anything. He didn't have to. I'd known about you and Hugo for years.'

'I don't believe you,' he whispered. 'If you'd known you couldn't possibly have kept silent for all this time.'

I stared at him coldly. 'And what could I have possibly said that could have made you other than you are.'

He recoiled from me as if I had struck him and stood staring at me with pain and bewilderment in his eyes. I felt his misery so intensely, his fear and confusion. Suddenly I remembered the child I had loved so passionately, the small boy with the velvet eyes and the angelic smile, unrecognisable now in this neurotic and fearful man.

My anger evaporated. 'Jack, I'm so sorry. Please forgive me for saying that.'

He smiled painfully. 'You see! It's happening already. He's teaching you to despise me, to forget that I'm your son.'

He turned to face me, his eyes glistening with tears. 'But I'm not going to let you forget. I'm not going to let him take you away from me. You're the only person I've ever loved — the only person who's ever loved me.'

'Jack, please,' I said, hardening my heart against this

emotional appeal. 'You're not a child any more ...'

'Yes, I am,' he shouted suddenly. 'I'm your child. I'll always be your child — and if you marry that bastard then you're going to destroy me.' He stared at me. 'Think about that before you make up your mind.'

'I have made up my mind,' I replied calmly. 'You'll have to accept that I'm going to marry Max Claremont.'

He slammed out of the room, out of the house. I didn't see him for another two days.

'He'll get over it,' said Max when I recounted to him my emotional but carefully edited version of events.

'After all,' Max went on, 'he was bound to react. You didn't expect him to congratulate you, did you?'

'No, I didn't expect that ...' I paused and prodded at the olive floating in my drink. 'But I didn't expect him to react quite so violently though. I didn't expect him to be — well, so terrified. He seems genuinely afraid of you. He thinks you're marrying me as some subtle sort of revenge.'

Max shrugged. 'Well, he would, wouldn't he? One can always rely on Jack to make a drama out of a thing.'

It wasn't exactly the strenuous denial I'd hoped for but for some reason I was reluctant to press the subject too far. Instinctively I knew that neither was telling me the absolute truth, but equally instinctively I felt that the truth was something it was better not to know. I knew there were questions I should ask but I also knew I wasn't going to like the answers. I felt it would be like prizing up the lid of some ghastly Pandora's box.

'I was wondering,' I said, when the silence between us was on the point of becoming strained, 'you see, I'd rather assumed that after we were married we would live at Eldon Square, but if Jack is going to be difficult, perhaps we should make other plans.'

'Certainly not,' he said, strangely animated. 'That's the worst thing you could do. Jack obviously intends to martyr himself, and if you walk out on him then you'll just be adding another branch to the pyre. We must just carry on normally. You must make it quite clear that it's he who must fall in with your plans rather than you fitting in with his.'

237

'But if he's going to make things unpleasant ...' I sighed, 'Sometimes I wish we could go away.'

'Go away? You mean run away?'

'All right. Get away then. I'm beginning to feel like some sort of criminal.'

'We are getting away. We're spending three months with Veronica and Sydney in New York. By the time we get back everything will have calmed down. You know what people are like. We'll be considered stale news within a week.'

I thought of Jack's violent resentment and felt it was going to take a bit longer than that. And I was suddenly irritated by Max's bland and unsympathetic manner, that impenetrable air of spiritual aloofness that seemed to shut me out. I wanted to tell him how traumatic the last few days had been. I wanted to explain to him about Jack, to try and put into words that strange love–hate relationship. Then I realised that I never was going to be able to talk to Max like that. I had to accept that our relationship had certain limitations. For all we were so close and alike, I would never understand Max as I would a man of my own generation. For one thing, my ideas and attitudes were no longer fluid. My own personality had hardened in the mould. I could talk to Max about morality and politics but emotionally, when it came to my deepest feelings, I found myself struck dumb.

I said, resorting to the despicable feminine device of quarrelling when all other means of getting attention have failed: 'You know, Max! Sometimes I get the impression that our marriage falls into the same category as defying the Pope and getting sent down from university. It's a deliberate act of defiance, like a small boy refusing to eat his lunch just to get Nanny's attention. I actually think you enjoy being the object of gossip and scandal.'

He looked at me, amused. 'Frankly, I couldn't care less what anyone thinks.'

'Have you told your mother yet?'

'No.' A slight pause. 'I haven't told her.'

'Why not? Because you're concerned about what she thinks.'

'That's a very irritating habit of yours, Lydia. Asking a question and then supplying the answer yourself. I haven't

told her because I haven't yet had the opportunity to do so —
and far from being concerned about what she thinks, I
couldn't care less what she thinks, I told you, I don't care
what anybody thinks.'

'And does that include me?' I enquired archly.

'Everything includes you,' he answered quietly. 'I don't
think or breathe without including you. How much more of
me do you want?'

'I'm sorry,' I began but he grabbed my hand.

'It's going to be all right.' He smiled. 'Trust me, Lydia,
won't you?'

It was just nerves, of course, as I felt myself being swept inex-
orably towards the point of no return. This was the first time
in my life I had acted out of pure emotion. I always felt
happier when my decisions were based on logic and hard
fact. And I was also feeling wildly unhappy about Jack. His
resentment wasn't something I could completely ignore. We
had to talk. I had to try and make him understand, so when
he returned home after two nights spent sulking at his club, I
went up to his room to speak to him.

I paused outside the door, listening to the delicate strains
of a Chopin polonaise.

'Please don't stop,' I said as he sprang guiltily to his feet
when I entered the room. 'That's one of my favourite pieces,
if you remember.'

After a moment's hesitation he began to play again and I
stood quietly, watching his face. A feeling of sadness swept
over me as I saw his rapt and tender expression. He played
with such emotion, such sensitivity — I was listening to a real
musician playing rather than an exhibition of practised
keyboard technique.

I glanced round the room, unmistakably inhabited by a
man who cared deeply about beauty and art; The Burne
Jones mezzotints, the vases of pale, icy, Lalique glass,
Dante's Inferno illustrated by Doré lying open on a stand.

'That was quite lovely,' I said as he finished playing.
'You're a very talented musician, you know.'

His face lit momentarily, then darkened again to an
expression of Byronic gloom. 'I was,' he said, 'or I could

have been.' He got up from the piano and slammed the lid. 'Unfortunately, Father had other plans.'

'Yes I know. I'm sorry. I suppose I should have protested more.'

He shrugged. 'It doesn't matter now. I really don't care.'

'Yes, you do.' I argued gently. 'You couldn't play like that if you didn't care.'

He didn't answer and I went on, seized with a sudden desire to make amends. 'It's still not too late, Jack. You're relatively young. You could go to Paris, study at the Conservatoire. There's nothing to stop you from doing what you want now.'

His eyes grew dark and dreamy. A wistful smile lit his face. 'It's a wonderful thought and bless you for thinking it, but ...' his eyes hardened. 'Oh, I see. How stupid of me. I suppose this is Max's idea for getting me out of the way? Pack me off to Europe whilst he steps into my shoes at the bank.'

I wanted to cry. I felt the tears welling up in my throat. 'Oh Jack, don't be silly. You couldn't be more wrong.'

'Well, it's strange that you've only just thought of it. Father's been dead three years and you've never so much as hinted at it before.'

'Yes, I know. I can't explain. Perhaps I didn't realise how unhappy you were before. I suppose because I'm so happy I want you to be happy too.'

'Well, that's perfectly simple,' he snapped. 'What will make me happy, ecstatic in fact, is for you never to see Max Claremont again.'

'Jack. Please don't ask that. It isn't fair. I love Max very much. It would cause me great unhappiness to have to give him up. Don't spoil it for me, Jack. Indulge me this once as I have so often indulged you.'

'It's not a question of indulging you. What you feel for Max, what you do with him, is none of my business. God knows, after the life you had with Father, I'd be the last one to object to you having a bit of fun. Don't marry him, that's all. That's all I'm asking. Don't you see how different that makes things? Marriage gives him rights. It gives him a say, it gives him power — and if he has power over you, then to

240

some extent he has power over me. I don't trust him not to use it against me.'

'Jack,' I said firmly. 'You must get this idea out of your head that Max wants to harm you, it's only your own guilt that makes you keep harping on this theme of revenge. Max has changed. I can't explain to you in exactly what way, but the Max Claremont that came out of prison certainly isn't the one that went in. He just wants to forget all about it. He's suffered enough. Can't you at least make an effort to meet him halfway. After all, you were friends once ...'

'No, we wen't,' Jack said. 'I wanted to be, but' — he smiled bitterly — 'people like me don't have friends really, at least not male friends. Women are all right because they think they're safe, but men are inclined to shy away. They all think I want to seduce them as if being a homosexual deprives one of normal values like selectiveness and taste.'

Then he smiled his sweet Satanic smile. 'Has it ever occurred to you, Mother, that might be another reason why I don't want you to marry him? Perhaps I'm jealous. Perhaps I want him too?'

He just says these things. They don't mean anything. They're just reflections of his inner bitterness and pain. I'm trying to be patient, understanding and sympathetic. Obviously, it has all been the most terrible shock, and although he hasn't mentioned it yet, he must have considered the financial aspect as well. Except for his salary at the bank and the income from his shares, Jack has no real capital to speak of. Edward had left me his money outright and naturally Jack had always expected his father's fortune to pass to him when I eventually died. A husband upon the scene, especially one who was unlikely to predecease him, considerably reduced his expectations. I decided the fairest thing to do was to settle an immediate lump sum on Jack outright, but before I could put this generous gesture into practice, Jack stormed into my office at the bank and demanded with menaces what previously I had been perfectly happy to give.

'How much did you have in mind?' I enquired coolly.

'A third. That seems fair, doesn't it?' he sneered. 'Equal shares all round!'

'Now who's after my money?' I snapped.

'I'm entitled to it. Max Claremont's not.'

I stared at him. He looked untidy and seedy and reeked of brandy.

'To be perfectly frank, Jack, before I made a decision like that I should have to be completely sure you were in full control of yourself. Judging by your appearance and your manner, this is obviously not the case.'

'My God!' he screeched. 'You've got the nerve to talk about self control when for the last six months you've been sniffing round Max Claremont like a bitch on heat!'

I repressed the urge to slap him hard. 'That remark merely justifies everything I have said.'

'All right. I'm sorry. I didn't mean to say that.' He sat down and attempted a conciliatory smile. 'Let's stop talking tempers,' he said using a childhood phrase. 'I'm not being completely unreasonable, you know. All I'm asking is for enough capital to make myself independent.'

'You are independent. You've a more than adequate income if you didn't spend it all on gambling and champagne.'

'Oh, I see. I've got to drink Vichy water whilst you and Claremont guzzle yourself sick on Veuve Cliquot.'

'I'm sorry, Jack,' I said coldly. 'But as far as I'm concerned the discussion is at an end. I have absolutely no intention of handing your father's fortune out piecemeal, either to you or to Max or anyone else.'

'Don't put me in the same category as that conniving bastard,' he yelled. 'I'm your son and I've got a right to my father's money.'

'It's not your father's money now. It belongs to me. That was his wish, that I retained control of the bank and the estate for my lifetime. I'm afraid you'll have to wait until I'm dead.'

'Assuming that there's anything left by then,' he said bitterly. 'I mean, after your boyfriend's had his share.'

'Please don't be persistent, Jack. The answer is no.'

I rose to my feet and moved towards the door.

'It would be in your own interest, you know,' he called after me. 'Have you thought how unpleasant it's going to be having me hanging around at Eldon Square — the cuckoo in the love nest, so to speak. Of course, if I had any cash I could soon make arrangements to live elsewhere.

I turned to face him. 'Well, you're supposed to be a banker, Jack,' I smiled grimly. 'Negotiate yourself a loan.'

Of course, I feel even guiltier now. I was far harder on him than I had ever intended, and as always when I've made a particularly harsh decision, within hours I begin to renege. And he's quite right of course, his presence at Eldon Square will be decidedly *de trop*, inhibiting to say the least. So without actually capitulating to what seems to me like a very subtle form of blackmail, I have decided that when I get back from America, I shall do something for Jack. It will all be a *fait accompli* then and he'll have no choice but to become reconciled to the idea. After all, what else can he possibly do?

August 30th, 1927
I think it might be going to be all right after all. What promised to be a disastrous day has ended, if not in complete reconciliation between myself and Jack, at least on a hopeful note.

I made a bad start. I was late getting up, late for a board meeting; in fact, until my secretary reminded me, I had forgotten that there was one scheduled for today. That brought it home to me. So obsessed had I become with my emotional affairs, I had lost track of what else was going on.

I applied myself assiduously to the morning papers. There was no political news of any interest. Baldwin's government continued to snooze its way through its second term. Financially, things were livelier. The pound was still having a bad time, struggling for parity with the almighty dollar and the revalued French franc — the days were gone when we'd all made fortunes out of borrowing from France at two per cent and lending it on to Germany at eight — but the City was pricking its ears up at the news of a proposed merger between armament giants Armstrong and Vickers with a new share capital of £21 million. The index had risen a very satisfactory seven points.

Then considering myself adequately informed, I set off for

243

the bank, entering the boardroom ten minutes late.

I could see at a glance that Jack had already briefed them regarding my marriage to Max. Five pairs of male eyes swept over me in a swift furtive glance. I spoke into an embarrassed silence.

'Good morning, gentlemen. I'm so sorry to be late.'

I made my way to my usual place at the head of the table, only, to my utter amazement, to find it already occupied by a smirking Jack. This was very significant. By usurping my place he was usurping my power. The gesture implied that I had forfeited both my influence and status. Despite being the senior director and major shareholder, I had suddenly been relegated to a nonentity.

I said nothing. I wasn't going to make a scene — that was just what he wanted. I slipped quietly into a seat farther down the table. Whilst the minutes of the last meeting were being read, I scanned faces and judged reactions. there were four other directors apart from myself and Jack; Leonard Baines and George Holly had been on the board since Edward's time; Roland Keith and Alan Crowley were more recent acquisitions. None of them looked at me directly and I felt in the avoidance of their glances a diminishing respect. I felt I had confirmed their prejudice that women in business were not to be relied on. I wasn't Edward Rochester's widow any more but a foolish emotional woman ruled by her heart and the prospect of having a good time in bed.

I tried to concentrate on the business in hand. The main topic, of course, was the Vickers–Armstrong takeover and how the merger would affect the clients of the bank. Then for a while we discussed whether interest rates would rise in an effort to prop sterling against the franc. Officially, all exchange rates were fixed but Britain's insistence on clinging to the nostalgia of the gold standard allowed it to fluctuate when depositors moved their money around.

Then Jack coolly raised the subject of my proposed absence from the bank. Normally when I was to be away I gave him my proxy vote but I was so irritated by his behaviour that for once I demurred. 'You can cable me in New York if anything comes up. There's no reason why I can't vote from there.'

Jack's eyes dropped to the notes on his blotter. 'Very well,' he said expressionlessly. 'If that's what you want.'

The meeting broke up. The other directors muttered embarrassed goodbyes and drifted off. Jack rose to his feet and gathered his papers up.

'Sit down, will you, Jack. I have something to say.'

He hesitated and I thought for a moment he was going to defy me, then sulkily he subsided into his chair.

'Now I'm not going to say anything about your childish behaviour today except to warn you that next time I enter this room I shall expect to find that chair vacant.'

'Oh, I beg your pardon,' he said in a flippant tone. 'Actually, I didn't think you were coming in today, I thought you'd be too busy attending to your trousseau.'

'Jack,' I said heavily. 'Let's get one thing absolutely clear. My marriage isn't going to make any difference to things here at the bank.'

'You don't think so?' he cried, leaping to his feet. 'Well, that just shows how naive you really are. You saw their faces, didn't you? You saw how embarrassed and uneasy they were. Who's going to take you seriously now you've made a fool of yourself over a damn schoolboy.'

'Just remember that this *schoolboy*, as you put it, is a year older than you and if *he* isn't old enough to be treated with courtesy and respect then neither are you.'

'Oh, I dare say everyone will treat Max with courtesy and respect. After all, in money-making circles he's pulled off something of a coup.'

With an effort I kept my voice and expression cool. 'Why must you provoke me, Jack? Do you think it will make any difference now? Do you think I'll change my mind just because you don't approve?'

'No.' His own voice took on a calmer note. 'No, I don't think that. I've already accepted that Claremont has far more influence over you than I. That's what makes me so angry, that he's got you so tamely eating out of his hand ...' He looked at me with dark moist eyes. 'I thought I could help you but I see that I can't.'

Then he came round the table and, as if we were mere acquaintances, held out his hand. 'Well,' he said stiffly. 'I

245

don't suppose I'll see very much of you till you get back from America. I'm thinking of going down to Farnfield for a few days. I — er —' he gave a tremulous smile. 'I expect things will probably be easier for you if I'm out of the way.'

I swallowed. 'Yes. Yes, of course, I understand.'

He leant forward to kiss me. 'I hope you'll be happy, Mother. I really do.'

'Thank you, Jack,' I answered in an emotional voice. 'I hope I shall be happy too.'

September 4th, 1927, on board the *Atlantic Princess*
We were married two days ago in a quiet civil ceremony; an intensely private and unromantic affair with my secretary and my personal maid as the only witnesses. Max had insisted that everything be kept to the minimum; no flowers, no fuss, no reception, no guests — I felt like a pregnant housemaid being rushed up the aisle before the onset of labour.

We left immediately for Southampton. Max had arranged to meet Veronica and Sydney aboard the *Atlantic Princess*, the flagship of Sydney's luxurious transatlantic fleet which was due to sail that evening. That explained the rush but it didn't explain Max's furtive and secretive behaviour. He might have been a criminal fleeing justice. Of course — I reasoned with myself on the train journey down — I was being foolish and sentimental to expect hearts and flowers. After all, in our case marriage was a mere formality. But I couldn't help feeling disappointed. I was overcome with a sense of complete anti-climax. After all my heart-searching, all the mental agony I had gone through, the occasion had passed off without even a glass of champagne. It certainly wasn't a memory I was going to treasure.

We reached Southampton at six o'clock, just twenty minutes before the ship was due to sail. As we hurried up the gangway, Max took my hand. 'Now we're going to do it properly,' he said, smiling.

So three hours later I was married for the second time in the vast Grecian ballroom. A thirty-piece orchestra played the Wedding March as I walked down a red carpet on

Sydney Elsworth's arm to take my vows with all due ceremony before the ship's captain.

They say that in everyone's life, there is a single moment of pure happiness and as Max turned to look at me and I saw the expression in his eyes, I knew that this was mine and that whatever had gone before, whatever was to come, I would be sustained by this one perfect moment.

There followed a lavish reception, a thousand guests — the entire first-class complement. It was completely bizarre; I was being congratulated by hundreds of people I didn't even know. But Max had planned it like that, so the moment couldn't possibly be spoilt by the cynical looks of so-called friends.

We danced to a Strauss waltz. I felt about eighteen. I had never felt so beautiful or desirable in all my life.

Max smiled down at me. 'No regrets,' he whispered.

'No. No regrets. Not ever.'

September 6th, 1927.

We are now just a day out of New York, a smooth and luxurious voyage so far. Sydney has proved to be the most marvellous host. I have to admit that in the beginning I'd had mild reservations about the presence of two virtual strangers on what, after all, was my honeymoon. I had only known Sydney Elsworth vaguely, more by reputation than anything else. Veronica of course I knew — at least we were socially acquainted. I had always thought her vain, frivolous, empty-headed and selfish and, although I doubted that she cared enough about anybody except herself to have any strong opinions about my marriage to Max, I was prepared for a fairly luke-warm reception. I expected coolness, reserve, to be treated in a polite but off-hand way, so when I was faced with this smiling creature exuding friendship and warmth, I was completely taken aback. In fact, I found her behaviour quite inexplicable. Despite her overt friendliness I sensed that she disliked me. She seemed on edge in my company yet she made determined efforts to seek me out. I felt she listened to my conversations, that she was watching me, waiting — but of course, I hadn't the faintest idea what for.

Then on the third day out, we were alone together on the promenade deck. Sydney had taken Max for a tour of the ship, leaving Veronica and I to amuse ourselves till lunch. I was pretending to read but I found myself observing Veronica as she flicked disinterestedly through a copy of *Harpers*. And as I watched her so she watched me, discreetly of course, glancing away before our eyes should meet. I suppose my curiosity had originally been aroused by her very obvious efforts to ingratiate herself with someone who could mean absolutely nothing to her at all. I had already dismissed the idea of sisterly devotion, that she was trying to make things easier for Max. Veronica wasn't like that — in fact, I felt she was probably the most selfish person I knew. I also felt that she was weak, insensitive, her vision limited to an image of herself and her only interest was in things that could flatter that image such as clothes, cosmetics and jewels. I wasn't exactly a stranger to *haute couture* myself but Veronica could have made a Worth mannequin feel shabby. Her complete dedication to her appearance might have been laughable if she hadn't taken it so seriously herself. She ate very little; she didn't seem to drink — to preserve her faultless figure I presumed. One could imagine her going into a positive decline if she ever put on an extra pound. And yet, strangely enough, I didn't think she was either stupid or uninformed. Her knowledge was merely selective. She knew nothing about politics or world affairs. She didn't even know who the President of America was, yet she could reel off the names of every New York couturier of any importance. I sensed a kind of feral intelligence, a ruthless instinct for self-preservation ... I glanced towards her suddenly and caught her hard speculative eyes dwelling thoughtfully on my face.

'Veronica,' I said abruptly. 'Is there something you want to say to me?'

She turned her perfect *maquillage* towards me. 'No,' she said innocently. 'Why do you say that?'

'You seem anxious — ill at ease whenever we're together. Naturally, I wondered why.'

'Oh, it's nothing to do with you. I'm just bored, that's all. I hate being at sea. There's nothing to do, is there? Nobody to talk to except a lot of dreary middle-aged people all trying to

248

pretend they're still young.'

I raised an eyebrow, momentarily wondering if this was a subtle gibe at me. I decided not. Veronica was as incapable of subtlety as she was of tact.

'I'll be all right as soon as we get to New York.' She gave her brilliant and superficial smile. 'We'll have a marvellous time, won't we, Lydia? They say they have the most wonderful stores and salons that make gowns up in three or four days instead of weeks and weeks like it is at home. But I forgot. Of course, you've been before.'

'Yes, several times. My late husband Edward often had business in the United States. Usually, I went with him.'

'What's it like?' she asked eagerly.

'Oh, busy, noisy — everyone goes round at a tearing pace.'

She smiled. 'I shall like that. I like life to move at a tearing pace.' She fitted a cigarette into an amber holder. 'Sydney has promised we shall dine at Delmonico's. Have you been there, Lydia? Sydney says all the rich and famous people go to Delmonico's.'

'Well, it was some time ago, but yes, I've been, although I've heard it's never been quite the same since Prohibition. One can still get a drink but at a price. Apparently, they serve it in china pots and pretend it's tea which I suppose might be quite fun.'

She looked at me blankly. 'Prohibition — what's that?'

'The Eighteenth Amendment. It means the sale and public consumption of alcohol is prohibited.'

I was amazed at her reaction. A look of baffled fury crossed her face, then as she saw me watching her she tried to laugh. 'Yes, of course. I'd forgotten. What an awful bore.' She rose to her feet. 'Well, seeing as it will soon be forbidden fruit, I'm going to indulge myself in a cocktail before lunch. Won't you join me, Lydia dear?'

We had a cocktail, and another — then to my astonishment Veronica ordered a large pink gin. More astonishing still was its effect. She became gushing, intimate, exhibiting the embarrassing sentimentality that only alcohol could produce.

'I'm so glad you're here, Lydia. It's really quite wonderful

249

to have a friend — somebody I can talk to, someone I can trust. Of course, when Max first told me that he was going to marry you I had my doubts. I couldn't see how it could work, knowing the way Max felt about Jack. You see, I thought that every time he looked at you he would think about Jack — and when he thought about Jack he'd think about Helen and he'd end up doing something silly again. I'm just glad to see that I was wrong and that Max is going to be sensible after all.'

Helen and Jack! What did she mean? She obviously thought I knew a lot more than I did. I resisted the urge to ask questions. One usually learned more by listening and letting the other person talk.

'After all, there's no point in bearing grudges, is there? It doesn't do anything, does it? One can't alter the past.'

She looked at me enquiringly, obviously expecting me to speak.

'Well, no. I quite agree ...' I began hesitantly.

'I mean — do you really think Max has decided to put the past behind him? Has he said anything about his feelings towards Jack? One never quite knows with Max. I can't ever tell what he's thinking these days. You see, he was so fond of Helen — well, of course, we all were ...'

She broke off, flushing guiltily. I followed her eyes and saw Sydney bearing down on us with a thunderous expression.

Veronica's eyes narrowed to a vindictive gleam. 'Sydney, darling,' she called out. 'Do come and join us. We're having the most delightful time.' She gave a spiteful little smile. 'I've just been saying to Lydia, how remarkably clever you've been. What a wonderful idea, darling, hauling me off to New York, the one place in the world where I can't get a drink.' She tilted back her head and drained the dregs from her glass. 'A secret drinker among a nation of secret drinkers. Obviously you meant me to feel at home.'

She slammed the glass down on the table. 'You didn't have to, you know. I was perfectly capable of managing things myself.'

'So I see,' said Sydney dryly. 'The first time I leave you alone you manage to get drunk.'

250

'That's your fault,' she snapped. 'If you're going to treat me like an idiot than I'm going to behave like one. You shouldn't have interfered.'

She stormed off leaving Sydney and I standing together in embarrassed silence. 'I'm sorry, Lydia,' he apologised. 'I'm afraid ...'

'No, please' — obviously, by now I had grasped what was going on. 'I didn't realise,' I said awkwardly. 'I would have done something if I'd known.'

'Why should you know?' said Sydney with a painful smile. 'It's not something that I've wanted to advertise.'

'I'm so sorry, Sydney. How terrible for you.'

'It's terrible for Veronica as well. That's why she needs our help and support.'

'Well of course,' I murmured. 'If there's anything I can do.'

'That's good of you, Lydia.' He gave me a grateful look. 'I don't want to burden you with my problems but if you could keep an eye on her when I'm not around. I can't be with her all the time.'

'Yes. Gladly. I'll do whatever I can.'

He nodded. 'I'd better go and see to Veronica now. She's always upset when she's had a lapse.'

He left me alone with the confusion of my thoughts. So Veronica was an alcoholic. Well, that explained a lot but it didn't explain Helen and Jack. Obviously she'd been implying that they'd been more than friends, and there'd been other implications that I couldn't even bring myself to think about just yet. But at least now I understood her, why she was so keen that we should be friends. She wanted to know how things stood between my son and Max and she considered me to be a prime source of information. But why did she care so much? I hadn't got the impression that she and Max were particularly close. And then it occurred to me that Veronica wasn't frightened *for* Max. She was frightened *of* him and what she thought he might do.

I felt I had to say something. I couldn't just let the incident pass. So as we were dressing for dinner I forced myself to say as casually as I could: 'Max! Why didn't you tell me about Helen and Jack?'

251

He frowned. 'From that remark I presume that Veronica has.'

'Is it a secret then?'

'No. It's not a secret. Let's just say it's a complication to our relationship that I wished to avoid.' He shrugged. 'I didn't tell you because I didn't think it would be something you'd want to hear.'

'But you'll tell me now?'

'If you insist.'

'Yes, I do.'

'All right then. It's perfectly simple. Your son seduced my sister. She was pregnant with his child so naturally I expected him to do the decent thing. When he refused, I hit him — and well, you already know the outcome of all that.'

'Oh my God!' I couldn't believe it. That poor innocent child. 'You should have come to me,' I said quietly.

'You weren't there,' he said. 'And by the time you were, it was too late.'

'But afterwards. You should have told me. I would have insisted that Jack marry ...'

'My God!' He turned on me. 'You don't think I'd have allowed Helen to marry that ...' For an instant I felt the full force of his hatred. It blazed across the space between us.

'It's all right,' I whispered. 'You needn't be tactful. I know all about Jack.'

I sat down. I felt sick, ashamed, unbearably guilty as I faced the appalling truth that if all this had come out at the time of his trial he never would have gone to prison.

'Why didn't you say something? Why on earth didn't you tell everyone the truth?'

He laughed bitterly. 'Oh, I had some outmoded ideas of chivalry then. I wanted to salvage what family honour Hugo had left us. I wanted to protect Helen.'

'And so,' I said with an ironic smile, 'because Jack seduced your sister you thought you'd get your own back by seducing me!'

He gave me a mocking look. 'If I remember, it was you who seduced me.'

'Don't joke about it,' I whispered. 'It's too awful for that.'

I moved away from him. I needed space to think. Obvi-

252

ously, what I had regarded as a schoolboy scrap had a very real basis of enmity. The repercussions were infinite and I could understand now why Jack had been so afraid. I looked at Max. 'This is obviously what Jack meant when he talked about you wanting revenge.'

'Yes — and in a way he was right. That was all I did think about for a while. And then Helen died and it all seemed so futile. Then when I saw Jack again I realised it wasn't so much hatred I felt but a strange kind of pity. I realised that nobody could punish him more than he was punishing himself. All I had to do was stand by and watch.'

'And by marrying me, of course you guaranteed yourself a ringside seat.'

'I married you because I loved you and I loved you long before this business with Jack. I agree he's a problem. I'm never going to like him or trust him or respect him.' He knelt down beside me and took my hands. 'But it's easier living with him than living without you. Really, you must believe that.'

Of course I believed him. I have to believe him. The alternative is unbelievable, that my husband is using me as a weapon against my only son.

September 12th, 1927, New York
New York is impressive, even for the fourth time; a city of monolithic towers that plunge the streets into darkness at noon; a kaleidoscope of shining steel and glittering glass with here and there the odd Gothic or neo-classical surprise. Of course, I found changes. That's part of New York's fascination, that it is never still. The old money still inhabited Madison Avenue and the upper east side between Fifth Avenue and the Park. Fifth Avenue was still lined with brownstone mansions, fake French chateaux and renaissance palaces. The Vanderbilts were still there opposite St Patricks but Saks had moved across town from Herald Square and Tiffany's had opened up on the corner of Fifty-Seventh and Fifth. But the atmosphere is the same; primitive yet sophisticated, barbaric yet genteel. And Sydney fits in perfectly. What is considered *outré* in London is perfectly usual in New

253

York and attitudes to wealth and success are completely different. In America only the artistocracy of money really counts and by Dow Jones standards Sydney Elsworth ranks somewhere between a duke and an earl.

'I'm surprised you ever went back to England,' I remarked as we sat together in his elegant apartment overlooking Central Park. 'You're quite obviously considered to be somebody here.'

He grinned. 'Anybody with enough money is considered somebody in New York. It's being somebody in Mayfair that really counts.'

'So why did you go back?'

'Oh, various reasons. I guess I felt I had something to prove. Local boy makes good and all that. Besides I wanted a wife, an English wife, just like I wanted an English car.' He smiled cynically. 'So I went out and bought myself a Bentley and then I went out and bought myself a wife.'

'I'm sure that's not true,' I began to protest.

'Oh yes. Veronica and I are strictly business — on her side at least. I've never kidded myself that it isn't my bank balance she's in love with.'

'And is that enough?'

'It has to be, doesn't it? There isn't anything else on offer as far as I am aware.' He hesitated. 'Look, tell me to go to hell if you think I'm stepping out of line — but, well, you married a man much older than yourself ...'

'You mean, did I marry Edward Rochester for his money too?' Strangely enough, I wasn't put out by this question, which from anyone else I would have thought impertinent. I had decided, after all, that I was going to like Sydney. My first impression of the archetypal self-made man had been changed by his attitude of concern towards his wife. I felt that inside Sydney Elsworth, shipping millionaire and property tycoon, was a vulnerable and sensitive man.

'Well I don't deny that I married Edward to escape from impossible circumstances. I didn't love him, although in the end I grew fond of him. I suppose I was grateful to him for never demanding any more than I was willing to give.'

Sydney pulled a wry face. 'Gratitude! That doesn't give me a great deal to look forward to, does it?'

254

'You can't take other people's experience as a pattern for your own life,' I objected. 'The circumstances were quite different. I was just a young girl. Veronica is a grown woman. Besides, Edward was an invalid for most of our married life. Perhaps if he had been able to be a loving husband, I might have been able to be a loving wife.'

Sydney nodded. 'Yes, I see. Well, thank you for being so understanding, Lydia ...'

'Look, Sydney,' I said. 'Have you ever told Veronica how much you care for her?'

He looked embarrassed. 'Not exactly,' he said.

'Why on earth not? It might make all the difference.'

Sydney shrugged carelessly. 'Probably because I couldn't trust her not take advantage of the fact. You don't know her as well as I do. She's entirely without scruples in her own particular way. I don't think there's anyone she wouldn't exploit to get what she wants.'

'But do you know what she wants?'

'No — and I don't think she knows either. She likes to spend money, she likes to drink. She seems to need a constant supply of excitement and diversion. That's why she drinks, because it excites her, makes her feel that life is exciting.' He gave me a diffident smile. 'That's why I hoped that the two of you would be friends. Veronica needs a steadying influence, someone sensible ...'

I interrupted him, laughing. 'Sydney, I can't say that I'm terribly flattered by this image you have of me as a matronly chaperone. I quite like a little excitement and diversion myself. That's why I married Max.'

'Yes, but you're in control. You'd think a thing over before you'd take the risk. Veronica doesn't think. She just goes for things, head on, never thinking of the consequences.'

I smiled reassuringly. 'Well, I'll do whatever I can to help.'

'You've helped just by listening. It makes a real difference having someone to confide in.' He gave a diffident smile. 'Perhaps we could help each other. After all, we've got a lot in common, you and I. We're both rich, mature, cynics at heart and we've both married people we feel in the long run might let us down.'

255

I remember forcing a smile. It was amazing how much it hurt to hear that small, unacknowledged but persistent doubt actually put into words. It's easy enough to dismiss Celia Richmond's spiteful insinuations and Jack's hysterical accusations, but when the doubts are expressed by someone as astute and balanced as Sydney, well, naturally, it makes one think.

Do I really think that Max will let me down? Do I really believe that like Veronica he saw marriage purely in financial terms? Am I the victim of some novelettish plot of greed and revenge? Having stared that rather ludicrous possibility full in the face, I have dismissed it as being completely unreal. Real life isn't like that. Such psychological complexities couldn't be maintained. Nearer the truth perhaps is the simple fact that Max loves me, loathes my son, but not enough to wreck all our lives. An over-simplification perhaps but the only one I feel I can live with.

It seems my mature years have cast me in the role of family confidante — everyone, except Max, seemed to want to tell me how they felt. First Sydney, and then yesterday, Veronica metaphorically baring her breast.

We had been shopping. Whilst Sydney and Max toured Wall Street and paid their homage to the House of Morgan and the Rockefeller banks, Chase and First National, Veronica and I descended on Seventh Avenue. All morning we had trailed in and out of silk-panelled salons and perfumed boutiques, and despite my resolve to set a good example to Veronica, I squandered a small fortune on a Franklin Simon original and bought shirts and ties and sleeve-links for Max. Four hours and three thousand dollars later we staggered into the Ritz Carlton for lunch.

'Heavens,' I said without thinking, 'I could do with a drink.'

'Oh, I'm sorry,' I added instantly. 'What a tactless thing to say.'

Veronica's eyes narrowed. 'It's all right. I'm not as sensitive as that.' She regarded me unsmilingly 'I presume Sydney's discussed my little weakness with you.'

'Only because he thought I could help. He's terribly concerned, you know.'

'Well, yes, that's the trouble, everyone being so frightfully

256

concerned. It would be much easier if they minded their own business.'

She lit a cigarette and blew the fumes in my face. 'I presume you're the new watchdog — under instructions to make sure that I don't go anywhere near a drink!'

I drew a deep breath. I was trying very hard to get on with Veronica despite the fact that I found her personality tiring and her vanity a bore. But having had my patience stretched by four hours of inane conversation about clothes, cosmetics and whether we had seen Carole Lombard in Saks or not, I found myself replying with a definite edge to my voice;

'Veronica. As far as I'm concerned you can drink as much as you like. Providing you don't embarrass me by actually getting drunk.'

She flushed. 'I'm sorry. I shouldn't have snapped.' She gave me a vaguely apologetic smile. 'But really, you know, it's not as bad as that. I don't go reeling about in public. In fact, I never even get vaguely drunk when I'm out. It's just at home, whenever I'm bored or upset. It's a kind of escape, you see.'

'From what? What's so awful about your life that you need to run away?'

'Well, I suppose nothing now, at least, not much. But in the past, after my brother Hugo died — and then my engagement was broken off and we had to leave Blanchland.' Her voice trembled. 'Everything was so awful, you see. Max went to prison, and then Helen died. That's how it all started. I had a drink now and then just to make things seem better, otherwise I really couldn't have coped. Sydney doesn't understand that. He's not very sensitive to things like nerves and depression.' She flung me a defiant and tearful look. 'I've had a great deal to put up with, you know.'

'Yes,' I said soothingly. 'I can see that you have.' I paused as the waiter set down a plate of hors d'oeuvres. 'Veronica. I wanted to ask you. About Helen ...'

'Oh God! I don't want to talk about Helen, please. Max has already torn me off a strip for mentioning it to you. But how on earth was I to know he hadn't told you?'

I persevered with my question. 'Max said something about Helen expecting a child ...'

257

Her reaction was startling. She stared at me with an expression of guilt and fear. 'Well, I wondered,' I went on, 'did that have anything to do with the way Helen died? I didn't like to ask Max. It was obvious that the subject was painful to him.'

'And why shouldn't it be painful to me too? She was my sister as well, you know.' She glared at me with that curious mixture of anger and fear. Then suddenly her shoulders slumped.'I knew this would happen,' she whispered miserably. 'I knew as soon as he married you, the whole wretched business would keep on coming up.'

'What wretched business? Won't you tell me what happened?'

'I can't. Max said I wasn't to discuss it with you. And if he hasn't told you himself, then obviously he doesn't want you to know. I should never have brought it up in the first place. I don't even know why I did!'

Well, by now I had put two and two together and arrived at the sickening number of four. 'Helen died as the result of a miscarriage, didn't she, Veronica?'

She hesitated, then nodded. 'But please don't tell Max I said anything, Lydia. He still can't bear to talk about it. Promise me you won't tell him that you know.'

'Yes, all right,' I agreed. 'I promise.'

She smiled gratefully. 'After all, it's best forgotten about, isn't it, Lydia?'

'Yes.' I nodded — but how on earth do you forget about something like that? Max certainly hasn't.

October 12th, 1927

The inevitable has happened. Our first real quarrel — if that bitter tight-lipped exchange can be called quarrelling. It was about money, of course, my excess of it and Max's lack of it, something that was bound to crop up before very long.

We had been lunching with Sydney's American partners: Jefferson Breck, a Southern gentleman with a virtually unintelligible Louisiana drawl and a frigid Bostonian called Eric Gill. Veronica had excused herself and gone up to her room and I had the impression that I was expected to do the same.

258

Understandably I was nettled. I had never subscribed to the Victorian ideas of the ladies withdrawing and leaving the gentlemen to their port. I liked port too and though in this instance the port was purely hypothetical, I made it quite clear that it was my intention to stay.

After a mildly awkward pause, cigarettes were lit and a bottle of illicit French brandy appeared. Conversation turned to the speculative boom produced by the Federal Reserve's reduction of interest rates and how we were all going to make the most of it.

I listened with interest, waiting for the right moment to express my views. I felt perfectly qualified to comment. If Edward had taught me about anything he had taught me about money and I could add dollars and francs, multiply by yen, divide by Deutsch marks and give the answer in sterling. But it soon became clear that I didn't know about Sydney's kind of money. I didn't know about pool operators and loan sharks, bootlegging and bond washing — fifteen minutes into the conversation I was completely out of my depth.

'It's easy money,' said Jefferson Breck. 'With interest rates down there'll be millions of dollars looking for a home. There's going to be a big boom in margin lending. Investment trusts will be the hot sector. Goldman Sachs are already sniffing the wind. I think we should move while there's still a wide market.'

'We issue a million shares of common stock,' Gill explained. 'Take ten per cent ourselves at, say, a hundred and sell the remaining ninety per cent to the public at a hundred and four. This gives us an instant profit of around three million dollars. We then re-invest the capital in the shares of other corporations ...'

I was mentally formulating a few obvious questions when Sydney said: 'How about coming in on this one, Lydia? A hundred thousand buys in and I guarantee you'll have trebled that in the first six months.'

I raised a cynical eyebrow. 'As you're so certain of easy profits, I'm surprised that you feel the need to raise capital from outside.'

'I find that an extraordinary remark for a supposed banker to make,' said Eric Gill. 'I wouldn't have thought it necessary

259

to explain the common practice of spreading risk in any large commercial venture.'

I was instantly irritated. 'The way Mr Breck was speaking, there didn't appear to be any risk,' I commented dryly. 'Besides, it's not the risk I would object to sharing but the stigma attached to what seems to me a fairly dubious enterprise.'

'Dubious!' Gill exclaimed in a chilly voice. 'In what way precisely, Mrs Claremont?'

'Well, forgive me for speaking plainly — but I got the distinct impression that this was a venture to make a quick profit rather than to promote the growth of long-term investment.'

'Well, naturally,' said Gill coolly, 'we intend to make a profit. I'm sure that even English bankers occasionally stoop to that. Otherwise, the Trust will be run, as with any other bona fide concern, for the benefit of the stockholders, whoever they are. Our investment policy will be conservative; blue-chip corporations rather than speculative high yield.' He smiled condescendingly. 'We are financiers, not gangsters, Mrs Claremont.'

I returned his smile. 'Perhaps in America the two things are the same.'

There was a little silence in which the room temperature dropped at least ten degrees: then Sydney said; 'Don't condemn it out of hand, Lydia. Believe me, you'll be missing a great chance. Max seemed to think you'd be with us all the way.'

'I naturally thought you'd want to participate, Lydia.' Max regarded me with an impatient frown. 'It seems an obvious venture for someone with large capital reserves. With sterling the way it is, anyone with any sense will be looking around for areas of dollar growth.'

'That's kind of you, Max,' I said, coldly furious at his patronising tone. 'But I'm perfectly capable of handling my investments myself. Please don't treat me like a silly housewife who doesn't know what to do with her allowance.'

'And don't treat me like an office clerk who's forgotten his place. I don't work for Rochester's now.'

I sat out the appalled and embarrassed silence that

followed, restraining the urge to burst into tears. Then I said, unable to keep the emotion from my voice; 'If you'll excuse me, gentlemen ...'

I fled up to my room. By the time I reached it I had lost the desire to weep. I was just angry now; angry with Max, angry with myself for making such a mess of things. I had intended to demonstrate that women were as able as men in the financial arena whereas I had only succeeded in proving the contrary view, that women couldn't argue without becoming emotional.

I took a bath, powdered my nose and brushed my hair. When I emerged Max was sitting there immersed in the *Herald Tribune.*

I didn't speak. He didn't speak — and after fifteen minutes of awful silence I eventually gave in.

'I suppose you're waiting for me to apologise,' I said.

'For what?' He fixed me with his glacial Anglo-Saxon stare. 'For treating me like the office boy? Oh, that's all right. I'm getting used to that.'

I flushed. 'All right, I'm sorry. I shouldn't have said what I did — but you must know how I dislike being patronised.'

'I wasn't trying to patronise you. I was trying to persuade you that you were missing out on an extremely lucrative deal.'

'Well, perhaps if you had discussed it with me first, instead of letting me jump in at the deep end to be savaged by that shark, Gill.'

'Discussed it with you!' His voice rose to an incredulous note. 'Since when have we ever been able to talk about money without you getting a suspicious look in your eye?'

'You're talking absolute nonsense,' I argued feebly. 'I've quite often attempted to discuss my business affairs with you but you've always seemed to shy away. I assumed you didn't want to be involved.'

'Only because you've always made it very clear exactly whose money it is. I don't like being patronised either.'

'Max,' I said, adopting my 'talking to sulky children' voice. 'There are some things we're going to have to get completely clear. I refuse to be continually apologising about my money. I'm a rich woman ...'

261

'Oh yes, I know that.' He jumped violently to his feet. 'That's one thing I don't have to be reminded of.' He strode to his dressing chest and wrenched open a drawer. 'And just in case it did happen to slip my mind' — ceremoniously he emptied the contents out. Silk shirts, silk ties, jewellery, gloves — 'what do you think I am? A bloody gigolo?'

I found myself flushing, embarrassed and enraged at his sneering refutal of my gifts. 'Max. I've no intention of altering my lifestyle just because it offends your pride. At the risk of repeating myself, I'm a wealthy woman and I have every intention of enjoying that wealth, and if you're going to turn a perfectly natural gesture between husband and wife into something sordid ...'

'It is sordid. It's offensive as well. Don't you see how humiliating it is to be always saying thank you and never being able to do anything in return.'

'I don't want anything in return ...'

'That's not the point. The point is that I can't compete with you financially on equal terms. I don't care how much money you spend on yourself but I'd rather live within my means. You don't have to buy me, Lydia. I'm not a child to be humoured with presents and gifts. Surely you can understand that?'

'Yes, of course I understand,' I bit my lip. 'Look, Max, I've been thinking ...'

'I suppose you're going to suggest making me an allowance,' he said in a dangerously quiet voice.

'No. I wasn't going to suggest that. I was thinking more of a settlement ...'

'No,' he said flatly. 'I'm not going to fall into that particular trap. You still don't understand, do you? I don't want your money — in fact, I'd rather starve than touch a penny piece of Rochester money.'

'Well, there's no answer then, is there?' I shouted wildly. 'You'd better start making plans for divorce because the money isn't going to disappear just because I'm your wife. When you married me you married the Rochester money as well ...'

We stared at each other in icy rage then weakly I subsided onto the bed. 'Oh Max, this is ridiculous. Most people quarrel

262

because they don't have enough money. We quarrel because we've got too much.'

'I haven't got too much ...'

'All right,' I said briskly, before we set off down that road again. 'Let's forget that we're married. Let's talk like banker and client instead. You're interested in this idea of an investment trust? You'd like to go in with Sydney?'

'Yes,' he cautiously. 'But ...'

'Well, then — I'll advance you the hundred thousand dollars you need to buy the partnership bond — that's roughly about twenty-five thousand pounds. You pay me back over five years at two per cent.'

He was silent. Shaking a cigarette out of a packet he struck a match. 'Two and a half per cent,' he said shortly. 'That's the going rate. I don't want any favours.'

'Is it a deal then?' I asked, holding out my hand.

He took it smiling. 'It's a deal.'

December 2nd, 1927

The last week in New York and just the thought of returning to England casts an air of gloom. Time has flown, every day of our stay has held a new experience from the furtive excitement of drinking applejack in a down-town speak-easy to the rapture of hearing Rachmaninov play his new concerto at Carnegie Hall. Max doesn't want to leave either. Having seen the Manhattan and North River Investment Trust successfully launched and the stock rise by seven points after only three days of issue, he's naturally uneasy at leaving his investment in the impersonal, albeit competent hands of Breck and Gill. So as the time draws nearer for our departure we're all beginning to feel a bit tense. Christmas and England loom and one can't help wondering what sort of reception we'll get. Being married to a younger man hardly raises an eyebrow in New York, but of course in England it will be different, as everything is different.

I haven't heard from Jack. My only contact with England has been two rather impossible transatlantic telephone calls to my secretary confirming that all was well at the bank. I'm rather dreading it all really, the moment when he and Max actually come face to face. We're all bound to feel awkward and I suppose it will be up to me not to let the situation become embarrassing or unpleasant. Divided loyalties are something I have already anticipated and I realise that I shall have to be scrupulously fair. Whatever happens I mustn't take sides. I have to make it quite clear that I care for them both equally but in a different way. Am I being unrealistic to think that it's going to be quite as simple as that? However, there is no point in anticipating the worst when there's still a chance that things will turn out for the best. I have a little while yet, a few days more of normality and peace. I'll think about England then.

December 16th, 1927, Eldon Square

Oh my God! What a homecoming! I couldn't have imagined anything more dreadful if I'd tried.

We docked at Southampton yesterday morning. I'd telephoned ahead to Mellon to expect us about eight. I was completely exhausted. Vanity had precluded that I sleep on the train, so I was quite dead on my feet by the time we pulled in. All I wanted was a quiet supper, a small brandy and the next two days in bed, so that I was horrified when we arrived at Eldon Square to see the house ablaze with lights.

Mellon opened the door looking apologetic and outraged. 'I'm so sorry, madam ...'

I pushed past him into the hall and stopped, aghast. Balloons and streamers festooned the stairs; a hideous tinsel banner proclaimed 'Welcome Home'. Then the drawing room doors opened. We were enveloped in a wave of heat and noise. A jazz band played the Wedding March; people were grinning, calling out stupid things like 'Congratulations' and 'Good Luck'. It was so cheap, so ugly — I thought I was going to be sick.

Then Jack was there, smiling slyly, stooping to kiss my cheek. 'Ah!' he exclaimed loudly, 'the blushing bride!' He looked at Max who was pink with embarrassment. 'And the blushing groom, flushed from the exertions of the honeymoon, no doubt — though I understand that in this case it was a mere formality.'

264

I rushed blindly towards the stairs; I was aware of Max behind me, shrill laughter following us up.

'How could he?' I sobbed. 'How could he deliberately humiliate me like that?' I wrenched off my gloves, flung my furs onto the bed. 'Well, that's it,' I raved. 'That's the absolute end. I want him out of this house first thing in the morning. It's my house. I'm under no obligation to allow him to live here. In fact, I'm not going to wait until the morning. I want him out of the house now and his ghastly crowd with him.'

'Calm down,' said Max. I was amazed at his coolness. I knew from his eyes that he was livid, beside himself with rage and yet here he was, telling me to relax and go to bed and sleep things off. 'Just behave as if nothing had happened. The last thing you must do is order him to clear out.'

I glared at him suspiciously. 'Why are you so keen to keep Jack with us. I'd have thought that was the last thing in the world you would have wanted.'

'It is — but I want the alternative even less. Don't you see that this entire charade has been engineered to provoke a scene. He wants you to throw him out because he knows that when you've calmed down you'll feel as guilty as hell, and once he's got you feeling like that . . .'

He drew me into his arms. 'You've got to ignore him, treat him as if he were a badly behaved child. He'll either get fed up and toe the line or he'll leave of his own accord. Either way, you'll have nothing to feel guilty about.'

I was too tired to argue. 'All right,' I said meekly. 'But I don't think it will work.'

'Perhaps not,' said Max, kissing my hands. 'But we'll have been seen to have done the right thing, won't we?'

December 25th, 1927, Ansty

Christmas at Ansty — my feeling of doom escalated the moment I set foot in that vast Victorian sham, looking even more of a fake since its restoration. The first small annoyance was that Max and I were to be in separate rooms in different parts of the house. I was shown to the gilded Empire splendour of Waterloo whilst Max was banished to the Jacobean

265

gloom of Naseby. I felt it was signficant, as if the fact we were man and wife was to be completely ignored. And then before I'd even had time to unpack my things, my new mother-in-law invited me to take tea in her rooms.

I accepted with some misgivings. Although I'd known Ursula Claremont for more than fifteen years, I couldn't say that I knew her well. In fact, we had hardly more than a nodding acquaintance. I knew *of* her of course, and whilst what I knew didn't endear me to her in any possible way, I was determined for Max's sake to be sympathetic and understanding. I even thought that by some wild stretch of the imagination we might become friends.

'Mrs Claremont. Do sit down.' She gestured authoritatively to a nearby chair. 'Although I suppose I must call you Lydia as there are two of us now.'

'Please do,' I said, smiling. 'It does seem rather silly to be formal.'

She returned my smile with a visible effort and for a few moments we exchanged pleasantries in a bland but guarded way whilst each of us summed the other up.

Then she said in an almost friendly tone, 'You must forgive me for asking you here before you've had time to settle in — but your marriage to my son came as something of a shock. I felt we should get to know each other as soon as possible.'

'Yes, I'm sorry,' I murmured. 'It was inconsiderate of us not to have let you know.'

'Max has always been inconsiderate. That's why I admire your courage in taking him on. You must enjoy taking risks, Lydia.'

I watched her hands moving among the tea things — beautiful hands, small and dainty, nails buffed to a rosy sheen — for some reason I found their pale perfection quite chilling.

'After all,' she paused to enquire whether I took milk or lemon — 'I'm sure you're far too sensible to expect such an arrangement to last ...'

'Please!' I stopped her. 'If you've asked me here merely to make unpleasant remarks ...'

'Well, I'm sorry if my remarks give offence, my dear, but you can hardly expect any mother to be enamoured of the

266

fact that her only son has married a woman nearly twice his age. It's nothing personal, I can assure you, but as usual Max has overlooked his duty to his family. Since his brother Hugo's tragic death, it has become Max's responsibility to provide an heir, if not to the family fortunes, at least to the family name.' She smiled her supercilious and condescending smile. 'Forgive me for being indelicate, but it occurs to me that in the circumstances it might be an obligation he will find difficult to fulfil.'

I set my cup down with a surprisingly steady hand. I had every intention of ending this unpleasant conversation by rising to my feet and making a dignified exit. Instead, to my horror, I found myself arguing the point.

'Max doesn't want any children.'

'All men want children. That just proves to me that Max is still only a boy.'

She stood up with a smooth and graceful movement. 'I can see that you don't understand us, Lydia. We're an old family. My late husband's ancestor received his lands directly from William the Conqueror, you know. Our survival is important, at least to us. And whatever he might tell you, it's important to Max. At the moment other considerations have taken precedence, that's all. But one day, when it dawns on him that he's the last of the line, that when he dies the Claremont name will also die, then he'll want children, he'll want a son ...'

I stood up quickly. 'Now look here,' I said firmly. 'I understand you're upset. I understand that everything has been a tremendous shock but there's no point in making things more difficult than they are. Whatever your private feelings, I am your son's wife and that's the way I intend things should remain. After all' — I couldn't resist it — 'as a devout Catholic, you couldn't possibly approve of divorce.'

'Well, that's just where you're wrong, my dear. Not being of the faith yourself, you perhaps don't understand that a purely civil marriage such as yours is not recognised by the Church. In the eyes of Rome you rank as no more than my son's mistress, so if he were to divorce you in law, it wouldn't be seen as such by either myself or the Church.'

'And I presume,' I said icily, 'that you intend to try and

267

influence Max to take that course?'

'Oh, I have no influence with Max. He does as he pleases. But if, as I think he will, he comes to feel like that; when he eventually realises that he's made a mistake, then of course I shall let him know he has my full approval.'

I made the dignified exit I should have made a full ten minutes ago. 'My God,' I thought wearily as I trekked back to my room. 'What on earth have I let myself in for?'

The brush with Ursula Claremont has left a bad taste in my mouth — in fact I find the entire family mildly nauseating. I've always rather despised people who can't speak their minds; people like the Anstys who sublimate their emotions to the mistaken high ideals of good breeding and etiquette and make their points through sly and secretive asides. At dinner tonight — an entirely Machiavellian affair with such a deadly atmosphere that at any moment I expected one of us to slide quietly beneath the table, a jewelled dagger between the ribs. Everyone was fiendishly and exquisitely polite but it didn't take me long to work out that Felicity Ansty loathed her sister-in-law and that the feeling was mutual; that Gerard Ansty, having spent Sydney's cash, now resented him bitterly and blamed Felicity for allowing this upstart to buy his way in. Only on one thing did they seem united and that was in their antipathy towards me. One had to admire the way they both included and excluded me, all in a very understated English way. At first I was amused. It was hard to take any of them seriously. Felicity I saw as an archetypal member of the English county set; good blood, no brains and a passion for quadrupeds. Gerard seemed a perfect model of aristocratic apathy; pompous, cruel and stupid, whose idea of a good time was blasting around with a gun. And Ursula — insanely pious, elegantly vicious, of all of them she struck me as the most sinister and bizarre. Beneath that air of moral rectitude I suspected there was the soul of a Medici poisoner.

Of course, these are exaggerated first impressions, but even so, as a family I found them quite unique. Individually they might pass as merely eccentric but *en masse* they became a complete anachronism in the post-war world. Their situation was common enough; landed gentry fallen on hard times. What made the Anstys different, especially Gerard and Ursula, was an intensely obsessive temperament that was only one step from fanaticism, an obvious flaw in character that narrowed their perspective on life to the fulfillment of a single aim, in their case to preserve Ansty and their luxurious way of life with as little personal effort as possible. Religion, of course, accounted for a lot. Catholicism survives because it clings so tenaciously to the glory of its past and it was this combination of religious bigotry and social prejudice that kept the Anstys isolated from reality and firmly anchored in the pre-war Edwardian haven in which all a gentleman had had to do was think about his own pleasure. Naturally, this made them ripe for exploitation by men like Sydney, and just how thoroughly he had done so was explained to me by Max as we sat in the library drinking a nightcap of brandy and milk and mulling over the extraordinary events of the day.

It seemed that the Anstys, having borrowed vast sums from Sydney, now found themselves embarrassed as to the means of paying it back. Now Sydney had suggested completely wiping out the loan, putting a further twenty thousand pounds in trust for Russell and Philippa, the twins, on the condition that when Lord Ansty died, Sydney or his heirs would inherit the entire estate. In the meantime, he and Veronica would take up residence, *en famille.*

'It seems a bit hard on Russell and Philippa,' I observed.

'That depends on which point of view you take. I suppose, morally, you could say it was sharp practice on Sydney's part. But realistically, if it weren't for Sydney, all Russell would have stood to inherit was a crumbling ruin. The only real asset would have been the value of the land which is more than covered by the value of the proposed trust. Legally, Sydney could have acted very differently from the way he did. He could have forced the sale of Ansty as Rochester's forced the sale of Blanchland ...' He stopped. 'I'm sorry. I didn't mean to bring that up.'

'It's hardly the same situation,' I argued defensively, unwilling to let the insinuation of sharp practice hang in the air. 'With Sydney the inference seems to be that he deliberately engineered a state of affairs that he knew in the end would benefit himself, that he encouraged Lord Ansty to get financially out of his depth . . .'

'Like Jack encouraged Hugo!'

'That's not true,' I protested. 'Jack lent Hugo money because they were friends.'

'But that friendship didn't extend to extending the mortgage on Blanchland. My God, the bank couldn't foreclose quickly enough.'

'As a matter of fact' — I felt myself flushing guiltily — 'As a matter of fact it wasn't Jack who insisted on calling the mortgage in.' I turned and looked at him. 'It was I.'

'Yes, I know.' He smiled. 'I looked up the file when I worked at the bank. I just wondered if you'd admit it.'

'And what if I hadn't?'

'But you did, so the question doesn't arise. Anyway, I've told you before, I don't hold you or Rochester's responsible. It was Hugo's fault entirely.'

'That wasn't what you said just now. You blamed the bank for foreclosing . . .'

'Hugo was the catalyst. It was his inadequacy that started everything off.'

'But Hugo's dead,' I reminded him. 'You can't pursue a dead man, and as it seems obvious that you feel the need to take it out on someone, it does occur to me that I might be next in line.'

'It's not revenge I want, Lydia. It's Blanchland.'

Somehow I missed the emotion in his voice and went on in a brisk and practical way. 'But you have to be realistic, Max. Blanchland's gone. It's in the past. You have to forget all about it.'

'I can't,' he said quietly. 'I won't.'

I stifled my irritation. It was all getting rather tiresome, all these people with their ideas and emotions fixed in the past. 'It's just a house, Max,' I said peevishly. 'Four walls and a roof.'

He turned and gave me an incredulous look. 'Obviously you've never been to Blanchland. You haven't seen it, have you?'

'Well, no . . .'

He took my hand and led me out into the hall and stood me in front of a vast landscape painted in oils. 'There,' he

270

said proudly, as if he were showing me the palace at Versailles. 'Now say that it's just a house.'

I looked and saw — still just a house; ugly, disproportionate, inhospitable and cold. And then I saw Max's face and his expression of longing, and just for a brief moment I was able to see Blanchland through his adoring eyes. At least I saw its nostalgic splendour; I felt the fascination of its antiquity, the fatal charm it had exercised for hundreds of years. I felt its malevolence too. It wasn't a house to be lived in. It was a house to be possessed, squabbled and fought over ...

Then Max said softly. 'One day I'll get it back, I've promised myself that, that I shall live there again before I die.'

Suddenly, uncomfortably, I was reminded of his mother as he turned upon me the same obsessive gaze.

'And how do you propose to do that?' I said in a down-to-earth voice.

He shrugged, his eyes quiescent again. 'I don't know yet,' he said. 'But I'll find a way. If you want something enough there's always a way.'

I struggled through Christmas Eve, surviving a bishop to lunch and the enforced ritual gaiety of the dressing of the tree. Children came from the village in the afternoon and sang carols in the hall, then after dinner and a tense evening of piquet and bridge, we all trooped down to the chapel for Midnight Mass. I staggered out in the early hours of Christmas Day, stupified by incense, embarrassment and boredom.

'Oh God,' I muttered sacrilegiously. 'I could do with a drink.'

'You should convert then,' said Max cynically. 'That was a Laffite '89 in the communion cup.'

We went upstairs, giggling like children, then as we passed his mother's room, her voice rang out;

'Maxwell!' She appeared in the doorway, her breviary still in her hand. 'May I speak with you privately for a moment.'

Max hesitated. 'It's very late,' he said. 'Can't it wait till the morning?'

'I shan't keep you more than a few moments.' A pause,

271

redolent with pique and obvious displeasure. 'Of course, if it's too much trouble.'

I squeezed his arm. 'It's all right,' I whispered. 'I'll go on up.'

But I didn't go up. I watched Max go in and saw that he didn't quite close the door. I could hear their voices quite clearly.

'Won't you sit down, Maxwell? Perhaps I could get you something to drink? I always keep a little cognac here ...'

There was a chink of glasses. I moved closer to the door so that I could see her face. I was amazed at her change of manner, her conciliatory tone.

'I do apologise for the late hour,' she went on in a quiet and diffident voice. 'Although, in a way this might be an appropriate moment; the birth of our Lord, a new beginning — the perfect time perhaps to make our peace.'

Max remained silent, understandably stunned by the olive branch after days of mute disapproval and silent reproach.

'Of course, I had hoped that you would come and see me of your own accord. As *pater familias*, so to speak, there are obviously things we must discuss.'

Max found his voice. 'Such as?' he enquired.

'Well, this business between Sydney and your Uncle Gerard for one thing. You must talk to Gerard before things develop into a family feud. I hold no brief for Sydney Elsworth as you probably know, but as I warned Gerard that this was likely to happen, I feel he must face the consequences for disregarding my advice. The only thing to do now is to accept Sydney and Veronica's offer as graciously as he can and allow them to make Ansty their home with as little fuss and unpleasantness as possible.'

'Why don't you speak to Gerard yourself? You've always been perfectly happy to give the orders before.'

'Well, yes — when you were all younger and there was nobody else. But you are head of the family now, Maxwell. You're a married man — with responsibilities — ' she paused and I saw her smile — 'and speaking of your marriage, I presume you don't expect me to congratulate you! What I will say, however, is that I was hurt and distressed to learn of the event through the medium of the newspapers and the gossip of my friends.'

272

I heard Max fidgeting uncomfortably. 'Yes, I'm sorry,' he said shortly. 'I should have let you know but everything was done in rather a rush.'

Oh Max, you fool, I thought. What a plum line to feed her, and of course she came back, right on cue.

'Marry in haste, repent at leisure. I hope that isn't going to turn out to be true.'

Max stood up. 'It's not something I intend to discuss, so if that's all, Mother ...'

'No, it isn't all,' she cried. 'It is most decidedly not all.' She was on her feet too, pale with supressed anger.

'All my children have disappointed me, marrying out of their religion and class, but you have surpassed yourself, Maxwell, marrying a woman quite old enough to be your own mother, a woman who has no intention of giving you children, even supposing she still could ...

'You've always made a virtue out of perversity, haven't you, Maxwell? You've abused the privilege of a good family ever since you were old enough to speak. You were sent down in ignominy from university. Until you went into the army you couldn't hold on to a job — then more disgrace — prison — I thought you might have learned your lesson by then. But no! Your very last chance to redeem yourself by marrying decently and producing heirs to carry on the family name and you throw it away by marrying, of all people, Lydia Rochester.

'I can only assume you did so to punish me; to deprive me of grandchildren, to let the Claremont name die as everything else I have cared about has died.'

I heard Max laugh. 'My God! You can't possibly conceive a situation that doesn't include you, can you? I married Lydia because I wanted to, because I loved her, something else you wouldn't know anything about.'

'Love!' Her voice rose, shrill with passion. 'You don't even know the real meaning of the word. Love is pain and sacrifice. It's something that grows between people, not something that happens overnight. You're just infatuated by her. You desire her but that won't last. Your desire will wither as she will wither. And then what will you have to sustain you? No family, no son, no heir to the money you're so busy

273

making. And what about Blanchland? You're always saying that one day you'll get it back. What's the point if, after you, there are no Claremonts left to inherit it. To whom will you leave it? Veronica's children — if she ever has any! Russell! Philippa! Family, yes, but none who bears the Claremont name. You're the last, the very last....'

'And whose fault is that? I wasn't always the eldest son.'

I saw her smile. 'All right. It's Hugo's fault. Is that what you wanted to hear? But in Hugo's defence, he did at least leave behind him an heir. He left you, Maxwell. Is Hugo still to blame because you haven't the courage to shoulder your responsibilities either? It's too late for Hugo to make amends but its not too late for you.'

Max was silent. I pressed closer to the door. Why on earth didn't he say something? Why on earth didn't he tell her to go to hell? Unashamedly I applied my eye to the crack in the door. Suddenly I needed to see Max's face. I needed to see the expression of scornful pity and tolerance that would explain the silence that could so easily have been taken for acceptance of Ursula Claremont's point of view.

'I just wanted you to know, Maxwell, that as far as I am concerned, as far as the Church is concerned, your marriage is far from indissoluble. I just wanted to say ...'

I moved away then and went slowly up to my room. Whatever else she had to say I didn't want to hear.

I haven't said anything — what could I say without admitting to eavesdropping. And is there any point in making a fuss? I feel it would be a mistake to take Ursula too seriously. Of course, I'm irritated that my age and fertility should be subjects for open discussion but I'm not going to feel guilty because I can't measure up to the Catholic standard of being pregnant every year. Physically, I'm still capable of bearing a child but every month my chances of conception must diminish. And pregnancy at my age wouldn't be without risk. Really, it would be quite foolish even to think about it. But I am thinking about it, partly because Ursula calling my fertility into question has thrown out a challenge and it would give me great delight to prove her wrong — but mostly because of Max, because I can't help being aware that whilst Ursula ranted on about tradition,

274

family and heritage, Max was actually listening to her, as if what she was saying was relevant, important, as if she really had a point. Has she, I wonder? Did I dismiss the subject much too easily? Is Ursula right — will Max come to regret not having a son? Will he feel cheated, resentful ...?

I'd like to talk it over with Max. I'd like to ask him why he stayed whispering with his mother till the early hours of the morning; I'd like to ask him why he didn't tell her firmly that our marriage wasn't any of her damn business, why he didn't walk out the moment she hinted at separation and divorce. But I can't say anything without revealing the apalling fact that I listen at doors. I can see how easy it would be, living here in this grotesquely Florentine atmosphere, to acquire the habit of emotional subterfuge. After only a few days, I find myself not being able to be completely honest with Max. And that's all it takes, isn't it? One small secret, one small omission, one tiny deviation from the absolute truth and from there all the deceptions multiply.

July 17th, 1928, Eldon Square
I found another grey hair this morning — the sixth in all this week. It's inevitable I know. One can't defy the years any more than one can defy the law of gravity, but one hopes to delay them, slow them down. So every morning begins with a careful scrutiny of my complexion, a pore by pore search for the first ugly line. My mirror reassures me; skin still smooth, flesh still firm — on a good day I could easily pass for thirty. But youth is more than just perfection of figure and face. Youth is optimism, enthusiasm, recklessness and laughter, the confidence of knowing that with the whole of life ahead of you, you can afford to make the odd mistake. Age is caution and complacency, cynicism and self doubt. Age is a woman of forty-five staring desperately into her mirror mourning her lost youth ...

Oh my God, how trivial, how incredibly vain. I'm getting like Veronica and becoming completely obsessed with my looks — surely I'm far too intelligent for that? But perhaps all women, deep down, are secretly afraid of becoming old and ugly and unattractive to men. It's all our own fault, of

275

course. Once we had decided to make ourselves creatures of sexual allure by decking ourselves out in jewels and perfumed silks, we lost all hope of real equality with men. Once we allowed physical beauty to be the yardstick by which we were judged and left things like character, courage, honesty and endeavour to become the sole prerogative of men, we were immediately hoist with our own petard. To base one's power on something so flimsy, on something that must so inevitably fade, seems only to confirm the male prejudice that women, on the whole, have no brains. That's an over-generalisation of course. There are women, I know, who retain the beauty of a perfect bone structure well into old age but the masses have to rely on the fleeting prettiness of youth. Youth is beautiful in itself, a radiance of skin and hair, a brightness of the eye that can overcome the most unfortunate arrangement of features. But when youth is gone — and nature herself joins in the conspiracy here by setting a time limit on a woman's fertility, so that one has to contend with unpleasant phrases like 'the change of life' which seem to sound the death knell to desire and femininity. What will change, I wonder? Will I grow hairs on my chest? Will my voice deepen? Will I develop a total aversion for sex?

Of course, all this bitter cynicism is just a mood. I'm vaguely depressed that I haven't become pregnant. After so much soul-searching, after so much inner turmoil convincing myself that it was worth the risk, my failure to conceive is a complete anti-climax.

I'm not feeling on top form in any case. After three months of being the buffer between my husband and son, my sense of humour is wearing thin. Jack's behaving appallingly. He's drinking a great deal and his personality alternates between that of a vicious homosexual and an abandoned child. I'd never thought it would be easy, the three of us living together, all in the same house, but I had expected Jack to have toed the line long before now. Of course, I understood his strategy perfectly. His continued presence was a subtle form of blackmail meant to induce me to sign a big fat cheque. It was an option I'd been on the verge of taking a dozen times, but as Max says, once you give in to a threat you only expose yourself to the threat of being threatened again.

276

It doesn't help that Max is doing so well and seems to be making money at an alarming rate. But then everyone is making money on Wall Street these days. Sydney had been right. The stock market had taken off exactly as he had predicted. Every day millions of people are pouring millions of dollars into Wall Street; every day new corporations spring up to keep pace with the avalanche of money coming into New York. Investment trusts were the hot sell and Manhattan and North were at a five-dollar premium only three months after issue. The forecast is that dividends will be high. Unfortunately, this isn't such good news for the rest of us. The flow of funds out of Europe has led to interest rates being raised and so, inevitably, to a decline in investment, which has produced stagnation and poor profits at the bank. It's pure irony of course, that the events which have led to Max's sudden prosperity should be the cause of Jack's financial decline. I feel that Max exploits the situation with a certain relish, mildly provoking Jack whenever he can. It's the pretence of amiability that I find so unnerving. Raised voices I could deal with and I find myself longing for a good, clean row. But all conversations between them are conducted in polite gentlemanly tones.

At breakfast yesterday morning:

'I see that Wall Street's taken off again after that little set-back last month,' observed Jack looking up from the *Financial Times*. 'The Dow Jones is up 69.'

'Oh, it'll go higher than that,' Max said confidently. 'This is going to be the share boom to beat all share booms, and if you've got any spare cash I'd certainly advise you to put it in.'

Jack smiles with sweet malevolence. 'Really!' he exclaims. 'Unfortunately spare cash is a bit of a problem with me and as I haven't got your propensity for scrounging ...'

'Oh, I wouldn't say that,' counters Max with mock earnestness. 'In fact, I'd say that importuning was almost instinctive with you. You're just not very good at it that's all.'

'Well, I haven't had as much practice as you, my dear chap — nor do I have the same means for repaying the considerable sums you extract from my mother. In my case it would be regarded as incest.'

277

I leave them to it at this point and go up to my room feeling sick and angry but knowing it would be pointless to interfere. Then Jack corners me the moment Max is out of the house:

'I knew it. You've been giving that swine money, haven't you? All right, I want to know. How much has he had?'

I looked at him coldly. 'It isn't Max who's constantly badgering me for money. It's you.'

His fine white skin turned an ugly crimson. 'Well, he doesn't have to badger you, does he? You obviously can't wait to hand it out. And don't bother to deny it. I'm not a complete fool. You don't just walk into a partnership with a man like Elsworth. So where did he get his capital from?'

He grabbed my arm. 'You gave it to him didn't you. You gave him the money to buy himself in but you won't part with a penny for your only son.'

'I didn't give it to him,' I answered calmly, shaking him off. 'I loaned it to him in a perfectly business-like way. If you want to know all the details, I loaned him twenty five thousand at two and a half per cent, most of which, I might add, he has already paid back. Now, are you quite satisfied? Is there anything else you want to know?'

'Yes, there is. How long had you been married before he asked you to cough up?'

'He didn't ask me. I offered to back him ...'

'But you won't offer to back me,' he cried furiously. 'I could be making money too if I had the capital. I suppose I'm not a good enough risk. I'm just your son, aren't I? Your own flesh and blood. You don't have to worry about buying me, about keeping me sweet ...'

'Shut up,' I said quietly. 'I won't allow you to speak to me in that filthy way.'

'Oh, that hurts, doesn't it? That really touches you on the raw.' He leered at me unpleasantly. 'My God. He must be an even bigger marvel in bed than he is on the exchange. Because that's really where he makes his money, isn't it? Doing his duty between the sheets?'

That was the final straw. I made up my mind that he could have his damn money just so long as he left me alone. I just couldn't cope with this grotesque *ménage à trois* any more

278

and, although I hated to admit defeat, I couldn't see any point in risking my sanity just for the sake of principle.

I tackled Max the minute he entered the house.

'I see,' he said thoughtfully. 'So you're going to give in — just like that?'

'I don't see it as giving in. I was going to make a settlement on him in any case. If he hadn't been so stupid as to try and force my hand . . .'

'Well, that's it, isn't it? Force is what we're really talking about. You're going to allow him to impose his will on you when what should be happening is the exact reverse. He's attempting to blackmail you financially and emotionally, and if you give in now then you're giving him a licence to make any demands he likes. You'll be setting a precedent that will operate for the rest of his life. Behave badly enough, be unpleasant enough, and in the end people will give him what he wants.'

'You're quite unpleasant towards him yourself sometimes, Max. That dreadful episode at breakfast this morning all blew up because you taunted him about his lack of money.'

Max raised his eyebrows. 'Taunted him! I made a perfectly innocent remark advising him that if he had any spare funds, the U.S. market was the place they should be. Why shouldn't he have spare funds? He has a perfectly adequate income — or he would have if he didn't squander it standing treats to his rather unsavoury friends. And that's another very good reason for not letting him get his hands on any amount of cash. How long do you think it would last among that questionable crowd he's been hanging about with lately? Frankly, Lydia, it's in Jack's own interest to keep him financially dependent until he's proved that he's grown up enough to handle a grown-up situation like his mother marrying again. Once he's proved he can be sensible, well, you can think again.'

I didn't speak. These were old arguments, at least to me. He wasn't saying anything I hadn't already thought of. And he made it all sound so reasonable, as if we were discussing a small child's demand for an extra bag of sweets instead of a grown man's financial independence.

'You've just got to be patient, that's all,' Max went on.

279

'You've got to be strong because you know that Jack is weak. Don't give in till he's got all this stupid resentment out of his system. Make it quite clear that, however hysterical or unpleasant he gets, he can't control your life.' He smiled as he slipped his arms round my waist. 'Sorry darling, but you've just got to persevere.'

So I persevere. I continue to be sweetly patient, understanding and supportive towards Jack. I continue to mediate, soothe, make allowances, reassure ... I sense that Jack is getting desperate, that sooner or later he's going to do something stupid and rash.

July 23rd, 1928

George Hollywell came to see me today. George is bald, cautious, unimaginative and staid. He had been a close friend of Edward's besides having been on the board for twenty years. His firm have been the bank's accountants for over thirty.

'George!' I exclaimed as Mellon showed him in. 'What a pleasant surprise.'

'I'm sorry to bother you at home, Lydia, but well, I wanted to speak to you privately.'

'That's perfectly all right, George. I'm always pleased to see you. Sit down, won't you? Can I offer you a drink?'

'Thank you, Lydia. You're very kind — but I'll say no, if you don't mind.'

My smile became a little less welcoming at the tone of his voice; embarrassed, apologetic, redolent of bad news. Obviously this wasn't a social call.

'How can I help you, George?' I sat down and awkwardly he followed suit. 'Is there something wrong?'

'Well, I hope not, Lydia. Probably it's nothing.' He forced a laugh. 'You know what sticklers for detail we accountants are. I'm sure there's a perfectly simple explanation.'

'For what?' I enquired in an apprehensive voice.

'Well, as you probably know, we began the bank's yearly audit this week and I've always made a point of doing your personal accounts at the same time. Well' — he opened his briefcase — 'as I was going through your cheques and receipts, I came across these; three cheques, all for cash, totalling three thousand pounds — all signed, Lydia Rochester.'

He laid the cheques on the table before me. 'It was the last cheque that caught my attention — dated as you can see after your marriage, so really it should have been signed Lydia Claremont. And well, of course, the date as well, September 10th, when actually you would have been in New York. Of course, I realise that there's nothing illegal involved, for according to the bank staff, it was Mr Rochester who cashed the cheques himself ...'

I stared at the cheques, at the signatures particularly. They were very good forgeries, almost perfect in fact, but how stupid of Jack to make such an obvious blunder. I really couldn't think what to say.

George helped me. 'I was wondering if perhaps, before your departure for the United States, you'd given Jack the cheques already signed to be cashed at his convenience in your absence.'

'Yes, of course,' I said, without meeting his eyes. 'I remember now. That's what happened.'

'Yes, I thought it would be something like that but I thought that I'd better bring it to your attention.'

I smiled with difficulty. 'Yes. Thank you, George, for letting me know.'

We both rose to our feet, both relieved that the interview was over. I walked with him to the door and, still without looking at him, held out my hand. 'Goodbye, George — and thank you again.'

I stood for a moment, collecting my thoughts, then I said; 'Mellon. Would you telephone the bank and ask Mr Rochester to return home straight away. Emphasise,' I added, 'that it's urgent.'

He looked guilty the moment he walked into the room.

'Jack,' I said without preamble, 'George Hollywell came to see me today. I presume you know what about.'

At first he tried bluster. 'Why on earth should I know? I'm not clairvoyant.' He shrugged. 'Probably some triviality he's managed to get himself worked up about.'

281

'If you consider theft a triviality, which with your casual attitude to other people's money I dare say that you do.'

'What do you mean by that? Now look here, if you're accusing me ...'

'Yes, I am accusing you — I'm not quite sure what the correct term is; fraud, forgery or just plain theft, but, whatever the form, it comes down to the fact that you have relieved me personally of three thousand pounds. Now, please Jack, no more displays of injured innocence.'

Then he went on the defensive; 'All right then? What if I did? If you weren't so bloody-minded about money I wouldn't have to resort to doing things like that.' He flung himself down aggressively in a chair. 'I'm entitled to it. After all, there's Max making money hand over fist. I just indulged in a bit of speculation myself but unfortunately it didn't come off.'

'Max speculates with his own money,' I reminded him coldly.

'Well, that's rich,' he yelled. 'That's bloody rich. His *own* money — when you've admitted that you lent him twenty five thousand. In my book that makes it your money.'

'Max has paid it all back and with interest I might add. Max is able to speculate successfully, you see. He makes money instead of losing it.' I gave him a look of bitter contempt. 'It doesn't seem that there is anything you are capable of doing with reasonable competence, not even, it seems, being a thief.'

He gave in then, burying his head in his hands. 'Oh my God,' he whispered. 'This is the bloody end. I suppose you're going to tell Max, give him something else to crow about.'

'No,' I said calmly. 'I won't tell him — at least I won't if you tell me the real truth. I can't believe that you could stoop to something so despicable without a very good reason.'

He smiled faintly. 'Well, thank you for that, at least — and yes, I did have a very good reason although you'll probably find it even more despicable.'

He stood up and went to stand by the fire. 'I didn't really have any choice, you see. I had to get the money from somewhere. I couldn't ask you outright so I had to resort to, well, helping myself. I had obligations you see, outstanding debts.'

'Gambling debts.'

'No, not exactly.' He gave a choked laugh. 'I was indiscreet, shall we say, with a gentleman I met a few months ago, apparently by chance in a bar. I was drunk of course and it later turned out that the encounter wasn't quite so fortuitous as I had previously thought. There are photographs apparently — not very flattering.' He smiled weakly. 'Not the sort of thing that's likely to get one on the front page of *Country Life*.'

'Blackmail!' I whispered. 'Oh my God! How could you have been such a fool?'

He laughed shakily. 'Well, yes. I was rather thinking along those lines myself, especially when I received a demand for ten thousand pounds in exchange for the negatives. Of course, I didn't have it, nowhere near, so I've been paying at the rate of five hundred a month to keep my little idiosyncracy out of the public eye and myself out of Wormwood Scrubs.'

I was silent, waiting for the feeling of shock and horror to subside and yet wasn't this something I'd been expecting for years?

'This person,' I said carefully, 'the person you give the money to, is he ...?'

'My partner in crime?' Jack said mockingly. 'No. I've never seen him again. I presume the party I deal with is the man behind the lens, the Cecil Beaton of the *demi-monde*. His name is Sudely or at least he says it is.'

Our eyes met and suddenly all his bravado dropped away. 'I'm sorry,' he said quietly. He came and knelt beside me and took my hands. 'I'd have done anything to have spared you this.'

'It's all right,' I murmured, registering his contrition with only half my mind. I was more conscious of my own reaction, at the tenderness I felt when I should have been feeling rage and disgust. I had hated Jack, despaired of him, sometimes I'd even wished that he'd never been born, yet the moment he was threatened, I reacted with all the primeval fury of a tigress defending her only cub. 'It's all right,' I said again. 'You needn't worry. From now on you can leave everything to me.'

283

It was exactly what I needed, a fight, a challenge, an antidote to my introspective and self-pitying mood. Psychologically, nothing could have been more perfect. I've always had a weakness for the underdog. I'm always the first to wave the flag for a hopeless cause. I'm the kind of person who finds far more gratification in being needed rather than loved. Edward had needed me so it had never occurred to me to let him down. Max had needed me once but now I suspected he needed success more. But Jack needed me now and I wasn't going to fail him, so three days later, after withdrawing seven thousand pounds in used notes from the bank, it was I who set off instead of Jack to keep a rendezvous with a despicable blackmailer.

I had expected some sleazy underworld character so I was surprised when this well-heeled, well-educated young man turned up. He was surprised too. He had expected Jack and he was sliding into the front seat of the car before he realised it was a woman at the wheel.

'I beg your pardon,' he said, raising his hat. 'I was expecting a friend who drives a similar vehicle.'

'Your friend, as you put it, happens to be my son. Please get in. From now on you're going to have to deal with me.'

He got in reluctantly. I felt his unease. 'Well, Mrs Rochester, I don't know if your son has made the terms of our arrangement clear to you?'

'Have you got the negatives?' I said crisply. I drew an envelope from my bag. 'I understand the asking price is ten thousand pounds — less the three thousand you've already had.'

'No, at least not with me. I don't carry them around.

'I could get them though,' he added as he saw me replace the envelope in my bag. 'If you wouldn't mind waiting. I shouldn't be more than ten minutes at the most.'

I nodded and he slipped quickly from the car and, with his departure, my courage departed too. I suddenly realised what an unenviable position I had placed myself in; alone in the dubious security of the car, alone in a strange and seedy neighbourhood, having foolishly revealed myself to be in possession of several thousand pounds.

I locked the car doors and glanced nervously at my watch. Ten minutes he had said and he'd been gone for fifteen already. I should have let Jack come as he had wanted to, except that I hadn't trusted him to be firm and businesslike — and yes, I had to admit it, there had been this very small doubt at the back of my mind that it might be one of Jack's fantasies; an ingenious ploy to get himself out of trouble and make a tidy profit of seven thousand pounds as well. Of course, I felt immeasurably guilty now ...

I was startled by the sudden rattling of the door. 'A wise precaution, Mrs Rochester. I should have suggested it myself. One can't be too careful these days.'

I held out my hand for the small manilla envelope he withdrew from his inside pocket.

'Money first, Mrs Rochester. That's the way these things are done.'

Reluctantly I handed the money over. After a quick glance inside he put it away. 'I won't insult you by counting it. In my experience bankers very rarely make mistakes — of a financial nature, that is.'

He laid the manilla envelope on the dashboard of the car. 'You're a very brave lady, if I may say so, Mrs Rochester. Not many women would venture out at this time of night alone, especially on such an errand.' Then he nodded towards the envelope which I had made no attempt to pick up. 'Shouldn't you check to make sure that what you're paying for is there? Perhaps you're not quite so brave as that. I must admit that they're not the sort of thing I'd care for my mother to see.'

I turned and looked at him. 'Well, if they're not there, Mr Sudely, you'd better watch out. I have paid you under protest in any case, so should there be any further demands, I can assure you they won't be met. It may interest you to know that my son has no money of his own, so should you continue to threaten him, he'll have no choice but to come to me, in which case I shouldn't hesitate to inform the police.'

He smiled unpleasantly. 'Do you know what the term of imprisonment is for sodomy, Mrs Rochester?'

I returned his smile. 'Yes, I do, Mr Sudely. About a quarter of what it is for extortion.'

285

He inclined his head. 'I take your point.' Then he opened the car door and raised his hat. 'Goodnight, Mrs Rochester. It's a pleasure to have done business with you, if I may say so.'

'So where do we go from here?' I said, after we had ceremoniously burnt the evidence in my sitting room fire.

Jack shrugged. 'I don't know. We carry on, I suppose.'

'Yes. But not in the same way. This has to be a turning point, wouldn't you agree?'

I regarded him with a stern and protective air. Having rescued him from the clutches of the odious Sudely, I didn't intend that he should fall into the same trap again. 'Don't you agree?' I repeated as he remained silent.

'Yes, of course I agree. But what do you want me to do?'

'Well, I'm not sure yet. It's something we're going to have to talk about — your ...' I paused awkwardly.

'Hellenic tendencies,' Jack supplied. 'It's a bit late for delicacy, isn't it?'

'Well, let's call it your problem then, for want of a better word. Isn't there something that can be done, medically I mean.'

'It's not a bloody disease,' Jack snapped. 'I can't take pills for it, if that's what you mean.'

'Please don't be aggressive, darling,' I said with a patient smile. 'I'm only trying to help, you know.'

'Yes. I'm sorry. Forgive me. It's just that it's not something I find easy to talk about.'

He lit a cigarette and sat fiddling with the spent match. 'I can't really explain — but to me, to people like me, we don't actually feel we're doing anything wrong. It seems perfectly natural to us, you see. It's only indecent because everyone else says that it is.' He gave a twisted and bitter smile. 'And don't think I haven't tried to find — well, not a cure, but a way of controlling it, you know. I even thought of becoming a priest once. Enforced celibacy seemed the only way of resisting temptation.'

'Perhaps if you married,' I suggested. 'Perhaps if you made a real effort to form a physical relationship with a woman ...'

'Well, I tried that with Helen, with absolutely disastrous results ...'

'Yes, I know — but at least it proves that with the right woman in the right circumstances, you could behave conventionally.'

He shook his head. 'It doesn't work like that. It might have worked with Helen. She was very special, you know. The ironical thing is that I really cared for her.'

'Why didn't you marry her then, when Max asked you to?'

'I don't know,' he whispered. 'Bad timing I suppose. I was so shocked when she told me she was pregnant. I got cold feet. I saw myself being forced into something I wasn't sure that I wanted. It wasn't so much that I didn't want to marry her but I didn't want to be forced to marry her. I didn't really know what I was saying when I suggested that she get rid of the child. I didn't realise the implications. I thought one just took a pill or something and it all went away. And then Max turned up. Of course, by then I was filthy drunk. I made everything worse. I told him everything, about Hugo, about Helen ...' he covered his face with his hands. 'If only he hadn't arrived just then. If only I'd had time to sober up and calm down a bit. Of course, I'd have married Helen. I loved her.'

'But afterwards,' I said gently.

'After he tried to kill me, you mean? I couldn't think of anything then but my own pain and terror. Yes, it was cowardly I know, but I'd never been so frightened of anyone in my whole life. I thought he meant to come back and finish me off. I thought I'd be safe if I had him arrested. And then of course, I realised, that still wouldn't stop him broadcasting to all and sundry that I was a pervert and a queer. I had to get in first, I had to have something equally damaging to throw back in his face so I invented that ridiculous story about him cooking the books.' He gave a bitter laugh. 'And then, after all my precautions, he didn't say a word. I waited but nothing happened.'

'Then why didn't you withdraw the charges when you saw he was going to remain silent?'

'I thought it was a trick. I thought he was just waiting to wriggle off the hook ... And it wasn't as easy as that. The police were involved. I couldn't admit to what had really happened, could I? I just played things down as best I could

287

and let the charges be reduced to the very minimum. But I still thought it was a trick, that he was going to denounce me in court, that he was just waiting for the biggest and most impressive audience. That's why I said I was too ill to attend. I just couldn't face being there when the truth came out. But it didn't come out. He didn't say anything after all. But that only made it worse. It meant that I owed him something ...'

'He didn't do it for you,' I interrupted. 'He did it for Helen.'

'Well, I know that — but that just made me feel even more inadequate. It meant that he was strong and I was weak. Oh, but I swore to make it up to him. I promised myself that when he came out of prison ...' his voice died away. He looked pale and ill. 'And then Helen died and I knew it was the absolute end. I knew he'd blame me — and why not? I blamed myself, my God, how I blamed myself ...'

'Jack, listen to me,' I said urgently. 'This is mostly in your own mind. You don't know what Max feels because you've never asked him.'

I took his hands. 'You're going to have to talk to Max, talk to him as you've talked to me.'

'I can't,' he said weakly. 'And anyway, it wouldn't do any good. He'll never forgive me, I know that.'

'You don't know that. To be forgiven you must first admit that you've been at fault. Confession has to come before absolution.

'Talk to him,' I urged. 'Speak to him as you've spoken to me. It's time this thing between you was brought out into the open.'

'All right,' he agreed reluctantly. 'But not just yet. I feel so done up by everything that's happened, I couldn't face another trauma just now.'

'Very well. I'll leave it to you to choose your own time — but it has to be said, Jack. I want you to promise ...'

'Yes, all right. I promise.' He rose to his feet and made a nervous movement with his hands. 'I don't suppose there's any chance that we could get away somewhere for a week or two. Just the two of us, you know, like old times.' He smiled diffidently. 'I just feel I'd like to get away from the town. Farnfield or somewhere. Perhaps we could go there?'

I looked at him with compassion. I could see he was quite devastated by the whole affair. I could understand now how traumatic and wretched the last year must have been; how threatened he must have felt by my marriage.

'All right,' I said, smiling. 'After all, why not. I'll speak to Max first thing in the morning.'

'Darling,' I said to Max as we drank our breakfast coffee. 'Would it put you out at all if I took Jack down to Farnfield for a week or two?'

Max looked up from *The Times*. 'Why? Is he ill?'

'No — at least not in the way you mean. I just think he could do with a change. He seems rather nervy and run down lately, that's all.'

'Oh, for God's sake, Lydia,' Max scoffed. 'Jack's got nerves of high tensile steel.'

'I don't agree,' I said defensively. 'Jack's very sensitive and highly strung underneath. He just tries to hide it, that's all.'

'Well, he's certainly made a good job of hiding it from me. Anyway, it's out of the question, as I promised Sydney we'd go down to Ansty for the start of the grouse on the twelfth. He's arranged a shooting and house party of about thirty guests, and as it's his first real social bash since he and Veronica moved in, I rather think he needs me to hold his hand.'

'I didn't promise him,' I pointed out coolly. 'You'll have to go without me if you can't put Sydney off.'

'Lydia,' he looked at me, frowning. 'Why are you making such a ridiculous fuss? I'm not going to let Sydney down at a moment's notice like this, and it will certainly look odd if I turn up at Ansty without you. Besides, I would have thought the last thing you wanted was to be incarcerated at Farnfield alone with Jack. A month ago you couldn't wait to get away from him.'

'Things have changed,' I said carefully.

'Since when?'

'Since he apologised to me for being so unbearable. We had a long talk and he's promised me that he's going to turn over a new leaf.'

'And you believe him, I suppose,' Max said scornfully.

289

'Well, that's up to you, of course, but I still don't see why you need to take him down to Farnfield as if he were some ailing girl. Don't fall for it, Lydia. This is just another of his publicity stunts.'

'I didn't realise,' I said coldly, 'just how hard and unfeeling you actually have become. Surely you can see how emotionally drained he is?'

'Quite frankly, Lydia, all I can see is a very clever young man who, having tried every other means to come between us, is now trying the "sick little boy" routine. Now, I've never tried to dictate to you before, but I'm afraid I'm going to insist that you come down to Ansty . . .'

'All right then,' I agreed with an icy smile. 'But if I come to Ansty, then Jack comes too.'

He stared at me in silence. 'Are you serious, Lydia?' he demanded at last.

'Yes, why not? You expect me to be pleasant to your family whether I like them or not. Well, they can be pleasant to mine for a change.'

'You do know that possibly my mother might refuse to receive him? You must know how she feels about Jack.'

'No, I don't,' I cried hotly. 'How would I know? She never talks about it. You never talk about it. None of you ever say exactly what you think. My God, you're not even honest with one another.'

Max fixed me with his cold cruel eyes. 'I wish I had your courage, Lydia. You're quite fearless when it comes to saying what's on your mind.'

'So were you once,' I reminded him.

'Yes, and look where it got me — six months in gaol. I just listen now and let fools like you do all the talking.'

August 17th, 1928, Ansty

We drove down to Ansty on Saturday the 11th; Max and myself sitting in strained silence in the front of the car, Jack pale and penitent in the back.

I could see that Jack's invalid appearance irritated Max. Several times he spoke to him unnecessarily sharply. He was even more irritated by Jack's meek replies; his eternal apologies for being a nuisance, getting in the way and so on. It crossed my mind that he was overdoing it a bit but I just hoped that in an effort to be on his best behaviour he was leaning too hard the other way.

However, we reached Ansty without incident about four o'clock. There were other guests which diffused the sensation of Jack's arrival. Lord and Lady Ansty were excrutiatingly polite, and though there was a nasty moment when Jack and Ursula Claremont came face to face I thought on the whole it went off very well.

Then, as I had feared, Max had a fit of temperament as soon as we reached our room.

'And just how long is he going to keep up this ridiculous act?'

'Max, please. You're not even giving him a chance. I don't blame you for being suspicious, but for my sake you could give him the benefit of the doubt. He's had a bad shock and sometimes it takes something really awful ...'

My voice tailed off. Too late. Max pounced.

'What kind of shock? I knew there was something. What the hell's been going on, Lydia?'

'I can't tell you,' I said miserably. 'I promised Jack.'

'Well, if you don't tell me I shall go and damn well ask him myself and you know where that will lead.'

I told him; the bare details, glossing over the more sordid bits. He listened in silence and still in silence he got up and began to pace round the room.

'Well, say something then?' I ventured nervously.

'What do you want me to say? Poor Jack — how dreadful — something like that?'

'Well, a little sympathy wouldn't be entirely out of place,' I said. 'It's not entirely his fault. He can't help being the way he is.'

'Of course, he can help it. That's like saying you can't help being a rapist or a child molester.'

'Well, I didn't expect you to understand,' I cried hotly. 'Of course, I expected you to be furious about the money but after all it is my money ...'

'Yes, it's your money — and if you want to give him the lot, well, that's up to you. That isn't what I'm furious about.

I'm furious because you didn't tell me, because you put yourself at risk in order to protect him. And I'm even more
furious that he let you do it, that he's so low and unprincipled as to involve you in his sordid affairs. He should have
come to me ...'

'And you would have helped him? Is that what you're
going to say?'

'Yes. I would have helped him. For your sake I would
have helped him because I'd do anything to stop you being
hurt. I'd have protected him in order to protect you.'

Well, what could I say? My defensive stance crumbled at
the look in his eyes. 'Oh darling, I'm sorry,' I said. 'You're
right, I should have confided in you but, you see, I just didn't
know how you'd react.'

He put his arms around me. 'Promise me that if anything
like this ever happens again you won't try to deal with it
alone. Promise me that you'll come to me, however dreadful
it is, you'll let me help?'

'Yes, of course.' I kissed him. 'I promise.'

The next few days passed off pleasantly enough. Country
house parties are predictable at the best of times. The men
shoot and play billiards, the women amuse themselves with
cards or tennis or croquet. In the evening one dines and
afterwards plays bridge before trudging up to chilly
bedrooms for the night, and then beginning the whole
process again. Few variations are possible. Walking the dogs
is an alternative outdoor pursuit and one can always ride or
hunt if it's the season. A great deal depends on the personality of one's fellow guests. They were a mixed bag; impover-
ished aristocracy and wealthy bourgeoisie; 'honourable'
young girls hoping to be dishonoured by rich young men.
There were a few of the old county set who made it clear that
they were only here because Gerard Ansty had invited them,
and whilst quietly despising Sydney were perfectly happy to
sit and guzzle his port.

Sydney himself has been quite magnificent and has given a
flawless performance of the genial, expansive, all-American
host. He has apparently given up protesting his English
origins as an American is obviously what his guests prefer

292

him to be. Allowances can always be made for Americans, you see. Colonials aren't expected to know how to behave, so any lack of social graces can be overlooked.

So for three days we were all on our best behaviour. Gerard was mostly drunk, Veronica mostly sober and Felicity floated happily somewhere in between. When she wasn't impressing upon everyone how much happier she and Gerard are in their cosy new quarters in the east wing, she was attempting to justify selling Russell and Philippa's birthright. — 'Well, of course, it's entirely for the children's sake that Gerard and I have made the sacrifice. I mean Russell will be able to go up to Cambridge when he's finished at Ampleforth, and at least Philippa will be able to come out in style. And it's not as if there's any guarantee that Russell would even want to be bothered with a huge estate. I mean, young people don't these days, do they? They all want to live in town in smart little flats.'

Thank God, Jack behaved beautifully. He was deferential to the men, attentive to the ladies. He had a kind of asexual charm that made him attractive to women, as if they knew instinctively that they were safe.

And Max — well, he was just Max, looking on with amused and practised cynicism at this demonstration of English Society taking its ease. Now after three days of relative harmony, most of the guests are beginning to take their leave and the family prepare to be left to their own devices again. Then, I feel certain, will the trouble begin.

Veronica was the first to crack. With just twelve of us left and most of the guests waiting to be ferried over to Shipley for the afternoon train, a cold buffet had been set out in the dining room. We had hardly sat down when Veronica lurched in, floating towards us on a palpable tide of gin.

'Yes, I'm drunk,' she announced. 'In fact, I don't think I'm quite drunk enough. Will you excuse me while I get a refill.'

She lurched out again. After a moment's strained silence everyone, with true English stoicism, resumed the conversation as if the incident had never happened.

I looked at Sydney. He was white with rage. He said with a calmness that one couldn't help but admire; 'Lydia. Would you mind ...'

293

I found her in the library, staring morosely into a half empty bottle of gin. Drunk and distressed, but she still managed to look like a Botticelli Venus.

'Veronica. What's wrong?' I was genuinely concerned.

She gave me a belligerent look. 'Why on earth should you care? No one else does.'

'Don't be silly,' I said firmly. 'Of course we care. I wouldn't have come looking for you if I didn't.'

She smiled faintly. 'You're really very decent, aren't you Lydia? Far too decent for us. I really don't know why you bother when we're all so rotten to you.'

'No. I don't know either,' I replied dryly. 'Now are you going to tell me what's the matter or shall I go away and leave you to finish the bottle?'

She gave a queer hiccoughing sigh. 'Oh, it's nothing really — at least it won't seem like anything to you.' Her mouth trembled. 'It's just that I thought I was pregnant and I've just discovered that I'm not.'

I smiled bitterly. My God, if only she knew how often I'd travelled that particular road only to arrive at the same dead end. I told myself I mustn't be anxious. Worrying about it only made my chances of conception worse. I would leave it in the hands of fate to decide whether I became pregnant, and so far fate had decreed that I should not. But because I understood so well Veronica's dejection, I slipped my arm round her shoulders and gently said; 'Don't worry about it, darling. You've heaps of time.'

'But it's been a year now,' she said tearfully. 'I'm beginning to think there must be something wrong. I've tried absolutely everything; taking my temperature and things like that.' She wrung her hands theatrically. 'I've got to have a baby. It's the only way I can make things up to Sydney, you see.'

'Perhaps,' I said soothingly, 'you're trying too hard. It happens like that sometimes. People want something so desperately that the strain of wanting it has exactly the opposite effect.'

She looked at me suspiciously. 'I expect you're just saying that to cheer me up.'

'No, I'm not. Any doctor would tell you exactly the same.

294

I read about a woman somewhere who'd been trying, unsuccessfully, to conceive for years. In desperation, she adopted a child ...'

'I don't want someone else's child,' Veronica broke in vehemently. 'I want my own child ...'

'I was going to say, that having adopted a child, within just a few months she found she was expecting one of her own. The point is that by adopting a child she took the pressure off herself. She'd stopped worrying about conceiving and so she did.'

'Do you think that could be it?' she asked eagerly. 'That I'm thinking and worrying about it all too much?'

'It must be it. After all, you've been pregnant before, so that you know there's nothing wrong with either you or Sydney.'

Her face clouded. She looked uneasy. She stretched out her hand for the bottle of gin.

'And that won't help,' I said firmly. 'In fact, drinking is the worst thing you could possibly do. I'm surprised you haven't thought of that yourself ...'

Then the door was flung open and Sydney walked in. 'Well, that was quite an entrance, wasn't it, Veronica?'

'Sydney!' I felt duty bound to intervene. 'Veronica's upset. She's had rather a disappointment ...'

'Well, it's a damn good job I don't hit the bottle every time something doesn't come off ...'

'Please Sydney,' I gave him a look of mute appeal. 'It's an entirely silly and feminine thing. Veronica thought she was pregnant but she's not.'

'Well, that's a relief,' Sydney shouted. 'I wouldn't want any child of mine to have a drunkard for a mother.'

Veronica began to cry. 'Oh Sydney, please don't ...'

'And it's no good trying that. That doesn't work any more.' He thrust his hands in his pockets and strode about the room. 'Now listen to me, Veronica. I've been as patient as hell; I've turned a blind eye; I've given you every damned mortal thing a woman could ask for. And all I've asked for in return is that you remain sober at least fifty per cent of the time and that you don't embarrass me in front of my friends ...'

'They're not your friends,' Veronica screamed. 'You haven't got any friends. They only come here for what they can get.'

'All right then. My guests — our guests — they're still going to talk whatever they are. Not that they'll be giving away any secrets. You're a standing joke already, do you know that?'

'Are you sure it's me they're laughing at, Sydney?' Veronica shrilled. 'If you knew how people sniggered about you behind your back ...'

I went out and closed the door. This was obviously going to be a very private quarrel. I felt I had heard more than enough.

That was drama number one and the second followed on smoothly, occurring the following day when all the guests had gone and the family was sprawled in the drawing room, trying to escape from the intense August heat.

Everyone groaned in unison as the wheels of a car were heard on the drive.

'Oh my God,' said Felicity. 'I can't face visitors today. Blake will have to tell them that we're all indisposed.'

The door opened and Blake stood there, the first time I had ever seen him out of countenance.

'Mrs Claremont,' he announced. 'Mrs Hugo Claremont' — and in walked a vision of expensive French chic.

It was Max who spoke first. 'Marcia,' he said — and then for some inexplicable reason he began to laugh.

Then Veronica, grimly sober, leapt from her chair. 'How dare you?' she screamed. 'How dare you show your face here again, you bitch, you thief?'

'Veronica!' Ursula took instant control. Breeding asserted itself with a visible effort.

'Marcia. Well, this is a surprise, although hardly a pleasant one. I suppose I must ask you to sit down.'

Marcia seated herself, crossing her legs with the seductive slither of silk. 'Forgive me for dropping in on you,' she said in her languid voice. 'I would have telephoned first but I didn't realise you'd had one installed.'

Silence. We all stared at her. 'Have you had lunch?' enquired Felicity vaguely, her thoughts, as always, turning to

296

food in a crisis. 'I'm afraid we have already eaten but I'm sure Cook could manage something if you're famished.'

'Thank you,' replied Marcia, 'but I lunched on the train. A cocktail would be nice though.'

'Blake. A cocktail for Mrs Hugo. In fact, I think we'll all have one.'

Then Ursula cut through the conversation in an ugly voice. 'Why have you come?' she demanded. 'What is it you want?'

Marcia regarded her coolly. 'What I always want,' she said candidly. 'Money of course.'

She smiled into the shocked and appalled silence. 'I met some mutual friends who were staying in Paris. They told me how well you were all doing, that the family fortunes had recovered. I've just come back to collect my share.'

'Everything you were entitled to you received on my son's death. In fact, you received more than your share if one includes the things that you stole.'

'Well, I'm afraid that's where you are wrong.' Marcia's voice took on a businesslike note. 'As I understand it, the estate was entailed, and as Hugo had left no obvious heir, anything that was left after the debts were paid went to Max. Of course, I realise it wasn't a great deal; a few thousand pounds, some furniture, paintings ...' She glanced smilingly round the assembly of stupified faces, clearly enjoying the sensation she made.

There was a bigger sensation to come. She glanced at Max; 'I'm sorry, darling, but you'll just have to hand it all back. You see, legally it belongs to my son — Hugo's son.'

Everyone stared at her. Nobody spoke. Then Ursula's harsh laughter broke the silence. 'You don't expect us to believe that, do you?'

'Now, look here, Marcia,' Lord Ansty roused himself from his alcoholic stupor. 'If you've come back here with the idea of passing some — er — well, some by-blow off as Hugo's son ...'

Then Marcia nodded to Blake. He went out of the room and returned holding the hand of a small boy of about two. I heard Ursula make a strangled noise in her throat. There was no doubt he was a Claremont; that Elsinore blondness, those mazarine eyes ... whose son could he have been except Hugo's.

All eyes were on the boy but I looked at Max. He was deathly pale and his hand trembled visibly as he raised a cigarette to his lips.

Then Ursula rose to her feet. 'It's a miracle,' she breathed. 'The answer to my prayers.' Her fanatical eyes swept over us all. 'Don't you see? It's a sign of divine intervention, a sign that Hugo has been released from Purgatory and taken up to be with God.'

'Oh my God,' Max muttered. 'Excuse me, won't you.' He added loudly as he walked from the room. 'I think I need some air.'

That broke the spell for everyone except Ursula. She moved in a trance-like state towards the boy. 'What is he called?' she asked tremulously.

Marcia smiled. 'Hugo. What else?'

'Yes. Yes, of course, as you say, what else.'

Then she knelt down beside him and stared into his face. Then to everyone's horror and complete amazement she suddenly began to weep.

Felicity took charge. 'Blake. Take Mrs Claremont up to her room, would you.' She gave the rest of us a pointed look. 'And I think perhaps ...'

We all took the hint and trooped outside.

'My God! What a show,' Jack crowed with delight. 'It's better than Hollywood, isn't it?'

I left him to a post-mortem discussion with Veronica and Sydney whilst I went in search of Max.

He was out on the terrace, his hands thrust in his pockets, a cigarette between his lips. I hesitated before approaching him, uncertain of his mood, and then just as I was about to step forward and call his name, I saw Marcia emerging from the French windows further down.

I hesitated again, shrinking back into the folds of the library curtains.

'Hello Max.'

'Hello Marcia.' Oh, what a wealth of explanation there was in those four simple words.

I saw Max smile. 'Well, I must say you know how to make an entrance — and an exit as well, come to that.'

She laughed. 'Yes, I'm sorry about that, Max.' She

298

shrugged. 'I thought it best to make a clean break.'

Max nodded. 'So,' he began after a little silence, 'when Hugo knocked you up before shuffling off this mortal coil, he managed to leave us yet another little surprise.'

'Well, I didn't expect you to be pleased. I realise that it makes things awkward for you.'

Max stared down at his feet. 'Did you know before you left — that you were going to have a child?'

'No. Why should I? I had given up hope of that years before.'

'But there must have been signs,' Max persisted indelicately.

'Well, that could have been anything; the shock of Hugo's death — anything.'

'How old is he?'

'He will be two in December. He was born on Christmas Day. I'm sure Ursula will find that significant.'

'Why didn't you come back before, as soon as you knew?'

'What was there to come back for? There was no money, no home for me, nothing.'

Another silence, then Marcia said. 'I didn't know you were married.' She accepted a cigarette as he offered his case. 'At least, not until I arrived in England.'

'Who told you that I was?'

'Everyone, darling. It's still the talk of the town that you married Lydia Rochester.' She inhaled on her cigarette. 'I congratulate you,' she added bitterly. 'You've done well for yourself, Max. I'm afraid I haven't been so fortunate.'

'Is that why you've come back? Just to see what you can get?'

'Yes. Why not? The family owe me something, don't you think, considering the shabby way they've always treated me. But things will be different this time. I've got something they want now. I've got Hugo.'

'You haven't got anything I want, Marcia.'

She laughed. 'No? Well then, you've changed, Max — but then I suppose we both have ...'

Max jerked himself away from the wall and with elation I saw the expression of scorn on his face. 'No, Marcia. You haven't changed. You're still as greedy and selfish as ever.'

299

He ground out his cigarette stub with the heel of his shoe. 'I don't know what your plans are — apart from the fact you're here to make as much trouble as you can — but I warn you now, whatever they are, make quite sure that they don't include me.'

Again I said nothing to Max — the inevitable consequence of eavesdropping has to be a still tongue. I felt I had Marcia fairly well summed up. I'd never cared for her very much when she was Hugo's wife and she appealed to me even less as his widow. My banker's instinct, despite the expensive clothes, told me that she was broke. My feminine instinct told me that at some time in the past she had slept with my husband. Of course, they were only suspicions and probably that's all they would have ever been if it hadn't been for Jack.

I went upstairs and found him sprawled on my bed. 'Well!' he demanded avidly. 'What do you think?'

'About what?' I said carefully.

'About Marcia and her brat. Quite biblical really — as the worthy Ursula said, something along the lines of a miracle.'

I suppressed the unpleasant thought that was forming in my head. 'Don't meddle, Jack,' I said shortly. 'It's none of our business.'

'Well, I thought it might be your business, old girl.'

I turned to look at him. 'In exactly what way?'

'Oh come on,' he scoffed. 'You're not that naive. You don't honestly believe the boy is Hugo's, do you?'

'Of course, it's Hugo's child,' I said with conviction. 'The resemblance is too strong for it to be otherwise.'

'Well, there's an alternative explanation to that, although I don't suppose it would appeal to you ...'

I winced. I hadn't actually got that far in my reasoning. I was vaguely aware that something wasn't quite right but I wasn't prepared yet to accept the conclusion that Jack had obviously reached.

I sat down in front of my mirror and violently powdered my nose. 'I don't know what you mean,' I said feebly.

'What I mean is that I don't believe the child is Hugo's. I spoke to Hugo the day before he died and he told me that he hadn't slept with Marcia for months. It was one of the reasons he was so depressed, the fact he wasn't able to produce an heir which was the main reason he married at all. And if you're asking me to believe that what Hugo couldn't achieve in eight years of marriage he managed in the last twenty-four hours of his life ...' He poked around in the box of chocolates beside my bed. 'So if it wasn't Hugo who knocked the lovely Marcia up, one can't help wondering who did.' He sank his teeth into a fondant creme and licked his lips. 'Frankly, my money's on Max.'

I shouldn't have allowed myself to be drawn but I just couldn't stop myself from arguing the point. 'Don't be ridiculous, Jack. The child was born on Christmas Day. I heard Marcia say so, which means that it must have been conceived in late March. Surely Max was still in India then?'

'He can't have been still in India. He was certainly back in England by the 22nd April because I spoke to him at the creditors' meeting then. Hugo died on the 31st March ...'

'This is a quite pointless discussion, Jack,' I cut him off shrilly. 'And although I'm sure it appeals vastly to your sense of mischief to suggest that Max ...'

'Why don't you ask him?' Jack suggested with his deceptively innocent smile. 'I think I'd certainly want to know if I were you.'

I went about it in an entirely roundabout way. It was our last day at Ansty and we were wandering in the gardens in the aimless way one does when departure is imminent.

I said casually, stooping to breathe the perfume of a rose. 'Have you decided anything about Marcia yet? I mean as regards to her claims.'

'No,' he answered absently. 'I suppose I'll have to see Ridgeway and get him to work something out.'

'Yes, I think that would be wise. I know it's unlikely, but if Marcia wanted to be difficult she could make out a case for restitution which might amount to more than you wanted to pay.'

He frowned. 'In what way?'

'I'm not sure really — but something along the lines that if Marcia, as the boy's trustee, had had access to the money at the time of Hugo's death, then she could have done this or

301

that ... Do you see what I mean?'

'Yes, I see what you mean — but I still don't think that legally she could claim more than the residue of the entail, plus interest.'

'No. I'm not saying that she could. I just thought it might be wiser to find out.'

'Yes, all right. I'll mention it to Ridgeway — although frankly, I think that will be the least of our problems. If Mother gets her way then we'll be saddled with the pair of them for life. Having glimpsed the resurrection and the life, as it were, she's going to fight tooth and nail to keep the boy here.'

'I suppose there's no doubt that Hugo was the father?'

'Hardly. I don't think Mother would be deceived about her own grandson.'

'I wasn't disputing that he was her grandson.' I stared down at my feet. 'That isn't the question I asked you.'

He shot me a startled and guilty look. 'What the hell do you mean?'

'Max,' I said gently. 'If the child is yours, I'd rather know.'

I watched his face. His reaction was important and I felt I had my answer in the way he avoided my eyes. 'It just struck me as curious,' I went on. 'They were childless for all those years — eight years, wasn't it — and then Marcia suddenly produces a posthumous heir.'

'Is it yours?' I persisted when he remained silent.

'Lydia. It's a silly question to ask ...'

'But you and Marcia were lovers once.'

I knew he wouldn't lie so I was quite prepared when he said: 'Yes. Just briefly. It doesn't mean anything now.'

'Then it could be your son ...'

'It's Hugo's son,' he said with sudden vehemence. 'Don't ever think of him as anything but that. I had to share everything else with Hugo, but I'm certainly not going to share his bloody son.'

I couldn't leave it at that and I made a few discreet investigations of my own. Naturally, amongst the family, the subject was under avid discussion and what I couldn't find out from the general conversation, I had become desperate enough to

302

ask. What I ended up with was this: Hugo had died on the 31st March when Max was already half way home on his leave. Gerard had actually cabled him the news on board the *Corinthia*. So really the period in question was as little as three weeks. If Marcia's statement that the boy had been born on December 25th was true, it could have been Hugo's child at full term, if one accepted the miracle of him finding his potency in the last few hours of his life. Equally, it could have been Max's child born three weeks prematurely, which really wasn't unusual at all. Either way, it was impossible to be sure.

In any event, I've made up my mind that I'm going to be eminently sensible. It's all in the past. It all happened before Max and I had even met and I'm certainly not going to allow a small indiscretion to wreck my happiness — except that the small indiscretion lives and breathes and is called Hugo and has soft curling blond hair and amazing blue eyes ... Oh my God, what a weapon, what a wonderful lever. Already Marcia's got the entire family dancing to her tune.

And Max! Well, of course he pretends to be aloof and disinterested, but I've seen him looking at Marcia, I've seen them exchanging their amused and private smile. I've seen him looking at the boy as well, covertly speculating, and that perhaps is the hardest thing to bear because in that sphere of course I can't compete.

But I'm going to be sensible. I'm not going to get myself worked up into a ridiculous jealous rage. We'll be gone tomorrow — and oh, I can't wait to get away. I can't wait to distance myself from that smug knowing look, that sensual smile, that perfect figure encased in perfectly cut Parisian clothes ...

It occurs to me that I'm not going to be sensible at all.

September 3rd, 1928, Eldon Square
Our lives have returned to some form of normality. Marcia and Hugo, despite Ursula Claremont's strenuous efforts to detain them, have returned to France, promising to return at Christmas by which time she expects some sort of settlement to have been worked out. Max doesn't mention it. Perhaps

303

he's embarrassed to discuss it with me, perhaps he feels I'll read something into his either being too generous or being too mean. I can see his dilemma. If the child were Hugo's then he'll feel no qualms about negotiating a fair but entirely impersonal settlement. But if it were his child — if he thought that he was being penny-pinching towards his own son ...

I mustn't think about it. I have a son of my own to concern myself about. I'm still very anxious that he should try and make his peace with Max. I've mentioned it once or twice, quite casually of course. Jack reminds me that I'd promised to let him choose his own time. He says he has other guilts to work off first and I have to admit that he seems to be taking a real interest in his work at the bank. He's even suggested that we should turn at least twenty per cent of its investment over to short-term American loans. Madly unpatriotic of course, with the Bank of England struggling to stem the outflow of gold — but one can't deny the attraction of paying our depositors five per cent and lending to New York at twelve. Everyone's doing it. We're all making money out of the great American boom. Even I wasn't able to resist a spin at the wheel, buying five hundred Goldman Sachs at $105 in July and selling them at $170 in August — a profit of thirty-two thousand dollars in less than a month.

So everything is going smoothly — on the surface at least, like a skin of thin ice concealing the rank water beneath. We all skate very cautiously. I don't mention Marcia, Max doesn't mention Jack, neither of us mention the boy, Hugo.

I'm dreading Christmas. The atmosphere is bound to be intensely Borghese, with everyone giving each other poisonous looks if not actually resorting to the real thing. I've thought of not going. I mean, technically, what happens to Hugo isn't anything to do with us. I suggested it to Max tentatively, that it might be nice to spend Christmas at Farnfield for a change.

'I have to go to Ansty,' he replied shortly. 'You know there are things to sort out.'

'Can't Ridgeway see to it for you. I thought that was what lawyers were for.'

We'd just finished breakfast. Jack had already left for the bank and Max was on the point of departure.

304

'Well, he could,' he said, stuffing the *Official List* into his monogrammed case. 'But I'd rather be there so I know exactly what's going on. You never know what Marcia might have up her sleeve.' He bent down and dropped a light kiss on my cheek. 'Look, I'll have to dash. I've got a meeting at ten.'

'It just seems,' I said peevishly, getting up and walking with him to the door. 'It just seems that lately your family's affairs take priority over everything. We spent last Christmas at Ansty. I thought it might be quite diverting to go somewhere I wanted to go for a change.'

He paused. 'Well, you don't have to come. Why don't you go down to Farnfield and I'll join you there as soon as I can.'

I froze. He couldn't have said anything more certain to rouse my suspicions.

'Oh, I see,' I said hotly. 'I'm to be packed off to Farnfield whilst you and Marcia walk down memory lane.'

His eyes hardened. 'Don't start that, Lydia. I tell you now you couldn't be wider of the mark.'

I wilted visibly beneath his scornful gaze. 'Well, I'm sorry but sometimes that's the way it looks to me.'

'Actually,' he said coldly, 'what I was going to suggest, if you hadn't jumped down my throat, was that I go down with Ridgeway on the 19th — Marcia isn't arriving till the 20th by the way — and then, after we've held our council of war, I'll drive up to Farnfield the next day or the day after perhaps, depending on how things go.'

But that still left two days for Marcia to exert her Continental wiles — and I didn't like 'depending on how it goes', a vague statement which might lead to others equally vague like 'something's cropped up' or 'I've been detained'.

I backed down which seemed the only sensible thing to do. 'No. It's all right'. I smiled ruefully. 'I was just being petty. Of course we'll go to Ansty.'

I'm being entirely unreasonable, I realise that, but jealousy isn't an emotion I've ever experienced before. It isn't even the normal kind of envy. I don't see Marcia herself as a rival; it's her position as the boy's mother that raises my hackles. And I can't believe that Max is as indifferent to the boy as he

305

would like me to believe. He's *too* indifferent, too vehement in his denials, and his refusal even to consider the possibility of paternity seems far too strenuous to me. It's out of character for him to be hostile towards a small boy in any case and quite inexplicable if Hugo is merely his nephew. All of which inclines one to think the worst. Marcia as a *femme fatale* I could easily match — but as the mother of Max's child, able to manipulate him through his natural feelings for his son — well, how could I possibly compete?

December 19th, 1928, Ansty
We met in the library, an uneasy alliance, all with our various hopes and vastly differing points of view. Ridgeway took the chair, calling us to order as if he were a judge at the bench.

'Now, I think we all know why we're here, to come to some agreement regarding the claims of ...'

'We're here to decide my grandson's future,' Ursula cut in. 'And I think we must all agree that it should be here with us.'

'If you'll just bear with me, Ursula,' Ridgeway said mildly. 'I was coming to that — but first, I want to acquaint you with what little information I have been able to glean from official sources. According to the child's mother, he was born at Puiseux, a small village between Chantilly and Paris on the 25th December, 1927. Unfortunately, there is no official documentation of the fact — the French, unfortunately, are notoriously lax in these matters. There is, however, a baptismal certificate in the name of Hugo Marcel Augustine Claremont dated January 17th, 1928.'

'Oh get on with it, Ridgeway,' Veronica said impatiently. 'No one is disputing that it's Hugo's child. We're not interested in when and where he was born.'

I was interested though. It seemed to me the most important thing — without a birth certificate the whole question of his paternity was thrown wide open. I glanced at Jack who flung me an openly triumphant look. Max just looked pale and grim.

Ridgeway continued. 'There's one other point before we proceed to the main agenda. Max has raised the question of his own personal liability regarding the limitation of restitution in any claim that Mrs Hugo Claremont should make. I say personal liability because, although in fact Max did not have sole enjoyment of such goods and chattels that were part of the Blanchland entail, in *law* he was the sole heir and therefore it falls to him to make restitution. Such of the contents of Blanchland that were not disposed of are, I understand, stored here at Ansty. Assuming the claim that the boy is Hugo Claremont's son is proved, these items now belong to him and his mother as trustee. I have instructions from Max to persuade Mrs Hugo Claremont to settle on a *quid pro quo* basis, i.e. a cash sum in lieu of goods, and accordingly I have taken the liberty of having a valuation made and have arrived at a figure of approximately six thousand pounds.

'There has been a suggestion that Mrs Hugo could have grounds to sue for further damages on the basis that had restitution been made earlier it could have altered her life, but as the delay in informing the estate that there was an heir by way of Hugo Claremont's legitimate progeny was entirely the fault of the plaintiff herself, I am advised by counsel that such a suit would not proceed very far. So I think you may rest assured that financially, at least, liability is restricted to the Blanchland entail.

'Having said that,' he went on, 'some of you may feel that the family has a moral obligation to Hugo's son by way of upbringing and education. There are two alternatives here; an annuity payment to the boy's mother to cover the cost of school fees and so on, the disadvantages of which are obvious in that the family would have little control over how the money was spent, insofar as it was being used for the sole benefit of the child. The other option is for the family to assume personal responsibility for the child's future, but of course this would depend on his mother being persuaded to relinquish control. In short, I am instructed to put it to Mrs Hugo when she arrives that the boy remain here and be legally adopted by his grandmother.'

'But Marcia will never agree,' Felicity argued. 'Personally, I think it's a dreadful idea.'

'I think you're overestimating Marcia's maternal feelings,' Ursula said tersely. 'It's perfectly clear to me that it's always

307

been Marcia's intention to leave the boy with us. I dare say he's become an inconvenience to her way of life and so she's decided to put the responsibility onto us and get as much out of it for herself as she can. As I see it, it's just a question of settling a price.'

'But who will pay?' demanded Veronica. 'That seems to me a more relevant point. It's all very well, Mother, making these *grande dame* gestures and spending other people's cash. But really it'll be Max or Sydney that will have to cough up. It's not as if you've got anything of your own.'

'It's the family's responsibility, therefore the family must pay, each according to his means.'

'And anyway,' continued Veronica sulkily, 'why must it be you who adopts Hugo? I mean you're not getting any younger, are you? I would have thought it more suitable that he come to Sydney and me.'

'Suitable!' exclaimed her mother. 'With your penchant for alcohol, I would hardly think that makes you suitable to mother an impressionable child.'

'All right. That's enough.' We all looked at Max. 'Stop squabbling over the boy as if he were a bargain hat. It's what's best for the child that matters.'

'Exactly,' Ursula pronouced. 'And what's best for Hugo is not to be dragged all over Europe by a mother whose morals, to say the least, have always been questionable. I don't care to hazard where Marcia's income comes from, but she didn't buy the clothes she was wearing at a market stall. I have no intention of allowing my only grandson to be raised in some Parisian bordello ...'

'Shut up,' Max said. 'It's up to Marcia to decide. In case you've forgotten it's her child as well. And if she's got any sense she'll take him as far away from us as she can.'

'Well, I can understand you feeling like that, Maxwell. His father always made you feel inadequate, didn't he ...'

'Please!' Ridgeway stood up, 'I think, as Max says, we are being a little premature. Now. I shall put our proposition to Marcia when she arrives' — he spread his hands — 'but it is up to her entirely what she decides.'

And of course Marcia loved it, being courted by Ursula and

Veronica in turn. At first she reacted with outrage to Ridgeway's proposals, but as the settlement figure grew — no one actually liked to call it a bribe — she became more amenable. She began saying things like 'I must think about Hugo, not myself' — and of course, she would need time. It wasn't a decision one could make overnight ...

'She'll be here till the spring,' said Max cynically, 'or at least until she's bored. Then, having milked the family for everything she can get, she'll take herself and the boy back to France until she runs out of money again. Then the whole dreadful business will start again.'

'I forgot you knew Marcia so well,' I remarked dryly.

'Oh yes,' he said grimly. 'I know Marcia.'

'And that's what you want? For Hugo to go back to France?'

'Yes,' he said, the impassive 'I don't want to discuss it' look descending on his face. 'I think that would be best for everyone, don't you?'

In all the wrangling, Hugo himself was almost forgotten. His vocabulary was limited and he spoke only French in any case. Apart from his mother, I seemed to be the only one fluent enough to understand his stumbling words. Perhaps it was that which made him attach himself to me. Russell and Philippa ignored him completely. He must have been frightened to find himself suddenly among strangers who squabbled and bickered in an unintelligible tongue. I think it reassured him to hear his own language spoken. So while Sydney and Max played billiards, Marcia stayed in bed till noon, and Ursula and Veronica argued over who was most suited to have control of the child, the child and I went for walks and watched the first snow of the winter falling on the lake, and at night I read him fairy tales in French. On Christmas Eve we built a snowman in the paddock and for the first time I saw him really laugh. My heart turned over; he looked so like Max and I felt a sudden rush of tenderness for this child who was so lovable yet seemed so unloved. I suppose Marcia loved him in her own way, except that I felt she loved herself more. Ursula saw him as a replacement for the son she had lost. Veronica saw him as some sort of fertility drug meant to induce a pregnancy of her own. It was then I suppose that the idea first took root. Why Ursula? Why Veronica? Why not me?

'No,' said Max. 'Don't even think about it.'

'Why not?' I pleaded. 'He's the most intelligent and adorable little boy.'

'I don't care. The answer is no.'

'But if there's a possibility that he's your son ...'

He turned on me violently. 'I don't care whose son he is. If he's Hugo's son, I don't want him, and if he's my son I still don't want him. I can't make it any clearer than that!'

'But I want him!' I cried.

'Why — just because everyone else does?'

'No, that's not true.' I pressed my hand over my mouth. I was near to tears. 'I want him because I can't give you a child myself ...'

'So you thought you'd buy me one ready-made?'

'Stop it,' I screamed. 'Just stop sneering for once and listen to me.'

'I have listened,' he said calmly. 'And the answer is still no and it will always be no. I've told you, don't even think about it, Lydia.'

But I do think about it. I can't stop thinking about it. Only one thing would divert me and that would be to have a child of my own.

July 10th, 1929

July already — where have the days gone? In my determination to become pregnant I seem to have willed the time away. As each month ends in bitter disappointment I then look forward impatiently to the end of the next. So the first three months of the new year have passed in an orgy of furtive temperature-taking and practically non-stop sex with absolutely no results at all. In April and May I was mildly diverted by the General Election and the return of a Labour government under Kier Hardie. There was the usual 'Socialist' panic in the City which was reflected at the bank. The plunging market set back the proposed takeover of

310

United Steel by the Austin Friars Trust, and as the bank had large investments in City Corporations, a subsidiary of the Trust, Jack flew into a panic when the share prices sagged. There was a bout of distress-selling but prices rallied marginally before the market's close. By then I had lost interest. I had other things on my mind. Marcia and Hugo were still entrenched at Ansty. I received regular bulletins from Veronica as to the state of play. Ursula apparently had been persuaded to drop out of the bidding in favour of Sydney and Veronica, and in April Marcia had agreed to Hugo's adoption in exchange for an income of three thousand a year. In May she had changed her mind about the terms and decided that she wanted a lump sum settlement instead. In June she changed her mind altogether and said she was thinking of taking Hugo back to France. Needless to say, at every change of plan, Veronica grew more desperate and as she grew more desperate so the price of settlement rose.

I understood how she felt. In June I was feeling a little desperate myself. My failure to conceive had become a mild obsession and I had only agreed to Sydney hauling us all off to Ascot because it gave me the opportunity to sneak off to Harley Street and get a professional view. It wasn't encouraging — possible but not probable was what he actually said. I took this to mean that it was hopeless.

Of course, I was desolate and yet mingled with my disappointment was relief that I wouldn't have to endure such a gruelling ordeal. I haven't given up though — at least I haven't given up the idea of giving Max a son. I'm thinking about Hugo of course. It's the perfect solution. If only I could get Max to agree.

July 29th, 1929
Veronica came to lunch today; exquisitely slim, intensely sober, obviously taking her role as an expectant mother seriously. Naturally, she talked about nothing else.

'The trouble is,' complained Veronica, 'she baulks at actually committing herself legally. What she really wants is to leave Hugo to be raised as an English gentleman while she pushes off back to Paris to spend her ill-gotten gains. Of

311

course, we're not having that. Sydney is most insistent on a formal adoption because otherwise, of course, Marcia could just come back for Hugo whenever she liked and we'd have no legal right to stop her.

'I mean she's been living off us for more than six months now and it's not as if she really enjoys a quiet life. She had that sort of life before at Blanchland and it didn't suit her then. Sydney thinks she's just hanging around waiting for the price to go up but really he's been quite fair; three thousand a year isn't to be sneezed at, especially as she won't have the responsibility of Hugo any more.'

'And how is Hugo?' I enquired.

'Oh, he's fine. I think. It's not always easy to tell. He doesn't say very much although he's beginning to pick up quite a bit of English now.'

'This must be very unsettling,' I said quietly. 'For Hugo, I mean.'

'That's exactly what I said to Marcia. If she had any real concern for him she'd have cleared out months ago and left him with us. It must be obvious, even to her, that he'd be heaps better off with Sydney and I.'

'You're fond of him then?'

'Of course. I adore him.'

'Only I remember you saying that you wouldn't want to accept somebody else's child.'

'But this isn't somebody else's child. This is Hugo's child, my own flesh and blood.'

Then she went on to say how she was having the nursery completely done up and Uncle Gerard had already put his name down for Ampleforth. 'And we've got a proper nurse. She speaks fluent French, although I'm not sure that it's a good thing to encourage him to chatter in French. After all, he's going to be English from now on, isn't he?'

I thought of the child — Max's child — unhappy and alone. I thought about him for a long time after Veronica had gone.

I'm still thinking about him and wondering if I have the courage to take matters into my own hands.

312

August 5th, 1929

At first I just meant to telephone Marcia — after all, I couldn't see any harm in sounding her out. Then I felt this was too impersonal. Much better, I thought, to just turn up casually at Ansty, although then I'd have to make sure that Veronica was out of the way. Then I remembered Veronica mentioning that she and Ursula were lunching with the Edgecombe's on Monday of the following week. With any luck, Marcia would be on her own.

I started off for Ansty as soon as Max left the house. I had timed my arrival for about mid-day.

Blake informed me that Mrs Hugo was still in her room and Master Hugo was out in the grounds with his nurse.

I went upstairs quickly. I felt if I hesitated I should lose my nerve. Even now my palms were sweating.

I knocked on the door. She called out 'Enter'.

She was still in bed. Obviously she had been expecting a servant; the sleek waves of her hair were preserved by a net; there was a luncheon tray on the floor — she'd stubbed out her cigarette in the remains of her meal.

'Forgive me,' I said politely. 'I didn't realise that you weren't up.'

'Oh, that's all right,' she said languidly. 'Frankly, I can't think of anything to get up for, Veronica's not here if that's who you wanted.'

'No, I know. Actually, it was you I wanted to see.'

She looked interested. 'Well, that makes a change. Everyone else only seems to want to see the back of me.'

She threw back the bedclothes and priggishly I averted my eyes as she slid to the floor. When I looked again the net had disappeared and she was wrapped in an ostrich feather and satin robe.

'Still,' she said, stretching herself out on a pillow-heaped couch. 'Even when Hugo was alive I was only a member of this family on sufferance, so really, nothing has changed.'

'You haven't come to any decision about Hugo then?'

'Agreement is a more suitable word — I don't suppose you have a cigarette?'

I handed her my case. She helped herself.

'No. We have come to no firm agreement. As always, the

313

family want something for nothing. They want to drink champagne but pay only for beer. They want to tie me up with string; I can have this but only if I let them do that.' She shrugged. 'I can wait though — and if it doesn't come off then I shall just take Hugo back to France. I shall be no worse off than before.'

I hadn't wanted to antagonise her but I was infuriated by her off-hand tone. 'Is it just a question of hard cash,' I asked coolly, 'or does what's best for Hugo come into it at all?'

She returned my cold look. 'What would be best for Hugo would be to allow him to grow up here in England with people he loves — but that includes me, you see, and I am not acceptable so I am to be banished. So if they want Hugo without me then they will have to pay.'

'Well, in a way I can see their point. People have to have some sort of certainty in their lives and Hugo needs that too. I mean, you're still young, Marcia. You might marry again and take Hugo away and that would be heartbreaking from — well, say Veronica's point of view.'

'So she has sent you to be her advocate then?'

'No. Far from it. I'm here entirely on my own behalf. What I wanted to say — to ask you — was that, if you should decide to allow Hugo to be formally adopted, that you think about him coming to live with myself and Max?'

She raised her eyebrows. 'Did Max send you to say that?'

'No. Max doesn't even know that I'm here.'

'But he wants the child though?'

'No. He doesn't —' I looked at her— 'but I do.'

'I see,' she said slowly and I saw she was trying to work out the advantages of this.

I helped her. 'You see, I'm not going to be able to give Max a child, so it would mean that if we adopted Hugo he would be Max's sole heir. Everything would eventually come to him.'

'Ah yes — eventually. But that is all in the future. That wouldn't help me now.'

'I understand,' I said smoothly. 'Naturally, I would see that you were ...' I couldn't think of better word than compensated. 'A lump sum outright. No strings attached.'

She was silent for a long time. 'May I think about it?' she said.

314

'Yes, of course.' I was disappointed not to get an immediate decision but I didn't think it was wise to push a conclusion just then. I gave her my card. 'Telephone me, won't you, if you want to talk about it any more.'

August 19th, 1929
She called this morning, after I had agonised and lurked by the telephone for two whole weeks. We had a brief businesslike conversation, and although she didn't promise anything definite I felt it was just a question of haggling over the settlement before having the papers drawn up.

All I have to do now is break the news to Max.

I sat motionless as the Lalique vase shattered into a thousand fragments upon the hearth; a bronze figurine splintered the door of the Sheraton bookcase.

I had never seen him so angry. I had never seen anyone so angry. This kind of mindless fury was quite alien to me.

'Max,' I said desperately. 'Please calm down ...' but this only seemed to infuriate him more. The Sevres garniture followed the Lalique vase.

'Look,' I said, getting a little hot under the collar myself. 'Don't you think you're overreacting a bit ...'

'Overreacting!' He leapt across the room and grabbed my arm. 'Overreacting — when you've been conniving behind my back with that heartless French bitch — and then tell me over dinner that you've arranged to adopt Hugo as coolly as if you'd arranged to have the bloody decorators in.'

He pushed me away from him. I nearly fell. For the first time in my life I was actually frightened; for the first time I understood how Jack must have felt faced with this terrifying, insane and murderous rage.

'Max,' I said helplessly, 'if you'd just let me explain. I thought it was what you wanted. I thought ...'

'What I wanted!' He stared at me incredulously. 'Are you mad? Why on earth should I want to foster my brother's child?'

'He's not Hugo's child. You know perfectly well that he's not. You wouldn't reject him so passionately if he was.'

315

'But I don't know,' Max said with exasperation in his voice. 'That's the point, Lydia. I don't know and I'll never know. That's what I couldn't stand, looking at him, loving him and never knowing whether he was mine or not.'

'But Marcia must know. You must make her tell you.'

He smiled dryly. 'Oh, I don't think Marcia will budge from her story, not even to me. She's taken the line that it's better for the boy to be Hugo's legitimate heir than my bastard.'

'But does it really matter?' I asked gently. 'He's still a child. He still needs love, affection and I could give him that. I could give him so much. What can Marcia give him? It's perfectly obvious she lives from hand to mouth. What sort of life will that be for him, trailing round Europe?'

'I can think of worse. Better that than be smothered by your appalling generosity, Lydia. If he is my son then he'd rather struggle on with nothing than lose his independence.'

'Independence! He's two years old. How can you talk about independence at that age.'

'He won't always be two though. And as soon as he's old enough to realise that you took him away from his mother, that you bought him ...'

'And that she sold him — don't forget that. I should think if he resented anyone it would be her.'

'It doesn't work like that. She's his mother.'

'He'll have forgotten about her by then. Don't you see? By the time he's fifteen I shall be the only real mother he's ever known.'

'Lydia, you can't equate a legal arrangement with a tie of blood.'

'You're wrong,' I argued desperately. 'You don't know anything about children. Hugo needs security, a family; he needs love and compassion.'

'And of course you're the only person in the world who can give him that. You specialise in compassion, don't you, Lydia? You can't resist taking another lame duck under your wing.'

I flushed at the sneer implicit in his voice. 'What on earth do you mean?'

'I mean that you never want people on equal terms. They always have to need you more than you ever need them.'

316

'That's not true,' I cried. 'Of course I want to be needed. Every woman does ...'

'But I need you,' he shouted. 'But not as a prop, a support, someone to lean on. That's what you want — you want to patronise, to pity, you want to dominate. That's why Jack's no use because you've always run his life for him. That's why you've taken this boy up so that you can dominate him.'

'That's not true,' I whispered. 'Whenever have I tried to dominate you?'

'You're trying to now — by foisting a responsibility on me that you know I don't want. You're using that boy, just like the others ...'

'No,' I cried. 'I'm fond of Hugo, more than fond ...'

'Well, I hope you are, Lydia,' he said in a dangerously quiet voice, 'because the minute that boy walks in through the door, I shall be walking out.'

August 25th, 1929, Farnfield

I decided I had to come to Farnfield for a few days and caught the first train the following morning. We hadn't spoken since our quarrel the previous night. He'd looked on in silence whilst I'd slung some things into a case. He hadn't replied to my stilted goodbye. He hadn't even asked me where I was going.

So here I am at Farnfield. The weather is very fine, long hot endless days; sometimes it isn't dark till nearly midnight. And wonderfully solitary, just Ellis and his wife, the couple who keep things up. I plan long bracing walks across the moor; afternoons in the garden soaking up the sun, evenings spent writing letters and reading.

I've already written to Marcia, telling her how things are. Strangely enough, I don't feel anything now when I think of the boy. My longing for him ceased when I realised that instead of bringing Max and I together he was going to drive us apart. Max was right. After all, my intentions weren't so pure. I *was* just like the rest of them. I hadn't wanted Hugo, I'd just wanted Max's son. I'd wanted to deprive Marcia of her weapon purely because I'd wanted to use it myself. And of course I had absolutely no right to try and force the child

317

on Max. He had every reason in the world to be angry. I feel ashamed, guilty. This glimpse of myself as an interfering martinet has completely shattered my self-esteem. Am I really that kind of person? Do I deliberately look for weakness so that I can demonstrate my strength? Am I only capable with people who are incapable themselves? I don't deny that I'm never happier than when I'm taking up the cudgels on behalf of the oppressed, that I am, by nature, compassionate. But that these should be seen as faults! That my generosity should be seen as self-righteous charity, my compassion as condescension — that my good intentions should be so appallingly misconstrued. It's not as if I don't know what it's like to be on the receiving end. I was the object of my grandfather's charity for years. But perhaps that's not the same. Something grudgingly given and as grudgingly received makes for a kind of equality, I suppose. I never felt grateful and it's the need to be grateful that people seem to resent, to be the object of charity and pity. Gratitude offends against pride and self-esteem. What a masochistic species the English are, that the majority would rather starve than accept a sixpence they hadn't earned themselves. That sort of pride is admirable if insane. It's not the sort of pride that keeps me sitting here, hoping that I won't have to humble myself completely, that Max will meet me half way and want a reconciliation enough to telephone. Of course, I'll have to go back. There's absolutely no point in sulking down here but it would be too humiliating to go back so soon. I'll wait just one more day.

I spent this morning wandering restlessly though the uninhabited rooms. We don't come here nearly often enough now. Before I married Max we used the house quite a lot, every other weekend, and always at Christmas, a houseful of guests. Edward had always loved it, especially towards the end ...

I went and sat in his room, as if the surroundings that had been so familiar to him might conjure him up. I wondered if he too had resented my compassion. Had he thought me patronising, condescending and supercilious? Had he resented the need to be grateful for my affection and care?

318

They were questions I couldn't answer now. My perspective on life seemed completely distorted. I felt I should never feel quite the same about myself again.

I went outside and walked in the grounds. I stopped for a word with the gardener and admired the hedges, neatly clipped; the lurid display of bedding geraniums. The sun hurt my eyes. I went back inside. I rang for Mrs Arnold to bring me some tea. I read until it was time for supper. At seven o'clock the telephone rang.

'Max!' I said eagerly.

'No, it's me — Jack. Sorry, old girl.'

Disappointment sharpened my voice. 'You've been drinking,' I said shrewishly. 'I can tell by your voice.'

'Well, yes, all right. I've had one or two but nothing serious.' He cleared his throat. 'I've had some rather devastating news, actually.'

'What's happened?' I said faintly, expecting to hear something dreadful about Max.

'I'd rather not talk about it on the 'phone. I was wondering if you could come up. I need to talk to you.'

'What about? I insist on knowing what the problem is.'

There was a pause and then he said; 'Hatry's crashed.'

'Hatry — Clarence Hatry — Austin Friars Trust?'

'Yes. The Trust, all the subsidiaries. They're talking about suspending dealings on all related stock.'

'What's gone wrong?'

'I'm not completely sure but everyone is talking criminal fraud. Apparently, he's been churning out duplicate share certificates to finance his bid for United Steel.' His voice rose in panic. 'Now you've got to come up. I can't cope with this on my own.'

'But I don't see what you think I can do. We'll have to wait for some more definite news. I'll come up tomorrow . . .'

'No. That'll be too late — you see, I'm afraid there's a bit more to it than that.'

My heart sunk. 'In what way?'

'Well, I'm in a bit of a fix personally. I mean, there was absolutely no risk. You know Hatry, everything he touched seemed to come up trumps. No one could have expected this, could they?'

319

My own voice; cold, heavy with dread. 'I don't know what you're talking about, Jack.'

'Well, everyone's known for months that Hatry had his eye on United Steel. It was just a matter of time before he made a bid. All the smart money was in, so I thought I'd have a go at a bit of stagging myself. I bought thirty thousand Austin Friars at five on account, meaning to close at six. And at first everything went like clockwork. I was in line to make an absolute packet. And then that election business set everything back. The shares dropped and I had to get a continuance till the next account and even then things were a bit sticky so I had to fork out a cover of ten per cent. And now this fraud thing's blown up. I — well, the long and short of it is my brokers have made another call and I'm not able to settle. I've just got until tomorrow morning to find the money.'

'How much money?'

A pause. I could visualise him licking his lips in the nervous way he had.

'Well, work it out for yourself. Thirty thousand at five, less ten per cent — something like a hundred and thirty thousand.'

'Can't you sell now. Cut your losses?'

'Well, obviously I've thought of that but who's going to buy the way things are. There's absolutely no market. Everyone's got cold feet. That's why the brokers are insisting I take delivery of the stock.

'And of course, the worst thing is,' he went on after another nervous pause. 'You remember me saying I'd had to cough up ten per cent? Well of course, I didn't actually have that sort of cash so I — er — I borrowed it from the bank. I mean. I just thought it would be a matter of days before I paid it back ...'

I couldn't think. I couldn't speak. I felt physically sick. 'What do you expect me to do, Jack?' I said faintly.

'Well, I leave that to you — but you know what will happen if I don't meet that call. I'll be completely ruined — and I needn't add that if anyone finds out that one of our depositor's accounts is fifteen thousand short ...' Fear and panic crackled down the line. 'Look, you've got to help me.

320

You've got to get me out of this. I've got less than twenty-four hours.'

'Jack ...' My head was spinning, my mind numb with shock.

'Look, you've got to come up now ...'

'I can't,' I said. 'There isn't a train till tomorrow morning. I didn't bring the car.'

'I'll come and get you then. I can be there in an hour.'

'No. Listen. I have to think ...'

'Think in the car. We can put our heads together on the way back.'

I didn't answer. It was an effort to think, let alone speak.

'So I'll come down and get you then? — Mother, are you there?'

'Yes, I'm here.'

'I'll come down then?'

'I — yes, all right.'

October 12th, 1929, Royal Victoria Infirmary hospital

Looking back on that day now after an interval of nearly two months, I can see that it was madness even to have got in the car. Jack was obviously drunk, but by then I was more than a little drunk myself. I'd had a brandy to steady myself after speaking to Jack; then another to give me the courage to telephone Max, then another for consolation when Mellon informed me that he was out. I didn't bother counting after that. I sat drinking steadily whilst I waited for Jack to arrive, mulling over exactly what I was going to do.

What was I going to do? Pay up as I always did, as he seemed to expect? I considered the consequences if I refused to help him. At least it wasn't illegal, but it was no less catastrophic for that. Bankruptcy was equally damning. He'd be finished in business. He'd have to resign from the bank. Tears pricked my eyes. I thought of Edward. What would he have wanted me to do? Protect Jack; protect the bank — weren't they one and the same thing? The bank was going to be hard hit in any case. We held large amounts of City Corporation stock, one of Austin Friars subsidiaries. The bank would survive that but whether it would survive the

321

financial impeachment of its managing director ... So really, when I thought about it, I couldn't see that I had a choice. When one thought of the scandal, the shame and disgrace ...

I tried not to think about it. I tried to concentrate on something pleasant and bland; milk and biscuits in the nursery, my father reading aloud from the *Iliad*; 'As Dawn spread her saffron mantle over the world, Zeus, who delights in thunder, called the gods to the highest of Olympus' many peaks ...' — but I couldn't fix the images clearly in my mind.

Ellis brought me coffee and took my bags down to the hall. I stood by the window watching for the car. Then I laid down my cup as the headlights swept into the drive and, just a little unsteadily, made my way downstairs.

Jack was nervous, excitable. He flung my bag in the back of the car. We moved off with screeching tyres amid a hail of gravel.

Jack was talking. I wasn't listening. I was thinking about Max, wondering where he could be. Perhaps I would try his club. He could be dining there — except that Mellon had said 'white tie'. Dinner at the Northern Counties didn't warrant white tie. *White tie!* That meant a theatre or a ball, a smart restaurant at least. Of course, there were a dozen explanations; someone telephoning at the last minute with a spare ticket for a play, a spur-of-the-moment invitation to make up a party ... A dozen explanations besides the one that had leapt instantly into my mind. Why on earth should I think he was with Marcia?

Jack was still talking. What was he saying? Asking me for a cigarette. I remember his face, illuminated briefly as he struck a match, yellow and sickly with fear. The cigarette formed a red button of light in the darkness of the car. I watched it burn down, ash falling on his lap. We drove into the bend, he lifted a hand from the wheel to wind the window down. Cold air rushing against my face; the cigarette stub tumbling along the road in a vortex of orange sparks; the car drifting over to the wrong side of the road ... then headlights coming towards us, dazzling and white; Jack wrenching at the wheel, the car mounting the verge, a tree rushing towards us in the glare of the headlights ...

More lights, white and blinding but with a faint bluish

322

tinge; men with their faces masked in white gauze; the dull gleam of surgical steel; the sickly smell of ether ...

Then the slow climb back to consciousness, like trying to escape from an abyss by way of a sheer and slippery cliff. No sooner had I gained a foothold that I slid back into the darkness again.

'Max!' My voice, faint and hollow, whispering round the sterile walls of the hospital ward.

'Yes. Yes, I'm here.' He leant down and kissed me. 'It's all right, I'm here.'

For a few moments I couldn't think. I couldn't think where I was or why I was where I was. Then I remembered the car careering out of control ...

'Jack! Is he ...?'

'He's all right,' Max said soothingly. 'Just cuts and bruises, a few broken ribs ...'

A pause whilst I summoned up the courage to ask. 'Am I all right?'

'Well you will be in a few weeks. There's nothing to worry about. It's just a question of absolute rest.' He hesitated and I felt his fingers gently stroking my hair. 'Apparently,' he went on, 'you're suffering from something called spinal concussion. The doctor says it's quite common in cases of severe trauma.'

'What does that mean?' I said. 'It sounds terrifying.'

'Well, I'm not quite sure myself. You know what doctors are like. You can never really grasp what they're talking about.' He tried to smile. 'They didn't seem to think it was fatal, anyway.'

I tried to smile back, to force down the sudden feeling of fear and panic but I could feel my mouth trembling, tears springing in my eyes ...

'Are you all right, darling?' Max leant towards me in concern. 'You're not in any pain, are you?'

'No,' I answered weakly. 'Quite the reverse ...' I broke off as my muddled thoughts grasped this fact. No pain, no feeling, no sensation at all. From the neck down I was completely paralysed.

'It's only temporary, Mrs Claremont.' A doctor, smiling and

323

efficient in a long white coat, soothed my fears in a calm professional voice. 'As far as we can see there has been no permanent destruction of tissue. There is no sign of real vasomotor paralysis or engorgement of the superficial vessels. What you are experiencing is a temporary interruption of sensory and motor function of the limbs. Everything else is functioning quite normally, although you may experience some slight oedema until bladder action is re-established.'

I stared at him blankly, my mind numb with shock. 'I see,' I said — but I didn't see anything. I didn't feel anything. My thoughts seemed as completely paralysed as my limbs.

'How — how long will I have to stay here?' I managed to say at last.

'Well, that depends on how quickly you make progress of course — and that depends on doing as you're told and not trying to rush things, but I would expect the flexor reflexes to have re-appeared within the next four weeks.' His manner was reassuring. He made it sound as if I was suffering from nothing more serious than a very bad cold. I looked at Max. He had averted his face and was staring at the wall. What did that mean? Was it a gesture of despair, anger — revulsion!

'Well, thank you for explaining, Doctor.' I forced a smile.

He patted my shoulder. 'Don't worry, Mrs Claremont. We'll have you up and about in no time.'

He left us alone but for a few moments we didn't speak. We couldn't seem to look at each other either, as if suddenly this dreadful thing was a source of mutual embarrassment between us.

Then I said with forced lightness. 'Well, this is going to be a bore, isn't it?'

He tried to smile. 'The rest will do you the world of good. In fact, you must be quite exhausted now. I should go and let you get some rest ...'

'No. Don't go.' Suddenly I was terrified of being left alone. I had been given a sedative but it didn't seem to be having any effect. I felt wide awake, my mind painfully alert as if to compensate for the anaesthesia of my limbs.

'You said Jack wasn't badly hurt?' I said, attempting to turn my thoughts away from myself.

324

'Yes. He was lucky — far luckier than he deserved to be. What on earth induced you to get into that car? It must have been obvious that he was drunk.'

For a moment I couldn't remember — then it all came back; 'I wanted to speak to you,' I said. 'I tried to get you on the telephone but Mellon said you'd gone out.'

'Yes,' he said. 'Veronica dragged me in to make up a box at the theatre.'

'Was Marcia there?' I enquired casually.

'No. She'd left the previous day. I presume that she's returned to Paris.'

'Did you speak to her before she left? What happened to Hugo?'

He frowned. 'No, I didn't speak to her before she left and the boy is with Veronica at Ansty, which is where, so she tells me, he is going to stay.'

'So Marcia agreed to the adoption then?'

I could see he was making an effort to keep his temper. 'Not as far as I know,' he replied stiffly — then he added hotly. 'Forget about him, Lydia. He's none of our concern. You can't even control the son you've got, never mind anyone else's.'

Then I remembered Jack; I remembered the money and Hatry. 'Jack's in trouble,' I blurted out. 'He came to me for money ...'

'Yes, I know,' Max said evenly. 'He told me.'

'He came to you?' I couldn't conceal my surprise.

'He didn't have much choice, did he? There wasn't anyone else who'd oblige him with a hundred and fifty thousand pounds?'

'You loaned him the money then?'

'No, not exactly.' He looked me straight in the eye. 'I forced him to sell me his stock in the bank, well, ten per cent of it, anyway.'

I didn't know what to say. I kept thinking; 'Poor Jack' although sympathy was the last thing he deserved.

'Well, you got a bargain,' I said at last. 'The stock is worth twice that if you should ever want to sell.'

'Why should I want to sell?' I saw him frown. 'I presume you don't approve.'

325

'I don't disapprove,' I said slowly. 'Unless, of course, it proves detrimental to the bank. After all, it could hardly be said that you and Jack get on. I wouldn't want that hostility to be taken into the bank.'

He shrugged. 'Why should it?' he said casually.

'Well, you must know that a ten per cent shareholding entitles you to a seat on the board.'

Was it my imagination or did I see him smile? 'Yes, of course, I know that — but it's not an option I would take up without your full approval and consent.'

That didn't sound like Max either. That air of humility didn't ring quite true ... But I was too tired to care. I felt my eyelids droop as at last the sedative began to take effect. I nodded drowsily. 'We'll talk about it,' I murmured and fell instantly asleep.

I didn't wake until noon the next day and after I had endured the dismal routine of bed pan and blanket bath and been spoon-fed my lunch, I was told that Jack was waiting to see me.

I steeled myself mentally for a scene and the minute he entered the room I knew he was furious. 'How are you then, old girl? They tell me you're going to be laid up for quite a few weeks?'

After this perfunctory enquiry about my health he drew up a chair and lit a cigarette.

'I suppose you've heard the news — that the bank has another major shareholder now?' He was smiling but I could feel his suppressed fury, his blistering rage. He looked a wreck too; stunned, beaten, but his eyes had a wild hysterical look.

'Well, he's got what he always wanted. He's got his foot well and truly in the door at the bank. No doubt he'll be voted in as Chairman within the week. My God, I can just see those old fools eating out of his hand ...'

'Jack,' I said quietly — it was difficult to be assertive from an entirely prone position. 'It's hardly Max's fault that you put yourself in a position where you had no choice but to sell. He didn't plan that you should make a fool of yourself, you know.'

326

He looked at me. 'Didn't he? Well, if he didn't, then it's quite amazing how everything has worked out his way. Don't you feel that?' he said savagely. 'Doesn't it strike you that, however badly things turn out for the rest of us, Max always comes up with a perfect result? Doesn't it strike you as a bit cold-blooded that whilst you were being pieced together on the operating table Max was coolly negotiating for ten per cent of the bank?'

'And doesn't it strike you, that if you hadn't been so stupid, if you hadn't got drunk and crashed the car ...'

'Oh, of course, I'm to blame. I always am. It's amazing how you can always cast me as the villain of the piece. I don't suppose you care to think about the fact that if you hadn't married him — if I hadn't had to watch him making such a wonderful bloody success of things — if I hadn't had to try so hard to keep up ...' Then with that characteristically abrupt change of position and mood he sprang to his feet. 'I'm sorry,' he said. 'I shouldn't be bullying you like this.'

He came and stood by the bed. 'I'm sorry,' he said again. 'Of course, you're quite right, it's entirely my own fault. I've been well and truly — what's the expression — hoist with my own petard?' He smiled weakly. 'It's bloody ironic, isn't it? The one thing that really mattered to me was to keep Max out of the bank and yet I've been the very one to let him in.'

'You haven't exactly let him in,' I protested. 'He's a shareholder, that's all, like thousands of others.'

'But he'll want a seat on the board, won't he? He's got an automatic option on that.'

'Yes, but he won't take it up without my express consent.'

That was a bad mistake. His face lit up. 'Then promise me you won't give it,' he demanded forcibly. 'You know what it would be like. We'd never be able to agree. Inevitably, we'd always be at each other's throats and that wouldn't be good for the bank, would it?

'At least give me a breathing space,' he pressed as he saw my indecision. 'Wait until you're back on your feet before you do anything. That's not too much to ask is it?'

'Jack,' I said wearily. I was growing tired now. 'You might need all the help you can get. There's this Hatry business to clear up ...'

327

'I can handle that,' he said eagerly. 'In fact, it's just the challenge I need. And I wouldn't feel so bad about Max coming in if I'd been able to get things back on an even keel. At least, I'd feel I could face him then on reasonably equal terms. Look, I know I've made a mess of things but I've learned my lesson, truly I have. You have to give me this last chance to prove myself.'

'All right,' I agreed. 'One more chance — but it will be the last one. I can't afford to take risks with the bank.'

I passed a bad night. The nights were always the worst and that night was the very worst of all. The silence and the darkness and the acute mental awareness of the flaccid numbness of my limbs. I became truly frightened. I imagined the worst. Supposing I didn't get better? Supposing I was like this for the rest of my life? But it wouldn't be life, would it? It would be a living death, like being buried alive; the body trapped, helpless but the mind so knowing, so utterly aware ...

I cried a little, cursed a little, and then pulled myself together as I always did. I was going to face this as I had faced all the other disasters of my life. It was no good feeling sorry for myself. Self-pity led to despair and that led to resignation and giving in. I reminded myself that I didn't give in easily.

The main thing, I felt, was to keep myself occupied, to maintain a cheerful and resolute front. I saw it as a challenge. Everything and everyone was to carry on normally but, instead of my going to the bank, I arranged for the bank to come to me. So every morning, sharp at nine, my secretary arrived and I spent the morning dictating letters and memos, and after lunch she read aloud to me from the financial journals so that I felt I knew exactly what was going on. Jack came every morning and Max every night and in between I was visited by my fellow directors, family and friends. It soon became quite clear to anyone who might have thought of offering sympathy that, though my bodily functions were temporarily impaired, my brain continued to function quite normally.

Under this stimulation I made rapid progress and by the beginning of October I had regained the full use of my arms

328

and hands. This was a milestone as I was now able to feed myself, use the telephone and read unaided. I read with interest and satisfaction the news of Hatry's arrest — and with dismay, the City's gloomy predictions that losses to investors could amount to twenty million overall. This was bad news for the bank with a quarter of a million worthless Corporation and General Security shares locked away in its vaults. It occurred to me to wonder if news of our commitment had somehow leaked out. Rochester Mercantile had dropped eight points since Hatry's exposure though I reasoned that this was probably just the market trend. All equities were down. Everyone seemed to be making a rush for gilts. Even Wall Street had turned sickly; unable to sustain its September peak, the market had turned soft in early October. So I convinced myself that the fall in Rochester Mercantile was just part of a loss of confidence in financial institutions generally. Things were bound to be sticky until after Hatry's trial.

The bank's stock continued to fall over the next two days but it wasn't until I had news of nervous depositors transferring funds that I sensed an impending crisis. I realised now that my accident coming so hard on the heels of the Hatry crash and the disposal, albeit privately, of a large block of shares, didn't inspire confidence amongst our shareholders. It was obviously common knowledge that the bank would sustain a heavy loss over the Hatry affair and, added to that, the knowledge that the bank was controlled by a sickly woman from her hospital bed. Something had to be done. A gesture had to be made to restore confidence. Despite my promise to Jack, I saw no choice but to make that gesture, and when Max came to see me that night, I formally offered him a seat on the board.

October 20th, 1929
Confrontation was inevitable. There was a lull of only a few days before the first conflict arose. It had been a bad week on Wall Street; three days of heavy selling had forced the market down, culminating in six million shares changing hands in the first hours of Monday trading. Despite a slight recovery towards closing, Max felt it was time to get out and

329

for the bank to call in its American loans. Jack, naturally, didn't agree.

'Well, I'm sorry,' he said to Max as they sat facing each other across my hospital bed. 'But I think you're over-reacting. A fall of twelve points in the Dow is hardly a cause for panic. I would need a far sounder reason for calling in investments that are making the bank a very healthy ten per cent. I agree that things aren't quite as rosy as they were, but they're bound to pick up. They always have before — in fact, some people are saying that by December the market will be higher than ever.'

'That's because nobody wants to admit that the good times are over,' Max argued. 'It's perfectly obvious that the market's top heavy. In my opinion a substantial fall is inevitable.'

'Well, nobody else seems to be getting cold feet. I hear Goldman Sachs have just launched another six hundred million dollars' worth of investment. That doesn't sound like a declining market to me but obviously you think you know better than Goldman Sachs.'

'I didn't say that. I agree that speculation is still very high. That's my point — it's too high. The Federal Reserve's figures for brokers' loans reached six hundred and seventy million dollars last week. That means a hell of a lot of investors are carrying stocks purely on margin. The bank is no longer funding real investment with a sound economic foundation. We're just providing the nickels and dimes for the American public to feed into an oversized gambling machine that might break down any minute.'

'Well, of course, it's that kind of negative thinking that pushes prices down in the first place,' Jack persisted stubbornly. 'If everyone had thought like that there'd never have been a boom at all.

'And quite frankly,' he added, jumping up from his chair, 'I'm getting a bit tired of you trying to force your dismal views down everyone's throat. You've only been at the bank five minutes and you think you know it all.'

'Look, Rochester,' said Max reasonably. 'I'm not interested in winning a personal argument, you know. I just want to do whatever is in the best interests of the bank.'

330

'And you think I don't?' Jack's voice rose to a screech. 'You've got a nerve, Claremont. Just let me remind you that you only own ten per cent, not the whole bloody bank.'

'Well, that's not quite true,' Max said easily. 'Actually, I own fifteen per cent.'

I thought Jack was going to faint. White-faced and trembling he rounded on Max. 'What the hell do you mean — fifteen per cent? Who did you swindle out of the other five?'

'I didn't swindle anyone. Rochester Mercantile shares are readily available on the open market, you know. I didn't realise I needed your permission to deal.'

Jack sat down, pale with shock. I felt mildly shocked myself, not so much at Max's possession of the shares but because he'd never mentioned it, because he'd kept it a secret, all to himself.

'Five per cent is a great many shares and a great deal of money,' I remarked quietly. 'You must have been buying up for some time.'

Max shrugged. 'Now and then, whenever I had the cash. You see, I did rather well out of some American shares quite early on.' He smiled. 'One speculates in America but invests in England. What better investment than the family bank?'

'Well, do I really need to say anything else?' Jack said triumphantly. 'All this time he's been slyly buying up our stock. If that isn't underhand I don't know what is.'

'I don't see that it's any of your business,' snapped Max. 'I merely mentioned it to demonstrate that I have an even greater interest than you in the bank's profit and loss, that I don't raise these points just to score off you.'

He looked at me in appeal. 'You know I'm right, Lydia. It might only be a small risk but I don't think it's one that we dare to take. After this Hatry business the bank couldn't stand another heavy loss ...'

'Don't listen to him,' Jack cried hotly. 'He's just trying to unnerve you. I'm the one who put the American deal together so it should be my decision whether or not we pull out.'

In an effort to prevaricate, I said, 'Perhaps it would be better if we put the matter before the full board and took a vote.'

'Why wait,' said Max. 'Let's take the vote now. Between us we have the necessary fifty-one per cent, Lydia. We can settle it here and now. It's up to you.'

I took a deep breath. I didn't have any choice. 'All right,' I said, without looking at Jack. 'Call the money in.'

October 24th, 1929

We got out just in time, just hours it seemed before the mad scramble by the European banks to get their money out.

Yesterday, Wednesday, the 23rd, the market index continued its fall, sliding from 415 to 384 during the morning session. Still nobody panicked. The financial journals described the market's erratic behaviour as a '*technical readjustment after the summer peak*'. Jefferson Breck cabled further reassurance from New York; *No cause for concern. Market fundamentally sound. Expect recovery within the next few days.*

Today, Thursday the 24th, thirteen million shares have been traded. Brokers are sending calls out to their margin clients for more collateral, inability to meet the calls has led to forced selling which has led to prices falling even further, more calls going out ... The New York banks intervened, desperate to avoid a full-scale collapse. The market firmed instantly and closed just a miraculous twelve points down. Jefferson Breck cabled from New York, a little less optimistically. '*Situation tense but early recovery expected. Intervention of House of Morgan turned the tide.*'

He cabled again four hours later. '*Continued deterioration against all expectations. Suggest immediate disposal of all speculative stock. Please advise re support of M.N.I.*'

Sydney is taking the next boat to New York.

October 29th, 1929

Despite the steady stream of cables and transatlantic calls, for those of us watching on this side of the Atlantic, it's virtually impossible to know exactly what's going on. Apart from the distance of three thousand miles there's a time difference of five hours which meant that Wall Street opened just as

London closed. It adds to the confusion, the sense of panic. It makes the compulsion to sell irresistible.

All we really have to go on are the grim figures churned out by the Trans Lux at the bank, but as prices continue to plunge even the wire is unable to keep pace with the mounting volume of sales. It means that most of the time no one really knows what's happening until long after it's happened. So over the weekend of the 25th and 26th, whilst we were celebrating Friday's marginal steadying of prices as the beginning of the end, three thousand miles away on Wall Street the end was just beginning.

It's like watching a brutal massacre. Even those who have nothing to lose watch in stunned and silent horror as the market continues its vertical plunge. On Monday the 28th, the market had opened quietly but sales had mounted in volume throughout the day, three and a half million changing hands within the final hour of trading. Yesterday the carnage reached its height as sixteen and a half million shares were flung hysterically into the market. Huge blocks of shares were sold for whatever they would fetch. Blue chips that had once been at a premium were changing hands for just a few dollars and for speculatives there were no buyers at all. It was like the toll of some grisly battle. We scan the Dow Jones like anxious relatives scanning casualty lists. Manhattan and North Island are very much among the dead. All that's necessary now is the post mortem.

November 2nd, 1929
It's over and yet it isn't over. In financial terms it won't be over for years. Already people are referring to it as the Crash, with a capital letter. People are saying 'before the Crash' as they had once said 'before the war'. For those who have lost it must seem like a disaster of equal proportions. Like the war, the repercussions are going to be worldwide. Predictions are for a slump, an international monetary crisis. Some form of recession seems inevitable.

'How's Sydney taking it?' I asked Max when Manhattan and North Island had settled at three dollars compared to its glorious summer high of a hundred and fifty.

'Philosophically, I suppose — like flood and famine, earthquake and plague. He's lost money of course, but nothing like as much as he made when things were good. That was the beauty of the investment trust. Its only assets were other people's money. Its the investors who have really lost.'

'And you,' I enquired cautiously. 'Have things turned out as well for you? You held ten per cent of the stock equally with Sydney, Breck and Gill. You must have made losses too.'

He looked faintly embarrassed. 'As a matter of fact I came out of it rather well. I sold out my interest in August when the market was still high. I sold everything in my portfolio, actually. I had to, you see, to buy Jack's shares in the bank.'

'More secrets,' I said lightly. 'I wonder what else I don't know.'

He gave me a quizzical look. 'You're angry, aren't you? I can't think why. I thought you would have been pleased that I hadn't gone under.'

'Well of course I'm pleased. It's just — well, I suppose it irritates me that you never discuss anything with me.'

He smiled. 'It isn't anything personal. I'm naturally secretive, that's all. A good gambler always plays his hand close to his chest.' He leaned forward, smiling. 'The trouble with you, darling, is that you have a penchant for losers rather than winners, that's all. In that respect, at least, I hope always to disappoint you.'

'Don't be ridiculous, Max. Nobody wants you to be successful more than I. It would just be nice if sometimes you'd tell me things rather than me having to always dig things out.'

'All right.' He laughed. 'When I make my first million you'll be the first to know.'

We went on to talk of other things — namely whether I could expect to be home by Christmas or not.

'You know, Lydia,' he said thoughtfully. 'I'm wondering if perhaps we shouldn't get a second opinion. Things do seem to be rather dragging on.'

'It's only just over two months, Max. The consultant told us to be prepared for three. We have to give things a fair chance.'

334

'I don't see the harm in letting someone else have a look. There's a chap at one of the Edinburgh hospitals. He's a specialist in this sort of thing and they have one of those marvellous ray machines there. At least then we'd know exactly what was going on.'

'I don't know,' I said doubtfully. 'I think I'd rather wait a few more weeks.'

'But where's the harm in just letting this chap have a look?' He leant forward and took my hand. 'Look, I'm sorry to be so impatient, but I do miss you, you know. I'd just feel better if we were doing something constructive.'

He was so persuasive that eventually I agreed. 'After all,' he added, 'what have you got to lose?'

Looking at his face I felt a queer sense of premonition which startled me into sharply withdrawing my hand. The gesture startled me even more. It seemed an extravagant reaction to such an ordinary remark.

It wasn't till after he'd gone that I realised why. I have, in fact, absolutely everything to lose if this specialist concludes that the damage is more than superficial. Perhaps, subconsciously, I'm afraid of that, and in a cowardly way I'm trying to postpone that reality for as long as I can. And it's true that secretly I've been worried about my lack of progress. There is still neither sensation nor movement in either of my legs. The doctors counsel patience and optimism but this seems to me an echo of the soothing platitudes that came out of Wall Street just before the Crash. But that's negative thinking. I've never believed in that. I mustn't allow myself to think the unthinkable.

November 19th, 1929
The days drag by. I try not to think about the man in Edinburgh and his wonderful machine — I have an appointment to see him in two weeks' time. His name is Carson and this fact of his identity makes him unpleasantly real — I preferred it when he was completely anonymous.

I try to keep myself occupied. I have the wireless and the telephone and an endless supply of newspapers and magazines. I have plenty of visitors too; Jack every day, Max

335

comes at least twice. Even Ursula has been, purely in order to view her handiwork I felt, and having satisfied herself that the wrath of God had been well and truly visited upon me, she went away with a quiet and triumphant smile. And Veronica of course. Yesterday she dropped in looking radiant in a Chanel suit and a huge silver fox. She seemed more beautiful and more selfish than ever. She brought me fashion magazines that she'd obviously read on the train coming up and a box of Benticks which she proceeded to eat herself.

Just for once she didn't talk entirely about herself — although, because she sees the boy Hugo as an extension of herself, I suppose it's the same thing really.

'Oh, he's such a darling, Lydia. Everyone adores him. I wish I could have brought him with me but Sydney thought it unwise. You never know with hospitals, do you? There might be all sorts of germs floating about.'

A pause whilst she searched for the last violet creme.

'It's amazing how things have turned out, isn't it? How wonderfully little Hugo has fitted in. He's a real Claremont, you know, and most people think I'm his natural mother in any case. We look so alike, you see.'

'Do you ever hear from Marcia?' I asked brutally.

Her expression darkened. 'No. There's been nothing. Not even a postcard to ask how he is. I'm not sure whether that's a good or a bad thing. Sometimes I think she's forgotten all about him, and as long as she gets her allowance she won't bother us. And then at other times I think it's just part of her plan, that she means us to forget all about her so that when she turns up again it will be all the more devastating.'

'You think she will turn up?'

'Well, Sydney thinks so. He thinks that if Marcia intended to stay away for good, she'd have let us adopt Hugo outright. He thinks it's a subtle form of blackmail. The fonder we get of Hugo, the more we're likely to pay to keep him with us.'

She stayed for an hour. I was relieved when she left. I found myself wondering why utterly useless people like Veronica manage to sail through life unscathed ... I was jealous of course, furious at her obvious pity for me, resentful of her possession of the child that could have been mine. It

336

was unfortunate that I should have started thinking about Hugo again. How different things might have been if Max hadn't been so violent in his refusal to let me adopt the boy. We would never have quarrelled, I'd never have gone to Farnfield. Jack wouldn't have been able to bring me back ... Why is life so terribly unfair?

November 15th, 1929
Things are bad at the bank. Losses on Corporation and General Securities stock are expected to be around half a million. For the first time in twenty years we shan't be able to pay a full dividend. Poor Edward will be turning in his grave.

There's a general air of depression all round. Prices on the London exchange are still falling though their decline is a dignified diagonal slide rather than a vertical collapse. What's happening now is that the people who refused to sell out of panic are now being forced to do so out of need. In America, everyone was hit by the Crash but in England it seems to be mainly the most innocent people who are likely to suffer in the long term, people whose only income was derived from managed investments which have suddenly been rendered worthless. The magazines are full of discreet little advertisements for the disposal of 'unwanted gifts'. Property too is tumbling into the market. All this uncertainty merely adds to my own. Inactivity of the mind coupled with that of the body is a certain recipe for gloom. What I need is some form of distraction.

Something always turns up — my father used to say that — so just as I was thinking I should go quite mad with boredom, there it was, the perfect therapy.

I had been leafing idly through the latest copy of *Country Life*. As I had predicted, the property section was twice its usual length, full of large old houses, impossible to staff, expensive to run. And then I saw it: 'For sale by private treaty. "Blanchland". Large country estate of fifteen hundred acres with three farms producing income of eight hundred pounds a year ...'

My first instinct was to telephone Max. Probably he

337

already knew, probably he was signing contracts this very minute ... And then it occurred to me, knowing how depleted his reserves were after buying the shares in the bank, that he might have trouble finding that amount of cash. He'd have to borrow. He'd have to approach either Sydney or myself; I couldn't imagine pride keeping him from Blanchland.

I decided to make a few more enquiries before I mentioned it to Max. A telephone call to the agents revealed that as yet they had received no firm bids but the vendor would consider offers of around fifty thousand pounds. I didn't even hesitate. Entirely on impulse I met the price. After all, I reasoned, we couldn't risk someone else stepping in before Max had time to raise the necessary cash. Then I thought what a wonderful surprise it would make. If I could spin things out till Christmas it could be my gift. Max would be lamenting the loss of Blanchland again and calmly, on Christmas day, I'd hand him the deeds.

I telephoned Ridgeway immediately and asked him to come over and, after swearing him to secrecy, instructed him to handle the purchase on my behalf, though I emphasised it was to be made in Max's name.

I felt wonderfully elated and passed hours of happy speculation, imagining his surprise, his pleasure, his delight. This would be one gift that he couldn't refuse. I intended of course to be equally generous with Jack. I would make him a gift of the Eldon Square house. After all, Max and I would be living at Blanchland, and it occurred to me that there was an added bonus in the fact that, with the estate to run, Max wouldn't have so much time for the bank which would make things more bearable for Jack.

And so engrossed did I become that I didn't notice the time passing. Suddenly it was time for my journey to Edinburgh.

November 26th, 1929
I insisted on going alone — at least, despite his arguments, I refused to let Max accompany me. I felt his presence would make the tension unbearable. I was nervous as it was. I found

338

the closed ambulance oppressive and the sound of the engine reminded me that the last time I had been in a moving vehicle ... This made me so agitated that I was given a sedative and the remainder of the journey passed in a pleasurable blur.

The ray machine was daunting, a massive device which omitted a beam of radiation which could pierce the flesh and record the image of the bones on a photographic plate. It was not painful as I had imagined but I felt slightly sick for an hour or two afterwards and it was a disappointment that I was not to be told the results straight away. I was going to have to wait till the morning.

I passed a restless night, despite a sleeping pill. I awoke early whilst it was still completely dark. My thoughts were chaotic, veering between wild optimism and nihilistic gloom. It was the uncertainty, you see, that was so unbearable.

He came after breakfast, which I couldn't eat.

'Mrs Claremont!' His smile was so cheerful that I felt there couldn't be much wrong.

He perched himself easily on the edge of the bed. 'Not feeling any discomfort, I hope? No headaches, nausea, anything like that?'

'No,' I replied steadily. 'Nothing like that.'

'Good. That's good. You may find some slight reddening of the skin in about ten days' time. This isn't anything to worry about. It fades quite quickly.'

He smiled again but this time I wasn't so reassured. 'Now I've written a full report to your physician. It's probably better if he explains things to you ...'

'Please tell me,' I said suddenly. 'I want to know. I can tell by your face that it's not good news but I'd like to know all the same.'

He hesitated. I could see that he was quietly weighing me up. Was I the hysterical type who'd make a fuss? Then he said gently: 'Well, your condition is a little more complicated than was at first thought. The X-ray shows definite tissue damage to the seventh lumbar segment ...' He paused. 'It's irreversible, I'm afraid, Mrs Claremont. There's really nothing else we can do.'

I swallowed hard. 'Does that mean' — I swallowed again

339

— 'does that mean that I shan't ever be able to walk?'

'Yes, I'm afraid so.'

'Well, thank you for telling me,' I heard myself saying in a calm and steady voice. *Thank you for telling me!* What a ridiculous thing to say! Thank you for destroying my hopes, for destroying my life, for turning me into a helpless cripple ...

I wanted to cry but I found myself smiling weakly and shaking his hand. 'Thank you for telling me,' I said again.

I felt the worst thing would be telling Max, and all through that long and horrific journey home I was formulating in my mind exactly what I would say.

In the event I didn't have to say anything at all. I saw by his face that he already knew. Of course, he too would have been waiting impatiently for the results. He probably knew before I did.

He came and sat by the bed, his shoulders hunched, his face obscured. He was so still, so silent — and for so long that I felt I was going to have to be the one to speak but I couldn't get the words past the constriction of my throat.

Then still without looking at me, he reached blindly for my hand. 'Oh Max,' I whispered, 'what am I going to do?'

He looked up at me then, the fairness of his lashes darkened with tears. 'Don't worry,' he said. 'We'll manage somehow. The main thing is you're alive.'

But it isn't, is it? There's life and life, and I'm only half alive, half a woman, from the waist down I'm dead and buried.

December 1st, 1929, Eldon Square

So I am home in time for Christmas exactly as I had planned, though not at all in the way I had imagined. I made a desperate effort to be cheerful. Things certainly looked better from the vertical instead of the horizontal, and I was mobile after a fashion in one of the latest type of invalid carriages in which, for short distances, I could propel myself.

It was only when I actually entered Eldon Square that I realised how difficult life was going to be. My own home where I had expected to feel so safe and comfortable was

340

suddenly an alien and dangerous place. Furniture had to be rearranged to allow passage for my chair. I had to get used to seeing things from a different level, to being looked down on, talked down to, to addressing waistcoat buttons before I remembered to look up.

I have a nurse called Emily Shaw, a robust middle-aged woman combining the necessary qualifications of professional cheerfulness with muscular strength. Shaw regulates my life with military thoroughness. At nine she brings me my breakfast on a tray. At ten, she carries me through to my bath. I take luncheon in my room unless I am expecting guests. Then I read until five when she helps me dress for dinner and carries me downstairs and settles me comfortably in my chair.

Then Max comes home. Over cocktails he tells me whether he's had a good day or not. Jack arrives shortly afterwards. He kisses my cheek, tells me I look well — the same words every night, the same false cheerfulness, the same forced effort to be pleasant to Max. They never quarrel now, or if they do they restrict their squabbles to the bank. I assume that for my sake some sort of truce has been declared. It appears I am to be cosseted, protected, shielded from unpleasantness of any kind which of course is the last thing I want.

At ten o'clock Max carries me upstairs and delivers me into Shaw's capable hands. He kisses me goodnight, tenderly, without passion, his mouth on mine cool and undemanding.

Shaw undresses me and puts my night-things on. I try not to look at my legs, to see how limp and flaccid and ugly my body has become. Then deftly, impersonally, Shaw slips me between the sheets — no silk sheets now but sensible ones, lined with a sturdy drawsheet and the crackle of a mackintosh beneath.

Then my sleeping pills and warm milk. Shaw disappears into the dressing room where she sleeps on a day bed in case I should wake in the night. She emerges minutes later in dressing gown and plaits.

'Goodnight, madam. I'll leave the door open in case you should call.'

I close my eyes, longing for privacy. I think that's what I

341

resent the most, that every aspect of my life seems to be public and exposed, that even the most intimate of acts is open to scrutiny.

I'm still wide awake. It's always a little while before the sleeping pills take effect. I lie thinking of Max, remembering what it was like to fall asleep in his arms, remembering how in the mornings he would kiss me awake. I'm faintly surprised that I should still feel desire — or perhaps it's just the memory of past desire that's still very strong, because as soon as I think of Max touching my withered and unresponsive flesh I am revolted rather than aroused. Of course I realise that that side of things must be over between us. I can accept celibacy for myself but it would be completely unfair to expect it of Max. Naturally, sooner or later he'll take a mistress, and I, equally naturally, will turn a blind eye. She'll be young and pretty and I shall resent her existence bitterly, as no doubt she will eventually come to resent mine. How strange that I can consider the prospect with a kind of equanimity now where once I would have been plunged into a jealous frenzy. One's values change. What was once important seems no longer so. I can bear the thought of his infidelity far easier than I can bear the thought of him looking at me with pity in his eyes. It hasn't come to that yet; sympathy and compassion aren't the same as pity, but even now I find myself intolerant of his solicitude, his consideration, his perfect patience. How ironic, thinking of all the compassion I have lavished on other people all my life, and yet when it is offered to me I can't accept it.

December 28th, 1929
We spent Christmas quietly at Eldon Square. To my secret relief, Jack had got up a party of friends and gone down to Farnfield, and though Max and I had been invited to Ansty as usual we politely declined.

So it was just the two of us exchanging gifts on Christmas morning, and, after I had exclaimed in delight over a pearl monogram brooch, I smilingly handed him the beribboned box that contained the deeds of Blanchland.

I held my breath. It was a big moment for me. For weeks I

342

had hugged my secret close and the vision of Max's pleasure had warded off many a bout of pain and depression. So I was a little taken aback to see the blank look on his face.

'You know what they are, don't you?' I enquired with a fond smile.

'Yes, I know what they are.'

'Aren't you pleased?' I asked anxiously.

'Yes, of course. I'm just rather — well — overwhelmed, that's all.' He looked at me with mild irritation. 'I wish I'd known you were going to be so generous, Lydia. This makes my own offering rather shoddy in comparison.'

I was stung by his sarcasm. 'You're angry, aren't you?' I cried in amazement. 'But why? Isn't this what you've always wanted? Hasn't it always been your ambition to buy Blanchland back?'

'Yes — *my* ambition, *my* achievement. I wanted to work for it, fight for it. I didn't want it given to me, tied up with ribbon.'

He jumped to his feet and began to pace irritably around me. 'And of course it never occurred to you, the anger and disappointment I felt when I realised that Blanchland had been sold to someone else.'

'Well, it might have been, if I hadn't stepped in. What if you couldn't have raised the money in time?'

'I'd have raised it, don't worry. And even if I hadn't that would have been my affair. Don't you see how galling it is to have to admit that everything I have is directly or indirectly due to you?'

'Oh, for goodness' sake, does it matter?' I snapped, irritable myself. 'Are you telling me that you'd have been happier to see Blanchland go to someone else rather than take it from me?'

'Yes, I would,' he yelled, his face reddening with fury. 'So you can keep these' — he flung the deeds into my lap — 'until such time as I've raised the money to buy them back.'

Of course, we made it up ten minutes later, and I suppose I should be glad that our relationship is still normal enough to allow us to quarrel. But for me the day had turned sour. My grand gesture was meaningless. It had now taken on the appearance of a bribe. As always I had been overgenerous so that it seemed as if I was offering him some form of consolation, a compensation for his ruined and dreary life.

That's the worst thing about being a chronic invalid; it's not just coming to terms with the physical aspect of illness, it's coming to terms with the effect it has on the mind. One becomes increasingly sensitive. One's judgement becomes impaired. One is always on the defensive, looking for a slight, imagining that people are being condescending when they're only being kind. And people are kind — too kind, so that I think they are pitying me, that their kindness comes from a feeling of guilt. But that's an invalid's prerogative, to make people feel guilty for being healthy and whole. I remember Edward used it to marvellous effect. He made me feel guilty about everything so that in the end the smallest and most innocent of pleasures appeared iniquitous.

I often find myself thinking of Edward now. There's an obvious parallel of course. What has happened to Max is almost exactly what happened to me and it's because of the life I had with Edward that I think about the future with such concern. I remember how quickly love turns to pity and pity becomes guilt, and guilt turns to resentment and hatred. I remember the feeling of being trapped, of struggling to conceal my impatience and disgust, I remember thinking how unfair it was that Edward should get all the sympathy. People said what a tragedy it was for a man like Edward to be struck down in his prime. They never saw the equal tragedy of a young woman trapped, all her youth wasted ... Oh God, I mustn't ever let that happen to Max.

January 10th, 1930
I'm beginning to take a very strong dislike to Shaw. I sense a mildly sadistic streak, that beneath that jolly and overtly kindly disposition lurks a cruel and tyrannical personality. Of course it's natural to resent the person who, in every other way a complete and utter stranger, is witness to the most personal and intimate details of one's life. Yet I feel Shaw observes my struggle for modesty with a ghoulish relish, that she thrills to my humiliation and shame. And she is

344

beginning to bully me in a playful 'Mother knows best' kind of way. I am a 'good girl' or a 'bad girl' accordingly.

I find myself increasingly revolted by her presence and chilled by the thought that for the rest of my life I shall have to endure this forced intimacy, that I shall always be at the mercy of Shaw or someone like her. It's just another of the little ironies that occur to me these days — that my dread of being alone is transformed into a dread of never being alone again.

January 28th, 1930

I have spent the last few days in bed, for no better reason than that I cannot face getting up. Edward had days like that, days of depression and inertia, of creeping despair, when even the effort to speak was too much.

And really, life goes on, with or without me. It's amazing how quickly one becomes divorced from the real world. Every day I grow more detached, more distanced from reality, like a small and diminishing star on the edge of some vast universe. People will hardly notice that I'm not there.

I think a great deal about death; Edward's, my own — if only I could be sure of an equally swift and peaceful end. In retrospect, it seems a pity that I wasn't killed outright. Sudden death is always preferable to a slow decline.

I have considered suicide of course, in a purely impersonal and academic way. Even though I have no real religion, I have respect for the sanctity of life, and self-destruction has never been a serious option. One contemplates it, but not seriously. As Nietzche said: 'It's the thought of suicide that gets me through many a bad night.' It's like money hoarded, never to be spent. One has the comfort of knowing it is there.

But there must come a point when even my courage fails, when the heroic struggle for survival ceases to he heroic and becomes merely an act of stubborn stupidity. When one is completely helpless and dependent in every other way it seems the only decision one can actually make oneself. Then death begins to exert a fatal fascination. It holds out the promise of relief, a way of escape. It's no longer a terrifying prospect and one begins to think about it as a haven, a

345

retreat. One begins to weigh up the issues, to balance years of pain and incontinence against the prospect of a quiet and dignified end.

And even more persuasive to the argument, at least to me, is the fact that death for me would mean life for Max. All I have left to give him now is freedom.

February 20th, 1930

I'm quite calm, quite certain. It's amazing how suddenly and swiftly I've achieved peace of mind. I'm not sure of the exact moment when I actually made my decision, the moment when the whole purpose of Marcia's visit became clear. Perhaps, subconsciously, I made it the moment Max handed me Veronica's wire.

I was still in bed, conscious of my tangled hair and unpowdered nose. I read with a curious feeling of sickly excitement: *'Marcia's back. Obviously it's pay-day. Sending Hugo and nurse up on first possible train. Can you accommodate whilst we haggle.'*

I handed the telegram back. 'Why is she sending Hugo here?'

Max shrugged. 'Obviously she's trying to keep him out of Marcia's way. You know how stupid Vee can be. She's got absolutely no right to keep them apart. After all, the boy is still Marcia's son.'

And yours, I thought bleakly, and reflected that sometimes fate could be particularly cruel. Not content with having pushed me to the very edge of the abyss, it now seemed that I must actually jump in.

'Will you mind him being here?' I asked, remembering the last time we had talked about Hugo.

'I suppose not,' he answered, then as he remembered too, he added gently: 'Will you?'

'No, of course not.' I spoke lightly, mentally closing the door on the past. 'It will make a pleasant diversion to have Hugo here.'

Max glanced at his watch. 'Do you want me to stay? I can telephone the bank if you like ...'

'Don't be silly,' I said, suddenly irritated by his solicitude.

346

'I'm perfectly capable of making conversation with a three-year-old child, probably more capable than any of you, seeing as everyone seems to treat me as if I were a similar age.'

'Sorry,' he said and pulled a face. 'I keep forgetting how you hate people making a fuss.'

'Not people,' I said, smiling. 'Just you.'

He leant down and kissed me. 'I'll get off then,' he said. 'Telephone me at the bank as soon as he arrives and I'll try to get away early.'

'Darling, I've just told you there's no need to make a fuss ...'

'I'm not fussing,' he said. 'I'd quite like to see him too.'

Of course I pondered on that all morning. Did it mean after all that he was fond of the boy? What a travesty it would be if, after that first violent reaction, he had changed his mind, that if I hadn't swept off to Farnfield we might have talked again more quietly and he might have agreed ... It was a possibility I didn't dare explore.

Hugo and his nurse arrived after lunch and my heart twisted within me as I saw how he'd grown and how, even more, he resembled Max.

He regarded me gravely. 'Hugo,' said his nurse, 'this is your Aunt Lydia. Say "How do you do, Aunt Lydia."'

'How do you do, Aunt Lydia,' he repeated in his quiet childish voice.

'Hello Hugo,' I smiled. 'Do you remember me?'

'Yes,' he said doubtfully. He gave the nurse an anxious glance.

'The snowman,' I said. 'Do you remember the snowman we made together in the field?'

His face lit up. 'Snowman,' he lisped and gave a gurgling laugh. Then his face fell again. 'Snowman went away. You went away — and Maman.'

'Now come along, Hugo dear,' the nurse said briskly. 'We must get you upstairs. It's quite time for your nap ...'

'No. Goway!' Hugo screamed suddenly and even I was shocked by the violence in his voice.

Smithers grabbed at his arm. 'Now that won't do, will it. What will your Aunt Lydia think? She'll think you're a

347

naughty little boy who won't do as you're told and we all know what happens to naughty boys, don't we?'

Hugo yelled even louder and struggled in her grip. His small face was contorted with fury and hatred, and as Smithers tried to drag him out of the room he jerked his head round and bit deeply into her hand.

With a scream of pain, the nurse loosed her grip and Hugo ran and flung himself down sobbing on the couch.

'Oh, I'm so sorry, madam. What a disgraceful exhibition. What on earth must you think?'

'I think the child is tired and frightened,' I answered her mildly. 'And until he's calmed down I suggest you leave him here with me.'

'Oh, I couldn't do that, madam. Mrs Elsworth's very strict about Hugo having his nap . . .'

'Well, Mrs Elsworth isn't here, is she? And whilst you're in my house you take your orders from me.' I tugged at the bell rope beside my chair. 'Mellon will show you to your rooms now and when Hugo is ready to go up I'll send for you.'

She departed with a sullen look. Hugo, who had stopped crying, stared at me cautiously.

'Why don't you come over here, Hugo, and let me take off your outdoor things.'

He approached me slowly, with something like distrust. I unbuttoned his coat and smoothed down his hair. 'There now. Sit down by the fire. Your hands are quite cold.'

He sat obediently, cross-legged at my feet.

'You were rather horrid to Smithers, weren't you?' I looked at him with mild reproach. 'Perhaps later on you might like to say that you're sorry.'

'Not sorry,' he said, his face sulky again.

'No, I know you're not — but that doesn't matter as long as Smithers thinks you are. You see, I know how you feel. I have a nurse too. Her name is Shaw and she tries to bully me like Smithers bullies you.'

He stared at me solemnly, as though he was quietly considering what I had said. I doubted that he fully understood but he seemed quite happy just to listen to my voice so I went on talking in a gentle reassuring voice. Within ten minutes he was fast asleep.

348

Max came home about four and we all had tea in the library. I was watching of course, but even so I couldn't have missed the searching way Max looked at the boy. It was as if he was trying to make up his mind, as if he were searching Hugo's face for some sign, some clue that would resolve the doubt that was in both our minds.

He didn't say much, except to keep asking Hugo if he wanted some more cake.

'Max,' I protested, 'you'll make the child sick.'

Simultaneously they looked at each other and simultaneously they smiled and the resemblance between them was so acute that I wondered how Max could still doubt their obvious relationship. I myself was convinced that Max was his father.

We dined alone. Jack had gone up to town with friends to see the new Coward play. We were unusually silent. I felt that we both wanted to talk about Hugo but neither of us wanted to broach the subject first. Then, just as we were finishing, the doorbell rang with an impatient and imperious note. Intuitively I knew it was Marcia.

'Hello Max' — accompanied by that lazy feline smile. She nodded casually towards me. 'How are you, Lydia?'

Max didn't speak but he rose from his chair and went towards her. I sensed immediately the antagonism between them, the curious antipathy felt by people who've once been passionate lovers but who now don't care to be reminded of the fact.

'What the hell are you doing here?' Max demanded.

Marcia peeled off her gloves. 'I should have thought that was obvious,' she replied coolly. 'I am here because my son is here.'

'Does Veronica know about you coming here?'

'Probably. I did not actually say so. When I left we were not exactly on speaking terms. I dare say that she's guessed.'

She extracted a cigarette from a gold case and placed it between her lips, waiting pointedly for Max to light it.

'What's the problem this time?' Max said, lighting one himself. 'I presume that Sydney didn't offer enough.'

349

'Nothing like enough,' Marcia agreed airily. 'Everything costs so much these days, don't you agree? Unfortunately for all of you, I have to live as well.' She laughed at Max's disgusted expression. 'Oh, I know what you are thinking, darling, except that you are too English and well bred to tell me.' She shrugged. 'I have to make the best of my assets and the only asset I have left is Hugo.'

'I'm going to telephone Veronica,' said Max in a grim hard voice. 'And then I'm going into the library to have a drink, otherwise I might be tempted to forget just how English and well bred I am.'

He went out and slammed the door. Marcia shrugged and began to stroll restlessly around the room. Just the sight of that slim swaying body, those silk-clad legs . . .

'Marcia,' I said crisply, 'would you mind sitting down? I prefer to hold conversations at eye level.'

I could see that she hadn't noticed the wheelchair until then. 'Lydia!' she exclaimed. 'What has happened?'

'There was an accident. I was injured. I thought Veronica would have told you.'

'No. She didn't mention it. Is it serious?' she said.

'I'm paralysed from the waist down, if that's what you wanted to know.'

Her eyes widened. 'For good?'

'Yes, it seems so.'

'I'm sorry,' she murmured. 'What terribly bad luck.'

She sat down, lit another cigarette and regarded me thoughtfully. 'I shouldn't have come,' she said with a sigh. 'At least not whilst Max was around. I'd forgotten how much he resents me.' She gave a faint smile. 'That must please you very much.'

I raised my eyebrows, aware of the implication behind her words, as if she considered herself a rival. I was also aware of something new in her glance, a look of appraisal, of thoughtful speculation. She was obviously weighing up the possibility of being able to provide physical consolation to Max.

Suddenly I felt such a burning sense of grievance, a raging anger against life and particularly against this woman who kept turning up like a bad penny and bringing turmoil to our lives.

350

'Marcia,' I said quietly, 'has it ever occurred to you how dangerous it is to meddle as you do with people's emotions, how cruel it is to play with their lives?'

'Yes, of course it has occurred to me. That is half the fun, to have people like Veronica and Ursula dangling from my hook. You don't know what I had to put up with when I was married to Hugo. Well, now it's their turn to squirm.'

'Yes, I understand that. You told me before. But what about Hugo? Is it fair to use your own son as bait? Look, Marcia. Why don't you just take your son and go quietly back to France. If it's a question of money ...'

'Ah yes. I remember you offered me money before — but you wanted Hugo yourself then, didn't you, Lydia? And now you're offering me money to take him away? So now who's meddling with other people's lives?'

'Perhaps I am,' I admitted. 'But from quite different motives. It's the child I care about and I don't like to see him passed around like this. You obviously don't care to bring him up yourself, so, if it's just money you're bothered about, why not let Sydney and Veronica adopt the boy outright. You must know that Veronica would pay whatever you asked. It would break her heart to have to give him up.'

'And you don't think it would break mine? You think this is easy for me — having to beg, knowing that I am only tolerated because I'm the mother of Hugo Claremont's son.'

'Are you?' I asked softly. 'It occurred to me that you might be the mother of Hugo Claremont's nephew instead.'

'Ah, so Max has told you that we were lovers. That wasn't very chivalrous of him. I didn't think English gentlemen betrayed their bedroom secrets.'

'He didn't have to tell me. I guessed.'

'And you're also guessing that Max is the father of my son?' She shrugged carelessly. 'He might be. He might not be. Who can say? I'm a woman who likes to keep her options open.' She looked at me with her hard eyes. 'Of course I might not be so vague if Max were free. I suppose, in the circumstances, that might be possible now. You do not strike me as a woman who would keep a man trapped in a marriage that, physically at least, can be no marriage at all.'

351

I smiled dryly. 'You mean, am I going to give Max a divorce?'

'Well, it would seem the decent thing to do. Of course, it's none of my business . . .'

'But you'd like it to be, wouldn't you? Perhaps you're thinking of offering your services as a correspondent?'

'Oh no,' she said. 'I've been a mistress too often. It's only marriage that interests me now.'

'And you think Max would marry you if he were free?'

'Well, he asked me once,' she said, smiling. 'I know one would never think so from the way he treats me, but he's never really forgiven me for walking out on him. He will get over that though. Things were different then. We didn't have the same choices. I mean it's not as if he needed to marry for money now.'

'But you need to, don't you, Marcia? You can't live like you want to on Sydney's three thousand a year. That's why you won't let Veronica adopt Hugo. You're hanging out for Max, hoping to use the child to get him to leave me.'

She had the grace to flush. 'I'm sorry. I shouldn't have said anything. Naturally, you are angry with me.'

But strangely enough, I wasn't any more. Whilst she had been speaking I had caught a glimpse of the frightened and lonely woman underneath, a woman so desperate for security, both financial and emotional, that she'd try every despicable means to get it.

'No, I'm not angry with you, Marcia. If I feel anything it's pity. One can't help but feel sorry for someone who's so desperately unhappy that they need to make other people unhappy as well.'

She returned my look unflinchingly. Obviously she's survived worse affronts than that. Coolly she rose to her feet. 'Would you mind if I went up to see my son now? I'm afraid I shall have to beg a lodging for the night — unless of course you'd rather I found a hotel.'

I rang for Mellon. 'Mrs Claremont will be staying the night. Perhaps you could have one of the maids prepare a room.' I looked at Marcia. 'Mellon will show you where Hugo is sleeping.' I gave her a faintly challenging look. 'When you look in to say goodnight to Max, as I'm sure you will, perhaps you'd tell him that I'm ready to go upstairs.'

'Yes, of course.' She hesitated. 'I hope our little talk hasn't upset you, Lydia.'

'Not in the least,' I replied casually. 'Why should it?'

It had of course. Despite my show of bravado it had disturbed me a great deal. I knew I wouldn't sleep however many pills I took. All sorts of unhappy thoughts were churning in my mind so, as Max lifted me into his arms to carry me upstairs, I asked him if we could go to his own room for a few minutes. I needed to talk out of earshot of the efficient and ubiquitous Shaw.

He laid me on the bed carefully as if I were made of glass. 'This can't be much fun for you,' I said ruefully.

'Or for you either,' he answered, smiling.

'No — but my choices are limited, yours are not.'

'What's that supposed to mean?'

'It means that the restrictions on my life are entirely physical. I have no choice but to live a certain kind of life. You do have one and for you to live the same kind of life requires an effort of will.'

He frowned. 'I know this is leading up to something but I'm not sure what.'

'What I'm trying to say is that — is that I'll understand if you can't — I mean if you should need to ...'

'You mean if I should ever want to take a mistress then it's quite all right.'

I felt myself blushing. 'Well, something like that ...'

'Well that's generous of you, Lydia,' he said with heavy sarcasm in his voice. 'Do I have to make the decision now or may I let you know?'

'Max, you're not taking me seriously.'

'Well, did you expect me to?'

I could see I had made a mistake, that my frankness had offended against his romantic ideals. It wasn't the suggestion of infidelity that so outraged him but the suggestion that he could commit the offence with my connivance and approval.

'Yes, I do expect you to take me seriously. It's important to me, Max. I have to know ...'

'Yes, you have to know — that's always been your trouble,

353

Lydia. *You have to know*. Everything has to be tabulated neatly in black and white. Life isn't like that. It's fluid, malleable. It changes from hour to hour, day to day.'

'My life doesn't,' I reminded him sharply. 'This is the best that it's ever going to be, so if you don't like what you see then I'm giving you a chance to say so now.'

'For God's sake, Lydia. What's brought all this on?' He gave me a hard searching look. 'Marcia, I suppose. What's she been saying?'

'Only that she thinks I should do the decent thing and divorce you.'

'Bitch,' he swore. 'You didn't take her seriously, I hope.'

'Perhaps I should,' I said quietly. 'It can't be much fun married to a permanent cripple — and don't say that it doesn't matter,' I added as he opened his mouth. 'It does matter and I want you to promise me that if you should ever want to be free you'll be honest with me. I want you to promise me that you'll never pretend!'

'Oh Lydia,' he groaned. 'What a strange conception you have of love. How can you talk about things like this in such a cold and practical way?'

'I can because I have to, because I know you won't. You've never been any good at facing reality. You can't go on pretending that nothing has happened, nothing has changed.'

He came and sat beside me and took my hands. 'The reality is that I love you, Lydia. And I'm not saying that nothing has changed. What I'm saying is that it hasn't changed enough for it to matter to me.'

'Perhaps not now, but in five years' time ...'

'Five years, ten years — I'll still be here. If it's promises and reassurance you want then I promise you that, whatever happens, I'll never leave you. You're my wife and I love you. Remember? For richer, for poorer — in sickness and in health' — he leant forward and kissed me — 'Till death do us part.'

So you see I'm quite safe. I have absolutely nothing to worry about. Max will never leave me — however empty and painful his life may become, he'll always stay with me

354

because he gave his word and a Claremont never goes back on his word. Poor Marcia will never have him — perhaps just for a few nights as she had him before — but he'll always come back to me. That's a wife's consolation, isn't it? Her claims upon her husband are legal and binding and when they are reinforced by duty and conscience that leaves no possible means of escape. It's a commitment for life. As Max said: till death us do part.

That's when I made up my mind. The words seemed symbolic, a concrete expression of something that for days I had been struggling to say. Just that simple phrase, as simple as swallowing a handful of pills — a quiet and dignified exit.

It's very quiet now, no sound in the world except the rhythmic scratching of the pen and Shaw's gentle breathing through the half-open door. Poor Shaw. Perhaps whilst I still can, I should absolve her from blame. There was nothing she could possibly have done. And Max, my darling Max, I have never loved you more or cared for myself less. You mustn't think you've failed. You mustn't think I've chosen this way because I believed that you would leave me — it's because I believed that you would not, that out of love or loyalty or a sense of honour, you were prepared to make me the gift of your life and the only way to stop you was to make you a gift of mine. So accept this freedom because it's freedom for me too. Don't grieve, because the woman that you loved was already dead and what dies now is merely the flesh. You kept your promise, Max. Only death could have parted us and only death has.

PART FOUR
Max

I was the one who found her — and at first I thought she was just asleep. She hadn't been dead long. Her cheek when I kissed her was still alive and warm. And then I saw that her eyes were not quite closed — I saw on the bedside table the empty bottle of pills. I knew then that she had left me.

My grief took the form of a bout of childish rage. I felt cheated, deprived, like a schoolboy left behind on a Sunday afternoon treat. And then I felt guilty. I was overwhelmed by that primitive emotion on which the Church relies to bring sinners whimpering back to the confessional begging for the lash. I went over the entire evening in my mind. What had I said? What had I done? What hadn't I said or done that I should have?

I recalled our last conversation, that rather curious exchange. I had suspected something then. There had been something in her voice, a concealed desperation, a note of despair ... It had kept me awake. I had remained wondering if I had reassured her enough. Clearly, she'd got it into her head that I was going to leave her, that because of the accident I couldn't care for her any more. This was nonsense, of course. If anything I loved her more because now she needed me and she hadn't needed anyone before. It had worried me enough to get up in the night and come to her room, only to discover that I was too late.

I went further back, through our brief stormy marriage and here the odds were stacked overwhelmingly against me. My love for Lydia had been the only genuine thing. Everything else had been a lie.

My first mistake had been in thinking I could separate the love I had for Lydia from the hatred I felt for her son. I should have either given up Lydia or given up the need to get

359

my own back on Rochester. It had been a point of honour. I couldn't abandon the medieval concept of letting a family insult go unrevenged. I hadn't planned on pistols at dawn or anything quite as dramatic as that. But I wanted him to suffer. I wanted him to feel uncertain and threatened. I wanted to deprive him as he had deprived me. To me he was a worthless, snivelling coward and I felt sure that, once we were married, Lydia would see he was worthless too. I hadn't reckoned with the maternal instinct, that genetic blindness that makes the mothers of mass murderers say things like: 'He was a good boy really. It wasn't his fault.' It was only when I realised that Lydia wasn't going to abandon him just because he was an unprincipled, unnatural, out-and-out bounder, that I thought up my master-plan.

I had known from the start that Rochester had no real money of his own and this suited my purpose admirably. What he did have, though, was twenty per cent of Rochester Mercantile stock and what I hoped to create was a serious debit situation which could only be restored by a disposal of assets, namely the disposal of his Rochester Mercantile stock to me. I knew instinctively that as soon as I married his mother he would have to compete. He saw me as a rival and he'd have to try and prove that he was better than me, and in this respect he played straight into my hands. So the first thing I had to do was make myself a success and this also proved easier than I had ever imagined. Thanks to Sydney, I had been virtually in at the beginning of the stock market boom. I discovered quite quickly that I had a flair for options, predicting the rise or fall of a share price over a three-month period. In this way with a small outlay one could make quite respectable sums. I was always cautious though. For one thing I never dealt on margin and never in stocks that were highly speculative. I soon developed an instinct for a flat market and went short just before prices fell, only to go back in again to pick up the bargains just before prices rose.

One might think this was a handicap in a raging bull market, that being a pessimist among millions of optimists was a dead end. But I clung tenaciously to my belief that what goes up always comes down again. It was just a question of being in the right place when it did. My first bit of luck came in the spring of '28 when a dozen options came in at a phenomenal profit. By then I had perfected the art of the bear squeeze, dumping stock to push prices down, then buying them back at a cheaper rate and selling them on when things looked up. Of course, I'd been caught once or twice but never to any great extent, and by the end of '28 I was sufficiently wealthy and with sufficient expertise to try out my tactics on Rochester.

I had made it my business to know all about him. I knew his income, his assets, his expectations and his debts. I knew his friends — his real friends — the effeminate arty crowd who hung round the theatres and music halls. I knew all about Roger, the struggling actor who obliged men like Rochester when he was 'resting between parts'. I knew all about Clive Rush, the intense young man who worked in the Foreign Deposits department of the bank. In particular, I knew all about Stevens, our shared valet, whom we both paid to spy on one another. For my purpose, of course, nothing could have been better. I just had to make sure that the right information went through.

At first I let him win. Like an amateur sitting down to a professional poker game, I had to allow him to grow confident before I produced my royal flush. For months, courtesy of Stevens, he had played the market with my expertise. But like me he was cautious. He ventured only small amounts and, as Sydney would say, to lose big you had to bet big. Obviously, I was going to have to think of something else.

It was then that I thought up the blackmail idea, using the contacts I had made in prison. For a serious financier, a six-month prison sentence should be compulsory; a nodding acquaintance with embezzlers and forgers is an absolute must.

I had assumed, of course, that in such a delicate and embarrassing moral dilemma, he would naturally come to me. I intended to rescue both his pride and his reputation but at a price which would turn out later to be far in excess of ten thousand pounds. It quite threw me when I discovered that he had thrown himself on Lydia's mercy and Lydia, predictably, had rushed to defend her only chick. Apart from

361

confirming my opinion of Rochester as a cad, I found myself no further forward.

Then the Hatry business came up. I couldn't believe my luck. Everyone in the City knew that Hatry was sailing close to the wind in an effort to finance his bid for United Steel. That he was overstretched was practically common knowledge. Involvement was strictly for high fliers; all the careful money stayed at home. I put my faith in the fact that Rochester was now too much in the habit of copying my moves. If I bought, he bought. If I sold so did he. He was so confident of my judgement that he never even bothered to check things for himself. He just followed blindly wherever I led. It was just a question of convincing him that I was putting thousands in and that if he didn't he'd be losing out on a multi-million deal. I knew this was the big one, big enough to force him into taking a risk. The thing was, you see, that I knew he didn't have the money to gamble with, and although I knew he could manipulate the account to a certain extent, on the sort of gamble I was hoping to persuade him to take, somewhere along the line he'd have to come up with some actual cash. In other words, I intended to force him to steal from the bank.

That I had succeeded beyond my wildest dreams was now a source of remorse and guilt. I tried to tell myself that I couldn't have foreseen the magnitude of Hatry's crash. I couldn't possibly have anticipated that Rochester's ruin would be so complete that he'd get blind drunk and drive his car into a tree — I couldn't have known that in destroying him I would destroy Lydia too.

Except that at the time I couldn't admit that. To have acknowledged then as I sat beside my wife's dead body that I was in some way responsible for her death would have been too grievous a burden to bear. Naturally I blamed Rochester instead.

I stayed beside her all night, holding her close in my arms, as if in some way the warmth of my body would somehow revive her and I wouldn't have to face the dawn alone.

Dawn came, grey and chilly. I supposed I ought to call a doctor or somebody although I couldn't see that there was any point. I woke the nurse who proved even more cheerful and more efficient in the presence of death. She made me some tea which I could not drink. I sat quietly, moving the spoon round and round in the cup while she made what she called the necessary arrangements.

I moved into the next room when the doctor came. He came in later and said something about an inquest and that there'd have to be a post-mortem. He asked me if she'd left a note and it was then that I remembered her journal, left neatly beside the bed.

I ran back into the bedroom and snatched it up. I knew that she had left it for me ... Then I looked down and saw that they had covered her face with the sheet. That's when I realised she'd really gone. All that was left of the woman I loved was this shrouded icy corpse.

Somehow I got through the day. Veronica turned up just as they were taking the body away. She insisted on staying and taking charge so I was able to think my own thoughts whilst she restored some semblance of order to the house. Overall, I didn't feel anything much. I was aware that things were happening around me but I wasn't always conscious of what they were. I didn't think beyond each separate moment of my existence. I didn't look back, I didn't look forward. I shut myself up in an emotional vacuum of the here and now and somehow I survived the brutality of the inquest and the verdict of 'suicide whilst of unsound mind'. In the same way I survived the funeral, a quiet almost furtive affair because, although they no longer buried suicides at crossroads, a lavish affair wouldn't have been the done thing. Only when all this was behind me did I dare think ahead, and when Ridgeway called Rochester and I together for the reading of Lydia's will the future seemed very real.

We stood facing each other on either side of Ridgeway's desk. We exchanged smiles of polite courtesy as he invited us to sit down.

Ridgeway cleared his throat. 'I, Lydia Fortesque Rochester Claremont ...' I stared at my hands as the bequests to servants and employees were got out of the way ... 'To my son, John Edward Fortesque Rochester, I bequeath half my personal fortune as at the time of my death, the house in Eldon Square and all the property known as Farnfield in the county of Northumberland.

'To my husband, Maxwell Francis Vivien Claremont; half my personal fortune as at the time of my death, all of my personal shareholding in Rochester Mercantile Marine ...'

I stared at him blankly. I was quite numb with shock, and as I glanced at Jack I saw that he was too.

Rochester was the first to recover. He leapt to his feet knocking the chair back. 'You bastard,' he yelled. 'You arranged all this. You talked her into cutting me out of the bank ... Well, I'll bloody well contest it. The coroner said she was of unsound mind and this bloody well proves it ...'

'Mr Rochester!' Ridgeway regarded him distastefully down the length of his nose. 'Apart from the doubtful taste of such a proceeding, I should point out that the greater part of this will was made as long ago as June when your mother was in full possession of her faculties. So, apart from casting an unforgivable slur on your mother's name, such a proceeding would prove quite ineffectual.'

'I don't bloody well care about that.' He looked at me in fury and hatred. 'I'll think of something. I'm not going to let you cheat me again.'

'Too late,' I smiled provokingly. 'I already have.'

I went back to Blanchland at the end of the month. Since being dispossessed from Eldon Square I had stayed at my club whilst workmen purged the Blanchland of the presence of the Prestons and finished installing the gadgets that I had intended to make life easier for Lydia but which I hadn't the heart to cancel.

By very bad timing it was the anniversary of Hugo's death and this preyed on my mind to a ridiculous extent. I felt acutely nervous. I kept thinking of the last time I had turned in at the gates of Blanchland expecting to be welcomed as the prodigal son. Every step of the way I fully expected to be turned back, to be told that, after all, there had been some terrible mistake. I kept thinking about my brother Hugo — I kept thinking that his presence in the house would still be so strong — I kept thinking that perhaps I'd have to share Blanchland after all ...

But not even these morbid thoughts could dim the glory of the moment of repossession, when I walked through the door and was greeted by a scene of such complete Victorian sentimentality that tears actually sprang in my eyes.

All the servants were lined up to greet me on either side of the hall. Lydia had had the forethought to keep the Prestons' staff on and as most of these had been local people inherited from us, there were still many faces that I knew. I was pleased and touched. It was the homecoming I had dreamed of, and after I had partaken of the fatted calf disguised as a sumptuous and succulent sirloin of beef I went up to my room, once my brother Hugo's room, fully expecting to find him there.

My things had been unpacked, though I had brought precious little with me; my clothes, cigarettes, a bottle of whisky, and Lydia's journal which, as soon as I felt the moment was right, I fully intended to read.

I stretched myself out on the ornate but uncomfortable four-poster bed in which Charles Stuart was reputed to have spent a night. There was nothing here of Charles Stuart now — and nothing of Hugo, though I closed my eyes, straining my ears for the ghostly echo of his voice.

I continued my proprietorial inspection of the house. I'd had all the original furniture and pictures shipped back from Ansty, so everything was more or less as it had been before. In fact, things were so essentially the same that it was almost as if I had never left and that the last four years had been a terrible dream. That made me think about Hugo again and I found myself scurrying round the house like a terrier looking for a rat, scouring every room for a sign of his presence, making mental notes to remove anything that reminded me too forcibly of him. When at last I was sure I was completely alone, I walked into the hall and stood beneath the glorious hammer-beam roof, in the very spot where four years and all but three months ago I had made my dramatic vow. And I had kept it hadn't I? I was back, I was home, I was at Blanchland.

Then quietly I went upstairs, and in the house I loved, I

365

mourned the woman I loved. I sat down to read Lydia's journal.

It took me a long time because as soon as I picked it up I felt compelled to put it down. It seemed such an intrusion, to pry into her private thoughts, even though I knew that by leaving the journal she had meant to share them with me. Whisky helped, though it was inclined to make me tearful. Often I couldn't continue for the tears in my eyes as a phrase conjured up a poignant memory. It was like living my life with her all over again. But mostly I read with an air of bewilderment. I hardly recognised myself. I didn't recognise Lydia at all. Was it possible to know somebody so well and yet not know them at all?

The last entry, meant for me, I read over and over again. Don't grieve, she had said — my God, that was like saying don't think, don't breathe. I wept and drank more whisky and worked myself up into an hysterical rage. Then I flung the book across the room with a howl of pain and fury. 'You didn't have to do it, you silly bitch. I loved you. Didn't you know that?'

At the beginning of April I went back to the bank, conscious that with fifty-one per cent I had virtual autonomy so it followed that any failures would be considered a hundred per cent my fault. Things weren't good to begin with. The bank was still reeling from the financial shocks of 1929, and although we had limped bravely into 1930 I felt it was now that the bad times would really begin. With my nose for disaster I anticipated a world recession which made it difficult to plan any real strategy. But before I tackled that problem I needed to tackle the problem of Rochester first. The revelation via Lydia's journal of his complex and sensitive personality hadn't mellowed my feelings toward him in the least. If anything, I was more incensed, having read how he had lied to Lydia about Helen's death and how he'd persistently tried to poison her mind against me. Nevertheless, whether I liked it or not, we were going to have to work together until I had worked out a scheme to force him to sell out. I was just thinking about this when he slammed his way into my office.

'Well, how does it feel, Max? Rather good, I should think. So much for so very little.'

He pulled up a chair. 'Actually, you know, I've been working out just how incredibly well you've done. Even leaving Blanchland aside, there's nearly half a million in cash — I know, you see, because I got the same — and if you add to that the shares you were left in the bank, well, you're looking at over two million pounds. So taking that over the two-year period you were married to my mother, that works out at over eighty thousand pounds a month.' He smiled. 'It takes your breath away, doesn't it? I didn't realise gigolos were so highly paid. In fact, I'm almost tempted to take it up myself.'

'You might find that difficult, Rochester,' I commented dryly. 'I'm not aware of a market for ...'

'Queers is the word you're searching for, I think. But I'm entirely flexible in that department, you know. After all I managed pretty well with Helen.'

For a moment I saw red. I had half risen to my feet before I realised that this was exactly what he wanted. He was trying to provoke me into losing my temper, to recreate the very situation that had landed me in prison before.

He tried again. 'And talking about Helen,' he went on lightly. 'Can I take it she's been the reason or your persecution of me? I've always known that you married my mother solely to get back at me. I've always assumed it's because I made Helen pregnant. Do correct me if I'm wrong.'

I realised then how desperately he wanted to hurt me, even to the extent of hurting himself. I knew how terrified he was of physical violence. Well, I wasn't going to hurt him but I was going to frighten him to death.

Slowly I rose to my feet and walked round the desk. 'No,' I said quietly, 'it wasn't just because you made her pregnant. It was because you didn't have the decency to make amends for what you'd done. It's because you arranged for her to go to some filthy abortionist who, after he'd butchered her, left her to bleed to death ...'

For a moment he just stared at me, then his face turned pale.

'No!' He was on his feet, backing away. 'No. You're

367

wrong, quite wrong. I never saw Helen after she told me she was pregnant. I never even spoke to her.'

'Well, you would say that, wouldn't you?'

'Now listen, Claremont,' he was visibly trembling now, 'you've got this all wrong. I swear to you I had nothing to do with it. I admit I did suggest it when she first told me, but that was just panic. You know perfectly well I couldn't have gone through with anything like that. For God's sake, you must believe me.'

The terrible thing was that I did. There was no mistaking the shock and horror in his eyes. I sat down heavily, sick with shock and horror myself. Who else then? There was only one answer — Veronica.

'Max, darling. How lovely to see you?' She gave me a sisterly hug and drew me towards the fire. 'Goodness, you're freezing. Sit down and get warm and I'll ring for some tea.'

She sat down and immediately stood up again. 'Come up and see Hugo. He's having his tea. I always feel so incredibly mean making him eat in the nursery. I know we always did but there were four of us, weren't there ...'

She chattered on happily and I followed her up the stairs.

'Hugo, darling — look who's come to see you. Say hallo to your Uncle Max.'

The boy stared at me, a smear of jam on his mouth. 'Hello, Uncle Max,' he repeated, smiling.

'Hello Hugo,' I said quickly and equally quickly I looked away. It was like looking at a small replica of myself.

Veronica knelt down beside him and kissed his cheek. 'Smithers tells me you have learnt another nursery rhyme today. Will you say it for me and Uncle Max, to show us what a clever boy you are.'

I watched as he recited 'Three Blind Mice' in a childish and lisping voice. I always watched him when I knew that he was not watching me, hoping that he would reveal some small idiosyncracy, some physical peculiarity, some quirk of manner so that I would know he was my son. By now I had admitted to myself that I wanted him to be and most of the time I was able to believe that he was. Vanity dictated that Hugo could never have produced such a personable and apparently intelligent child, and, added to that, his abysmal record in the reproduction stakes — well, how could there be any doubt? But there was doubt; there always would be. I didn't even think that Marcia knew the truth. I had to rely on my own instinct. I felt if I looked hard enough and long enough, I'd find something in his face, an expression in his eyes that would tell me whether he was Hugo's son or mine. Not that it mattered at that moment whose son he was, just so long as he was never Veronica's.

After having dutifully applauded Hugo's rendition, Veronica and I went back downstairs. The tea-things had arrived. Veronica poured.

'How's Mother?' I asked as she handed me my cup.

'Oh, you know,' she shrugged. 'She's in retreat at the moment. She's gone over to Minsteracres for a two-week stay. Quite frankly, it's a relief.'

'And Marcia?'

'Oh, Marcia's not here. I kicked her out a week ago. Apparently she's staying at some hotel in town, though what she's still hanging about for I've no idea. She's got her allowance, so why doesn't she just go back to France? It's really not good for Hugo to have her continually coming and going like she does. I mean, I accept the fact that for the moment at least she's not going to let us adopt Hugo, but if Sydney and I are supposed to be bringing him up then really she's got to keep away.'

She glanced across at me. 'Is that why you came — to see Marcia?'

'No.'

'Well, if you came to see Sydney, he's still in Leeds ...'

'I didn't come to see Sydney either. I came to see you. I wanted to talk to you — about Helen.'

She grew visibly pale. 'Helen! What about her? What do you mean?'

'I thought you might want to tell me exactly what happened.' I paused to light a cigarette. 'Or would you prefer it if I told you.'

'I don't know what you mean,' she said faintly.

'Yes, you do, Vee. It's no good pretending any more. I know that you killed Helen.'

369

'I didn't,' she protested weakly. 'At least I didn't mean to ...' She broke off and buried her face in her hands. 'Oh my God,' she groaned, 'I always knew that you'd find out one day.'

'Well, I have found out, so you might as well tell me everything. I'm not leaving here until I know.'

She told me; the whole sordid story. The entire tissue of lies. I had been prepared to be horrified but not to such a degree.

Then she looked at me, here eyes brimming with tears. 'Oh Max,' she sobbed, 'can you ever forgive me?'

I rose to my feet. I had never felt such cold hatred in my entire life. 'No, Veronica. I'm sorry, but I don't think that I can.'

I didn't sleep that night — in fact, I thought I'd never sleep again. I kept thinking of Veronica in her fine house with her furs and her jewels, her servants and her cars. And then I thought of Helen, suffering and in pain, dying alone and afraid ... I even thought of Rochester, persecuted for a crime he hadn't committed — hanging was too good for her really.

In the morning I telephoned Ridgeway and gave him my instructions. Then I telephoned the bank to say I wouldn't be in — I wasn't up to facing Rochester just yet. Then finally I telephoned every Newcastle hotel until I found where Marcia was staying. I asked her to meet me in the bar for cocktails at six.

I spent the rest of the day quite calmly, going about the usual business of the estate. I half expected Veronica to telephone, and as I had vowed never to speak to her again, I felt it better to stay out of the house. Naturally I was aware that what I was about to do would probably finish me with Sydney, but that was a risk I felt I could afford to take. I didn't need Sydney any more and he didn't need me, so a parting of the ways would have been inevitable. Of course, I regretted the fact that it wouldn't be amicable, but as I had defended Helen in life I felt compelled to do so in death. Veronica must be made to pay.

It's queer looking back on that day after so many years. What a strange view we have of ourselves when we are young

370

— all that passion, that ego, the certainty of being right. I'm not capable of such feelings now, my blood has cooled. I have learnt the virtue of compassion and forgiveness. I have learnt that it's impossible to hurt other people without hurting yourself ... But I didn't know that then, so I set off for my rendezvous with Marcia with all the zealous virtue of a knight setting out on his first crusade, convinced that God and right were on my side.

Marcia was waiting for me in the hotel's 'Palm Lounge'. There were several women sitting there, obviously hotel residents; women of a certain age, a certain type, women who had nowhere else to go on a chilly April evening. I felt a flicker of compassion. I remember thinking: is this what happens to women when they've never been loved? Marcia stood out like an orchid in a cabbage patch — or did she? As she rose to greet me I noticed the strained brilliance of her smile, the lines of determination and desperation around her eyes and mouth. It occurred to me that nobody had ever really loved Marcia either.

This was a bad start. I couldn't afford to be sentimental but already I was beginning to feel a little shabby. It wasn't in my nature to treat women badly, especially a woman I had once slept with. I had to keep reminding myself that Marcia had shown fewer scruples when she'd walked out on me, and then there was that despicable conversation she'd had with Lydia the night she died. Even so, I knew it wasn't going to be easy.

I ordered cocktails. I supposed that really I should have asked her to dine but I now felt a compulsion to get the whole ghastly business over as soon as possible.

We settled ourselves in a corner under a dusty palm. She smiled at me uncertainly. 'Well, this is very pleasant, Max. I must say I'm surprised. I didn't think we'd ever have a civil conversation again.'

I smiled back. 'Well, things are different now, Marcia, aren't they?' (I meant that I was prepared to be nice to her because she had something I wanted. She thought I meant that because I was now a widower this let her in with a chance.)

Then I said with a disarming smile. 'Actually, I have to

371

admit to an ulterior motive. I wanted to talk to you about Hugo — your son.'

'Our son, Max. Why continue to pretend?'

I couldn't help it. I said without thinking. 'How do you know? He could just as easily be Hugo's. You told me that he made love to you just before he died.'

She shrugged. 'I know, that's all. Women do know these things.'

I nodded, and having apparently accepted paternity on the grounds of feminine intuition, I went on to say in what I hoped was a fond and fatherly voice. 'Well, having agreed that then, I hope you'll also agree that I have some say in the boy's future.'

'Well, yes — I suppose so.'

'Quite frankly, I don't want him brought up by Veronica and Sydney, especially I don't want him to have too much contact with my mother,' I paused. 'But whether you'll agree to what I do want, well, that's another matter.'

'Oh,' she fluttered her lashes. 'I'm interested. Go on.'

'I want to adopt Hugo,' I said shortly. 'I want him to be brought up at Blanchland as my son.'

'Why do you need to adopt him? Why can't he just live with you at Blanchland as he does with Veronica at Ansty.'

'Because I'm not prepared to get fond of him and designate him my heir unless I have some legal claim. At the moment, legally, he's Hugo's son. If he were simply living at Blanchland he'd still be Hugo's son. I'm not prepared to accept that.'

'I see,' she said. 'And what happens to me?'

'That would be up to you,' I said. 'Naturally, I intend to make a generous settlement. A lump sum. No strings attached. You'd be free, independent. You could do as you pleased.'

'How much of a lump sum,' she demanded bluntly.

'Fifty thousand pounds or half a million francs, whichever you would prefer.'

'But only if I allow you to adopt Hugo?'

'Yes,' I answered firmly. 'I must insist on that.'

She didn't speak and I could see from her expression this wasn't what she'd had in mind. 'There is an easier way,' she

372

said at last with a hesitant smile. 'You could marry me. After all, you did ask me once.'

I stared at her coldly. 'Don't you think a proposal is in rather bad taste considering that my wife has only been dead two months.'

She flushed. 'I don't see why. You want Hugo. I want a home and security. That way we both get something we want.'

I shuddered inwardly, forcing down my utter revulsion. I could see that I had entirely miscalculated here. Marcia was after more than money. After all, what was fifty thousand pounds compared to Blanchland and the prospect of a husband who was a near millionaire.

'Well' — I forced myself to smile and tried to look as if I were really considering the idea. I only hoped that, if Lydia was watching, she'd understand — 'even if I found the idea agreeable,' I answered evasively, 'you must see that I couldn't marry again for some considerable time.'

'Why not?'

'Because at the moment I don't know that I want to commit myself to that extent, and in the second place it would cause a great deal of comment if it were seen that I couldn't wait to get somebody else up the aisle.

'Look, Marcia,' I went on when she remained silent, 'you don't have to pretend with me, you know. If it's more money you want, just name your price.'

'No, it isn't more money I want, Max, I realise that now. I've always settled for the money because there was never anything else. But money is just money. It's quickly spent and one still ends up with nothing. It's security I need, to know that there's somewhere I really belong, someone I really belong to.' She smiled wistfully. 'I should have married you when you asked me, Max. We'd probably have had a dozen children by now. It's sad, isn't it, that it takes people so long to discover that the things that make them happy cost nothing at all.'

Well, I had to admire her performance. If I hadn't known her so thoroughly I might have been deceived. I laughed aloud. I couldn't help it. My credulity had been stretched to the utter limit.

373

'Oh, I don't expect you to understand, Max. I'm not even sure I understand myself. But lately I've looked at myself and I don't like what I see. Perhaps if I could like myself, other people might like me too.' She looked at me with a moist tender gaze. 'I want you to like me, Max. More than anything in the world I want you to like me.'

'Look, Marcia,' I began awkwardly.

'Don't worry, Max. I shan't embarrass you any more. You can have Hugo with my blessing. I'll sign the adoption papers as soon as you like.'

'And the money ...'

'I don't want the money. I told you, Max, money isn't important any more.'

I stared at her, stunned, so thoroughly off course now that I didn't quite know what to say. It occurred to me that either Marcia was being very clever or I was being very stupid. 'But how will you manage?' I wanted to know. 'What will you do?'

'I shall go back to Paris. I still have friends there. I can soon get a job modelling again. It won't do me any harm to work for my living again.'

She looked at me and smiled. 'And after a while perhaps I'll come back and see how you and Hugo are getting on and then perhaps' — she shrugged — 'who knows?'

Then I saw the trap yawning beneath my feet. By adopting Hugo I bound myself to her irrevocably for the rest of my life, but Marcia was far too clever to pursue that advantage now. She'd go back to Paris for as long as it suited her, long enough to allow for her transformation from slut to saint. Then she'd turn up at Blanchland, a reformed character, and because she was Hugo's mother I wouldn't be able to keep her out. I'd never be rid of her then. She'd hang around until, out of conscience, I asked her to marry me ... For a few moments it all hung in the balance — then I thought of Veronica, I thought of Helen, I thought of the small boy we were both using as a pawn ...

'Yes,' I smiled bleakly. 'Who knows?'

I drove home in a mood of both triumph and despair. On the one hand, having won the battle for Hugo, I had achieved the means of dealing my sister Veronica a mortal blow, but on the other I had put myself under obligation to a woman I loathed.

Of course, I reasoned throughout the sleepless night that followed, there was still time to back out. I wasn't committed to anything yet — except the boy, except Hugo ... It wasn't till then I realised how desperately I wanted him to be my son.

So, as arranged, I met Marcia at Ridgeway's office the following day, and Hugo Marcel Augustine Claremont became my legally adopted son and the object of my love and despair for the next thirty years. But of course at the time I didn't know that, so I was still in moderately high spirits as I bid Marcia farewell at the Central Station. Then with Ridgeway in tow, I motored down to Ansty to tell Veronica the good news.

Naturally, I wanted to be in at the kill; in fact, I was actually tempted to wield the axe myself, but this seemed too much of an indulgence so I left things to Ridgeway whilst I waited outside in the car. Then this seemed cowardly, as if I couldn't face her, and besides I had to admit that the boy now meant far more to me than a means of doing Veronica down. After fifteen minutes of heart searching and nervous indecision, I got out of the car and went in.

Veronica was alone in the drawing room. She looked up as I came in and gave me a vaguely enquiring look as if she wasn't quite sure who I was.

'Where's Ridgeway?' I said.

'He's upstairs with Smithers. They're getting Hugo's things together, I think.'

She spoke quite calmly and it was this calmness that angered me. I had expected hysteria, pleading, violent abuse. I found myself irritated that I was to be deprived of the signs of her suffering.

Then without looking at me she said; 'Why, Max? Because of Helen?'

I didn't answer and she gave a faint tired smile. 'Well, it's quite a relief in a way — to know that I can't be punished any more, that the very worst has happened and that there's nothing else any one can do to hurt me.' She stood up and

375

took a cigarette from a box on the table. 'You don't believe in God, do you, Max? Well, I didn't either, but there's definitely something or someone — someone who decides whether we should be happy or not. It all comes back, you see. All our selfishness and cruelty are turned against us in the end.' She looked at me with her pale, calm eyes. 'This will come back on you, Max. You just see.'

'Is Sydney here?' I asked. I really didn't think she should be left alone.

'No. I don't expect him back till tomorrow.' She smiled. 'Oh, you needn't worry about Sydney. He'll probably be quite pleased. He never really wanted Hugo in any case. Men never do want other people's sons, do they? That's why I don't understand why you do, Max. Oh, yes, I can see it was the most perfect way to punish me, but it doesn't end there, does it? You've had your revenge but you've still got Hugo. What are you going to do with him? You don't know anything about children. You don't even like children. All you've ever cared about is Blanchland and I would have thought Hugo's son was the last person in the world you'd have wanted to share Blanchland with. You hated Hugo. I can't believe that you could really bring yourself to care about his son.'

I couldn't help it. It just came out. 'He's not Hugo's son,' I said. 'He's mine.'

Her eyes widened. 'Yours! I don't believe you. You and Marcia? For God's sake, when?'

'Does it matter? Just take my word for it. He's mine.'

Then suddenly she began to laugh hysterically. 'Oh Max, you fool. What a mad thing to have done just to get your own back on me. That's going to be your punishment, don't you see? Because, whatever Marcia has told you, that child isn't yours. He might look just like you but he looks like Hugo too. He's got Hugo's temperament, his personality, his mannerisms, his smile . . .'

I turned and walked out. Her shrill laughter followed me. 'It all comes back, Max. It all comes back in the end.'

I sat in the car shivering. I wasn't even going to think about it. Veronica would say anything. It was just pure spite . . .

Then the door of the house opened; Hugo and Ridgeway and Nurse Smithers came out. It was too late to turn back now.

I dropped Ridgeway at the station, then turned north for home. It seemed a long drive. The child was silent. The nurse chattered non-stop. I felt I ought to say something to reassure the boy but I felt myself inhibited by the presence of the nurse.

We turned in at the gates of Blanchland and I ordered the car to stop and instructed my driver to take Nurse Smithers on up to the house. I said that Hugo and I would walk from here.

We walked for a while in silence. He seemed so ridiculously small staggering along on his short legs beside me that after a few yards I picked him up.

He regarded me thoughtfully. 'Where are we going, Uncle Max?'

'We're going home, Hugo,' I answered, smiling. 'We're going home to Blanchland.'

Then as we came in sight of the house I set him down. I stood for a moment drinking in its grandeur, its timelessness, its ravaged beauty. 'That's Blanchland, Hugo,' I said with passionate pride, 'and one day it will be yours.'

Then he turned and looked at me. I stared at him and he stared at me, and suddenly in the wide childish eyes I found my answer. Suddenly, I knew with absolute certainty whose son he was.

I smiled with bitter irony. 'Welcome back, Hugo,' I said.